"THE TRUTH IS THAT I LIKE YOU AND THAT FRIGHTENS ME."

The next thing she knew, Will was leaning in front of her, his presence powerful, unnerving, both her hands clasped between his own. His gaze raked her face as if he could see into the secrets of her soul.

"You're afraid to *like* me? Why, Louisa? I pose no threat to you. We've established that I'm not bent on seduction or stealing. Surely, given that, you can let me be your friend?"

Shivering violently, Louisa looked away. "I'm not sure that is possible." The only thing she was sure of was that if he carried on looking at her with that direct, intense gaze, they'd be much more than friends in a matter of minutes. Desire coursed through her, leaving her weak and shaken to the core. . . .

Dell Books by Katherine Kingsley

IN THE WAKE OF THE WIND
ONCE UPON A DREAM
CALL DOWN THE MOON
THE SOUND OF SNOW
IN THE PRESENCE OF ANGELS

KATHERINE KINGSLEY

In the Presence of Angels

Published by
Dell Publishing
a division of
Random House, Inc.
1540 Broadway
New York, New York 10036

This novel is a work of fiction. Names, characters, places, and incidents either are the product of the author's imagination or are used fictitiously. Any resemblance to actual persons, living or dead, events, or locales is entirely coincidental.

Cover art by Tree Trapanese.
Insert art by John Ennis.
Hand lettering by David Gatti.

Dell® is a registered trademark of Random House, Inc., and the colophon is a trademark of Random House, Inc.

ISBN: 0-440-23599-5

Printed in the United States of America

Published simultaneously in Canada

March 2000

10 9 8 7 6 5 4 3 2 1

OPM

Acknowledgments

I owe thanks to many people for their help while I gnashed my teeth and fiddled around and moaned and groaned while writing this book. For their patience, I thank them all, but in particular I owe a special debt of gratitude to Francie Stark, Jan Hiland, and Jane Woodward. They are not only dear friends but were good enough to read the work-in-progress and make careful comments. They also laughed and cried in all the right places, which makes them real stars.

George Platt lent me not only his ear but also his years of veterinary experience with horses. Thanks, George. You were an enormous help.

Last but not least, I thank Sam Morse, who one lazy autumn afternoon in Mykonos insisted that a character called Samantha Davenport appear. Here she is, Sam, in all her glory. I hope I've done her justice.

To the readers: Please do write me at P.O. Box 37, Wolcott, CO 81655, with your thoughts and comments. I always reply to letters that include a SASE. You can also e-mail me at kkingsley@compuserve.com or visit my web page at http://ourworld.compuserve.com/homepages/kkingsley for information and updates.

Enjoy!

Katherine Kingsley

Stone walls do not a prison make
  Nor iron bars a cage;
Minds innocent and quiet take
  That for an hermitage;
If I have freedom in my love,
  And in my soul am free;
Angels alone, that soar above,
  Enjoy such liberty.

Richard Lovelace

Prologue

Waterloo
June 18, 1815

"Will—oh, God, Will, I've been hit!"

Major Lord William Fitzpatrick heard Val's panicked cry through the thunderous roar of the cannons and staggered to his feet, his ribs burning as if they were on fire. His own horse lay on its side, bleeding profusely from a lance attack, its eyes wide with fear and pain, its nostrils flared, saliva pouring from its mouth.

"I'll be back, Maestro, I swear it," Will gasped, reluctant to leave his mount and taking a brief moment to stroke the gelding's head, although bending down nearly made him fall to his knees again. Maestro's weight had come down on Will's side as they both went down in the attack.

Val's voice came again, desperate, pleading. "Will—for God's sake, help me! I think I'm done for! Don't forsake me now, not now . . ."

"Hold on, man, I'm coming!" His heart pounding with fear for Val's safety, Will peered through the black smoke, his eyes red and smarting, the late-afternoon sun all but dimmed by the thick fog and clouds of gunpowder. He stumbled along in the direction of Val's voice, his hearing his only guide. Musket fire rained down, staccato bursts contrasting with the deep boom of the cannons, the clash of sword against sword as men valiantly fought for their lives.

At least half of the horses that pounded around him ran riderless and terrified, adding to the chaos.

Dazed and sickened, Will walked in the midst of hell itself. All around him men cried out in agony, the slaughter beyond description. The earth seemed to vibrate beneath thundering hooves, and the mud ran red with blood.

Groping his way toward Val's ever-weakening voice, Will stepped over bodies as he went, animal and human alike. He finally dropped to his knees, his broken ribs forcing him to fight for every breath, but he willed himself on, refusing to let Val, his dearest friend and comrade these last five years, die on this godforsaken field alone.

He almost tripped over Val's body, so covered in mud was he that Will barely recognized him. If Val hadn't spoken at that moment, Will might have stumbled past him.

"Will—thank God," Val murmured, one hand reaching up and grabbing Will by the collar. Blood streamed from the corner of Val's mouth and covered his entire front. Will quickly pulled open his friend's coat. With a sinking heart he saw that beneath the sticky mess, Val's chest has been pierced by a bullet, the skin and muscle ripped open, blood steadily pumping from the hideous wound.

Will had to turn his face away for a moment. "I'll try to find an orderly," he said, fighting for composure, knowing no one could help Val now.

"It's no use," Val whispered. "I'm dying, Will. There's no point lying to me. Please, stay with me until I'm gone, I beg you."

"I would never leave you," Will said, pulling Val up into his arms, although the effort nearly undid him. He steadied Val's body against his own, his arms holding him close.

His heart breaking, he murmured words of comfort against his friend's hair, the blond now black with blood and mud. "You'll be remembered as a hero," Will said. "Know you've been the finest soldier a man could hope to serve with and as fine a husband and father. I will count you always as my friend and be grateful for the time we had together, for everything we shared."

A cannonball roared over them and Will instinctively bent his body protectively over Val's, as if he might somehow keep him safe. But he was too late. Far too late.

Val coughed weakly and turned his head against Will's shoulder. "It hurts," he moaned. "Oh *God*, how did this happen? We should have . . . should have taken the day, but instead we rode straight into suicide."

"We pushed our advantage too far and the damned French cut us off from behind. Never mind, we'll win yet. Don't think about it now."

Will struggled not to cry, not to show his own weakness. He was so tired, so damned tired, but that was nothing in the face of Val's impending death. His chest ached horribly, not just from his broken ribs but also with the knowledge that he was about to lose the best friend he'd ever had. So senseless, so bloody senseless.

"Will? One last thing?" Val's voice was now so low, Will could hardly hear it.

He bent his ear to Val's mouth. "What is it? Ask anything, my friend, anything at all."

"Please . . . please, will you see my body buried? I do not wish to be picked apart by the crows or the looters, and with the number of men lost today it will be a long time before I am tended to. My family, you understand . . ."

Will understood. It would be hard enough for Louisa, Val's wife, to bear the pain of learning of his death—Will knew well enough the love that was between them since Val had shared with him all of Louisa's letters over the years.

She would at least have peace of mind about his burial. "As you wish," he said. "I will see to it."

"Thank you," Val mumbled, then licked his lips. "I am cold, Will, so very cold."

Looking up, Will saw two beings of light descending and knew the moment was at hand. He bent down and pressed his mouth against Val's pale brow, wet with rain and cold as ice. "Go with God," he said, then silently commended Val's spirit into the care of His Heavenly Father's angels.

Val's mouth curved up in an ironic smile. "You know I don't believe in that nonsense."

"You shall soon enough," Will whispered. "Be at peace, my friend. I shall say prayers for your soul."

Val choked, and his eyes opened wide. "Maria," he gasped. "Maria!"

And then his eyes closed and his head dropped to the side as he released one last long, shuddering breath.

Oblivious to the fighting that raged around him, Will sat perfectly still for a long time, holding Val's lifeless body tight in his arms.

1

*W*ill fastened his saddlebag with a firm snap of the straps, then mounted Maestro, who had miraculously survived the fierce fighting of Waterloo none the worse for his injury. Breathing in a long, fresh breath of the salt air blowing in off the Devonshire coast, he settled himself more comfortably in the saddle and smiled down at his soldier servant who had been every bit as loyal as his horse and for as many years.

"I think that's it, Sergeant," he said. "Thank you for all your help."

"Are you sure you don't want me coming with you, Major?" Harold Tibbins asked, looking anxious and concerned. "Norfolk isn't exactly around the corner."

"Not around the corner, no," Will agreed. "Still, I think that this is something that I best do on my own. There's no point dragging anyone else into the reception I'm bound to receive when I return to Alconleigh. Perhaps it's a good thing my brother isn't expecting me." His voice held a touch of irony. Even Tibbins didn't know the whole of the story, and Will had no inclination to enlighten him. "In any case," he added, "your own family will be expecting you. Make the most of your leave, won't you? You deserve every moment of it."

Tibbins shrugged a shoulder. "I don't know how much I'll enjoy myself knowing that you're on your own and facing your brother down, but I'll do my best." He placed a hand on the horse's flank. "Are you sure your decision to resign your commission is for the best, Major? You made a fine place for yourself in the King's Dragoons."

"Ten years of service is more than enough for me," Will said. "Now that Napoleon is safely shut away, and this time for good, I doubt the king will have any further need of me, let alone notice my absence."

"Not a soul would have any idea that you were ever a soldier, never mind the son of a marquess with the way you look now," Tibbins said, pointedly running his gaze over his master.

Will glanced down at the civilian clothes that Tibbins had found him in the Plymouth market only that morning. They weren't the garb of a gentleman by any means, but Will had been in a tearing hurry to leave his uniform behind, wanting no further reminder of his time in the army. He'd have some decent clothes made up at another time.

For now, the simple doeskin breeches, coarse linen shirt, and the clumsily tailored cotton jacket were comfortable enough, even if the fit left something to be desired. He had a change of clothing in his saddlebag along with his shaving kit and a day's worth of food, and he honestly didn't care how he looked, as long as it wasn't like a soldier.

"I'd better be on my way if I'm to make any distance before nightfall," he said, reaching down and shaking Tibbins's hand. "Thank you again for all you have done," he said, straightening. "I wish you the best of luck."

"Don't you be a stranger, Major. We'll miss you in the regiment." Tibbins turned abruptly away, but not before Will had caught the sheen of tears in his eyes.

He felt like crying himself, only with relief.

Will nudged Maestro into a walk and didn't once bother to look back, not at the ketch that had brought him from Cherbourg, now anchored in Plymouth harbor, not at the soldiers and officers who milled around the pier, many of whom he had called his friends, not even at the pretty girls who circled them flirtatiously.

Instead, he fixed his gaze firmly on the road ahead that led out of town and away from the memories of acrid smoke and the stench of blood, the roar of cannon fire and the heartrending screams of dying men. Waterloo had left an impression on him that the ensuing eleven months had not managed to erase and that would probably stay with him for the rest of his life.

Whatever awaited him down the road could never in a million years be worse than that, not even if he discovered that his brother had permanently exiled him from his family home.

At least he'd never have to kill again, and he could think of no greater blessing.

Broadhurst Farm
Maidencombe, Devon
May 21, 1816

"What on earth am I to do?" Louisa muttered to herself for the tenth time, the pages of the farm ledger blurring before her eyes. "Anyone would think that I could pull miracles out of thin air, the way they all go on." She rubbed her eyes and made a face, hearing the constant drone in her head.

You'll work something out, Louisa . . . Don't you worry, Mrs.

Merriem, something always comes along when you need it the most . . . Oh, but Mama, you're so clever, you're bound to think of something.

Louisa threw her pen down and collapsed back in her chair. "Well, I'm glad they all think I'm so perfectly wonderful and clever and resourceful, but little do they know. The only miracle is that we've managed to scrape by for this long."

She impatiently pushed the thick braid that had tumbled over her shoulder out of the way before the ends landed in the inkpot, then picked up the rough draft of the notice she'd posted at the local pub five days earlier.

> *Wanted Urgently: Man-of-all-work. Room, board, and reasonable salary provided. Experience and a responsible nature mandatory. No fighting men need apply. Please reply to Mrs. Merriem, Broadhurst Farm, near Maidencombe.*

She hadn't had a single answer.

"*Blast* you, Frank Hillbarrow, for a drunk and a thief," she said vehemently, cursing the day she'd ever hired the last farm manager. "And damn you, Valentine Merriem, for a drunk, a thief, a liar, and an idiot," she added, her fingers tightening around the large glass paperweight on the desk as if it might be her late husband's sorry neck.

Too late for that, though. Val had been dead and buried these last eleven months and she never had had a chance to tell him exactly what she thought of him. Too late for that, too, not that it would have done any good. Val had never listened to a word she said.

Shoving her forehead into her hands, Louisa forced back angry tears. So many lives had been affected by Val's selfishness. Her father's health had been broken by Val's bad investment advice and its devastating financial results. They'd lost Broadhurst Hall, where Louisa had grown up, and the generous income that had always sustained them. All that was left was Broadhurst Farm and whatever money she could eke from it. She was responsible not only for herself and her daughter, but also for her father and the few servants from the old days whom she'd be damned to see put out into the cold.

And what had Val done when he'd realized the extent of his folly? Louisa's eyes narrowed in fury at the memory. He'd taken the last of her dowry and bought himself a commission in the army, running away to become a hero.

Some kind of hero, she thought resentfully, wearily rising to stir the smoldering fire back into life. He hadn't even bothered to tell her to her face what he'd been planning, sneaking off in the night like the coward he was, leaving her to find a note propped on the mantelpiece the following morning.

Gone to serve his God, king, and country indeed! Five years, and the outrage she still felt had the ability to make her shake as if she had a bad case of the ague. Val was a lucky man that a bullet had taken his life on the battlefield of Waterloo, or he would have met one on the doorstep delivered by Louisa herself, if he'd had the nerve to return.

But there again Val had had his own way, dying a hero's death and never having to face up to the responsibility of his actions or the endless grind of staving off poverty. Not that she'd let him know about that—anything but. She'd written him every single week, glowing letters, warm, loving letters, to make sure he didn't forget for a minute the family he'd left behind. She'd described life on the farm down to every last conceivable detail, made it out to be an idyllic existence. Her pride would allow her to do nothing else, and she hoped Val had regretted his decision to desert them for the thankless life of war.

Somehow she suspected that all her efforts had been in vain. According to his rare and brief letters, Val had loved every minute of battle. He was the type that would.

Louisa stabbed the poker into the crumbling log, sending sparks flying in all directions, then jumped back with an alarmed cry as a fragment of wood detached itself and flew her way, almost as if Val were sending one more insult in her direction.

"That would suit you perfectly, wouldn't it, Val Merriem," she said with a scowl, stepping hard on the glowing particle that had landed on the hearth, crushing it beneath her heel before it could burn the house down.

"You wouldn't mind seeing Broadhurst Farm go the way of everything else since it no longer affects you. Nothing was ever of consequence unless it somehow had bearing on your own creature comforts. In which case I sincerely pray that there are monks' cells in heaven and the good Lord has assigned you one, since nothing would annoy you so much as to feel you are being deprived."

"Mama? Are you talking to yourself again?"

Louisa turned abruptly at the sound of her daughter's voice from the doorway. "Portia," she said more severely than she intended, her color rising. "You mustn't creep up on me like that." Louisa *hated* being caught in a vulnerable moment, especially by Pip, for whom she was supposed to be a tower of strength.

"Sorry, Mama, but you were so busy with your conversation that you didn't hear me."

"I was—I was just having a little chat with um . . . with God. I was asking Him to look after some unfinished business." As she spoke she quickly moved to the desk and closed the ledger, then gathered up the pages of manuscript she'd been working on earlier. She didn't want Pip, or anyone else for that matter, to know about the book she'd been writing over the course of the last two years. It was her little secret, the one thing that was hers alone.

Pip grinned and tugged on both her braids, her freckled nose wrinkling. "Don't fib. You were in a temper and taking it out on the fire. You always do when you're having trouble with the books." She danced over to her mother and hugged her around the waist. "Don't worry, dear Mama. You'll fix it. You always do."

Louisa squeezed her eyes shut and made a valiant effort to suppress a scream of frustration. "I am sure I will," she said in a strangled voice. "We could use an answer to the notice in no short order, however. I keep praying, but that hasn't done a bit of good to date."

"There's always tomorrow," Pip said cheerfully. "Come along now. Cook has baked a ham for dinner and Grandpapa says he is as hungry as a wolf and will eat me if you don't hurry."

Louisa looked down at her beloved daughter and managed a smile. Pip, still so innocent, still so hopeful. Life had not yet left its harsh marks on her, despite the struggles she had already experienced in her brief eight years.

Making an effort to cast away her dismal mood, she gently ran her hand over Pip's fiery hair that rebelled against the braids her grandfather had so painstakingly put in that morning. "Then we had better hurry. It won't do to have Grandpapa making a meal out of you—who would help to milk the cows or collect the eggs in the morning?"

"Certainly not Grandpapa," Pip said with a wicked chuckle. "He's henpecked enough as it is and has no use for cows or chickens."

"Just so," said Louisa, and taking Pip's small hand in hers, led her from the room, firmly closing the door on her troubles.

Will drew up his horse and stared at the sign at the crossroads. Maidencombe. He could hardly believe his eyes or his luck. Only a day and a half on the road and here he'd inadvertently stumbled across the one place he'd never expected to see, but which had been on his mind for the last five years. More than on his mind. Broadhurst Farm had been a waking dream, culled from the letters that Louisa Merriem had written to her husband on a weekly basis, letters that Will had since read over and over until he'd memorized their contents.

Will felt torn as he tried to figure out what the right thing to do might be. Should he turn left, find Broadhurst Farm, personally deliver the letters to Louisa? Or should he mind his own business, send the letters by post, and continue on his way and get his own nasty business over with without further delay?

He dismounted and led Maestro to the small stream that ran only a few yards from the road. Hot and tired, he sank down into the cool grass, the old injury to his ribs aching from exertion. He needed the rest, no matter what he decided.

Images played through his mind of Louisa Merriem's vivid descriptions of Broadhurst, so enticing, so evocative of a happy family life that had always eluded him. He felt as if he'd watched little Portia grow up, felt as if he'd been there when the harvest was planted and later brought in. Damn, he felt as if he knew each member of the small staff, every site of every daffodil that bloomed in April, exactly where the sun rose and set at any given time of year, just how Cook's delicious treacle tart melted on the tongue.

All of this due to Louisa, a woman he'd half fallen in love with only by virtue of words on a page, not a single one written to him, but to the husband she loved.

Broadhurst and Louisa had given Val and Will something to talk about, a respite from the incessant war, a place to retreat to, even if it seemed a million miles away, but he knew, too, that he'd created a fantasy world that probably bore no resemblance to the truth, and that he was bound to be disappointed by the reality.

Still, he'd go to Broadhurst in a heartbeat.

The trouble was that Broadhurst and its inhabitants were none of his business. Will lay back in the grass.

What use was confronting a grieving widow with a packet of letters that would cause her renewed distress, remind her of everything she'd lost? He could only imagine how she felt—he already knew that Val's heart had been torn when he'd heeded the call of country and forced himself to leave Louisa, his daughter, everything he held dear, for the hellhole of war. He'd been a true hero, losing everything in the end for what he believed.

Will had had nothing to lose, nothing at all save perhaps his sanity, and he'd managed to hang on to that for the most part. His only real indulgence during his time in the army had been pretending in his very weakest moments that he, instead of Val, lived at Broadhurst, that it was he who loved Louisa, that it was he who slept in her bed at night and made her cry out in pleasure. That it was she who slipped wild strawberries between his lips and whispered words of endless love.

That those moments of fantasy had been brought on by fear and a constant sense of helplessness was no excuse at all. He'd always felt guilty that he'd imagined them at all, because the real flesh-and-blood woman belonged to his dearest friend.

Surely he owed Louisa Merriem her privacy. Surely she would not thank him for intruding on her grief.

Will pushed himself upright. On the other hand, he could tell her stories that might comfort her. He could even tell her of Val's last moments, of how he'd held Val in his arms as he lay dying. He didn't have to say that Val hadn't actually spoken Louisa's name in that moment, that in his anguish and madness he'd choked out someone else's— Will still didn't understand that, although he prayed that maybe Val had been calling to the Virgin Mother, despite his insistence that he didn't believe.

He could perhaps, in some small way, offer Louisa comfort. He owed her a brief visit. If he didn't stop, he might be remiss in his duties to a fellow officer.

Once in the village, Will received directions to Broadhurst Farm with no trouble, but he couldn't help the erratic pounding of his heart as he made the turn into the drive leading to the house itself. Louisa Merriem had described it exactly, painting an evocative picture with words that neither stinted nor glorified. He pulled Maestro to a stop and drank in the sight before him, a sight that previously had lived only in his imagination. He'd imagined it well.

There, in a gentle dip of valley, stood a Tudor farmhouse, hugged on both sides by large stands of trees, fronted by a lawn and terraces with yew and beech hedges. The house was simple, built of gray stone, one wing gabled. To the right, a south-facing orchard, covered in blossoms of white and pink, promised a heavy yield of fruit later in the year. To the left a rose garden nodded sleepily in the light breeze, the flowers just unfurling from tight buds.

Will's heart tightened in his chest. He had never in his life seen such a welcoming sight.

A thin plume of smoke rose from one of the four chimneys, a sure sign that someone was there. He leaned down and ran his hand over his horse's smooth neck. "Perhaps I'm mad, Maestro, but I feel as if I've come home."

He grimaced at his folly. This was not his home, and he'd be well served to remember it. He was here but for a few brief moments, his mission to deliver a packet of letters that didn't belong to him either, as much as he felt they did.

Swinging down from Maestro's back, he took the reins and led his horse up the path to the front door, tethering him to a ring in the mounting post. He swept his cap from his head, and gathering his courage, he raised the door knocker and sharply rapped it twice. The sound echoed hollowly and then silence fell.

Will gazed down at one foot, the surface of his boot dusty from travel. He quickly bent over and rubbed his hand over one boot and then the other, then straightened and ran his fingers through his hair, trying to tidy that as well. Belatedly realizing what a sight he must be, he wished he'd had the foresight to stop first at a posting inn, where at least he could have washed and changed.

Louisa, if she was at home at all, might well turn him away after one look, taking him for a vagrant. Maybe he'd go into the village and get a room, come back tomorrow looking more presentable. Or maybe he'd just carry on now that he'd seen the farm and stick to his original plan, posting the letters at another time. From another place. A place far away from here.

He'd just turned away when the sound of the door suddenly opening caused him to spin back around.

Will's mouth fell open at the sight of the woman standing before him. She could be no one but Louisa, but nothing had prepared him for the sight of this slim woman, her mass of auburn hair loosely pulled back by a simple ribbon, her brilliant blue eyes regarding him in clear surprise and something he almost interpreted as horror, though he could think of no cause.

"Mrs.—er, Mrs. Merriem?" he stammered like an idiot.

"That is correct," she said, her gaze raking him up and down, then snapping back to his face, her color high. "Thank goodness you're here. Did you bring references?"

"References?" he repeated awkwardly, feeling like a callow youth. Lord, but she was the most beautiful woman he'd ever seen. That was the one thing he hadn't imagined. Val had said only that she was attractive in her own way but hadn't elaborated beyond that. "References," Will said again, desperately trying to pull himself together.

"Indeed, although I cannot afford to be too picky at this point. Do you drink?"

Will blinked. "On occasion," he managed to say. "Not—not often."

"That will have to do, I suppose," she said, her full, wide mouth pursing slightly. "You have come from . . . ?"

"Plymouth," he said in a daze, thinking that he was missing a vital point, but he had no idea what it was. He dragged his gaze from her lovely mouth and cleared his throat. "I have come from Plymouth. Does it matter?"

"Not as long as you're not a seaman or a soldier, God forbid." She frowned. "You do have experience? How old are you?"

"Thirty years of age," he replied, knowing now that she had surely mistaken him for someone else. *Not a soldier?* What in hell was that supposed to mean? "What, um, what sort of experience did you have in mind?"

"As I clearly stated in the notice posted at the pub, I need a man-of-all-work. That means carpentry, expertise in farming, lambing, all of that sort of thing. The hours are long, as you might expect, but if you prove your competency you will have decent quarters, nourishing meals three times a day, and six shillings a week. The job is yours if you want it? Do you?"

Will quickly ducked his head, trying desperately not to laugh. He saw it all now. His shabby dress had created the illusion that he'd come in answer to a notice posted at the pub for a farm laborer. God help him. It was perfect, too good to be true.

Why not? a small, treacherous voice whispered in the back of his head. Why the hell not? He was in no rush to get home, and no one expected him in any case. Here was a golden opportunity to spend some time with the woman and the place he'd been dreaming about for five long years. She was obviously desperate for a man-of-all-work, and here he was, able and willing, and although he might not be entirely experienced, he could learn soon enough. He felt almost as if God had finally smiled on him . . .

No, his better side told him firmly. *That would be deceitful. That's not why you came. Stop this farce, cut her off now, while you still have a chance. Cut her off. Cut her—*

"Has the cat got your tongue?" she asked. "I have just offered you a job that you've come all the way from Plymouth to apply for. What is your name, man?"

He raised his head. "Will," he said, unable to help himself. "Will Cutter," he added, supplying the last sane thought he'd had, although he hadn't cut her off after all. "I accept the job, ma'am. Show me what is needed and I will do everything in my power to earn your trust and my wages."

Making her way back to the house after showing Will Cutter to his quarters above the stables, Louisa wondered if she had just made one of the larger mistakes of her life. No mistake would ever equal choosing Val as a husband, but she couldn't help a sense of misgiving in hiring this particular man.

For one thing, he was far too good-looking and more than likely knew it—how could he not? Hiring a handsome man was a mistake in itself, since excessively handsome men tended to have an equally excessive high opinion of themselves that was seldom, if ever, warranted. She'd learned that lesson from Val.

Then there was the matter of his horse. She stopped and turned, gazing thoughtfully back at the stables. What was a man in Will Cutter's lowly station doing with a magnificent horse like that? He could never have afforded it, so she could not discount the possibility out of hand that the gelding had been stolen.

On the other hand, his speech led her to believe that he was not a peasant by any stretch of the imagination, so she supposed he might be a man of good birth who had fallen on hard times. His finely chiseled cheekbones, thick, wavy dark hair and equally dark eyes, along with the narrow, high-bridged line of nose and squared chin with the slight cleft, all indicated good breeding of some kind.

She'd nearly fallen over when she'd opened the door and

seen him standing there, a dark angel cast in Lucifer's own image. She wouldn't even think about the shiver that had gone through her when she'd taken in his broad shoulders, narrow waist, and powerful thighs.

He couldn't have been more different from Val, who had been green-eyed and blond-haired, his build slight. This man towered over her, exerting a powerful presence that had forced the breath from her body and very nearly caused her to slam the door straight in his face. Will Cutter was not what she'd had in mind when she'd posted her notice. Indeed, he was the last sort of man she'd expected to turn up on her doorstep.

Men of low birth did *not* exert such an air of quiet command, nor did they generally have a look of sharp intelligence. He looked as if he had seen the world and then some. She imagined he probably had, and hadn't much liked it, given the expression behind the dark brown eyes that she could only describe as haunted. Or at least that was the impression she'd had when he first looked at her, before he'd masked his expression so that she could see nothing at all.

Louisa ran a hand over her aching forehead. What did it really matter in the end who Will Cutter was or where he hailed from? Whatever his birth, he clearly had to make his own way in the world, and if this was the way he chose do it, what business was that of hers?

He'd appeared at her door and she needed him. Short of his being a murderer, which she sincerely doubted, she had no argument with him. He appeared strong and able, and she couldn't ask for more than that.

At any rate, who was she to question God's generosity, whatever form it had arrived in? She had a planting season to see to and a harvest to be brought in at the end of it.

Fences needed mending and animals needed looking after. Food had to be put on the table and with a little luck, there'd be some extra money to get them all through the winter. With a lot of luck, Will Cutter would help to make that happen.

2

Once he'd fed and watered Maestro and settled him into a stall, Will went back up the stairs and surveyed the room that would be his home for as long as he chose to stay.

The space was simple but clean, and a decent amount of light streamed in from the attic windows. The iron bedstead, covered in a simple white counterpane, looked comfortable enough, if perhaps a little on the small size for a man of his height, but he'd slept in conditions far more cramped.

He tested the mattress, which creaked slightly under his weight but appeared mercifully free of lumps, so he tossed his satchel to one side and stretched out, folding his arms behind his head.

A slow grin crept across his face. Will Cutter, indeed. What *had* he done? He'd never been a creature of impulse, always thinking his decisions carefully through before acting, and yet twice in one day he'd succumbed to spontaneous behavior. Hiring himself to Louisa Merriem as her man-of-all-work had to be the single craziest thing he'd done in his life.

And yet . . . and yet he had not a moment's regret. He felt freer than he ever had, unfettered by family or military obligations, with no history save that which he chose to create for himself.

Propping himself up on his elbow, he considered his situation. He would need to reinvent himself, come up with some kind of plausible background, for questions would surely be asked despite the ease with which Louisa had taken him on. So who was this Will Cutter, and what had he been doing before his arrival at Broadhurst?

Soldiering was clearly out of the question, given Louisa's opinion on that subject. So was any story that came close to the truth of his real life. He suspected that Val had occasionally mentioned him in letters he'd written home, and the last thing Will needed was for Louisa to make any connection between Major Lord William Fitzpatrick and Will Cutter.

Will frowned. There was the problem of his speech, not the usual accent of a laborer. Perhaps it would be enough to say that he'd been moving from place to place over the last few years, having fallen on some hard luck, and been forced to earn his living as best he could. That might do if he elaborated cleverly enough.

His hands appeared weathered, he supposed, and he had the advantage of having spent a great deal of time in the company of the laborers at Alconleigh, far more sympathetic people than either his father or brother. Some knowledge of farm management must have rubbed off on him. At least he was knowledgeable about horses.

Will settled back more comfortably and closed his eyes, hoping to catch an hour or so of sleep before he had to appear at the dinner table. He soon fell into a mercifully dreamless slumber.

A floorboard creaked and Will came instantly awake, shooting upright, his instincts finely honed by years of battle, his right hand going to his side as if to find a weapon there.

Instead of the enemy he'd reflexively expected, he saw only a small girl of eight years or so with carrot-colored hair, her braids sticking out in a haphazard fashion. Her wide blue eyes regarded him curiously and without alarm.

"Hello," she said, rubbing her nose with her fist, her gaze unwavering. "You must be the answer to Mama's prayers, unless you're a villain, but I don't think you look like one. I saw the horse downstairs in the stall and thought someone must finally have come."

Will knew without a doubt that this was Portia, Val's daughter. His heart tugged hard in his chest. As with Louisa, the reality of seeing Pip in the flesh sent him reeling, and he had to catch his breath and guard his expression.

She was exactly as he'd expected, freckles and all. He'd been reading about her exploits for five years and felt as if he knew her inside out. An imp, strong-willed but sweet of nature, highly imaginative and keenly intelligent, with a definite bent toward mischief. So Louisa had described her, and so she appeared with her hem muddied and bedraggled and her pinafore in no better shape. A long streak of dirt ran down one round cheek.

"Hello," he said, smiling at her. "I don't know about being an answer to anyone's prayers, but my name is Will. Will Cutter, at your service." He stood and swept her a bow. "What do you think of my horse? His name is Maestro and I think him very fine indeed."

She ran the tip of her tongue over her bottom lip. "He is the biggest horse I have ever seen in my entire life, truly magnificent. I have a pony, but she's round and pigheaded. Her name is Apple. Mine is Portia, but everyone calls me Pip—except Mama when she's trying to be severe with me. Portia seems like a very silly name, but Mama says I will grow into it." She wrinkled her nose. "Mama says I will also grow beautiful one day and have many fine suitors, but I do not think that is possible, and anyway, I don't want to marry anyone but John Henry, and he doesn't care what I look like."

"And who is John Henry?" Will asked, his heart completely lost. In the months since Val had been killed, Will had not heard another thing about life at Broadhurst, and he suddenly realized just how much he'd missed out on. John Henry was definitely a new development in Pip's life, and Will couldn't contain his curiosity.

"He is the boy who lives on the next farm. He doesn't mind that I'm a girl at all. He thinks I am every bit as good as a boy, even if I do have to wear silly clothes and study my books all the time. We have adventures together."

"Hmm," Will said. "John Henry sounds very jolly indeed, but do you not like studying your books?"

Pip considered. "It is not that I don't like studying, because I like to learn new things. It is only that studying takes too much time away from everything else." She flashed him a grin. "If I could ride my pony anywhere I wished and study at the same time, I would be very pleased, but I learned that is not possible. I tried it once last year and ended up in a ditch with a lump on my head. Mama was very cross with me."

"I should think she was more worried than cross. Bumps on the head can be nasty."

Pip shrugged. "My head is exceedingly hard. Mama says that all the time. I expect she is right."

"Is she?" Will cocked his head to one side, unable to resist the opportunity. "Tell me, Pip, what happened to the last man-of-all-work?"

"Oh, Frank Hillbarrow, the farm manager, you mean? He drank spirits all the time. He fiddled the books, too, and left in the dead of night with Mama's savings. She was very, very cross about that. She's been horribly worried ever since."

"I can imagine she has been." So Frank Hillbarrow had been farm manager, whereas Will had been appointed a job several notches lower, which apparently was not going to entail any sort of bookkeeping. Highly understandable, although unfortunate, since Will could probably sort a number of accounting problems out for Louisa, given his training and education. His heart went out to her. She'd clearly been struggling and had no one to turn to.

It might take him some time to gain her trust, but he'd do his best. "Never mind, Pip," he said, "we'll get it all sorted out somehow. The important thing is to make a start, and perhaps you can help to show me how things are done. I'll need a good helper if you don't mind taking on the job."

Pip's little face lit up with pleasure. "I am very good at that sort of thing. We can begin early tomorrow morning."

"I'd like that. In the meantime, if you will excuse me, I should wash and change for dinner." He tugged on his ear, for the first time realizing one of the inconveniences of his new life. "Um, can you tell me if there is anyone at Broadhurst who does general laundry? I am going to be in need of clean clothes by tomorrow."

Pip raised her eyebrows. "You are not in the habit of doing your own washing?"

"I am not, no," he said with complete honesty. "I am sure I can work out the process if it is required of me, but I was hoping that there might be someone who is more experienced?"

She burst into laughter. "I was teasing you. Of course we have a laundress. Mrs. Robbins would be mightily offended if you started hanging out your clothes on the fence posts. Bring your washing to the house when you come for dinner and leave it in the basket behind the back door."

"Thank you," Will said, meaning the words with all his heart. "I look forward to dinner. I have to confess I am starving."

"Good," Pip said. "Cook likes it when the plates are swept

clean. You won't get much, but if you don't eat every last morsel, you might well find yourself beaten with a broom and locked in the coal cellar overnight. Cook's temper is very, very precarious."

"Thank you for the warning. Is Cook, er, handy in the kitchen?"

Pip laughed. "That is for you to say. I would advise you to say yes."

Will chuckled, wanting to sweep the child he wished was his own into his arms and hug her hard. "I can see you are to be my godsend, Pip. Later then. And I beg you, speak of my shortcomings to no one."

She laid a finger alongside her nose and winked, although where she'd learned that vulgar gesture he could only imagine. "Later then," she said in a conspiratorial whisper, and scampered down the stairs.

Will sank onto the bed, half wanting to laugh, half wanting to cry. How was it possible to feel so complete and so empty at the same time?

His life had taken some extraordinary turns in the past, but for the last ten years he'd gained little pleasure from it. If anything, Louisa's letters had brought him those small moments of happiness. Now here he was in the heart of Broadhurst Farm and every bit as much an outsider as he'd been before. Meeting Pip had only driven the point home. Fantasy was one thing, reality something else altogether, although he couldn't say he was the least bit disappointed by the reality, not as he'd expected to be.

It was only that being here under false pretenses was not what he'd had in mind, and it served to make him feel like a fraud. Which he was, of course.

Will rubbed one hand over his face. The irony was that most people, when choosing to be someone they weren't, usually hiked themselves up the social ladder, whereas he had taken a number of very large steps down it. A short laugh escaped him at the absurdity of the situation.

Oh, well. He might as well make the best of circumstances while he could. In the process, he'd do his level best to set Broadhurst back in order and pray that he wouldn't be unmasked before he could do some good.

Pushing himself to his feet, he set off to have a good wash in the horse trough. So much for a return to a life of luxury.

"Please have a seat, Mr. Cutter," Louisa said after briefly introducing him to Cook, who gave him a characteristically sour and suspicious look with nothing more than a humph in reply to his greeting. Louisa indicated a chair at one end of the large kitchen table where they usually took their meals. "The others should be in a moment. I hope you have brought an appetite with you."

"Thank you, ma'am, I have," Will said, sitting down at the table. "Something smells delicious. Partridge, perhaps?"

"Rabbit," Louisa said, shooting him a look out of the corner of her eye. His dark hair was damp from washing, and she couldn't help but notice the cowlick that curled at the back of his head, or the way his hair waved in every direction, sweeping back off his forehead, behind his ears, falling onto the back of his neck. She also couldn't help noticing his winged eyebrows, equally dark, or the length of his thick lashes. Oh, he'd make a fine satyr indeed.

"Rabbit? Perfect. A stew, perhaps?"

"Yes, a stew, but if you prefer partridge, you might be good enough to shoot it yourself."

He glanced up at her, a flicker of something odd in his

gaze. "I'm—I'm not a very good shot," he said, dropping his gaze abruptly.

"Pity," she replied. "I'm an excellent shot but I have very little time for such pursuits. Ah, good, here are my daughter, Portia, and my father, Mr. Fleming. Mr. Cutter is the new farm help, Papa. And behind them are Tom Trueboot and his daughter, Violet, who run the dairy. Tom has been lending a hand elsewhere on the farm until we could find more help. He will be glad of your arrival."

She watched as Will stood and made a slight bow, speaking a few polite words to each of them. As simple as the gesture was, it spoke volumes about him. Will Cutter had been properly brought up, and she couldn't help but wonder anew at what had brought him to these circumstances.

Throughout dinner she continued to watch him. His table manners were in no way objectionable, although not overly refined either. He ate every last scrap on his plate, his attention fully focused on his food. The little conversation he made gave away nothing at all about himself, yet he followed the general conversation with ease and interest.

When he did speak, he was as comfortable with Pip as he was with her father, even though her father was as silent as ever. Will seemed equally relaxed with Cook, Tom, and Violet. Indeed, he behaved as if he'd been sitting at the kitchen table with them for years instead of one brief hour.

A mystery lay behind this man, and she burned to know what it was. But what truly astonished her was the way his eyes lit up when Cook produced the pudding.

"Is that—could that possibly be a treacle tart?" he said in wonder, looking like a child on Christmas morning.

"It is indeed, Mr. Cutter," Cook said, folding her plump hands on her apron and smiling at him. "Are you fond of treacle tart?"

Louisa could scarcely believe her eyes. Cook never smiled at anyone. She spent most of her time complaining. But throughout the meal, Cook had been casting surreptitious glances at Will, not bothering to hide her interest in him.

"Oh, I am," he said. "It has been years since I've had the pleasure of tasting one, and this looks exceptional. The smell alone is enough to make me weak at the knees."

"Then you shall have the first slice, and plenty of cream to go with it," Cook said, cutting him a huge wedge. Cook never cut huge wedges of anything, either, as parsimonious with her food as a miser was with his money. She proceeded to drown the wedge in cream.

Will's eyes briefly shut at the very first bite. When he opened them again, he looked as if he'd gone to heaven. "Thank you for preparing such a superb treat," he murmured, and didn't speak again until he'd finished every last morsel.

If Will Cutter hadn't been such a magnificent physical specimen, Louisa would have thought he'd been scrounging for food in the gutter for months. She'd never seen anyone take so much pleasure from a simple meal. Just watching him made her want to smile, and she hadn't had much to smile about for a very long time.

A person couldn't help liking Will Cutter. The instant the thought crossed her mind, she forcefully pushed it away. She didn't want to like Will Cutter, nor did she have any intention of trusting him. He was there to work.

Tom Trueboot broke into her thoughts. "Let me tell you, Mr. Cutter, about the fine racehorse that Mr. Fleming used to run, since I can see that you have an interest in the animals. I used to be groom in those days when we still had a large stable, and he was my pride, indeed he was. He was called Morning's Promise, and he was every bit as glorious as you could wish for," Tom said, warming to his tale. "I can tell you that he was one of the best, grandest horses ever to grace the earth, not unlike that fine specimen you rode in on today—aye, I saw him with my own eyes as I brought the butter up. I'd say you know something about the breed, owning a beast like that . . . well, Promise's finest hour came when he beat the odds against the champion of his day . . ."

Louisa glanced around the table. Her father remained silent, little surprise, but the others, who had heard the story from Tom a hundred times before, listened intently, then questioned Will avidly about his knowledge of horses. His answers were surprisingly modest, which only led her to suspect that he knew more than he was saying.

Cook, cleaning away the supper dishes, every now and then shot Will a look of undisguised adoration. Will responded with an occasional welcoming smile as if he expected nothing less.

The one person Will seemed oblivious to was herself. He'd barely spoken a word to her throughout the meal. Louisa knew she was being absurd, since she'd barely spoken to him, but she couldn't help feeling a prick of annoyance. This was her family, not his, although one would never know it by the way they were all behaving.

Was this the effect that handsome looks had on otherwise sensible people? Well, she'd learned her lesson in that regard, and learned it the hard way. Never again would she let a man sway her judgment with smooth words and charming smiles, and she'd be damned if she'd let her dear ones be swayed either.

"Thank you for supper, Cook," Louisa said, standing and signaling an end to the meal. "We all have an early start in the morning and should get to bed. I will check with you in the morning, Mr. Cutter, and we can go over a list of the most immediate tasks that need attending to."

"If you will forgive me, Mrs. Merriem, I was wondering . . . do you have any books I could borrow? I am without reading material at the moment, and I hoped you might have a small library. I sleep better if I read before I retire, and I do promise I will be careful with the books."

This was the first piece of personal information he had revealed about himself, and Louisa could hardly refuse such a simple request. Indeed, she admired people who read for pleasure.

"Indeed, Mr. Cutter. Let me show you to the study. You may take your pick."

"I am in your debt." He took a moment to say good night to each person, smiling as he bent down and whispering something in Pip's ear that made her giggle and nod. Then he followed Louisa down the corridor to the study, where the fire still glowed in the hearth.

She lit the lamps and led him to the library shelves. "Do you have any particular interests?" she asked, taking a few steps to the side, for his nearness unsettled her and she could practically feel the warmth of his breath on her neck, even though he stood a good foot behind her.

"I read anything and everything," he said. "Is there something you particularly recommend?"

She thought, forgetting for a moment that he was hired help, an intruder in her house. Books were her passion in life, and sharing them gave her great pleasure. "Are you fond of Chaucer?" she asked.

"In the extreme. I don't suppose you have a copy of *Troilus and Criseyde*? It is one of my favorites."

She turned in surprise. "And mine, although I would not have thought that you were inclined toward the medieval traditions of courtly love."

"No? But Chaucer is an excellent teller of tales as well as a brilliant poet. I find his depiction of character as well as his shrewd observations of human nature most enlightening. Shakespeare does the tale decent service, but I feel his setting and description lack the power of the original."

"Neither has a happy ending, Mr. Cutter."

"No, Mrs. Merriem, but where is the surprise? How many of us are fortunate enough to experience a happy ending? Life has a way of dealing its hand unexpectedly, and more often than not it deals a blow rather than a caress. It is left to us to make the best of our circumstances, whatever they might be."

Louisa bit her lip, sudden tears burning at the back of her eyes and thickening her throat. He was right, of course. She knew that better than anyone. She blinked hard and looked down. "I believe the fault should be laid equally at the door of human nature," she said in a low voice. "Very often where we anticipate honor we find the opposite."

"Ah, yes. Deception, dishonor, lack of loyalty, these are unfortunate aspects of man that all too often come to the fore." He shrugged a shoulder. "Naturally, I would prefer to hope for the kinder, nobler traits, but I would rather be pleasantly surprised than count myself a fool for expecting them."

Startled by his perception and his honesty, Louisa glanced up and nodded. "We are agreed."

"It must also be said that when we are fortunate enough to discover those very things in a person, we should hold on for dear life if we have any sense at all." He smiled at her then, his eyes infinitely gentle. "I believe that one of the greatest sorrows in life is to lose a person one has loved who had those traits."

She quickly dropped her gaze from his, thoroughly disconcerted by the probing expression in his dark eyes that made her feel as if he could see straight inside her to her savaged heart. Impossible, she told herself firmly. No one knew anything of her heart, savaged or otherwise. She made certain of it, and in any case that heart was now thoroughly hardened, especially against men like him. Charm had no effect on her, none at all. She couldn't think why she was behaving in such a foolish fashion. He was nothing more than a man-of-all-work, a complete stranger to her, and that is how he would stay.

"Here it is," she said, taking the volume from the shelf and handing it to him, hoping he didn't see that her fingers were trembling.

"Thank you," he said, not smiling now, not smiling at all. Instead, his face held an intensity that made her weak at the knees. "You are everything that is kind. I am grateful to you in more ways than I can say."

"Then perhaps it is best if you don't. I am glad if the job I have offered gives you a roof over your head and food in your mouth, but I expect you to work hard. And—and to respect your position and mine," she added in a desperate attempt to create distance between them, a distance he had somehow managed to breach with no trouble at all.

"You have nothing to fear from me," Will said in a quiet voice, running his thumb softly back and forth over the spine of the book in a fashion that made her wish he were touching her just so. "I intend only to help you in every way I can until such a time as you have no more need of me. You have merely to ask of me what you wish and I will do my best to fulfill those wishes."

"Why?" she asked, feeling as if she were being sucked into a magnetic pull entirely of his own making and helpless to resist.

Was *this* what he had done to her family at dinner, drawn them all into his orbit without any apparent effort, with no more than a smile and a few kind, attentive words? Were they all that needy? Was *she* that needy to be so affected by a man she knew not at all?

"Why do you care in the least?" she asked.

He pressed the book flat to his broad chest with one strong hand, the fingers long and square. "Because you do seem to need me. Because you should not be on your own in what appears to be a difficult situation. Because your family is a fine one and should no more be asked to suffer than you should. Is that answer enough?"

She blinked back hot tears, as unexpected as he was. "Yes. For the moment." She made a valiant effort to regain her composure and cleared her tight throat. "There is much I wish to know about you, Mr. Cutter, but I am too tired to ask you tonight. Had I not been so desperate for help, I would have insisted on references."

To her surprise, he burst into laughter. "Then let us both be relieved that you did not insist. I can give you no references, Mrs. Merriem. I am not in the habit of carrying them about with me. I am, however, in the habit of going from place to place, doing service where I am required. If that is not enough for you, then tell me now, and I will be off."

She chewed on her lip in an agony of indecision. Here was the perfect opportunity to be rid of him, and he had handed it to her on a platter. Yet by doing just that, he had also put her in a difficult position. He *knew* she was in terrible trouble; she'd said as much. She'd gleaned that his situation was equally difficult, although he hadn't said so.

Indeed, he'd said practically nothing at all, other than he thought he could help. In other words, he'd called her hand.

So why shouldn't she just let him do as he wanted and keep him on? It would serve them both. Aside from a meal here and there—no more than one a day in his company—she would have little contact with him.

He held the book out to her. "Would you like this back so that you can send me on my way?" he asked, one eyebrow cocked in question.

"Keep it for the moment, Mr. Cutter. We have an agreement. I will honor it as long as you will. Do not cross me, however, or think to play me for a fool."

He looked away, then drew in a deep breath before speaking. "I will honor our agreement, and I will do my best not to cross you unless I feel it is in the best interests of Broadhurst, in which case I will do my best to persuade you to my point of view. I will not cheat you, and I will not presume upon your goodwill. That is the most and the best I can promise." He looked back up at her. "I thank you for the loan of the book. Good night, Mrs. Merriem."

Turning abruptly, he left the room, his step silent on the carpet as he went, and disappeared into the dark of the hallway.

Louisa stared after him, wondering what on earth had gotten into her.

3

$\mathcal{T}$he day dawned fine and clear and Will quickly dressed, then went downstairs to saddle Maestro. He had an early appointment with Pip down at the dairy, but he first wanted time alone to have a look around the farm and make his own assessment of what needed doing before he conferred with Louisa.

Louisa. She'd surprised him last night on a number of counts, not least of which was her prickly attitude. This was not the woman he'd come to know through her writing—that was a different person entirely, one who was sensitive and thoughtful, who adored her family and her life. Perhaps Val's death had changed her, left bitterness in the place of what once had been joy. He could understand that: he knew well enough what a deep loss could do to the spirit, and Louisa, gentle soul that she was, had probably taken her beloved husband's death harder than most.

Still, he couldn't help but be saddened by the look of bleak unhappiness in her eyes, which she took such care to disguise. In those moments they'd had alone in the library, he'd had to force himself to keep his silence when his every instinct called him to reach out to her, to comfort her, reassure her that with time she would heal from the deep wound she'd suffered. Not that he was one to talk.

He'd had his share of pain, and although he'd covered up the traces well enough, his internal injuries still bled when he wasn't paying strict attention to keeping the memories at bay.

Dismissing that unpromising direction of thought, he

shielded his eyes and looked out over the fields, one planted with hay that appeared to be coming in nicely, the next one a smooth green expanse dotted with the fat white bodies of sheep grazing contentedly. In an adjoining pasture, close to where the dairy stood, a herd of cows had gathered near the gate, waiting to be milked.

All appeared well, although he saw that the fences needed mending and the dairy could do with some repairs to its roof where the tiles had come loose. His overall impression was one of moderate shabbiness, but on the whole, everything seemed to be running smoothly enough. He pushed his fingers through his hair and considered.

The problem couldn't be simply that Louisa was short a hand or two—she also had to be short of funds. There was the household to run as well as a farm, and a small family to support. Although he knew from Pip that the last manager had run off with some of her savings, he'd never been under the impression that Louisa was lacking in money. Val had been clear on that point: he said she was well off, that he didn't worry about her in the least, and Louisa herself had mentioned no financial concerns in her letters.

She didn't strike him as incompetent—indeed, from what he'd seen, she ran the household like a drill sergeant. Which led him back to wondering about the dichotomy in her personality.

Before he had a chance to ponder the matter any further, Pip's voice rang from behind him and he turned in his saddle to see her racing over the field on her pony, braids flying behind her, three motley dogs racing along beside.

Will couldn't help grinning. Little Miss Pip was a handful indeed, as free a spirit as he'd ever met. If he was fortunate enough to have a child of his own, someone like Pip would be everything he could hope for.

"Mr. Cutter, I thought you weren't going to wait for me!" she panted, pulling up her chubby mount next to his. "He *is* big, isn't he?" she said, looking up in awe at Maestro's height.

As if in reply, Maestro leaned his head down and nosed at Apple's neck, snorting gently.

"He won't bite her, will he?" Pip asked, her voice anxious. Still, she didn't pull away, which Will found admirable.

Will patted Maestro's neck. "No, he won't. He's just curious. I doubt he's ever seen anything quite like Apple in his entire life. She's not the sort of company he usually mixes in."

Pip's face split into a broad grin. "Now you sound like Grandpapa. He used to be the great squire, you know, and it's been hard for him having to lower his standards. He hasn't taken kindly to the notion."

"Your grandfather used to be a great squire?" Will said, seeing an opportunity arise to ferret out some useful information. "What was he a great squire of?"

"Of Broadhurst Hall, of course, and all the surrounding land for miles and miles. Then his circumstances became . . ." She screwed up her face and thought. "Became straight-lined."

"Straitened, perhaps?" Will supplied.

"Yes, that's it, whatever it's supposed to mean. He lost all his money and we had to come to live here."

"When was that?" Will asked, pulling Maestro's head up and away from his ongoing investigation of Apple, who looked as if she'd had enough.

"When I was little. I really don't remember living up at the Hall. Someone else owns it now, a Mr. Cumberland." She made a face. "He's a horrid man who makes Mama's life miserable."

"Really?" Will said, a small piece of the puzzle falling

into place. Perhaps Louisa hadn't mentioned the problem to Val in her letters, not wanting to worry him while he was at war and unable to do anything about it. "How does he make her life miserable?"

"Oh, he behaves as if he is very grand and we are nothing more than dirt beneath his feet. Then there's something about paying him rent and he's always raising it. I don't really know, except that Mama cries about it when she thinks she's alone. Still, she always manages to put on a brave face. Mama is very clever that way."

"I imagine she is," Will said softly. "Maybe we can help her to be even more clever if we're clever ourselves, Pip. I think we had better keep this conversation to ourselves, though. She wouldn't thank either of us if she thought we were in collusion."

"What's that? It sounds lovely and wicked."

Will chuckled. "It isn't wicked, exactly. It just means that sometimes people can be more useful when they put their heads together and the person they're trying to help doesn't know."

"Oh," Pip said, looking thoughtful. "That is a good idea. Mama loathes interference. Is that why you wanted me to show you how to milk cows, so that Mama won't know you're hopeless?"

Will grinned. Pip was nobody's fool, not that he was surprised. He felt as if he'd known her from early childhood and loved her just as long. He decided then and there that he'd better ingratiate himself with her if he was going to make any progress with her mother.

"Exactly," he said, "although I'm not entirely hopeless. There are things I do know how to do well. It's just that milking cows isn't one of them."

Pip nodded. "Come on, then. Old Tessie's good-natured

and won't mind your pulling the wrong way at her udders. You *do* know what an udder is?"

"That much I do, yes," Will said, trying to keep a straight face.

His face didn't stay so straight when Pip sat him down at a milking stool she'd fetched from the dairy and placed his hands on two of Tessie's swollen udders. All he managed to elicit from his squeezing was an indignant bellow from the cow.

"Not like that," Pip cried as he jerked his hands away in horror. "You have to pump from the top and down. Pump, squeeze, pump, squeeze. Do you want me to show you again?"

Will shook his head and reapplied himself to his task, determined to get it right. After a few more pumps and squeezes and some more bellows on Tessie's part, he finally managed to get two streams of milk going, although most of it missed the bucket and landed on him.

"The laundry basket's going to be full again tonight," Pip said, wiping tears of laughter off her face. "You really aren't very good at this, are you?"

"I warned you," Will said, wiping a splotch of warm milk off his cheek. "Give me a week, though, and I'll be an expert, I promise."

"You had better be, or you'll be mangling someone else's cows." Pip imperiously tossed one pigtail over her shoulder.

"Very well, Miss Bossy Boots, you show me you can do better. We had better have a full bucket or the game is up."

Pip instantly rose to the challenge, exactly as he'd hoped, her hands expertly squeezing away. Within minutes, fresh milk was frothing at the top of the pail and Tessie seemed content.

The process was accomplished in just the nick of time,

for as Will heaved the bucket up, Louisa appeared from inside the dairy.

"Oh. Mr. Cutter," she said, eyeing the bucket and then Will's stained trousers. "There you are. I see that you and Tessie have met. I trust that she gave you no trouble?"

"No trouble at all, thank you," he said, shooting Pip a look that threatened to level her if she so much as blinked.

"Tessie took to Mr. Cutter's hands very quickly," Pip supplied helpfully, her mouth trembling with the effort of sincerity. Her eyes said something entirely different.

"Apparently so," Louisa said, fortunately missing the exchange and taking the bucket from Will. She handed it to her daughter. "If you would be so kind as to take this into Mr. Trueboot, Pip, you can have your breakfast and begin your lessons with your grandfather. I'll be in to check on your progress later. Mr. Cutter and I have other business to attend to."

"Good luck," Pip murmured under her breath.

"Mincemeat of little girl for lunch," Will murmured back, also under his breath.

"I beg your pardon?" Louisa said, shooting him a suspicious glance.

"I said that I'm looking forward to lunch," Will replied, as if butter wouldn't melt in his mouth.

The sound of Pip's laughter trailed behind her as she disappeared into the dairy with Tessie's hard-won milk.

"You and my daughter seem to have struck up a friendship," Louisa said, looking after her daughter's retreating back. "I do hope that you will not let her distract you from your chores. Portia has a way of wrapping people around her little finger if she's given half a chance."

"Your daughter is a bright and charming child," Will said as he untied Maestro's reins from the railing. "You are to be complimented on the way you've raised her. She is spontaneous and natural, admirable qualities that so often are trained out of young people before they have a chance to develop their own personalities."

"You appear to know a great deal about children, Mr. Cutter."

"I know nothing at all about children, save for what I've been told," Will said, watching with interest as Louisa's hand absently stroked Maestro's neck and Maestro stretched it out to her in pleasure. "My only experience is in having been a child myself. But you, Mrs. Merriem, clearly know something about horses. Maestro will not let just anyone touch him."

"I learned what I know about horses from my father," Louisa said, dropping her hand as if suddenly self-conscious. "Your gelding is a magnificent animal. How does he happen to be in your possession?"

Will shot her a sidelong look. "What you are really asking is how can someone in my position afford to own a horse like this. The answer is that he was a gift from someone I once held dear. I've had Maestro for ten years."

He didn't add that Maestro had been given to him by his father when Will joined the army. Nor did he add that Maestro had been not only a gift but a salve to his father's conscience. A horse fit for war in exchange for Will's unwilling entry into the army. Into exile was more like it. Still, Will had thanked God every day for Maestro, whose courageous heart and loyalty to his master had become the stuff of legend in the Dragoons.

"Ten years? Goodness. He looks so young. How old is he?"

"Fourteen. He has a good many more years in him."

Louisa touched a long scar on Maestro's shoulder. "How did he come by this? It looks fairly recent."

Saving my life, Will thought silently, remembering with a shudder the lance thrust that Maestro had deliberately turned and protected him from, taking the full brunt of the blow himself. Without Maestro, Will would never have survived Waterloo, let alone the rest of the war.

"He cut himself on some wire," Will said instead, hating himself for the lie, hating even more the necessity for it. Will had always had a healthy regard for the truth, and he found lying to Louisa particularly distasteful.

"Poor boy. At least the cut was clean and looks as if it healed without trouble," Louisa said, her fingers skillfully examining the muscle beneath. "Does the injury trouble him?"

"No." Although touched by her concern, Will, quickly changed the subject, not wanting to dwell on a memory that gave him nothing but regret. "You appear to be without a horse of your own. Would that mare in the stable who is in, um, an interesting condition be yours, perhaps?"

"She is. Her name is Theodora, and I bred her to a very fine stallion, so I am hoping the foal will be equally fine."

"So for the moment you are without a mount."

"I am," she said, walking alongside him. "It is only a small hardship. With luck, I will be able to sell the foal in a year or two and make a fine profit. Of course, whether I'll be able to bring myself to sell is another question. I have a terrible tendency to become attached."

"I understand," he said, aware of just how attached to her animals she was. He knew all about Theodora, and had been pleased to see for himself that Louisa's breeding attempts had proved fruitful. He'd wondered whether she'd succeed in that particular venture. Lord, it was hard having to behave as if he knew nothing at all. The likelihood of tripping himself up was enormous and he had to guard every word, every reaction.

"I imagine you do understand, given your obvious devotion to Maestro. From your conversation with Tom last night, I gather that you know a good deal about horses."

Will sidestepped that issue, avoiding another pitfall. "I hope I know enough to be of use. Tell me, Mrs. Merriem, just what you do expect of me. You said last night that you wished to go over the tasks you expect me to see to."

"Oh. Yes, I do." She proceeded to fire off a rapid list of duties, most of which involved overseeing the plowing of fields, the mending of fences, and various other odds and ends that would be time-consuming but would not require a great deal of expertise. That was until she got to the part about branding the calves and docking their ears. It only got worse.

Will felt his stomach growing queasy. "You want me to . . . to do *what*?"

"I said that the majority of the calves have to be neutered, Mr. Cutter. Why do you look so surprised? It only involves tying off the necessary part. The rest will take care of itself." She regarded him curiously. "Are you all right? You appear positively ill."

He knew he did, for he felt positively ill. "Mrs. Merriem," he said through a dry throat, "you hired a man-of-all-work, as I recall. I took that to mean that you expected me to look after your odds and ends, not to mutilate innocent beasts."

Louisa stared at him, then burst into gales of laughter. "You do realize you are on a farm? These proceedings are a normal part of life here." Her laughter faded, to be replaced by puzzlement. "Why, I believe you are serious," she said, her eyes widening. "Who *are* you, Mr. Cutter?"

"I am a man who enjoys animals," he said, taking advantage of a fallen tree and sinking down onto the trunk. "I cannot bring myself to cause them pain. It is a failing of mine, I admit, but there it is."

"In which case life on a farm must have caused you a great deal of trouble in the past," she said, taking Maestro's reins from Will's hands and looping them over the horse's neck, setting him free to graze. She sat down next to him on the log. "Mr. Cutter, something tells me you are not all you try to appear to be. Would you care to explain yourself?"

"No. I wouldn't," he said, swallowing hard, still shaken by the idea of holding down a helpless calf and . . . the thought didn't bear repeating. "I told you I would help you to the best of my ability," he managed to say. "Those last tasks are not included in my repertoire. Anything else, just ask, and I will do my best, but killing or maiming—in short, no."

Louisa stroked one hand over her cheek, then looked down at the ground. "Very well," she said after a long moment. "There are others who can do the job. Does this have something to do with your being a bad shot?"

Will glanced over at her. At least in this he could be honest. "I can hit a target at fifty feet with no trouble. I would rather that target be inanimate, however."

"In other words, you have no lust for blood," she said, her voice so quiet that he only just heard her.

"I have not," he said, just as quietly.

Ah, if *only* he could tell her the truth and tell her from the very beginning. He'd never had a lust for blood— indeed, the very opposite, that every moment of fighting the war had been contrary to his nature, that in his childhood he'd wept when he'd been forced to "be a man" and kill game and birds.

Every gunshot had been a knife in his heart, and the day he'd been blooded with his first downed stag still remained a horrific memory. All of twelve, he stood there and tried to look as proud as his father as the fresh blood was smeared on his face, but he had to force back the tears and the guilt of being responsible for taking the magnificent beast's life. The effort had taken all of his self-control.

Taking a man's life had proved to be far worse, and he'd done more than his fair share of that, even if it had been in self-defense or in defense of his comrades.

"Mr. Cutter, there is no need to look so mortified. I admire a man who does not take pleasure from killing. There are far too many who think such an act proves their manhood but I happen to disagree. When I said I was a good shot, I told you the truth, but I did not say I enjoyed it—I would far rather someone else do the necessaries, which is why I asked you." She shook her head slowly. "I suppose one does what one must for survival's sake. I no more hold with killing than you do."

Will released a heavy sigh, shaking off his own dark thoughts, and looked over at her. The open, honest expression in Louisa's eyes nearly undid him; the mask she'd learned to assume had vanished, and his heart turned over in his chest at the sight of her.

She sat there in her simple gray dress of half-mourning, her blue eyes clouded, her hands gathered in her lap, a mass of auburn hair falling over one shoulder as she gazed off into the distance.

He saw her sadness, felt the despair at the root of it and knew it had nothing to do with their conversation, only that it had touched another, deeper cord. He imagined it was grief, still fresh and raw. She was a brave woman, the bravest he'd ever known.

She'd been embroiled in a terrible situation and never once given a hint of her troubles to her husband, writing him letters filled with life, giving him a reason to hope, to come home again, filling every page with vivid description so that he had something to cling to, a belief in the future.

He wondered if he would have been so brave if he'd been in her place.

He doubted it.

"Do you ever wonder if there's a grand plan?" he asked, shifting to face her on the log, suddenly, desperately wanting to know. "I don't mean anything specific, but something that God has set for us, a reason for the way things happen, for the bad as well as the good?"

She looked at him in surprise, her face soft and unguarded, and for the first time he saw her not as the woman of the letters but for exactly who she was. He took in a quick, painful breath, trying to steady himself.

"I've never thought of it like that before, at least not precisely that way," she said, her brow furrowing. "I suppose I've always thought that God meant us to do His will, but I never thought He might have a greater plan in mind, or at least not for me. Do you believe He has for you?"

Will briefly closed his eyes, too many emotions chasing through him. He couldn't risk having her divining his feelings, not when they were this close to the surface, too real for the first time, a real man caring for a real woman in a real world and for all the right reasons for once.

"I don't know," he said, turning his face away. "I've often wondered. Sometimes I think I'm fabricating the idea for my own comfort, but I cannot explain it away either. What sense is there in living a life that is nothing but a series of blind coincidences while we wait for our heavenly reward, when God might very well have given us the gift of making and rectifying mistakes so that we can learn from our humanity?"

"Oh," Louisa said. "I think I see what you mean. We do have free will, but God waits to see what we do with it. We can honor or dishonor His trust in us, is that it?"

"I think that is part of it, but I also believe that we each have a quest in this life, large or small. Some of us choose to acknowledge that quest, although most others choose to rely blindly on religious faith and feel that going to church every Sunday will take care of everything else." He scratched his cheek with one finger. "I cannot help but feel that it is the still, small voice we hear inside ourselves that leads us to the true nature of faith."

Will suspected that he sounded like a lunatic, but he didn't particularly care, not when he was talking to Louisa. He knew in his gut that she understood, although he couldn't explain why. He just knew and that was enough. "That viewpoint is probably also heresy in the eyes of the Church. Do you mind?"

Her rosy mouth curved up in a smile. "I do believe I'd rather listen to you any Sunday than the vicar, who rattles on about guilt and sins and our ever-failing weaknesses until I want to curl up and die."

"I don't think I need to meet your vicar, if that is the case," he replied, returning her smile. "I've had more than enough of hellfire and damnation." God knew he'd seen enough of it. "I'd rather concentrate on peace, thank you. I cannot believe that the Lord wishes us to live in a state of constant terror."

Louisa's smile widened. "I could not agree with you more, although I have to admit this is a rather peculiar conversation. Do you always launch into philosophical subjects at the drop of a hat, Mr. Cutter?"

"To tell you the absolute truth, I am in the habit of keeping my thoughts to myself. I cannot think what has come over me." *You, Louisa, just you*, he added silently, thinking himself a fool ten times over for allowing himself to feel this way at all.

"You intrigue me," she said. "Perhaps one day you will tell me more about yourself."

"Perhaps," he said, his voice neutral. He stood, not willing to trust himself with another word. Louisa had an uncanny ability to cut straight through his carefully constructed defenses, and he'd be damned if he'd let her drag another thing out of him. "I should get on with my duties. You've given me enough to keep me busy for the next year."

"Very well," she said, her voice assuming its previous brisk tone. "I will expect you to report to me on a weekly basis. If you have any questions, please do not hesitate to ask. Although I expect you to use your initiative, I also would like you to consult with me before doing anything that requires expenditure."

"Naturally," he said, busying himself with Maestro's reins. He swung up into the saddle and looked down at her, wishing she didn't look so damned lovely. "Although it works two ways, Mrs. Merriem. If you are in need of advice, you need only ask and I will do my best to provide it."

She colored. "I have done very well without your advice before now," she said, her eyes flashing with sudden anger. "I expect I will continue to do so. Just because I am a female does not mean I have an inadequate brain."

"My apologies," he said, wanting to kick himself for his thoughtless phrasing. "I did not mean to imply any such thing. I only meant—"

"I know what you meant," she said, glaring at him and planting her hands on her hips. "And in the future, keep your opinions to yourself, for I have no use for them. You are here to work, nothing more."

Will inclined his head. "As you wish," he said, stung to

the quick. He'd gone and revealed his innermost thoughts to a woman who clearly had no use for those either. He really was an idealistic fool for believing that she was anything like the fantasy he'd created in his head.

He turned Maestro and nudged him into a canter, wishing with all his heart that he'd never made the turn at the Maidencombe crossroads.

4

Putting down her pen in satisfaction, Louisa blotted the last page and placed it on top of the pile of closely written foolscap she'd painstakingly accumulated.

"Done," she murmured. "I'm actually done." She could scarcely believe it—her secret project, conceived as a last resort to bring in some extra income, had given her more satisfaction than she'd ever thought possible. She'd written a novel, actually written a full novel.

Best of all, she truly liked it. She'd started out to write something that she thought might be commercially viable, since her only intention had been to make money, not literature, and so had hit on the idea of an adventure story that centered on a pirate and his exploits in the last century. To her amazement the book had taken on its own movement and voice, and she'd enjoyed every last minute of Jack Kilblaine's life on the high seas, not to mention his roguish life on the shores of England and France.

Still, rogue that he was, Jack was also a man of honor, a latter-day Robin Hood, his intentions pure, although his behavior was anything but.

Louisa grinned. Who would have known she'd had it in her? She blushed to think of some of the warmer scenes she'd written, but how could it matter since she would never be identified as the author?

Chuckling to herself, she dipped her pen in the inkwell one last time and wrote out the title page.

The Adventures of Jack Kilblaine, Pirate.

She brushed her cheek with the tip of the quill. Now for

the author's name. Narrowing her eyes in thought, she mulled over the possibilities. Obviously, the name had to be a man's, for no self-respecting woman would write such brazen material—well, maybe with the exception of Caroline Lamb, whose publication of her roman à clef, *Glenarvon,* had created a monstrous scandal only last month.

God help Louisa if her father ever found out what she'd been doing in her stolen moments. He'd never speak to her again, not that he spoke much to her in any case.

M. J. Peter, she decided. M. J. for her mother, Mary Justine, and Peter for her beloved older brother, whose death at the age of sixteen had broken her heart.

Yes, that was good. Peter would have liked the book—indeed, he would have laughed himself silly over Louisa's daring. For daring it was. If she should ever be discovered, her name would be dragged through the mud and her reputation ruined for all time.

Stretching her stiff back, she leaned back in her chair and stuck her feet out in front of her. The odds of her novel's ever being published were minuscule, but she didn't really care at this point, as much as the extra money would help. She'd done what she'd set out to do, and for the moment that was satisfaction enough.

Tomorrow she'd send the manuscript off to the publisher she'd selected and try to put the whole thing out of her mind. Indeed, concentrating on finishing her book had one enormous bonus—she'd managed to forget about Will Cutter for the better part of a week.

She couldn't be sure whether she'd gone into a final writing frenzy as a reason to avoid him, or whether the book had taken over and she'd simply made the time to focus on it, but either way, the writing had accomplished its purpose. She'd seen hardly hide nor hair of the man since he'd ridden off after their conversation, and that was all to the good.

Their last encounter had been enough to thoroughly undo her. Who did he think he was, prying into her inner recesses like that, pulling things out of her that she'd never confided to another human being? He behaved as if he were father confessor and dearest confidant all at the same time, when he didn't know the first thing about her.

And she, being a complete idiot, had gone along with him, unable to help herself.

She shivered, the image of his direct, piercing gaze still far too clear in her mind, as was the memory of the way his broad, muscular shoulders had shifted under his coat as he'd leaned forward, his finely shaped hands resting on his strong thighs, his thick hair shifting gently in the light breeze. Her reaction to him had been nothing less than visceral, and she was still appalled by it. Surely she hadn't been swayed by his good looks alone? No, there was something else about him, something she'd never encountered before. He had a force of will, a power of persuasion, that left her feeling helpless.

Yes, she decided, that was what was at the root of the problem, and since feeling helpless was the last thing she ever wanted to experience again, Will Cutter would have to go. That was all there was to it. She'd dismiss him as soon as she had reason, and she would find one soon enough, since he was bound to prove unreliable. All men did in the end.

Louisa walked over to the window and looked out over the terraced gardens, gently washed in the light of the moon that was nearly full. This was her beloved Broadhurst, even if it was only just a tiny piece of what once had been, and she'd protect it—and her family—with everything she had in her. No one would ever steal from her again. She would see to that if it took the last breath in her body.

A knock sounded at the door and she jumped. "Just a moment," she called, hurriedly crossing over to the desk and depositing her manuscript in the lower right-hand drawer. She settled herself in the chair and pulled the accounts book out, opening it and picking up her pen as if she'd been hard at work on the numbers all evening.

She stiffened in surprise as Will Cutter appeared in the doorway, her cheeks suddenly flaming despite her resolution to feel nothing.

"Good evening, Mrs. Merriem. I trust I am not interrupting?" He was disheveled, his shirt open at the neck, and he wore no jacket.

She swallowed hard, wishing he'd bothered to dress properly instead of exposing such an unwelcome expanse of himself. "Not at all. Please come in," she said, indicating the chair opposite the desk, wishing with all her heart that she could make him vanish in a puff of smoke. Oh, Lord, *why* couldn't she keep her head about her when he appeared? She felt as if it were she who might go up in a puff of smoke at any moment.

She pressed her hands to her hot cheeks. "I suppose you've come about the weekly report?"

"No, Mrs. Merriem," he said, his face inscrutable. "I have come about your mare. She's about to foal. I thought you might want to know, since you put great store by her."

Louisa forgot everything that had gone before. "Theodora? But she's not due for another two weeks by my calculations—are you sure?"

"I am very sure. She is in her stall, and I believe your

presence might make her more comfortable. She is not having an easy time. This is her first foal?"

"Yes!" Louisa's heart began to pound in panic, and she jumped to her feet. "What do you mean? She is young and healthy and her pregnancy has been an easy one. Do you think she is in danger?"

"I honestly don't know," he said. "I think you should come, though."

Louisa blew out the lamps and rushed to the door. "Let us waste no time."

The lamps in the stables were already lit, and Louisa's heart fell into her stomach when she saw Theodora. Her black coat was covered in a fine layer of sweat, her eyes dark and dilated. She lay on her side, her sides heaving.

Louisa quickly opened the stall door and sank down onto the fresh straw, her hand stroking Theodora's neck. "Come now, my beauty, relax. There's nothing to be frightened of, nothing at all." She glanced up at Will, who had knelt down next to her. "Where is Maestro? Perhaps his presence is frightening her."

He shook his head. "Maestro is in the paddock. I decided this afternoon that this was no place for him to be."

"This afternoon? You've left her like this since the afternoon?" she demanded, anger rising quickly.

"She was restless, but her labor only became apparent in the last few hours. If you'd prefer someone else to attend to her, you have only to say the word. Whatever you decide, I suggest you keep your tone soothing and your feelings under control, no matter what you might think of me." His expression was stony.

Louisa instantly regretted her outburst. "Forgive me—I am just terribly concerned."

"Naturally you are," he said, his face softening slightly. "We both are. I am going to need your help. Are you willing? It might be a messy job."

"Of *course* I'm willing, you dunderhead," she said, then clamped her lips together, remembering that she'd just promised to stay calm. "I love this mare and will do anything necessary. It is you I am worried about, given your squeamish stomach."

Will ran one hand over his eyes. "I never said I had a squeamish stomach, I said I didn't enjoy killing. Although I might make an exception in your case if you don't get over whatever absurd grudge you're holding against me and help me get Theodora through this." He glared at her. "Do you think you can manage that much at least?"

"I just said as much, didn't I?" She dropped her gaze to her hands. "I'm sorry. My temper tends to run away with me, especially when I'm distressed. Just tell me what to do and I will do it without argument, I promise."

Will's eyes crinkled at the corners and she thought she saw a laugh lurking in them, which somehow helped to ease the tight knot in her chest.

"I doubt that, somehow," he said, "but I will hold you to your word. I'd like to examine her, see what I can discover, although God help me—I've never actually delivered a foal, let alone one that might be in distress."

"Do you really think the foal is in distress?" she asked, her voice no more than a whisper, worry eating away at her. "Maybe Theodora is just nervous, being a first-time mother."

"Maybe," Will said, stripping off his shirt and tossing it into the corner. "Let us hope that is the case, although I cannot like the way she is straining with no progress." He ran his hand over her swollen side. "I've seen mares give birth before, but I've never seen one in this condition."

Louisa smoothed her own hand over Theodora's belly, following Will's path. "I remember well giving birth to Pip. Her entrance into the world was tedious but uncomplicated. What does this mean?"

She tried not to look at Will's bare chest, but couldn't help herself. He was so beautifully made, his ribs muscled, his chest ridged, and oh . . . his shoulders were so broad and well defined. She felt ashamed of herself for noticing him at all under such dire circumstances.

Will picked up a piece of soap and thoroughly washed his hands and arms in a bucket of water he had standing nearby. "I think she might have a malpresentation. I've been reading some books your father loaned me last week—I wished I could have asked him his opinion myself, but he'd retired for the evening. To tell you the truth, I'm not sure how much information I could have elicited from him. He finds prolonged conversation difficult."

"My father suffers from ill health," Louisa said, not willing to elaborate. She couldn't, not without having to explain Val and his actions, and that was the last thing in the world she wished to do. Explaining Val at all was impossible, even to herself.

Will took a strip of linen and wrapped and tied Theodora's tail to get it out of the way, then washed her with soap and water from the bucket.

"What are you going to do?" Louisa asked uncertainly as he took up a position behind Theodora.

"I'm going to examine her, see what I can discover," he said, gingerly inserting his hand into the birth canal. "Your job is to reassure her." He looked unnerved, which didn't reassure Louisa in the least, and she couldn't imagine that Theodora felt any different.

She squeezed her eyes shut, praying that Will wouldn't

hurt Theodora, but amazingly enough the mare didn't seem to mind, since she made no protest. Instead, she blew softly through her nostrils and relaxed her head. Even a mare in hard labor trusted Will, Louisa thought, wondering why she found it impossible to do the same.

"I've found one leg," Will said with a grunt. "I think the head must be turned back and the other hock hung up."

"Can you do something?" Louisa said, opening her eyes and peering over at him. He looked as if he were in pain, his face screwed up, sweat beading on his brow.

"I'm going to try as soon as I can catch my breath. My arm feels as if it's caught in a vise. I think I'll wait until this contraction is over." He rested his head on his extended forearm. "I have to confess, I never thought I'd find myself hanging on for dear life to an unborn foal. Damnation, that hurts."

Louisa couldn't help grinning. Will Cutter did not appear to be his usual calm, assertive self. Indeed, he looked thoroughly disheveled and uncomfortable, and she had to confess she was enjoying the spectacle despite the seriousness of the situation and her very real alarm. "What will you do?" she asked, dropping a kiss onto Theodora's cheek.

"I'm going . . . going to try to back the foal up and pull her head straight to get her nose to come down. At least that's the plan. I don't suppose you have any other better idea?"

"Well, it stands to reason that you have to do something about getting that other leg straight. Do you have a plan for that?"

"Yes, as it happens, I do have a plan for that," he said between gritted teeth. "You are a woman of little faith, Mrs. Merriem. Perhaps you would rather take over?"

"Oh, no—you seem to be doing a fine job," she said quickly.

He raised his head, his dark eyes filled with wry humor. "How quick you are to see reason. Ah, that's better—she's easing up." Shifting slightly, he rotated his arm and pushed hard. "Good. I have some slack on the shoulders now." He looked off into space, fully focused on his task. "There. The body's moving back."

Another few minutes passed as Louisa watched him intently. Sweat trickled down his chest and back and he was clearly struggling. She didn't want to think about what he was doing, but he appeared confident. She, on the other hand, was anything but.

Finally he looked up, a triumphant smile on his face. "I have the nose—it's coming forward! Now for that blasted other leg." His lips compressed and his shoulders shifted. "Oh, that's excellent, just excellent, Theodora. You stay nice and relaxed."

Louisa watched his face intently, the strong planes accented by the light of the lamps. "Can you feel the other leg?" she asked, her heart pounding with anxiety. They were so close now, but still not out of the woods.

"I think . . . I think I have it. Yes, that has to be the other leg." He leaned forward and twisted his arm, then pulled his weight back with a slight groan. "That's—that's it, I think," he gasped, his face streaked with rivulets of sweat. "Yes, I've got both forelegs straight and the nose is right on top. Come on, Theodora, come *on*, girl. It's your turn."

As he carefully withdrew his arm, Theodora gave a mighty push and then another.

"Come and look," Will said softly. "I think you'll want to see this."

She instantly moved to his side, her eyes widening as two miniature hooves appeared, followed by slender fetlocks. With one more push the head emerged, eyes closed, ears folded flat.

Louisa sighed with amazement. "Oh . . . oh, it's a miracle," she whispered, overwhelmed and filled with infinite gratitude.

"It is that," Will said, clearing mucus away from the tiny nose and mouth. In another moment the rest of the body came sliding out, a beautiful little colt. He squirmed on the straw, snuffling as he took in his first breaths.

Silently staring in awe, Louisa was astonished by what she'd just witnessed.

"Let's introduce him to his mother, shall we?"

Will gently took him by his front legs and moved him up toward Theodora's head. She stretched her neck toward him, tentatively smelling him, and then, recognizing him as her own, began softly licking him.

"Mission accomplished," Will said, sinking back into the straw, a smile of supreme satisfaction on his face. "Thank God for small mercies."

"Thank God for you, Will Cutter," Louisa said, tears of relief streaming down her face. "I honestly didn't know if you would be able to manage." She ran trembling fingers over her eyes, wishing she had better control over her emotions.

"To be honest, neither did I." He stood and moved over to the bucket, sluicing his hands and face in water, then used his discarded shirt to dry himself off. "I should examine her for any tears or lacerations, but I think that we're free and clear. Could you fetch another bucket? I think there's one around the corner somewhere."

Louisa stood, surprised to find her knees wobbly. She

imagined she was suffering from delayed shock. Now that the crisis had passed, she shook from head to toe. The very thought of losing Theodora had frightened her more than she cared to admit—she'd raised her from a foal and doted on her. Theodora had never given her a moment's trouble, unlike most everyone else in her life.

"Oh," she said, reaching her hand out to steady herself as she nearly stumbled.

Will instantly appeared at her side, his arm going around her waist. "Feeling a little undone, are you?" he said, taking her weight against him. "Here, sit down. I'll get the bucket myself."

Louisa quickly obliged, as eager to escape his touch as she was to avoid keeling over and making even more of a fool of herself.

"I'll be right back," he said, giving her a long, appraising look before he disappeared.

The few moments he was gone gave her time to try to pull herself together. She put her head in her hands, wondering why Will Cutter had the ability to rattle her so completely. Just the feel of his arm wrapping around had set her heart racing and caused her breath to catch in her throat. She suspected that the dizziness she felt now had far more to do with Will than with Theodora, and she wanted to kick herself for being such an idiot.

Had she learned *nothing* from her experience with Val? Not that Val had ever made her feel light-headed, but still, she'd sworn she'd never let herself be drawn to any man ever again.

Louisa groaned, hearing her own thoughts. Was that what was happening? Could she possibly be attracted to Will? Impossible, she told herself. He was the man-of-all-work, a simple laborer, nothing more. One wasn't physically drawn to one's laborers, it just wasn't done. She'd spent her entire twenty-seven years trying to do the right thing, not that it had done her any good: she seemed to go from bad to worse with no trouble at all.

Her head shot up as Will reappeared, bucket in hand. "What—what is it for?" she asked for lack of anything better to say.

"Theodora has yet to deliver the placenta," he answered, crouching down next to her. "Good, you have some color back in your face. Feeling better?"

She nodded, wishing he'd keep his distance. "I think I'm just hungry," she said. "I missed dinner."

"You've been doing a lot of that. Cook says you usually have a better appetite—the trays she's been sending you have come back mostly untouched. Any reason?"

"I've had other things on my mind," Louisa said, looking away.

"Anything you care to discuss?" He moved back to Theodora and started to examine her. "Sometimes troubles shared are troubles lightened."

"Nothing, thank you," Louisa said, deliberately making her tone noncommittal.

"In other words, it is none of my business. Fine, Mrs. Merriem. Have it any way you want it, but it seems to me that you have a very great deal on your hands and no one else to help you out. I am here and willing to listen, so I'd suggest that you give up this pigheaded attitude of yours and let me help."

"*Pigheaded* attitude?" she said, sitting up straight, her cheeks flushing with anger. "Just who do you think you are?"

"The man you are paying to help you," he said evenly. "I can hardly be of help when you avoid me around every corner to the extent that you will not even take meals with your family. Cook also tells me that this is not your usual habit, so I can only assume that I am the problem."

He glanced over at her. "You might be so good as to tell me *why* I am the problem. Could it have anything to do with the last conversation we had? Did I leave you with a disgust of some kind—my deplorable views on life, perhaps? Allow me to apologize if that was the case, but I didn't realize that in speaking of my personal philosophy I was offending you."

She bit her lip, ashamed that he'd ever thought her to be so insensitive. "No, you didn't offend me in the least. I—I honestly have been busy."

He looked at her long and hard. "So busy that you've ignored everyone around you, including your daughter?"

"Did Pip say something to you?" Louisa said, horrified that she might have felt neglected. Her daughter was her entire reason for living, and Louisa had been so selfishly caught up in her writing that she hadn't even stopped to consider that Pip might be missing her. "Did she? Please tell me."

"Pip has said nothing. She would never say a word against you—you are her entire world and she loves you dearly. That much she did tell me. I am merely making an observation." He placed his hand on Theodora's belly. "I think she's ready now."

Louisa, feeling smaller than she ever had in her life, watched as Will delivered the placenta and examined its surfaces to make sure everything was whole, then placed the mass in the bucket. She wanted to curl up into a little ball, knowing that he was right: she had been negligent. She'd put her own feelings ahead of her family's, and to what end? So that she could finish writing her novel? So that she could make herself more comfortable by keeping as far away from him as possible? Those were poor excuses.

Will placed the bucket outside the stall door, then washed and dried his hands again, all of this in complete silence.

She wanted desperately to say something, to explain, but she didn't know how to begin.

Then he turned toward her and sat, his back leaning against the wall of the stall, one knee pulled up, his arm resting on top. "So. Are you ready to talk now?"

Her cheeks flamed. How could she possibly make him understand? "It's complicated," she said. "I don't know what else to tell you. There's too much . . . too much that's happened."

"Then tell me how you feel," he said. "Start there and the rest will come."

"Mr. Cutter—"

"Will," he said. "Just Will. There is no one here but the two of us." He smiled softly. "Except, of course, Theodora and her newborn foal, but I doubt they're listening to anyone save the angels."

"The angels," Louisa said, exhaling tiredly. "I suppose you believe in fairy dust as well."

"Not fairy dust. But angels, most definitely. Do you not, Louisa? Have you lost that much faith?"

"Not in God, but certainly in man," she said, forgetting to object to his using her given name. "As for anything in between, I haven't time. Life is hard enough without creating fantasies with which to delude oneself. I put those aside with my childhood."

A shadow passed over his face, and he looked down at his hands for a moment. "Yes," he said in a low voice, "I've learned that fantasies can be misleading, even if they do help in one's darkest moments. Still, there is a huge difference between recognizing fantasy and recognizing the presence of Divinity."

"And you think you know what that presence is?" she asked with a heavy note of sarcasm.

He raised his head and looked at her, his eyes clear and direct. "You just experienced life being born and you called it a miracle. You had no qualms about speaking of it that way. Why do you then question the presence of Divinity when it appears before you?"

"That's different," she said, flustered, although she couldn't in all honesty fault his reasoning. "You were talking about angels, not the miracle of birth. That happens hundreds of thousands of times every day."

"Is it any less preposterous that every birth, let alone every death, should be accompanied by angelic presence?"

"Am I to presume that you have direct experience?" she asked, tucking her legs up under her. "I begin to think you really have been sprinkled with fairy dust."

He chuckled. "No fairy dust, and I wouldn't encourage you to presume anything at all. My life to date has not been any sort of exultation, celestial or otherwise. All I am saying is that I do believe the Heavenly Father has taken enough pity upon the poor miserable, misguided creatures He created to provide us with a little extra help in the form of angels. God help them as well, for they certainly have their work cut out for them."

Louisa's face lit up with amusement. "Oh, so that's how it works? God's angels are actually little ants, forever moving earth when we cave it in around ourselves, staving off disaster?"

Will burst into laughter. "I've never thought of it quite

like that, but I reckon you have it precisely. Bless you for giving me your own unique perspective. I have a tendency to take life too seriously, and you've been a great antidote."

"I don't know if I should be complimented or insulted," she said, her own laughter bubbling over. "Do you mean that you think me featherbrained?"

"Oh, anything but," he said, his expression sobering. "Anything but, although I do think you lack a certain degree of common sense."

She stiffened in indignation. "My common sense is my finest quality."

"No. It is not. You might *think* it is, but you are wrong." He rested his chin on his fist. "Your finest quality is your heart, for that is what leads you. Your common sense is what you use as a secondary measure, and not always effectively, since it's not your strong suit. Say what you will, you know I am right."

She stared at him openmouthed, wondering how he could possibly know any of these things about her. The hell of it was that he was right, although she wasn't about to let him know that. "And what makes you such an authority?" she said, bristling defensively.

"Let's just say intuition and leave it at that. There is, however, a great deal more that I would like to know about you. This is your opportunity to set me straight."

"Why ever would I want to do that?" she said, reaching back and retying the ribbon around her hair, which had come loose in every direction.

"Why wouldn't you?" he replied, an amused glint in his eyes. "I cannot think you have anything to hide. Indulge me, Mrs. Merriem. I have nothing better to do than sit here and wait until Theodora and her foal get to their feet."

Wishing that Will Cutter wasn't sitting there before her,

bare-chested and looking so blasted *masculine*, Louisa sighed impatiently. "All right then. My husband is dead, as you've probably guessed. He was killed at Waterloo. I have a family to support and, as you've observed, very little help about the place. What else do you want to know?"

"What makes you so impossibly prickly. Anyone would think I was trying to extract your molars instead of a little information."

"You're not exactly subtle about your probing," she said, her voice tart. "What do I know about you, after all? You dropped onto my doorstep with no warning and no references."

"Oh, no you don't. You're not going to evade the question by turning it back on me," he said, shifting his position and resting the back of his head against the wall, his gaze trained on her face. "So why *do* your hackles go up so easily?"

"I was not aware that I possessed hackles," she said, shooting him an injured look. "They sound most unladylike."

"I think I will avoid a reply, as I dare not risk the consequences." The laughter left his eyes. "If you won't tell me about yourself, tell me about your father. You say he suffers from ill health. Has that always been the case?"

Louisa stiffened. "I cannot think that is any of your business either."

"Perhaps not, but I was hoping you would tell me anyway. Whatever you say I will keep in confidence—I'm not in the habit of disseminating other people's business, despite what you might think of me."

She hesitated. It would be such a relief to have someone to confide in. She'd spent so long trying to carry the burden by herself, and the effort weighed heavily on her.

"Very well," she finally said, although with great reluctance. "He had a financial setback some years ago. We lost nearly everything and he hasn't been the same since. The shock nearly broke his constitution, and he has not been well ever since."

Will nodded. "Pip told me you used to live up at the Hall. Your father was forced to sell it, then?"

"Yes, and everything else he possessed, save the farm," she said bitterly. "I think he has never been able to forgive himself for taking the advice of someone he ought not to have trusted. The stock he invested in collapsed, you see, and he'd put all his money in it."

"I see," Will said, his tone thoughtful, "and now the only money you have is the income from the farm, is that it?"

"Yes," she said miserably.

"Did your husband leave you nothing, then?"

Louisa stared down at her hands. "Nothing," she said in a low voice. "Val lost most of what we had in the same venture. Then he joined the King's Dragoons and went off to war."

"He joined up *after* this disaster?"

Louisa looked up, wondering why Will appeared so surprised. "Yes. He bought himself a commission. He thought his country needed him."

Will frowned. "He thought his country needed him more than you did?"

"Clearly," Louisa said, not wanting to talk about Val in the least. Just thinking about him was enough to make her blood boil. "So we moved down here, and I've done my best to make the farm turn a profit, but with little success, I'm afraid. One of the problems is the extortionate rate that the new owner of the Hall keeps demanding for lease of the outer fields. I just cannot get Mr. Cumberland to see reason."

"Hmm," Will said, picking up a piece of straw and examining it as if it were the most fascinating thing he'd ever seen. "Does this Mr. Cumberland have any particular ax to grind with you personally?"

Louisa drew in a sharp breath. "How on earth would you know that?" she said, for a horrified moment wondering if Will Cutter could read minds, then dismissing the idea as ridiculous.

"Just a guess," he said easily enough. "Would you mind telling me what that ax is?"

Louisa blushed down to her toes. "Is it important?"

"It might be." He tossed the straw to one side. "I've found that people are very often motivated by a sense of vengeance, caused by some real or even imagined slight."

"Your perception is frightening," she said, a shiver running down her spine. "As it happens, I rejected David Cumberland's offer of marriage a number of years ago. He never forgave me."

"So when he saw his chance to make your life a living hell, he took it. Typical," Will said with disgust. "What were the circumstances behind your turning him down?"

Louisa twined her fingers together.

"Louisa? Must I repeat the question?"

She scowled at him. She'd never met such an infuriatingly persistent man. "No, and don't call me Louisa. My name is Mrs. Merriem to you. I met my husband that same London Season. I had never considered Mr. Cumberland seriously, but he thought otherwise, and when I fell in love with Val and married him shortly thereafter, David Cumberland felt betrayed and humiliated."

"Was his courtship public knowledge?" Will asked, not looking at all perturbed that she'd put him in his place.

"His courtship was no secret, although I had made no favorite of him," she admitted reluctantly. "I suppose he thought his money would win out in the end. Val had very little, you see, although he did have a higher social standing, being the younger son of a baron—not that I cared about that."

She pressed her hands against her face, her cheeks flaming. "I cannot believe I am telling you all this."

"There is no need for embarrassment," he said. "You married for love, not money or position, which is as I think it should be. I have nothing against arranged marriages, mind you, if neither party objects, but I could no more marry without love than I could trade my honor for a profit."

Louisa studied him with fascination. "Why, Will Cutter, the way you talk, anyone would think you knew something about marriage."

He surprised her yet again, his color heightening as he quickly looked away from her inquiring gaze. "I didn't say that. I only said that such an arrangement would not suit my nature. I know nothing at all of marriage, never having experienced it."

"And now I've embarrassed you. Did I cut a little too close to the bone?" she asked, feeling as she'd finally seized the advantage, and high time, too, since he'd been cutting far too close to her own bone. "Or are you the only one who is allowed to pry?"

"I wasn't aware that I'd been prying," he replied. "I was trying to help, not an easy thing to do when you tie my hands behind my back at every other turn."

"Oh dear, Mr. Cutter. Something tells me that you don't like having the tables turned on you." She tapped her chin, her lips trembling with a suppressed smile. "It only seems fair that you should give back as much as I've given."

"You are a hard little taskmaster, aren't you?" he said, looking thoroughly uncomfortable. "Do keep in mind that I'm not paying you for your help—not that I need any."

"Don't you? Then explain to me why you, an obviously educated man, have been sitting here in my stable, up to your elbows in horse."

"Because your horse needed my assistance," he answered dryly. "I don't recall trying to teach her the alphabet."

Louisa leaned forward. "You, sir, are dodging the question, and I would point out that you've neatly dodged the entire subject every time I've brought it up."

"That is my prerogative," he said. "You claim the same privilege—why shouldn't I?"

"That's not fair," she cried, frustrated to her limit. The more he eluded her questions, the more her curiosity grew. "I told you what you asked; surely you can return the courtesy? You are the most impossible, intractable, evasive man I've ever had the misfortune to meet!"

"Why don't you try asking nicely?" he said, a sudden smile flashing across his face. "You don't catch flies with vinegar. Honey is much more effective."

"Very well." She folded her arms across her chest. "Please, Mr. Cutter, will you tell me something about your background?"

"Will. You might be Mrs. Merriem, but I prefer to be called Will."

"Will, then," she snapped, wanting to kick him. Oh, he really was impossible.

"Thank you." He blew out a long breath, then rested his hands on his raised knees. "I was born in a small town in Norfolk. I lived there until I was twenty, and yes, I was fortunate enough to be educated by a fine man who lived nearby and was dedicated to his profession. His passion was literature and the classics—oh, and history, so I was given a healthy dose of all three. At the age of twenty I went out on my own and have been moving about ever since, relying on my wits to stay alive." He tilted his head. "Will that do?"

"No," she said bluntly, refusing to let him off the hook now that she was finally getting somewhere. "What about your parents?"

His eyes darkened. "My mother died when I was eight, giving birth to a daughter who also died. My father survived her by another fourteen years, although he was never in good health after that. He eventually succumbed to an illness of the lungs. I don't think he ever really recovered from her death."

"I'm sorry," Louisa said softly, knowing well what it was like to lose a mother at a young age and, although her father was very much alive, also knowing how it had felt to lose him in spirit. She and Will Cutter had more in common than she'd realized. "Why did you leave home? Your father was still alive, was he not?"

"He was," Will said, gazing up at the ceiling. "The truth is that I didn't get along with my elder brother. We were too different and there was—there was bitterness between us. I thought it better to go than to stay and subject my father to any more acrimony. He was fragile enough as it was, and . . ." His voice trailed off and he shook his head, his eyes clouded, his brow drawn down. "I felt at the time that I had no choice. I suppose I could have fought harder to defend myself, but I didn't see any point in making a volatile situation any worse."

"What did you have to defend yourself against?" Louisa asked, her heart going out to him. He'd suffered, that much was obvious, and she very nearly regretted having asked him at all.

Will shook his head again. "It's not important. Suffice it to say that my leaving prevented a full-blown confrontation that would have injured my brother's reputation, even if it could have saved mine. It wasn't worth the trouble. He wasn't worth the trouble, and my father's health was of more concern to me than anything else."

"So you simply left, turned your back on them both?"

Will laughed, a harsh sound that held no humor. "I'd say it was the other way around. Yes, I left, but didn't turn my back. I never forgot them, not for an instant. When I received news from my brother of my father's death, I was naturally distraught, although the fashion in which the news was delivered brought no comfort."

He raked up a handful of straw and let it fall through his fingers. "I realized then that my brother would never let there be peace between us, that the anger in him ran too deep. Oddly enough, I'd put aside my anger toward him long before. Enough time had gone by that I wanted nothing more than to have a family, even if it was just the two of us left. I was a fool to be so naive as to think it might be possible."

"How awful for you," Louisa murmured, feeling dreadful for him. She might have lost almost everything else, but at least she still had her beloved father and daughter, not to mention the few members of the staff who had stayed on, always loyal. "Is there truly not any hope of making peace with your brother?"

He closed his eyes for a moment, then looked directly at her. "I doubt it. It would take a miracle, and I think I've used up my allotment of those. I briefly thought at one time that I might at least try, but something else came along that was more important."

"What?" she asked. "What could possibly be more important than trying to make amends with your brother?"

"You," he said simply. "You and Broadhurst Farm."

5

Will stood up abruptly, cursing his loose tongue. Louisa stared at him as if he'd lost his mind, and he began to wonder if he hadn't. As hard as he tried to keep his guard up, she always managed to find a way to bring it down. He'd really gone and put his foot in it now, talking about his family like that, and his last ill-advised statement . . . he cringed internally. She must think him a proper lunatic, and she had every reason to.

"What on earth do you mean by 'me and Broadhurst Farm'?" she demanded, two spots of color flaming in her cheeks. He knew his own were doing the same.

Will's mind raced as he tried to think of a way to cover himself. "I meant only that when I arrived at Broadhurst, I didn't expect to find the situation that I did. I thought that I would work for a time before continuing on my way. Clearly I'm not going anywhere soon, or at least not until you are back on your feet financially."

"Oh," she said, looking relieved. "Forgive me—for a moment I thought . . . never mind. It's not important."

Will chose not to answer, knowing perfectly well what she'd thought and not trusting himself to say another word. He moved to Theodora's head and crouched down. "Come on, girl, time to get you both up." He gently pushed at her shoulder, urging her to stand.

After a few moments she grunted and obliged him, then reached her head down and encouraged her newborn to do the same. The foal floundered about, and then instinct took over and he found his footing, his feet wobbling about as he put his weight on them.

"He's a handsome fellow," Will said, pleased to see the foal stagger to his mother's side and butt his nose into her belly, beginning to nurse. "What will you call him?"

Louisa thought for a minute. "Achilles," she said. "I think it's appropriate, since a vulnerable foreleg nearly proved to be his undoing. It's a loose analogy, but I think the name will do."

"A good choice." Will chuckled as he smoothed his hand over Theodora's withers. "Let us hope that he triumphs in all other things. He has the look of a fine racehorse about him."

"He has, hasn't he?" Louisa said with satisfaction. "His father is well known for his victories. I had to sell my finest necklace to pay the stud fee, but I think it was worth every penny."

"I have to agree." Will risked a glance at her. Louisa had never looked more attractive to him than she did at this moment, disheveled, her hair escaping once again from its ribbon, one cheek smudged with dirt, her eyes alight with pleasure. His loins began to tighten with desire and he forced his gaze away, appalled with himself. If he didn't get away from her soon, he was in danger of doing something disgraceful, and he'd done enough damage for one night.

"We should probably leave them alone," he said. "I'll clean the stall up in the morning, rather than disturb them any further."

She nodded. "Thank you. I owe you a great deal for this night's work." But she didn't move.

He pulled in a deep breath, forcing down the urge to march over to her, take her in his arms, and kiss her breathless. One did not assault grieving widows, especially not the grieving widow of a dear friend.

"Good night then," he said, drawing on an inner reserve of strength that he'd never had to touch before, at least not in this capacity. He'd always enjoyed the company of women, and taking a night or two's pleasure here and there was enough for him. But then his heart had never been in danger. Now it was seriously in jeopardy and had been from the first moment he'd laid eyes on her, already knowing too much about her own heart.

"Good night," she said, giving him an unexpected smile that threatened to send him to his knees. "I thank you again for saving Theodora and Achilles. I really don't know what I would have done without you."

She turned and quietly let herself out.

Will sank down into the straw as he heard the stable door close behind her, and covered his face with his hands.

"Damn," he muttered. "Damn and damnation, and God's bleeding teeth on top of all that." He clenched his fists together and pounded them into his forehead hard. "You are a great blockhead, my man, and deserve everything that's coming to you, may God give you strength to deal with it."

Raising his head, he stared hard at the opposite wall.

So many thoughts crashed through his mind that he hardly knew where to begin to sort them out. Val. He needed to start with Val. What had the man been thinking to leave his family when they were in the middle of a terrible crisis? He couldn't make head nor tail of that one. Val had adored his family. His wife and daughter meant the world to him, he'd said as much time and time again.

Still, Louisa had been clear about the manner in which Val had left, and the deep unhappiness in her eyes had given him the truth—but surely there had to be more to the story? He *knew* Val, or thought he had, indeed had counted him as his closest friend. The two pieces didn't fit. Val was no coward, and only cowards deserted their families in times of trouble.

Too tired to think any more, Will stood and extinguished the lamps, leaving mare and foal to sleep in peace.

He was not so lucky, spending hours tossing and turning. His dreams were a tangled skein of battle and bloodshed, of holding Val in his arms as his friend lay dying, and then, suddenly, as if he were the man who had been dying, he was the one held in Louisa's arms as she stanched his blood and kissed his brow.

Will woke with a start, covered in cold sweat. Nightmares about battle were nothing new to him—he'd been plagued by them since Waterloo—but having Louisa appear in one shook him to his core. She belonged to a place of peace, not to a scene of unspeakable horror that no man should ever have to experience. He had no right dragging her into that, even if it was only a dream.

"What are you thinking about, Mr. Cutter? I do not think it is my Latin translation." Pip closed the book in her lap and leaned back against the tree trunk. "Was it that bad? Would you like to finish it? I am sure that Mama would be far more pleased with your translation than mine."

"Not at all," Will said, smiling down at her. "You were doing a fine job."

He enjoyed these sessions with Pip, helping her with her schoolwork, although he knew perfectly well that she took every opportunity to have him do it for her. He wasn't entirely sure why Pip had allotted him the role of tutor, but her grandfather had been confined to bed with a chill for the last fortnight and had not felt strong enough to take her through her lessons.

Pip appeared at his shoulder every noon, bringing a basket with both their lunches in it as well as her books. They'd fallen into the habit of spending the next hour together, eating and chatting, but he did manage to encourage Pip to get some studying done.

"Then why were you staring off into space?" Pip persisted.

"I was thinking that I need to get into town to buy myself some new clothes," he lied.

In truth, as usual he'd been thinking about Louisa, but her daughter didn't need to know that. He took every care to be sure that no one knew he thought about Louisa at all. The only bright note was that he was so exhausted by the end of the day that he could barely think of anything at all, a blessing now that Louisa had resumed having dinner with them in the kitchen.

"New clothes?" Pip said. "Whatever for? You'll only get them filthy by the end of the day."

"That's the point. Mrs. Robbins has been working overtime to keep what I have clean, and since I have only one change, she has to do my washing every day."

"I don't think Mrs. Robbins minds in the least," Pip said. "I think she *likes* doing your washing. She's always singing when she's pressing your shirt."

"Mrs. Robbins is a cheerful soul," he replied, taking a bite of his apple. He had the distinct feeling that Betsy Robbins was interested in a good deal more than his washing, but he didn't think that Pip needed to hear that either. Although, knowing Pip, she'd already worked it out for herself, given the mischievous grin on her face.

"Why don't you just ask Grandpapa for some of his old things?" Pip said. "He's big like you, and I'm sure he must have some clothes that he no longer uses. It's silly for you to spend good money when you can make do with his."

"I wouldn't dream of asking him," Will said firmly, the idea of wearing someone else's castoffs going against his upbringing. It wasn't as if he didn't have more money than he knew what to do with, not that he could tell Pip that. He was supposed to be impoverished. He was beginning to *loathe* being impoverished, just as he was beginning to loathe all sorts of absurdities about his new life. When he wasn't dreaming impossibilities about Louisa, he dreamed of soft mattresses, smallclothes that didn't scratch, bathing in a steaming tub of water instead of a freezing horse trough, about soft breasts pressing against his chest and warm, welcoming thighs . . .

"Don't be silly," Pip said, interrupting the dangerously lascivious direction of his thoughts. "Mama always says 'waste not, want not.' Look, here comes Grandpapa now— he must finally be feeling better! We can ask him."

"No, don't trouble him—" Will started to say, knowing that Louisa's father would no more like the idea than Will did, but Pip had already jumped up, racing down the path toward her grandfather. She began to chatter away, hands flying about as she put forth her request.

Will groaned, wishing Pip wasn't always quite so impulsive. He groaned a second time, wishing he had better control over his usually disciplined mind. How could he face Mr. Fleming, knowing he'd just been thinking about his daughter's most intimate parts?

He stood as Mr. Fleming came toward him, the older man's face drawn into its usual melancholy lines, his shoulders stooped, reducing his height. Will thought he must have been a strong, good-looking man once, but now he looked old beyond his years and defeated, his blue eyes bleary, his clothes hanging on his frame.

During his years in the army, Will had seen a few men

whose spirit had been broken by battle, and Charles Fleming fit the description. From what Louisa had said, Will could understand the reason. Fleming must feel like an utter failure, his pride shattered by his reduced circumstances, unable to support his family, no longer a part of the privileged world into which he'd been born. For a man who had once been wealthy and powerful, his life must now be a living hell.

The only pleasure he seemed to take from life was his granddaughter, whom he clearly doted on. Even now he held her hand tightly clasped in his, as if she were a lifeline he didn't want to let loose.

"Good day, Mr. Fleming," Will said. "I am pleased to see you are feeling better. Please don't give another thought to what Pip has been pouring into your ear about clothing. I assure you I had nothing to do with her suggestion. I can easily enough buy my own."

"Not at all, Mr. Cutter," Fleming replied in his quiet voice. "I believe that Pip's suggestion has merit, as I have an entire trunk of clothes that I no longer need. Indeed, I cannot see why they should not be put to good use. There's no point letting the moths have their way with them, and I would take satisfaction from feeling that I can be of some help to somebody."

Sympathy stabbed through Will's heart. The poor man had been brought so low that giving his clothing away to a menial laborer would make him feel helpful? Will couldn't possibly refuse him now, not if the small gesture might help. "Then I thank you for your generosity," he said. "You are very kind."

"I am in your debt," Fleming said. "You saved the life of my daughter's mare and her foal, and I have nothing but respect for your skill."

"I'd have been lost if you hadn't loaned me your veterinary books," Will said. "I can tell you that I had a few bad moments, but thank goodness everything worked out."

"Yes. How is young Achilles coming along?"

"Well, thank you. He's out in the paddock with his mother, if you care to take a look. He's a strong lad, full of vinegar."

"That is good news indeed. I must also thank you for taking on Pip while I was ill. She tells me that you have been helping her with her studies."

"I've been doing my best to keep up with her, sir," Will said, raising an eyebrow at Pip. "Your granddaughter has a fine future ahead of her as an expert cardplayer, I believe. She combines an impossible degree of charm with a quickness of mind that leaves me wondering whether I haven't been totally bamboozled into doing her lessons for her."

A slow smile spread across Charles Fleming's face. "You've caught on to that trick, have you?" He fondly smoothed his hand over Pip's bright head. "One has to be constantly on one's toes with this little imp."

"I am not an imp, Grandpapa," Pip said with strong objection. "I am a well-behaved child who takes the invective."

"I believe you mean you take the initiative," Will said. "And yes, you do. No one can fault you for lack of resourcefulness, although your behavior could benefit from a little more—restraint in certain areas."

"Mr. Cutter has a point, child. Like your mother, you have a tendency toward being headstrong. I believe we would all breathe a little easier if you listened more closely to the wisdom of your elders and a little less to your own opinions."

"You are not being fair, Grandpapa," Pip said, her little face assuming a mutinous expression. "Mr. Cutter says that originality of thought is what keeps civilization moving forward. He says that—"

"What I said," Will said, quickly interrupting before Pip could give her grandfather entirely the wrong impression of what he'd been trying to teach her, "is that originality of thought is essential to man's progress, but that it is based in a thorough understanding of the disciplines. What came before gives us the ability to move forward, but we must never lose sight of the essentials, which is why a sound education is so important." He fixed her with a firm eye. "Isn't that right, Miss Pip?"

"Yes," she said, tugging on one braid. "But you *also* said that a person should not be a slave to—to convenient thought."

"*Conventional* thought, and what I meant, as you well know, is that although you do always have a right to your own opinion, you must be careful about how and to whom you express that opinion. I believe I also said that an educated opinion is worth a great deal more than an uneducated one."

Charles Fleming directed a long, thoughtful look at Will. "You surprise me, Mr. Cutter. I thought you were assisting my granddaughter merely with the rudiments of Latin declensions, but now I discover that you have been embarking on the bases of philosophic thought. She is but eight years of age."

"The Jesuits believe that at seven years a child reaches the beginning of the age of reason, Mr. Fleming, and although I have little else in common with Jesuit belief, I agree with that much. Your granddaughter is surely bright enough to be given a grounding in such reason."

"My granddaughter is indeed bright enough, but to expect her to reason as an adult is like asking a calf to produce milk."

Will impatiently shoved a lock of hair off his forehead.

"Forgive me if I have overstepped myself. My conversations with Pip have naturally evolved from the material we've been addressing, even if it does strike you as overly advanced. She nevertheless receives it well, even if she cannot grasp it all at her tender age." He smiled apologetically. "I also have to admit that I enjoy the opportunity to voice my opinions. The cows do not take the same interest when I hold forth to them, despite their more advanced years."

"I have no objection to your discussions with my granddaughter," Fleming said, his eyes suddenly sharp and keenly focused for the first time in Will's brief acquaintance with him. "None at all. My surprise has more to do with the nature of your own education."

Thoroughly fed up with disguising nearly everything about himself, Will merely shrugged. He might be forced to lie about his station in life, even his name, but he drew the line at denying his education, especially since he could not explain that away so easily.

"As I told your daughter when she asked me the same question," he replied, "I had the benefit of a good man's tutelage. What he taught me has given me a healthy regard for well-rounded schooling, however one comes by it."

"Then you have been most fortunate indeed. I, too, have always believed that a sound education is the cornerstone of life, if it is to be lived to the fullest. As it is said, man cannot live by bread alone. You remind me, Mr. Cutter, of something I had forgotten." He gazed down at the top of Pip's head. "You remind me of a great deal I had forgotten."

Will looked down, deeply shaken by the thought that his words might somehow have broken through the man's misery and stimulated him in some positive way. "If I have reminded you of anything of value, sir," he said in a low voice, "I can only be grateful that we have had this conversation."

"I would like to have many more conversations with you, Mr. Cutter. I believe we have much in common. It has been a long time since I have had a desire to engage in discourse, but I feel a resurgent interest—most unexpected, I confess, but there it is."

Will inclined his head, immensely grateful that a real interest in life still stirred in this man. If he could encourage that interest, he would do anything in his power—he'd seen enough of lives destroyed and spirits crushed. "You have only to say the word, Mr. Fleming. I am busy for all of the day, but come evening I have some time off. I warn you, I am generally dog-tired by the time dinner is finished, but I will do my best to keep up my part of the conversation, if conversation is what you wish."

Pip, who had been listening to their interchange with enormous interest and unusual silence, finally spoke. "You both eat dinner, and now that you are better you will be joining us at the table again, Grandpapa, so why can you not talk together then? I want to hear, even if you think I am too little."

Charles Fleming laughed. He actually laughed, a ringing sound that came from his belly, and his face lit up with humor. "Why not, little Pip? We might brighten up the gloom and educate you better in the process, although goodness only knows what Cook will say."

"Very little," Pip retorted. "Cook already hangs on Mr. Cutter's every word, no matter what he says. *She* thinks he's wonderful, and so do Violet and Mr. Trueboot—and if Mrs. Robbins ever came to dinner, she'd never stop talking to him, so it's a good thing she has her children to look after. It's only Mama we have to worry about. Anyone would think she was sucking on a sour lemon, the way her face looks whenever Mr. Cutter says anything at all."

"Does it?" Charles Fleming said, looking perplexed. "I hadn't noticed."

"You hadn't noticed because Pip is exaggerating," Will retorted. "Mrs. Merriem is merely preoccupied with farm business, and I can understand why, since this is a busy and taxing time of year. I think some good conversation at the table would be a blessing to us all."

Actually, Will thought the idea brilliant, for not only would intellectual discourse engage Charles Fleming's interest, it would also give Will something to think about other than Louisa during dinner. He'd been going out of his mind in her presence, so maybe putting that mind to some good use would prove to be a tonic.

Louisa, on the other hand, might not agree. Pip had a point. Louisa didn't care to hear anything he had to say, giving him only the most absent of glances when he did speak. If he didn't know better, that night in the stables might never have happened, nor the intimate conversation they'd shared. Louisa treated him like a complete stranger. He supposed he shouldn't be surprised by her lack of regard, given that he'd forced her to speak of things she'd rather not have revealed, and on top of that he had unburdened a small part of his own story on her, the last thing she needed in view of everything else she had to contend with.

Why should anything he said be of the least import to her? He was, as she was forever pointing out, only the farm laborer, a situation he could only blame himself for.

Recalling his never-ending list of duties, he realized that he'd tarried long enough.

"Forgive me, Mr. Fleming, but I need to get back to work. We are cutting the first of the hay and I'd like to bring it in before rain threatens."

"Of course. I'll have Mrs. Robbins send over some of the clothing I promised this very afternoon. I hope it will do."

"Anything you can send my way, sir, I will be grateful for," Will said, resigned to the small humiliation. "I thank you for your thoughtfulness."

Fleming waved his hand in dismissal. "Nothing at all. I shall think upon the matter of this evening's discourse. Perhaps we might begin with Plato's *Dialogues*. Yes, that might do nicely."

Calling the dogs, he continued on his walk, his head bowed in thought, but to Will's eye his back seemed straighter and his shoulders just a little less stooped.

6

"Oh, there you are, Mr. Cutter," Betsy Robbins trilled, coming out of the stables just as Will came around the corner late that afternoon. "I just delivered a whole case full of Mr. Fleming's clothing. Isn't that nice of the old gentleman? I do declare, I think he's becoming less crusty. The case is upstairs on your bed, and I've aired and refolded the clothes for you—I think you should look very fine in them, not that you're not already fine enough as it is."

Will tried to ignore the way she batted her big brown eyes at him. He ought to be used to her overt flirting by now, he told himself. She was probably just lonely, a widow and still young. She was also very pretty in an earthy sort of way.

"Thank you for bringing it over. You are very kind." He smiled at her with a weak attempt at sincerity, too tired for anything else.

"Oh, my pleasure, indeed it is," Betsy said, fiddling with her bodice as if to bring attention to her ample cleavage.

Will tried not to look, although he didn't find it easy, not with two plump mounds of flesh swelling up enticingly from her low neckline. He was only a man, for the love of God, and with the way his loins had been aching since he'd come to Broadhurst, he thought himself a true stoic for not taking advantage of her unspoken invitation and tumbling her in the hay as a quick release. The problem was that he didn't want Betsy Robbins, he wanted Louisa, and with a ferocity that amazed him. Burying himself in Betsy Robbins's full curves wasn't going to change that simple fact and would only create more problems.

Betsy raised her hand to her blond curls. "My, but how the hour is getting on. I suppose I should be on my way home. The children will be wanting their supper. At least after that it's upstairs to bed for them and I'll have some time to myself. I do enjoy my time to myself, I do, although I enjoy it even more when I have someone to share it with."

Will didn't think he'd ever heard a broader hint in his life. "Then good day to you," he said, touching his finger to his cap, wishing she'd be true to her word and leave. "I thank you again for your trouble."

"Nothing is ever any trouble for you, Mr. Cutter. Anything I can do for you, just say the word. Anything at all."

"I cannot think of another thing," he replied, focusing his gaze on her red, chapped hands. What pleasure could he ever gain from having them run over his skin? None at all.

Now, Louisa's hands—they were a different matter entirely, milky white and smooth. He could easily imagine the course her hands might take over his flesh. The heat rose in his face at the very thought, and he had to look away.

"Oh, I dunno, it looks to me as if you could do with a bit of looking after, Mr. Will Cutter, and I surely know all about that, make no mistake about it," Betsy said with a saucy smile. She turned and sashayed off, her hips swaying so provocatively.

He closed his eyes and ran his hand over his forehead, thinking for the thousandth time that if he had any sense, he'd get on Maestro and leave Broadhurst without a backward glance instead of subjecting himself to an ongoing hell of unrequited desire for a woman he could never have.

"Why, Mr. Cutter, did I just catch you ogling Betsy Robbins?" the object of that desire said from a few feet away.

Will started and spun around, only to find Louisa gazing at him with an expression of high amusement, although behind the amusement he could have sworn he saw severe annoyance.

"I—I beg your pardon?" he stammered, thoroughly taken aback. "I was doing no such thing." He felt his face growing hot and cursed himself for that too.

"Weren't you? Well, in that case, a word of warning. Mrs. Robbins has had her way with more than one farm laborer in the pursuit of a new husband, so if you do not wish to find yourself with three children and a wife to support, I should not travel down that road."

"It seems to me," he grated out, trying to get a grip on himself, "that what I do or do not do in my free time is my business alone. You are such a stickler for my minding my own business that I'd think you'd be happy I'm doing my best to stay out of yours."

"You've been doing such a good job of it that I've just had to come down here to request a word from you," she shot back, her eyes flashing angrily. "You haven't given me a report on your progress in the last fortnight. Is that because you have made no progress, or because you assumed such a report unnecessary?"

Thinking that Louisa had one hell of a tongue on her when she chose, and barely able to control his temper, Will drew in a sharp breath between his teeth and slowly released it.

"I have not given you a report," he retorted, "because you have not given me a spare moment of your time. At dinner you ignore me, and you vanish immediately after into the inner sanctum of the study, which you have made very clear is inviolate. I assumed that if you wanted information, you would ask for it, and since you finally have, then I will tell you that all is proceeding as best it can, given there is no money and very few hands."

To his surprise, Louisa dropped her challenging stare. "Forgive me," she said in a low voice. "You are right, of course. I know you are doing your best with the limited resources available to you."

Will instantly felt remorseful about his show of temper, which had stemmed more from Louisa's erroneous assumption that he was interested in Betsy Robbins than from her challenge as to his competency. "I understand your frustration," he replied more evenly. "I have my own."

God, how he wished he could just throw his money at her, make all her problems go away, but sadly that wasn't possible. He'd have to reveal his true identity, and even then she probably would be too stubborn and angry to take a penny from him.

"The good news is that the hay is nearly in and should go for a good price. On top of that, the wheat crop is coming along nicely, as are the barley and the corn. Providing God does not decide to do something untoward with the weather, you should have a fine yield by autumn."

"I am glad to hear it," she said, but the unmistakable gleam of tears shone in her eyes and a stab of guilt shot through him. He'd upset her, and it was no one's fault but his own.

"It is I who should ask for forgiveness," he said softly, throwing his pride to the wind. "I should not have spoken so harshly to you."

She looked up at him, the tears spilling over. She brushed them away with the back of one hand. "No," she said on a gulp. "You had every right. I've just—just been so worried, and when I am frightened, I tend to make everyone around me miserable. It's a great failing of mine that I've never been able to control." She pressed a shaking hand against her mouth. "I want—I want so much to make everything right again for my father, my daughter, and I cannot seem to manage it." Her face crumpled and her breath caught on a sob. She covered her eyes with her hands.

Will couldn't help himself. He stepped forward and gathered her into his arms, her slim body trembling against his, so soft, so sweet, and although he despised the circumstances, he felt infinitely grateful that he was holding her at all.

"There's no need to cry," he murmured against soft hair that smelled like lavender with a hint of roses. Smoothing one hand over the top of her head, he let her weep into his shoulder, her tears soaking his shirt. Will thought his own heart might break with her distress, but there was little he could say to comfort her.

"S-sorry," she mumbled, pulling away. "I shouldn't behave in such a lily-livered fashion. I despise my own weakness." She gulped back another sob.

"You should not be so harsh on yourself," he said, gently wiping her cheeks with his thumbs. "You're only human, and you cannot carry this huge burden all by yourself. Of course you're concerned and have every right to be, but as I've said countless times, I'll help you in any way I can. You must believe that by now. Trust me, please. It's all I ask of you."

Her azure eyes gazed into his, filled with confusion. "I don't *distrust* you, Mr. Cutter. I just—I just have learned that the only person I can truly trust is myself. So many people depend on me, and I cannot let them down. The responsibility is my own, and my fault that I let it come to this."

"What on earth do you mean?" Will said, taking her hand and leading her over to the bench set against the stable wall. He pulled her down next to him. "It is not your fault that your father made a bad investment decision, any more than it is your fault you are in this position now."

"But it is," she said, looking down at her lap, her hands tightly clenched together. "I do not want to say anything more than that, but if I hadn't made a series of bad decisions myself, we would still be up at the Hall, my father's health would not be compromised, and I would not be worrying about how to provide food on the table every night." She sniffed and wiped the back of her hand over her nose, the unladylike gesture only endearing her more to Will.

He struggled to find words that might comfort her without offending, at the same time searching his pocket for a handkerchief. The handkerchief he found, but the words were not as easily attainable. "Listen to me," he said, thinking hard as he put the linen square into her hand and waited while she wiped her eyes and blew her nose. "Life always presents its challenges, but God is never so unkind as to not also present solutions to those challenges, if we will only pay attention to what He puts before us."

She raised her head and glared at him. "Are you always so infuriatingly sure of yourself?"

"Most of the time I'd have to say yes, but no, not always." God knew that was the truth, or at least had been ever since he'd taken up this ridiculous charade.

"Oh, and that is supposed to give me confidence?" she said, her face relaxing into the beginnings of a smile. "You confuse me. You have always behaved as if you are accustomed to commanding armies, your word law. Which is it, Mr. Cutter?"

"Forgive me if I have been in any way overbearing," he said, knowing she was absolutely right. He was accustomed to being in command, but he honestly didn't know any other way to behave. "You are, of course, mistress of Broadhurst and, as such, your word is law."

"Why do I doubt that?" Her mouth curved into a genuine smile. "Servility does not come easily to you, that much is clear. I wonder if you have given your other employers so much trouble."

"No one but you has complained to date," he replied. "I believe you have once again very handily changed the subject, though. We were talking about you, if you recall. Why did you say that you thought you had made a number of bad decisions that led to this situation? Surely you were not responsible for your father's mistakes."

A slight tremor went through her body and the merriment left her eyes. "I was not directly responsible, no, but I cannot help feeling that if I had made him privy to certain information I had, he would not have pursued the course he took. Still, it is water under the bridge."

"You must have had your reasons for keeping silent," Will said, intrigued, wondering what information Louisa could possibly have had regarding the complicated world of investing. It was not an area in which women were involved, although Louisa tended to defy all the usual rules. "Perhaps you were afraid to interfere in your father's business?" he prompted.

"No, nothing like that." She stared down at the ground. "If you must know, I felt that if I spoke out, I would be behaving in a disloyal fashion."

"Ah," Will said, knowing full well how important loyalty

was to her. He could easily understand that she would not want to challenge her father's decisions. "So you kept your opinion to yourself, is that it?"

"I did," she said, looking utterly miserable. "I wish I hadn't, but it's no good wishing now, is it? What's done is done."

He reached over and covered her small hand with his own. "If it helps at all, I've been guilty of the same thing. We think we are protecting the people we love and only realize in hindsight that we might have protected them better if we'd been a little less noble and a bit more forthcoming."

She nodded, fresh tears pooling in her eyes and spilling down her cheeks. "I believe you do understand," she said in a thick voice, pressing the handkerchief to her face. "You're speaking about your own father, aren't you? The problem that drove you from your home."

"I am." He shook his head, his own regret still deeply painful. "Not a day goes by that I don't wish I had made a different decision, that I had chosen to speak the truth instead of taking on the burden of someone else's falsehood. In the end, I don't think I served any of us well. I suspect my silence contributed to my father's death, even if not directly."

"What do you mean?" she asked, looking over at him in puzzlement. "You were gone."

"Yes. I was gone, but I left him believing something about me that broke his heart. At the risk of sounding impossibly conceited, I was his favorite child—I think I reminded him of my mother. The point is that I, too, know what it's like to carry blame." He picked her hand up and weighed her fingers in his, his thumb stroking over them. "As time goes by, I understand better that punishing myself helps no one, least of all me. The only thing to do is to go on, and the only way to do that is by absolving oneself of guilt as best one can."

Louisa bowed her head. "But you have seen my father.

You've seen how his health suffers. If you had only known him as he once was, you would understand better . . ."

"I think I had a glimpse of that man today," Will said, tightening his fingers around hers. "I think I might have a way to bring him back around, for I do not believe his health is the problem, it is his heart."

"What do you mean?" she said, an expression of panic in her eyes. "There's nothing wrong with his heart that I know of. Did he say something to you? You must tell me if he did."

"No," he said quickly. "I meant his inner heart, not his physical one." He chose his words with care, wanting her to understand his reasoning without alarming her any further. "I believe your father lost his sense of purpose when he lost the material things to which he was accustomed and the power and influence that went along with them. He lives now only for you and Pip, and you don't need his help, or at least you don't let him think you do."

"But I—I don't want to make any demands on him that he cannot cope with. He's not strong, and I fear that he might collapse if I let him know how dire our circumstances really are."

"You didn't tell him about Frank Hillbarrow stealing your savings, did you?"

Louisa gazed at him in horror. "How on earth did you know about that?" she gasped, one hand flying to her throat. "I told no one!"

"Pip," he said succinctly. "Your daughter knows a great deal more than you realize. How she knows, I cannot say, although I suspect that she probably overheard something."

Louisa squeezed her eyes shut and pressed her hand against her cheek. "I must have been talking to myself again," she muttered. "Pip is forever catching me at it."

Will couldn't help laughing. "Ah," he said. "A dangerous habit. Maybe you'd be better off writing down your thoughts and then locking the pages away where no one can read them if you don't want to be found out."

He didn't understand why her eyes snapped wide open and her cheeks stained with sudden color. "What—what are you talking about?" she demanded, abruptly pulling her hand from his.

Will regarded her with fascination, seeing that he'd hit some sort of mark but having no idea what it was. Louisa was the most complicated woman he'd ever encountered, a puzzle he was beginning to think he'd never piece together. "I only meant that you might be better off writing in a journal. Why are you looking at me as if I'd just suggested you commit a heinous crime? I keep a journal myself."

"Oh," she said, releasing a sharp breath. "I thought you meant—never mind. Tell me more about how you think you can help my father."

Will, still not accustomed to the abrupt shifts in conversation that Louisa was so adept at, had to forcibly turn his attention back to the previous subject. "I think we can all help him. What he needs is to feel he is useful, and although I agree that he's not up to dealing with the immediate problems you are faced with, he might benefit from being actively involved in something. He apparently has a great interest in literature and philosophy, and he suggested himself that we might have, um . . . *conversations* over dinner that address those topics."

"He wants to lecture us at dinner?" Louisa said, sitting back abruptly. "Oh, no. You cannot be serious."

"Perfectly," Will said, suppressing an urge to crow with laughter at Louisa's appalled expression. "Why does the idea strike you with such horror?"

"Cook will mutiny! She cannot abide anything but plain-speaking. And, Pip—oh, poor Pip. She has enough of studying during the day. Surely you don't want to let my father force it down her throat in the evening as well?"

"Actually, Pip suggested it herself," he said mildly. "She didn't like the idea that her grandfather and I vanish after dinner and leave her out. Or at least I believe that was her reason. As for Cook, leave her to me."

"You seem to want me to leave everything to you," Louisa said, but she chuckled. "What about Violet and her father? They'll be completely at sea."

"Not if I have anything to say about it. I'll be challenged to make these discussions palatable to everyone, but it will be an interesting challenge. The point is that your father appeared truly enthusiastic for the first time in my experience."

Louisa rubbed her forehead with her finger. "Perhaps. Perhaps you're right. But I warn you, Will Cutter, should Cook pack her bags and Mr. Trueboot and Violet defect along with her, you had better be prepared to take over the kitchen and the dairy as well."

"Then I shall have to make certain that they find the conversation positively scintillating," Will said. "Otherwise we shall all starve." He rose and offered her his hand. "The thing about challenges is that they are meant to be met and overcome. I expect nothing less than a positive result."

"Then you are either an optimistic fool or will prove yourself a genius," Louisa retorted, but took his hand and stood, smoothing down her skirt. She looked at him, her eyes dancing. "I'll be fascinated to see which you are."

"Count on nothing more than an optimistic fool," Will said, returning her smile. "That way we'll both be surprised when I prove myself a genius."

Louisa burst into laughter, and he was well pleased. She

needed to laugh more often, and he set himself that challenge as well. Nothing would give him more pleasure than to see Louisa Merriem remember what happiness was.

Louisa paced up and down her bedroom, her hands pressed to her hot cheeks, appalled by her actions. She had—she had allowed herself to be drawn into Will Cutter's arms, had made an absolute fool of herself crying on his shoulder, but far, far worse than that, she'd actually enjoyed the experience. He'd felt so *safe*, a harbor in a storm, had smelled so good, a mixture of clean sweat and something musky and male. Essence of Will, she thought, then squeezed her eyes tightly shut.

"Oh, dear God," she muttered, "protect me from myself." She wrapped her arms tightly about herself. The truth of the matter was that she was physically drawn to Will Cutter. Just the memory of his touch made her weak at the knees, and oh—the way his hard chest had felt against her cheek, the way his strong body holding her close against his own had set her heart to pounding. But had she pulled away? No, she had not. She'd just pressed closer like the wanton woman she was, not wanting the moment to end. She was no better than Betsy Robbins—and there was another truth: She hadn't liked the way Betsy had been looking at Will, and liked the way Will looked back even less.

"Oh, you really are a fool, Louisa," she whispered. "You were *jealous*, admit it to yourself. The very thought of Will going to Betsy's bed made you want to slap both their faces. There. I said it."

She marched over to the looking glass and glared at herself, the reflection staring straight back as if challenging her. *Prissy miss, do you think yourself so much better than me? At least I don't make any bones about what I want. Who would know if you went a few rounds in the hay with Will? Just imagine the pleasure you'd take from it . . .*

Louisa quickly turned her back, refusing to have a conversation with her wicked side. That part of her had already had one victory today, and she wasn't about to give it another. She'd lost too many battles to the dark Louisa in the past, and look where she was as a result. Once before she'd let her baser urges and foolish heart get in the way of her common sense, and she'd ended up married to Valentine Merriem.

She'd have been better off in a nunnery, wearing a hair shirt. Indeed . . . torturing herself wasn't a bad idea. Maybe she should take to wearing a corset laced so tightly that her ribs cracked every time she moved. Severe physical pain would take her mind off Will Cutter fast enough.

She couldn't help but laugh when she realized how absurd she was being. She was a full-grown woman, and just because she'd had a foolish moment didn't mean she was condemned to repeat it or act on it in any way. Will Cutter was merely a man, a farm laborer at that, and had no control over her. None at all, even if he did smell nice and feel nice and say kind things and make her feel as if she wasn't hopeless and useless and incompetent, as if she *mattered* to him.

Plopping down on the bed, Louisa stared miserably at the ground. Maybe that was the crux of the matter. Will made her feel as if she mattered to him. She was lonely and desperate, and he paid her some attention, talked to her about things no one had ever talked to her about before, asked her how *she* felt, and he listened, actually listened to her replies, carefully and thoughtfully, as if they meant something.

She frowned, trying to think if anyone had ever given her that much consideration, but couldn't come up with any recollection, or at least not since her dear mother had died. Louisa's role had always been clear—first the dutiful daughter, then the dutiful wife and mother, and now the dutiful mistress of Broadhurst Farm, whose job was to be sure that everyone in her care was looked after.

No one ever thought that she might need some looking after, and indeed, until this moment, the idea hadn't even occurred to her. Maybe that was it! she thought with a sudden leap of excitement. Maybe that was exactly what he was after—creating a vulnerability in her that until now had not existed.

Releasing a breath of relief that she'd finally pinpointed the cause of her weakness, she nodded decisively. If that was the problem, then she could defuse it easily enough: She had only to allow Will Cutter to do what he said he wanted to do. If, for whatever reasons of his own, he so badly wanted to help, then where was the harm in that? She could kill two birds with one stone.

He might be able to help her with the books and even with some financial strategy, since he was obviously an educated man. She would be relieved of some of the immediate pressure on her, and after all, two minds were better than one. She'd be watching him like a hawk, of course, since she didn't believe for a moment that he didn't have an ulterior motive in mind—she wasn't so foolish as to think he wanted to do all this extra work out of the goodness of his heart. . . .

Her eyes narrowed in thought. "Well, well, Will Cutter," she murmured. "I wonder what you really did come here for. Perhaps you thought from the notice that you might take advantage of a widow and her difficult circumstances, take your time to gain her trust, then rob her blind. You've done nothing since you arrived but insist that I could trust you, and to what purpose, I wonder."

Tapping her forefinger against her mouth, Louisa ran over the possibilities. He didn't have a penny to his name, despite his speech and education. He'd given her a plausible enough story for that, but thinking it over, a man with his attributes could have done far better for himself. He'd been clever enough to make himself appear entirely earnest, even going so far as to admit he knew about Frank Hillbarrow's stealing. Yet Will himself had arrived without a single reference or explanation for that salient lack. She wouldn't be surprised if he didn't have a long history of the exact same crime. Look at Val's long history, after all. If she hadn't learned from that, she never would.

Will probably even had a seduction in mind, given the way he'd been carrying on. He must believe that once she'd succumbed to him, she would be an easy mark.

"Yes," she said, feeling very much better. "You are definitely up to something, Will Cutter, and I very nearly fell into your trap, giving you far more personal information than I ever should have, letting you worm your way into my affairs and into the affections of my family, even believing for a moment that you might care a tuppence about me."

She stood up and marched over to the window, looking out over the gardens—*her* gardens, into which she had put so much time and effort. She'd be damned if she let anyone take anything else away from her or her family ever again.

"I even felt sorry for you when you fed me a bill of goods about your own sad life, Mr. Will Cutter. Well, two can play at that game, and I shall derive great pleasure from doing precisely that. I shall allow you to think me the poor, weak, defenseless widow drawn helplessly to your charms, and you will fall directly into *my* trap. I shall expose you for the charlatan you are, and you will be very sorry you ever trifled with me."

All she had to do was to take a page from Betsy Robbins's book and play the tease. She'd seen Betsy in action often enough to know how it was done—how hard could it be? The rest would follow.

With visions dancing in her head of the constabulary coming to arrest Will Cutter, of his protesting his innocence wildly while she handed over solid evidence of his guilt, Louisa happily dressed for dinner.

7

$\mathscr{H}$aving gone to the trouble of giving himself a proper bath and shave, using buckets of water that he'd painstakingly heated over the small stove in the stable's supply room and deposited in an unused old barrel that sat just outside the door, Will proceeded to dress in Mr. Fleming's clothes.

The fine linen of the shirt was a vast improvement over the coarse material he'd become marginally accustomed to, and the cut of the jersey breeches was enormously more comfortable than those he'd been wearing. He carefully tied his neckcloth in a simple knot and shrugged on one of the coats, which to his surprise fit well.

Will felt more like himself than he had in some time, although he could have done with a decent haircut. His own identity would have been even nicer, but one couldn't wish for every comfort. Decent clothing was enough for one day, and he had to admit that he owed Pip a vote of gratitude for insisting he accept when his pride would not otherwise have let him.

He brushed his wet hair, trying to tame it into some kind of order, not easy when the length fell over his collar and the natural wave insisted on going its own way.

He examined himself as best he could in the small, cracked piece of glass over the bureau. Presentable, he decided, although anyone moving in better circles would shudder at the sight of him. But since there was no one to care, or shudder for that matter, he couldn't see what difference it made.

He pulled in a deep breath, then released it. He didn't know why, precisely, but this evening marked some sort of watershed. He couldn't help but wonder if it didn't have something to do with Louisa's sweet response to him two hours earlier, when she'd come so easily into his arms, shed tears he never thought to see, poured out a part of her heart to him.

Never having dared to hope for even that much, he'd been deeply touched by her unexpected trust in him. Just allowing him to hold her, to cry without reservation, to confide in him without his having to pull each and every word out of her, had meant the world. She humbled him with her honesty, but he was ashamed that she'd given him so much of her own truth whereas he had left her with lies.

He couldn't for the life of him think of a way to rectify the situation, as much as he wanted to. He'd spent the last two hours battling with his conscience, and the only conclusion he'd reached was that if he was to truly aid her in her struggle, he had to continue his charade—anything else would turn her against him in short order and she'd be left again with no one to give her the help she so desperately needed.

"But I don't understand, Grandpapa," Pip said between mouthfuls of pigeon pie. "You've been going on and on about these people Plato and Socrates and what they said— or wrote—or, I don't know. Who is the one we're supposed to listen to? It's all so *confusing*."

Will privately agreed. The way Charles Fleming went about presenting the subject, they might all have been in a lecture hall at Oxford University. Will was already beginning to question the wisdom of these discussions at the table, regardless of Fleming's raised spirits. Everyone else looked thoroughly downcast.

Everyone except Louisa, that was. She'd been giving him

warm smiles ever since he'd walked into the kitchen, a definite change from her past behavior. He was certainly pleased, but he couldn't help being confused—Louisa had never been so solicitous toward him, and despite their encounter late that afternoon he had to wonder why her attitude had changed so dramatically. The woman sitting across from him was completely unlike the Louisa he'd come to know. If he hadn't known better, he could have sworn she was actually flirting with him.

"It is confusing, isn't it?" he said quickly to Pip, as much to distract himself as to forestall Fleming from complicating the issue any further. "Let me see if I can't clear it up for you a little. Socrates was a great teacher and Plato was his greatest pupil. Plato went on to write his *Dialogues,* using an imaginary Socrates to present his points. The real Socrates was simply the man on whose ideas Plato based his writings, although he expanded them greatly."

He tried hard not to look at Louisa, who was gazing at him in fascination, enough to make him lose his train of thought entirely. "Um . . . let's see," he said, trying desperately to concentrate. "Socrates, the real person, was tried and condemned to death."

"Oooh," Violet said, her eyes opening wide, her interest engaged for the first time. "They killed him just for saying what he thought?"

"It's not a new concept to kill someone for his theories, especially when they are politically threatening, but yes, that's what the Athenians did. The interesting part is that Socrates went willingly to his death, despite all the efforts of his friends to save him."

"Why would he do a thing like that?" Cook demanded. "For a wise man, he sounds like a downright fool to me." She made a loud *humph* of disapproval.

"It's a good question," Will replied, wiping his mouth with his napkin, trying to think how to explain simply. "I suppose he had a point to prove, given that his entire philosophy was based on the root of justice and virtue, and since he'd been unfairly accused of corrupting the minds of youths, he wasn't going to shift from his position."

"Did they hang him?" Violet asked breathlessly.

"Don't be silly, girl," Tom Trueboot said with a snort. "They didn't hang people back then, they cut off their heads sure enough."

Violet shivered. "Like Madame Guillotine?"

"With an ax, more likely than not," her father said, shoveling another piece of pie into his mouth.

"Actually, Socrates drank a cup of hemlock, a deadly poison," Will replied, highly amused by the shift in conversation. Give them a grizzly tale of death and he had their complete attention.

"Nasty stuff, hemlock," Cook said, nodding wisely. "Doesn't take long to do its work, does it?"

"No, it doesn't. Furthermore, Socrates was devoted to the study of medicine, and insisted that every last detail of his death be recorded so that it might prove educational."

"Lawks!" Violet exclaimed. "Can you imagine such a thing, writhing about in agony while someone writes about it in his notebook?"

"I think that's quite enough on that particular subject," Louisa said firmly. "We'll all lose our appetites, and Cook's made a lovely blackberry tart."

Will risked meeting her eyes, which were dancing with laughter, the blue an impossible color of cerulean, like the sky on a hot summer's day. She grinned at him, and he knew exactly what she was thinking. *Optimistic fool.*

"Perhaps we could return our attention to the original subject," Charles Fleming said, clearing his throat. "We are meant to be improving our minds, not lowering them into the gutter."

Louisa rolled her eyes and then quickly dropped her gaze to her plate, her mouth trembling at the corners.

Will wanted to tell her she had a crumb of crust on one of those delicious corners, but instead he forced his attention back to her father, trying desperately not to laugh.

"Do go on, sir," he said, not meaning a word of it. He'd already decided that despite Pip's suggestion to the contrary, these conversations would be better held in private— and without Louisa anywhere in sight if he was to make any sense at all.

"If any of you wishes to know more about Socrates' death, you can read about it in Plato's *Apology*, *Crito*, and *Phaedo*," Fleming said. "Now, as I was saying, Plato used the Socratic method of dialectic to put forth the view, or form, of goodness. The good person finds the highest pleasure in the pursuit of knowledge—"

"Forgive me," Will interrupted, seeing that this fresh attack was only going to lead to more glazed eyes all around the table. "Perhaps we might clarify by saying that goodness really comes from the knowledge of one's true self. Isn't that the most important point?"

Charles Fleming nodded in acknowledgment. "It is true indeed. But then one must go on to pose the question, as Plato did, that although goodness is objective, we do not necessarily have reason to act upon that knowledge. Why should one act justly if one can profit by doing the opposite?"

Frank Hillbarrow immediately sprang to Will's mind, and judging by the dark expression on Louisa's face, he'd sprung to her mind too. Actually, there were a number of people he could think of who acted entirely in their own self-interest, his brother leading the pack.

"I can only believe what Plato said about that as well," Will replied quietly. "Those who are unjust live in a state of internal discord and will never find the harmony of soul that is the domain of those who balance intellect, emotion, and desire."

Not that he was doing such a fine job in that department. His last bastion of reason, his intellect, had been run over roughshod by emotion and desire, and he wouldn't have a day's peace until he either worked Louisa out of his system or shot himself. Sadly, the latter wasn't an option, and he had no earthly idea how to work Louisa out of his system. From all indications, she was there to stay, a nagging pain in his heart and loins.

A cold sweat broke out on his brow as she leaned over to take a piece of bread from the basket, the delicate swell of her breasts tightening against her bodice. He tried not to look, but couldn't seem to tear his gaze away from the tantalizing sight.

"Mr. Cutter? Do you not agree?" Mr. Fleming's insistent voice broke into his highly unesoteric thoughts.

"I beg your pardon," Will said, trying to clear his mind, hard to do when his erection had raised his napkin off his lap. "You were saying, sir?"

"I was saying that Plato believed that human happiness was dependent on doing what is virtuous simply for the sake of it, not for pursuing any personal gain."

Will was beginning to think that human happiness was dependent on his getting Louisa Merriem into his bed and to hell with what was virtuous. To hell with Plato altogether.

"Grandpapa," Pip said, "do you think we could just eat our blackberry tart now? I cannot take in another word."

"Of course, my dear," her grandfather replied, smiling at her. "I expect too much of you. As I said to Mr. Cutter earlier, you cannot possibly absorb the implications of complicated philosophic thought at your age."

"Oh, it's not that," she said, smiling engagingly at Cook. "It's just that the tart smells so good that I cannot think of anything else, and I think Mr. Cutter is afflicted with the same problem, since he's not paying any attention."

Cook, looking immensely gratified, raised her bulk from the table and marched over to the windowsill where the tart was cooling. "We can't let our working men go hungry, not when there's a tart to be had," she said with a backward wink at Will.

He nearly fell off his chair, and Louisa covered her face with her napkin, a sudden series of coughs emerging.

"My dear, you're not coming down with a cold?" Mr. Fleming said with concern. "Your eyes are watering."

"No, Papa, I think not—something must have gotten into my throat," she said, her voice muffled through the linen. "I'll be fine in a moment."

"Are you sure, my dear? You have been silent this evening, when conversations of this sort normally engage your interest. We haven't had such discourse for a very long time, but perhaps you too are thinking about the tart," he added, smiling uncertainly.

"Forgive me. I—I was. That and how to instruct Mrs. Robbins in looking after Mr. Cutter . . . his fine new clothing, that is." She averted her face, her shoulders starting to shake with what Will knew without a doubt to be repressed hilarity.

He wanted to take her by the throat and shake the rest of her, the subtle dig going straight through him. She couldn't really still believe that he had any interest in Betsy Robbins, could she?

Had Louisa forgotten it was she he'd held that afternoon, her he'd comforted? Perhaps that had meant nothing to her at all. For all he knew, she'd confided in Frank Hillbarrow, let him hold her in his arms while she cried. The thought made him burn with anger even though he had no right to it. He had no right to anything when it came to Louisa, and he needed to remember that.

Will had to force himself to smile up at Cook as she slid a plate in front of him, but the blackberry tart had suddenly lost its appeal. He made an effort to do it justice, but every nerve in his body felt on edge. Louisa was not at fault, he told himself; he was the one with the problem and he could not in any fairness blame her for what she thought of him. Why should she think anything of him at all? He was nothing to her and would remain nothing.

So why was he so damned furious with her and with himself?

"Mr. Cutter?" Louisa said, her voice sweet as honey, and his gaze jerked to her face. Her eyes were wide and far too innocent.

Comprehension suddenly dawned. Louisa had been playing him for a fool, using every feminine wile she had at her disposal, and God knew, she had an entire arsenal. He couldn't begin to imagine what ultimate end she had in mind, for he was damned sure she had no interest in luring him into her bed. He could only think this still had something to do with her assumption about him and Betsy Robbins, as ridiculous as the idea was.

"Yes?" he replied in a neutral tone, determined to give her absolutely nothing else to use against him.

She lowered her lashes. "Would you be so kind as to meet me in my study when you are finished with your meal? We have some business to attend to."

He nodded in assent, watching as she rose, kissed her father and daughter good night, and serenely drifted out of the room.

Oh, yes. Louisa was definitely up to something and he suspected it was no good. He smiled to himself, thinking that he'd play right along with her until he worked out where she was heading with this silly game. He might even enjoy himself in the process.

Louisa clutched her hands together, waiting for Will to appear. She was as ready as she would ever be, although she wished she had her nerves under better control. She hadn't expected Will to appear at dinner looking quite so—so *elegant*. Decidedly handsome, in fact, as if he'd been born to wear finery. Her heart had tightened in her chest just at the sight of him, and she'd had to struggle to keep her composure throughout dinner, had to force herself to smile and flirt.

She'd nearly expired from embarrassment when she'd deliberately leaned over to expose her cleavage, and she hadn't missed his reaction. At least that had confirmed her suspicions—he was nothing more than a rogue at heart, masquerading as a man of honor.

"Come in," Louisa called, her heart jerking as a tap sounded on the closed door. She steeled her resolve as Will walked into the room, truly wondering if she could possibly go through with the plan that had seemed like such a fine idea only two hours before. Bringing Will to the point of seduction suddenly seemed like the most dangerous game she'd ever embarked upon.

"What can I do for you?" he said, strolling over to the fireplace and turning to face her. He casually rested his arm on the mantelpiece.

"You can look at my books," she replied, gesturing at the ledger in front of her. "I thought over what you said earlier, and I've come to the conclusion that you might be able to do a better job than I have at sorting through them. Clearly, I do not excel at dealing with my own affairs. I seem to have made a terrible hash of them." She tried hard to look helpless.

"I would be happy to," he said, but he made no move toward the desk. "Perhaps tomorrow morning would be better, when my head is clearer."

"Oh," she said, surprised. She'd thought he'd take the first opportunity to get close to her, ogle her bosom some more. "Could you not have a quick look tonight? I'd sleep so much better." She tossed her head and bit the corner of her lip for good measure. Oh, God, what had ever made her think she could play the coquette?

"I did not realize that you anticipated losing sleep. Is that something that happens to you often?"

She had to force herself not to scowl at him. This was *not* going as she'd expected. "I am usually so tired that I sleep like the dead. And you, Will? Do you sleep soundly, or is your mind taken up with other matters?" She fluttered her eyelashes.

"If you are asking whether my conscience is clear, it is." He gazed at her levelly. "On the other hand, if you are not sleeping well, then there must be a reason for it."

"I told you, I am constantly worried about making ends meet," she snapped, then quickly averted her gaze. No, the conversation was not going at all as she'd intended. "Forgive me," she said, staring down at her hands. "I am not myself."

"No, you're not," Will replied, straightening and crossing his arms against his chest. "Maybe you'd like to tell me why."

"I cannot think what you mean. I merely asked you to look at the books."

"And I told you I'd be happy to. Somehow, though, I have to wonder at your sudden shift of position. You have been behaving in a most peculiar manner this evening."

"I have no idea what you mean," she said, wanting to sink through the floor. She felt like an utter fool, for Will was clearly calling her bluff. She'd have to switch tactics and do it fast. "I am grateful to you for your offer to help, no more than that. Why would you find my acceptance peculiar?"

"Louisa. You cannot possibly think me so stupid. Prevarication does not suit you. I have no idea what has brought on this need to present yourself as some sort of temptress, but it doesn't wash." He chuckled. "Not that I've been unappreciative of your efforts, but they are entirely unnecessary. I have no interest in pursuing Betsy Robbins, if that's what you're still thinking, nor have I any intentions of forcing myself on you."

"You haven't?" she said, utterly confused and, to her shock, hugely disappointed. Furthermore, she could hardly object to his calling her Louisa after the familiar manner in which she'd behaved.

"No, I haven't, so you can forget about trying to lure me in so that you can slap my face soundly. Slap it now, if you must, but I have no intention of dishonoring you in any way."

"Oh," she said again, coloring to the roots of her hair. "I

hadn't thought—that is, I didn't mean to . . ." Her voice trailed off in an agony of embarrassment.

He laughed. "Don't give your mistaken assumption a second thought. It's perfectly natural, especially given that I took you in my arms today. Forgive me for that intimacy, but I thought you needed to be held just then. Trying to force me to the point of revealing my true motives is understandable, although entirely misguided."

Louisa pressed her fingertips against her eyes. She couldn't think of a single thing to say, caught out in the most stupid behavior of her life. "I—I'm sorry," she whispered.

She sat up with a start as his hands came to rest on her shoulders. He'd moved so quietly that she'd had no idea he'd walked across the room at all.

"There's no need to be sorry. You'd be foolish not to protect yourself, given everything you've been through," he said gently.

She trembled involuntarily as the heat of his palms burned into her skin. Oh, *why* did she find him so physically desirable? Val had never made her heart pound violently, not like this, nor had he ever made her stomach feel as if it had been turned inside out. She was at the mercy of her treacherous body and she didn't have the first idea how to bring it under control.

Abruptly jumping up, she moved quickly out of his reach, her back turned to him. "Don't," she said, her voice low and thick. "Don't start being nice to me now. I don't think I can bear it." Tears stung at her eyes and she angrily brushed them away.

"Would you prefer me to start behaving like an ogre?" he asked, a laugh catching in his throat. "I'm not sure I can—it would take such effort and I'm far too tired. Hmm. What's this?"

She risked a glimpse over her shoulder. Will bent over her desk, casually perusing her ledger, one finger arrested on the open page. "What is what?" she asked, curiosity getting the best of her.

"This entry. Louisa, whoever you've been buying your grain from is robbing you blind. You're paying twice what you should be."

"But—but I buy it from the miller," she protested. "He is always fair."

"Let me guess. You sell him your crop, he grinds it, and he gives you a discount for what you buy back in exchange for a good price on the original harvest."

She nodded, wondering what was wrong with that.

"The problem is that if you sold your crop on the open market, you'd be making far more. He knows that. He also knows that for you to get the crop to market and go through all the negotiations would be difficult. I wouldn't be surprised if Frank Hillbarrow and the miller hadn't had an arrangement that suited them both and Frank was taking a nice cut on the side."

Louisa stared at him, aghast. "But that's—that's robbery!" She moaned, hearing herself. When had someone *not* tried to rob her?

"It's also business as usual," Will said. "Louisa, I'm sorry to say it, but you're a woman doing business in a man's world. Men are going to try to take advantage of you as if it's their natural right. They presume upon your lack of experience and your sex and have no qualms of conscience about profiting off either." He tapped his finger on the ledger. "I'll have a close look at this, and if you could provide me with the books from the last five years, that would be helpful. We will get this sorted out, I promise you. There's no good reason why Broadhurst shouldn't be making a fine profit once we can find the money to put into improvements."

"Why, Will? Why are you so good to me when all I've done is to treat you badly?"

"You haven't treated me badly in the least," he said, closing the ledger and straightening. "You've done exactly what you said you would—you've given me a roof over my head, three meals a day, and a salary."

"And you've been nothing but patient and kind with me, even when I've behaved like a harridan."

"As I said earlier, you've had your reasons. It's not for me to judge you—God knows you've been through absolute hell. First you lost your house, then your husband, and you've had to look after everyone and everything else for the last five years. I know I rub against every last independent bone in your body, but I cannot see the harm in taking a bit of the weight off your shoulders, as much as I might annoy you."

Louisa sank into an armchair, her face averted. "You don't annoy me," she said miserably. "Maybe I would find it easier if you did. The truth is that I like you and that frightens me."

The next thing she knew, Will was leaning in front of her, both of her hands clasped between his own. His gaze raked her face as if he could see into the secrets of her soul. "You're afraid to *like* me? Why, Louisa? I pose no threat to you. We've established that I'm not bent on seduction or stealing. Surely, given that, you can let me be your friend?"

Shivering violently, Louisa looked away. "I'm not sure that is possible." She was only sure that if he carried on looking at her with that direct, intense gaze, they'd be much more than friends in a manner of minutes. Desire coursed through her in molten waves, leaving her weak and shaken to the core.

"Not possible because you still refuse to trust me, or not possible because I am only your employee, nothing more than a man-of-all-work? Perhaps it is my lack of station in life that you object to."

Startled by the bitterness in his voice, she looked back at him. "No! Oh, no, not that at all. You must think me the most terrible snob for you to say such a thing."

"What then, Louisa? If I told you I was the son of a marquess instead of a simple laborer, would it make a difference to you?"

"Don't be absurd," she said, coloring. "I have no use for the aristocracy, none. I have found them to be nothing but shallow and selfish, caring only about their own amusement."

He bowed his head. "I see. Yet you married a man born to the aristocracy, did you not?"

"I would have been better off staying well away," she said in a low voice. "I did not know then what I know now."

He looked back up at her, a frown marking his brow, his grip tightening on her hands. "What would that be? You told me you married for love."

"Yes. I married for love. My husband, on the other hand, married for something else."

Will abruptly released her hands, standing and walking over to the fireplace. He rested his palm against the mantelpiece, his back to her. "What are you saying exactly—that your husband married you for some ulterior motive? What could that possibly have been?"

Louisa, surprised by the harshness in his voice, swallowed hard. "Val was forced to marry for money," she said. "He made no secret of it, indeed, he was entirely honest, or at least he was when we first met. I, of course, had the money that he needed, but I didn't believe for a minute that was why he pursued me, for my standing in society was merely respectable. Val could probably have had most anyone he wanted in the lower echelons of the *ton*, but he chose me."

Will turned, his eyes fixed on her face, the expression unreadable. "In which case, why do you believe he did choose you? You've just implied that he did not marry you for love."

Louisa's throat was so tight that she could barely speak. "He married me because I was conveniently there and because he knew that I loved him, which would make me more malleable. I was young and foolish and without experience, not that it is any excuse for poor judgment." She bit her lip hard, all the old feelings flooding back—the pain of disillusionment, the anger, the misery when she realized what a terrible mistake she'd made. "I do believe that in the beginning Val thought he loved me, but he had no idea of what love really was. In the end, I was sure of it."

"How?" Will asked, his frown deepening.

Louisa shook her head and laughed, then shook her head again. "It didn't take an endless parade of infidelities or lengthy absences to make me aware that Val was never going to be constant—he made that clear in the first few months of our marriage when he mostly lost interest in sharing our marriage bed. Once he gained what he wanted, I was no longer appealing to him. He had made his conquest. It was time to move on."

She blushed furiously. She'd never told another living soul the truth about her marriage. "Please pretend you didn't hear that. I cannot think what has come over me to reveal such things."

"Truth," Will said succinctly. "And yet you let the world

believe that you loved and supported your husband completely, even after he left for war without so much as a direct word to you."

Staring down at her lap, Louisa could only nod. "Yes," she finally said. "What else could I do? I had a young child by that time. She was my miracle, my reason for going on. I didn't want anything to sully her memories of her father, or give her any reason to wonder why he wasn't with us." Louisa shrugged. "I thought it best to let her believe he was a hero, gone to do his duty for his country. What would be the point in saying anything else to her or others? People talk, Will. Word gets around and the gossips do their part, usually in a malicious fashion. I wanted to protect Pip as well as Val's memory, and I hope I've managed to do so."

Will ran his thumb over his mouth, his head lowered so that she could only see the shadow of his face. She wondered if he understood at all. She barely understood herself.

After a long silence, he finally spoke. "Did you ever let your husband know how you felt?"

Since she'd gone this far, Louisa couldn't see the point in keeping much else back. Her pride was already in shreds. "No. Oh, he knew I wasn't pleased about his behavior, but I tried to keep my tongue between my teeth. Val only became enraged when I confronted him, and I learned quickly enough that confrontation led to more of the same conduct, so I tried to be the dutiful wife, hoping against hope that he'd eventually mature and take his responsibilities more seriously—obviously, that never happened." She pressed a shaking hand against her mouth. "In the end, Val died a hero in the eyes of the world, but not in mine."

Will said nothing. Instead he moved over to the sideboard and poured a large glass of cognac, but instead of drinking himself, he pressed it into her hand.

"Here. Try to get this down. It might help."

She took the snifter between both hands, her teeth chattering against the edge of the glass as she sipped. The liquid burned painfully in her throat but warmed her nonetheless. Her hands trembled so badly that she nearly dropped the glass, and she coughed harshly against the unaccustomed spirits. Still, she managed to finish the cognac off, and to her surprise she felt slightly steadier.

"Filthy stuff," she said, leaning her head back against the chair.

"It has its purpose. Better now?"

"A little," she admitted. "Are you finished extracting painful and humiliating confessions from me?"

"For the moment. I think what you need now more than anything is sleep. Do you think you can manage that?"

Nodding, she suddenly realized that she was exhausted. The idea of sleep had never been more seductive. A hiccup of laughter escaped her throat, then another. Sleep was the last sort of seduction she'd had in mind, but far more welcoming than what she'd originally planned.

"Oh, Will, I am sorry," she chortled. "I very nearly led you astray, didn't I, and I really didn't mean it at all. Or at least I did, but for all the wrong reasons." She burst into laughter.

"Bed," he said firmly. "If you're ever to lead me astray, I'd rather you did it with a clear head and even clearer judgment."

For some reason she found that remark outrageously funny. "I would think that clear judgment would be the last thing you'd want." Her head wobbled slightly and a genuine hiccup shook her. "Oh, dear. I beg your pardon."

"Not at all. I fear you are slightly in your cups, madam,

so might I suggest that I help you up the stairs, since I am entirely responsible for your compromised position?"

"Help away. It's all you ever seem to want to do anyway."

"For good reason," Will said, reaching down and assisting her to stand, one arm firmly around her waist, the most perfectly lovely sensation she'd ever experienced. She wished he'd use both arms, since that would surely be more efficacious than one all by itself. Sadly, he didn't understand the logistics as well as she did, for he just slung her arm around his neck, the corded muscles of his shoulder shifting as he supported her weight.

She couldn't help leaning into his side, drinking in that lovely, elusive masculine scent.

Daringly moving her other arm around his lean waist, she dropped her head against his shoulder, allowing him to lead her out of the room and up the stairs, wishing it wasn't just one brief flight.

"Which room?" he asked as they reached the landing.

"I don't think I should tell you," she replied. "The next thing I know you'll be scaling the vine and climbing in through my window in the dead of night."

"Why would I do a foolish thing like that when the door would work far better?"

Louisa considered. "I don't know—it sounds more dastardly the other way."

"Dastardly, perhaps, but decidedly more dangerous." He looked down the hallway. "First on the right?"

Louisa gasped. "How did you know that?" she demanded.

"I didn't. It was a lucky guess." He shifted his position and walked her to the door, opening it with his free hand. "In you go, Rosebud. This is where I leave you."

"Rosebud?" she said indignantly. "What a silly name."

"Not at all," he replied. "It suits you—rosebuds are soft and sweet, but have thorns ready to draw blood if one doesn't handle them with care."

Louisa grinned and poked a fingernail into his ribs. "Like that?"

"That was mild punishment compared to what I know you can deal out when you put your mind to it." He released her and stepped away. "Bedtime, madam. I suggest you drink a large glass of water or two before you retire to save yourself a headache in the morning."

Sorry that he'd let her go, Louisa rested one hand on the door frame. "Thank you for your help," she said, gazing up at him. "Not just up the stairs, but for listening."

"Any time. I'd far rather have you feel you can speak to me about what is on your mind than devise schemes to compromise me."

"Do not remind me," she said with a groan. "I feel foolish enough as it is."

Will smiled softly. He leaned down and pressed a light kiss to her forehead. "Sleep well, Rosebud. I'll see you tomorrow."

Before Louisa could answer, he'd turned and gone back down the hall, disappearing down the stairs. She heard the light tread of his footsteps as he walked into the study. He came back out again a moment later and went out the front door, quietly closing it behind him.

Louisa leaned back against the wall, her shaking hands pressed to her flaming cheeks. She could still feel the warm imprint of Will's lips on her brow and wouldn't have been surprised to look in the mirror and find their outline, for they'd burned into her skin like a brand.

8

Slumping onto his bed, Will tossed the ledger he'd taken from the study to one side and put his head in his hands with a groan.

He could hardly take in the enormity of what Louisa had told him that evening about her marriage to Val. He didn't doubt her story; her distress had been too obvious. But every last word had been a knife in his heart, for each one had roundly condemned Val, painting an entirely different picture of the man he'd thought he'd known so well.

He'd kept his word and buried his dead friend, for the love of God, laid him on poor Maestro's back, as injured as Maestro was, and led them both from the battlefield, ignoring the pain of his own broken ribs. He'd believed Val to be worth every effort.

To learn now that Val had not only behaved in such a dishonorable fashion to his wife, but also had lied about it to Will time and time again, was a shattering disillusionment.

He raised his head and stared at a crack in the wall, as if it represented the fissure that had opened in his heart. Anger coursed through his veins at Val, but even more at himself for his own gullibility. This wasn't the first time that the fabric of his life had been unmade by someone else's falsehoods, but he was supposed to be older and wiser now, no longer a callow youth who believed that those close to him could be trusted.

He should have guessed something of the truth when Louisa had told him about Val's deserting his family to join the Dragoons, but he'd managed to push his doubts away.

He yanked off one boot, then the other, and threw them both hard against the wall, where they hit with a thud and fell to the floor.

Nothing made sense, not a thing. He'd *read* Louisa's letters, every last one, time and time again. Not one word gave any indication that she was anything but in love with her husband. . . .

He frowned heavily and rubbed his aching temples hard. Come to think of it, she'd never actually written those exact words. He'd assumed them, just as he had assumed she was reticent to put such private feelings on paper lest her letters fall into the wrong hands.

But then why, *why* would she write such long, evocative descriptions of Broadhurst, filling Val in on every last particular as if she thought to comfort him with reminders of their life together? It wasn't even a life they'd shared, he knew that now from what Louisa had said—Val had left before the move to the farm.

Louisa didn't know how to prevaricate even when she tried, and she had no reason to mislead him in this regard that he could imagine. In which case, why had she written the letters, and why had Val been so willing to share the contents with Will? Val had made a point of it, saying that he liked to share his happiness.

As hard as he tried, Will couldn't make any sense of the situation, and he was too tired to go on racking his brain. The truth was that Louisa harbored deep resentment against a husband who had made her life miserable, and that husband, far away from home, had put up a convincing pretense that all was blissful between them. What had been the point in either of them pretending?

Pulling off his coat, he wearily hung it over the back of

a chair, his shirt and breeches following. He picked up the pitcher of cold water on the stand by the window and poured it into the bowl next to it, splashing his face as if it might clear his mind, but to no avail.

How would Louisa react if she knew that Will had read all her letters, that he'd kept so many things from her that she had a right to know?

He shuddered to think how betrayed she'd feel. She'd been hurt enough by her husband, and he was damned if he'd do the same. His back was against the wall. If he told her the truth, he'd lose her, and if he didn't, she was lost to him anyway.

As he finally fell into bed and pulled the covers up over his body, the irony of the whole blasted situation struck him. He'd just learned that Louisa's heart was free and might eventually have been his for the asking, but now Louisa's heart was the one thing he could never have, as much as he longed for it.

Sacrifice really was hell.

"Nothing again," Louisa murmured, trying not to let her disappointment get the best of her as she went through the mail Will Cutter had picked up for her at the inn. She'd hoped against hope as she did every day that there might be some word from Mr. Sandringham of Sandringham and Basil, Publishers, but as usual, she'd received nothing but bills.

For all she knew, her manuscript had been lost in the post, a horrifying thought. She considered writing another letter, just to inquire whether Mr. Sandringham had received it, but she didn't want to irritate him. He was probably a busy man, she told herself. Perhaps months went by before a publisher actually looked at a manuscript from an unknown author.

She sank into her chair and tossed the bills onto her desk, not wanting to deal with them. The butcher would have to wait, and so would everyone else, for there was no extra money to be had at the moment, not until the hay could be sold.

Picking up a letter addressed in David Cumberland's scrappy handwriting, she tore it open and glared down at it, the usual demand for rent curtly written out, with another hike in the rate. She was convinced that he made a personal effort to write the bill himself instead of letting his steward deal with it, just to irritate her.

Maybe Will could do something. She'd have to remember to ask him.

Thinking of Will, which she'd been making a steadfast effort not to do all morning, made her cheeks go hot. How could she have been such a nitwit, first behaving like a strumpet and getting caught out, and then telling Will all those deeply personal things about herself and Val? She had to be out of her mind.

And to make matters worse, she'd let him press spirits on her, actually allowed him take her upstairs, let him kiss her. He'd only kissed her forehead, but still . . . she was walking down the road to ruin, she could see it all now. Next thing she knew she'd be a confirmed drunkard, her skirts hitched up for every attractive man who came along, spending all her time in the hayloft. Betsy Robbins would look like a nun in comparison.

What kind of example was she setting for Pip? Louisa knew she should count herself extremely lucky that neither

Pip nor her father had heard the two of them at her bedroom door last night. The very roof would have come down.

Will should certainly have known better, but what did he care about her reputation? Nothing at all, if his behavior last night was anything to go by.

By all rights she should loathe him, should at least toss him out on his ear, but unfortunately she needed him at the moment. That was the problem. She *needed* him.

Louisa pressed her hands against her throbbing temples, none the better for drink. Typical. A totally unsuitable man had come along and managed to insinuate himself into her life, just as Val had. Will had been so clever about it that she hadn't even realized what had happened until too late, and now her emotions were in turmoil and she couldn't think how to get along without him.

Well. She realized now, and she would make good and sure that he never insinuated himself again into any place but the fields or—or wherever else he had duties.

Thinking of which, she had duties of her own, and the day was getting on. Pushing the bills to one side, Louisa stood and set off for the dairy to oversee the making of the cheese. She'd deal with Will Cutter later.

Gazing up at the blazing sun, Will rested his pitchfork and pulled out a handkerchief. He wiped his streaming brow, thinking it was a miracle he hadn't managed to stab himself through the leg out of sheer distraction. Keeping his mind off his problems had been far more of a strain than heaving huge amounts of hay into a stack for the last ten hours.

"Mr. Cutter?"

"Yes, Pip?" Will glanced over at her and had to smile at the sight of her little body almost lost behind the huge bundle of hay she struggled with. She'd been doing her level best to help, working as hard as everyone else, never once complaining. Pip was a true soldier, although he was beginning to think her resolve came more from her mother than her father.

"Do you think we're nearly done for the day?"

"Why don't you sit down in the shade and take a rest? You've been going nonstop, little one." Indeed, she had refused any respite from her work, as hard as he'd tried to persuade her.

"I don't mind," Pip said, throwing her load next to the stack and collapsing in a heap against it. "And I'm not so little. As I keep telling you, I'm much stronger than I look." She ladled a long drink of water from the pail that sat in the shade, her face flushed red with exertion and heat.

"You are strong indeed, and a fine worker, as fine as any. However, we don't want you to expire of exhaustion. What would your mother say?"

"Why don't you ask her yourself? Here she comes now."

Will looked in the direction Pip pointed, his heart tightening painfully in his chest. He'd been wondering all day how to deal with Louisa when he next saw her. He couldn't allow even a hint of his feelings to show, although God only knew how he was going to keep those from her on top of everything else. Still, he had no choice. He was now going to have to convince her that he saw her as no more than his employer, and that was going to be no easy task. He needed to keep as far away from her as possible for both their sakes.

He started to reached for the shirt he'd long ago tossed to one side, but he was too late. Louisa, who'd been walking at full clip, appeared directly in front of him, her expression anything but amicable. He prayed that the result of the brandy was not the reason, but part of him prayed it was. The folly of that kiss he'd bestowed, even if it was only on her forehead, had been haunting him ever since. How was he going to make her believe that he had absolutely no interest in her after a gesture like that?

She planted her hands on her slim hips. "So, Mr. Cutter. How goes it?"

"It goes well, Mrs. Merriem. We should have all the hay gathered by the morrow."

"Have you examined the ledger yet?"

"I confess I have not. I haven't had the time."

"I'd appreciate your turning your attention to it as soon as possible." She didn't meet his eyes.

Will inclined his head. Oh, Louisa. She was at her most imperious when most unsettled, and if his own feelings were anything to go by, he could just imagine how unsettled she was. "When I have a moment," he replied. "Bringing in the hay must take first priority."

"Then I suggest you get back to it. Pip, what are you doing here?"

"Helping, Mama. I thought you would like it."

Louisa's face softened ever so slightly, and he was happy to see it. "I do like your willingness, but you are obviously tired and should go in. Mr. Cutter ought to have seen that you have had too much sun and exertion."

"I am fine, Mama, but I will do as you wish." Pip shot both of them a long, incisive look, then scampered off without another word.

Will looked directly at Louisa. "Mr. Cutter, madam, has been trying to persuade the valiant Miss Merriem to cease and desist all of the afternoon. Would you now like to take a lash to Mr. Cutter's back for failing to dissuade madam's headstrong daughter?"

"Don't start your sarcasm with me," Louisa said, her eyes narrowing. "My daughter is eight years of age. She is not a Clydesdale horse built for labor."

"Believe it or not, neither am I, but I do my best," Will said coolly. He knew what was bothering Louisa and he decided to address the problem head-on in order to diffuse it. "It was only a kiss on your forehead, Louisa, not a full-out frontal assault. Are you going to make my life a living misery for such a harmless gesture?"

She colored deeply, the flush spreading from her bosom all the way to her hairline. "I was not . . . not referring to—to *that*," she sputtered. "Why would you think such a thing?"

"Because it's the truth. If you must be angry with me, then at least be honest about it." Not that he had a leg to stand on when it came to being honest.

She glared at him, at least ten different emotions flashing across her face in a matter of seconds. "I—I only feel that I must draw a line. You work for me. Personal conversations are not a good idea."

"I agree with you," he said, wanting nothing more than to take her into his arms and smooth away her frown.

"You do?" she said, looking completely taken aback.

"Yes," he said, hating himself for lying, as necessary as it was. "I thought the situation through myself today, and I do." Louisa was staring hard at his bare chest as if it offended her, and he quickly reached for his shirt and shrugged it on. "However, we do have a great deal more to speak of."

"What—what do you mean? I—I just said that I do not wish to embark on any more conversations," she said, her gaze flying to his in confusion.

"And I just agreed. You also said that you wanted me to help you sort out some of your business matters. That will take some thought on my part, and I can hardly expect you to divine what those thoughts are. A certain amount of conversation will be necessary."

She twisted her hands together. "Very well. Think away. I would be grateful, that is *interested*, in what you might have to say."

"I will give you the best advice I can, once I come up with an appropriate strategy. I don't have an infinite number of hours to devote."

"No, of course not. Whatever you can spare." Her eyes had clouded over and she didn't meet his gaze.

He felt absolutely terrible about being so cold to her, knowing in his gut that what she really needed was to be held and reassured. He could see her vulnerability and confusion as easily as he could see how hard she tried to disguise it, but he could never again act on those impulses. He'd caused enough damage as it was.

"I'll let you know if and when I have something useful to tell you," he said, making his tone dismissive. "Until then, I'd appreciate your letting me get on with my work. I haven't the time to spare for these confrontations you seem to enjoy."

Louisa blinked. He might just as well have struck her, she looked so stunned, and he hated himself all the more for having been deliberately cruel.

"Very well, Mr. Cutter," she said, her back stiffening, her chin rising. "I won't trouble you again. Just let me know if and when you *do* find the time."

Will nodded, then turned back to pick up the pitchfork. He couldn't do it. He couldn't leave her like this, her pride hurt along with her feelings.

Turning around, he put a hand on her arm to stay her.

"Louisa, wait. Forgive me. I didn't mean to be so harsh with you. The truth is that I've been kicking myself for having pushed you to the point of distress last night. You have every reason to be angry with me, and I'm angry enough with myself for both of us."

Her shoulders slumped and she squeezed her eyes shut, covering them with one hand. "There is no need to apologize," she whispered, turning her back to disguise the tears he hadn't missed, tears that twisted at his heart, for he'd caused them.

"Yes, there is. I wanted to understand, but I went too far in my questions. I asked you for answers I had no right to." He gently turned her around to face him. "I promise that I will never again ask you anything personal, nor behave in so familiar a fashion."

"I am equally at fault," she said, her voice choked. "I should have exercised more discretion, but I was . . . I was feeling so alone and you were there, and—and it all came out despite myself." She tried to smile but failed miserably. "I woke up this morning berating myself for having allowed you to be so intimate, and I came out here to give you a piece of my mind."

"You did well enough," he said, reaching one hand out and brushing away her tears with his thumb, a gesture that had become second nature. "I think you're right. I need to remember my place, and you need to remember to keep me in it. Perhaps if we both bear that in mind, we'll avoid any more difficulties of this sort." He dropped his hand to his side.

She bowed her head. "Yes, of course. I am relieved that you feel the same way." She glanced back up at him, her expression uncertain. "Does that mean that you really do want to help me with my other problems? You didn't sound very interested just now. I thought maybe you only said what you did last night in order to make me more amenable toward you."

"Yes. I really do want to help. I probably will need a week or so to think everything through, but I promise you that I will apply myself to coming up with a solution."

"Thank you," she said simply. "I've just been through the bills and I cannot pay most of them as things stand. I've had another demand from Mr. Cumberland. He's raised the rate again."

"Has he? Hmm. I'll put David Cumberland first on my list of things to be dealt with."

She put out her hand solemnly. "I'm happy we set things straight. It will make life so much easier for us both."

"Yes, it will." He took her small hand in his and shook it firmly, although he could think of a number of other things he would have liked to do with it.

"Good heavens . . . it can't be," she said suddenly, pulling her hand away and peering around his shoulder. He turned, wondering what she was staring at with such astonishment.

A carriage clattered down the road, coming to a halt alongside them. An older woman's head poked out of the window. "Yoo-hoo," she called, waving her handkerchief vigorously. "Is that you, Louisa dearest? How perfect! I was just on my way to your house."

"Lady Samantha!" Louisa cried. "What on earth are you doing here?"

Will didn't waste a moment. He leapt behind the haystack, unable to believe his bad luck. It was Lady Samantha Davenport, if he wasn't mistaken, and he knew he wasn't. He groaned, then cautiously peered around the corner. Louisa had gone running over to the carriage and was now engaged in animated conversation.

Will pulled his head back and groaned again. Samantha Davenport was a paragon of society and knew everyone and everything about them.

She was a professional houseguest, spending all her time visiting her friends and making sure that no one was left uninformed of the very latest. That she knew Louisa didn't surprise him, not if Louisa had had a London Season, but Lady Samantha was the last person he'd have expected to see down here. If she recognized him, he was done for. He'd just have to be sure she didn't spot him.

To Will's infinite relief, her carriage started down the road again a few minutes later, and Louisa came hurrying back.

"Will," she called. "Will, where have you gone to?"

He stepped out from behind the haystack. "I'm right here."

"You'll never believe it—that was Lady Samantha Davenport," she said, her face a picture of panic. "She wants to stay the night. What am I going to do?"

"Give her a bed, I imagine," Will said, trying very hard not to let his own alarm show.

"No, you don't understand. She was very, very good to me when I was in London and we've written letters back and forth ever since, but I didn't tell her the truth about anything! Oh, Will—I couldn't turn her away, but I don't want her to know how awful things are, which she's bound to learn since she always ferrets everything out."

You're not telling me anything I don't already know, Will thought darkly. "Then you'll have to be sure you keep up a good pretense," he said.

"But how? I can't possibly have her dine at the kitchen table, but if we eat in the dining room, she'll expect everything to be perfect. She knows, of course, that we had to sell the Hall, but I made it sound as if life has been perfectly pleasant, since for Papa's sake I didn't want all of England to know how difficult our situation is."

"I don't see why you can't eat in the dining room," Will said logically. "You have a perfectly decent table and chairs."

"That's not the point! I have no footman, no butler. Lady Samantha will *never* understand. Her father was Duke of Coventry and he left her his fortune. She's never had to do without, not ever!"

Will knew perfectly well who Lady Samantha's father had been. His own father had been one of the duke's good friends and Will's childhood had been punctuated by visits from the duke and his only child. "I'm sure she can manage just for this one night. Cook can serve, can she not?"

Louisa heaved a sigh of exasperation. "I can't possibly expect you to grasp this, but one's cook does *not* serve the quality at table. Anyway, Cook would be bound to make some sour comment or other, and Lady Samantha would figure everything out in a flash. And before you go suggesting Tom Trueboot for the job, I can tell you that he'd be even more of a giveaway, since Tom hasn't the first notion of table manners, let alone how to serve those who do."

Will's eyes narrowed. "You're not suggesting that I play your footman? Because if you are, you can forget the idea right now. It's absurd."

"Oh, but Will," she said, grabbing his hand. "You could do it, I know you could."

"It's out of the question," he said firmly, trying to ignore the pleading expression in her eyes.

"But why? You'd be helping me out of the most enormous trouble, and I'd be forever grateful to you, truly I would. You've managed everything else—how hard could this be?"

"No. Absolutely not." Will wished she'd stop looking at

him with such glowing expectation. "I've never waited at table in my life."

"I could coach you now. It doesn't take much, honestly it doesn't. You just have to remember to serve from the left with your left hand and remove from the right with your right hand—oh, and remember to keep the wineglasses filled, and to stand with your back to the sideboard, facing the table." She frowned in concentration. "What else—oh, not to speak unless you're asked a direct question, and then to answer in a quiet voice, and of course to be careful not to spill anything."

Will ran a hand over his face. "No, Louisa. I must put my foot down, I really must."

"But—but *why*?" she cried in frustration. "You're absolutely perfect, and there's no one else, no one at all. Please? Won't you do it for me? It really is a matter of the utmost urgency."

Will slipped his hand down to his mouth and rubbed it hard. He didn't know how to refuse her without explaining why, which for obvious reasons he couldn't do. "I feel a headache coming on," he said. "Too much sun, I expect. And more than likely I'd drop something as I strained my shoulder today."

"It doesn't look strained to me, and I can give you lavender water for your head. She probably won't even notice you, she'll be so busy talking. People of her station never take any notice of the servants in any case, not unless they do something really outrageous. Servants are meant to be invisible."

"Thank you for pointing that out," Will said, amused. "How reassuring." But Louisa did have a point, he considered. Lady Samantha most likely would take absolutely no notice of him, and even if she did, more than ten years had passed since she'd laid eyes on him.

"Will? Please won't you save my skin? In the name of the friendship you offered last night?"

"Oh, I see. You would invoke that offer now that you need something, when you roundly told me off not half an hour ago for being too familiar with you?"

Louisa blushed furiously. "I'm sorry—I did not mean to . . . well, to take *advantage*. I'm just desperate."

She bit her lip in dismay, and Will had to force himself not to laugh at her confusion. He only loved her more for her transparency.

People saw what they expected to see, he told himself. Samantha Davenport would not be expecting to see a marquess's son, especially when that son was supposed to be in France with his regiment, as good as exiled from England.

"Will?"

He was mad to consider the notion for an instant, even if he did it for Louisa's sake. He made the fatal mistake of looking at her. She regarded him as she might the goose that would lay the golden egg. That he was as stupid as a goose was the only correct piece of that assumption.

"Very well," he said, laying his neck straight on the proverbial chopping block and fully expecting his head to be missing by evening's end. "Whatever I can do I will. But never again, Louisa. Is that clearly understood?"

"Perfectly. Oh, Will, *thank* you!" She threw her arms around his neck in glee. "You are the kindest person ever."

He quickly grasped her wrists and detached her from himself. Louisa had the ability to set his blood on fire with the slightest touch, and he really couldn't take much more. "I do not think it correct for you to be embracing the footman, madam, most certainly not in daylight," he said lightly, although his breath came short.

Louisa chortled. "I beg your pardon. Oh—as to your clothing. I'll send Pip over with something. We must have proper garb somewhere about, although it will be challenging to find something that fits a man of your size." She tapped a finger against her mouth. "I know, Papa's old breeches and stockings should do, and he's bound to have a dress coat. I must go now as I don't want to keep Lady Samantha waiting."

"I draw the line at powdering my hair," he said on a warning note, dismally imagining himself decked out as a footman.

"Oh, very well. Your hair is just long enough for you to pull it back in a queue, I suppose. I'll find a ribbon."

Will shuddered at the thought. "Whatever madam wishes," he said, resigning himself to the necessary evil. Maybe it was all for the best, since Lady Samantha was hardly likely to recognize him turned out like an eighteenth-century fop.

"I'll explain everything to Cook. She will have to work quickly to produce a decent meal. I can just hear her now, having a proper breakdown."

"Cook will manage. Whether I will is another question entirely."

"You'll be brilliant, I just know it."

Louisa shot him a dazzling smile, then sped away, leaving Will wondering whether there was a history of insanity in his family that no one had bothered to mention.

9

"Please, Papa, won't you reconsider and have dinner with us? Lady Samantha would be so happy to see you again." Louisa leaned down and took her father's hands in hers, squeezing them. "You might even enjoy yourself—think of what a nice time you had last night talking with Mr. Cutter."

"Mr. Cutter is an entirely different matter from Lady Samantha Davenport. I have removed myself from society, as you well know, and I have no intention of returning to it in any fashion. Furthermore, I have no wish to endure Lady Samantha's questioning. She is a busybody."

"Papa! She is a good, generous woman who stepped in and sponsored me when I had no one else. How can you say anything negative about her?"

"I didn't say her heart wasn't in the right place, I merely said that she likes knowing everyone's business." Charles Fleming removed his hands from his daughter's and picked up the newspaper. "I must say, Louisa, this scheme of yours to press Mr. Cutter into service as a footman just to please Lady Samantha is ludicrous. I cannot help but feel sorry for the man."

"He'll be fine," Louisa said, praying that she wasn't wrong. She'd practically forced him to take on the job. "Mr. Cutter is very resourceful."

"He is indeed, and you should have more respect for his position, for you cannot afford to lose him. You forget that men have their pride, even those not born to station." Fleming frowned. "I've been meaning to ask—what do you really know of Will Cutter, Louisa? I confess, he puzzles me. He's an educated man and a thoughtful one, his speech is most correct, and yet he works as a laborer."

Louisa shrugged. "You know as much as I. He doesn't like to speak of himself. I've gathered only that there were some problems with his family and so he left his home to make his own way in the world."

"He can't have done a very good job of it if he has to borrow other people's clothing. I don't understand why he doesn't hire himself out as a tutor in a good house. His qualifications seem perfectly adequate from the little discussion we've had, and he'd certainly make more money."

"Maybe he likes working outdoors, Papa. Or maybe he doesn't want to have to provide references, which would be a necessity if he were to take up a situation with a wellborn family." She shook her head, having asked herself the same question at least a dozen times. "He is a mystery to be sure, but his past is not our concern. As long as he does his job correctly I am satisfied."

"I wonder if there is not some scandal there," Fleming persisted, looking up at his daughter over his reading spectacles. "You watch yourself, Louisa. For all you know, the man is a rakehell whose family tossed him out for unconscionable behavior."

"I don't believe that is the case," Louisa said, not that she hadn't entertained the same possibility. "The problem was with his brother—some sort of argument as I recall. I really don't know the details."

"As long as he behaves correctly toward you, my dear. I won't tolerate any improprieties under my roof. I brought you up to be a gentlewoman."

Louisa colored at the implied reprimand. Her father couldn't *possibly* know about last night, could he? Not that anything improper had happened—or at least not truly improper.

"Louisa?" Fleming said severely, lowering his paper. "Why have you turned as red as a beetroot? Nothing has passed between you, has it? You have an unfortunate weakness for handsome men, Valentine Merriem being a case in point."

"No!" she objected quickly, before he could say another word. The last thing she needed was to be reminded of her alarming attraction to Will, although she was beginning to think that Will could have looked like the backside of a hound and she'd still be drawn to him for his kindness. "How could you think such a thing, Papa? I blush because you embarrass me."

"Mmm. You keep your head on straight, my girl. We don't need any more trouble. He may be handsome, but he is most unsuitable, and just you remember it."

"You are being unfair to Mr. Cutter," Louisa replied tartly. "We have a working relationship and he understands that as well as I." At least she was telling the truth in that regard. "I begin to think you are interrogating me because you are trying to distract me from my mission, which is for you to dine with Lady Samantha tonight."

"I have already given you my answer in that regard. I will take a tray here in my room, and you may give Lady Samantha my apologies and tell her I am indisposed."

Louisa sighed, knowing she was defeated. She'd simply have to put a good face on the matter and do her best to keep Lady Samantha entertained and distracted. "Very well, Papa. Thank you for the loan of the breeches and stockings and the dress coat."

"I have no further use for them," he said, turning his face toward the window, his shoulders stiff. "Why should they not now be fit for a footman? I'd play the part myself if

I didn't know the woman. At least I'd know the role in-side out, having had footmen of my own until the last five years."

"Oh, Papa . . ." Louisa's heart fell. She rested her cheek on the top of his head. "I'm so sorry. If I hadn't made the mistake of marrying Val, none of this would ever have hap-pened. I am to blame, no one else."

"That is not entirely true," her father said, his voice low. "I blame myself every day for allowing the marriage at all, for I should have known that he was a weak man. I thought only to see you married into the aristocracy, but that was pride on my part. A man like Valentine Merriem could never have made you happy, and that should have been my first consideration."

"Do not forget that I thought I loved him, Papa. You told me at the time that you wanted me to be as happy as you and Mama had been, and you gave me your blessing based on that. Anything else is hindsight now. We weren't to know that Val was unreliable and selfish."

"Humph," her father said gruffly, reaching up to take her hand. "I also couldn't imagine you married to that David Cumberland, which seemed to be the way the wind was blowing."

Louisa dropped a kiss on his cheek. "I wouldn't have married David Cumberland in a thousand years. He was a bore."

"Never mind, my dear. It's all water under the bridge now. I was a fool ever to listen to your husband's investment advice, but he was so persuasive about his sources. If I'd only resisted the temptation to double my fortune, we'd still be very well off."

"And Val would never have run off to join the army and

I'd still be married to him," she said with an attempt at humor. "Every cloud has its silver lining."

He looked up at her over his shoulder, his eyes shimmering. "If that is yours," he said, his voice choked, "then you are my silver lining, Louisa, you and Pip. I might have lost everything else, but I still have both of you, and I am grateful for that. I do not know what I'd do if I lost either of you." He composed himself. "Now go and ready yourself for dinner. You can tell me all about it tomorrow, after Lady Samantha has taken herself away."

Louisa straightened and smoothed his hair. "I will. Just pray everything goes smoothly tonight. I cannot afford any mistakes."

"No, you cannot, but I know you, Louisa. You are strong, far stronger than I. You will manage beautifully. You always do."

As Louisa left, the bundle of clothing in her arms, she wished she had as much confidence in herself as her father had.

"Oh, Mr. Cutter, you do look silly," Pip said with a peal of laughter as Will walked into the kitchen.

"I feel like an organ-grinder's monkey," he replied succinctly. "What your mother is thinking of, I do not know. Pray God this is the last time I ever have to perform this particular task."

"There's naught to fear," Cook said, turning from the stove, but she, too, burst into laughter when she saw Will. "You look like a right milord," she said, her gaze raking him up and down, her eyes tearing with mirth. "Wherever did you get that foolish ribbon for your hair?"

"Mrs. Merriem was kind enough to supply it. If I'd had any sense I would have had my hair cut last week and saved myself the embarrassment of a pigtail."

"It's not so bad. I must say, I never knew what fine calves you had." Cook winked at him. "Best watch out that Lady Samantha doesn't give them a little feel when you get close."

Will marched over to her and wrapped an arm around her waist. "Watch yourself, Cook, my love, or you'll know more about my calves than you ever wished," he said in a lowered voice. "A man can only take so much admiration."

She threw her head back and howled with laughter. "Now that's the most attractive offer I've had in donkey's years. Don't waste yourself on me, Mr. Cutter. The only treacle I've got left is in my tarts." Wiping her eyes on the corner of her apron, she patted his cheek. "It's a good thing for you Betsy Robbins has gone home for the day, or you'd never get to the table at all."

"Why," he said with growing frustration, "is everyone interested in Betsy Robbins but me?"

"Because she's got an appetite on her that devours everything in its path, my lad. We're just waiting to see where the bones land."

"What do you mean, Cook?" Pip said, chewing on a piece of bread. "What bones?"

"Not mine, you can be sure of that," Will said, then quickly changed the subject. "I pray I do not spill soup down Lady Samantha's bodice."

"Don't you worry, Mr. Cutter," Cook said. "You'll do well enough as long as you keep your eyes where they belong. I've seen them go out on stalks before, I have, and the strain hasn't done you a bit of good." She stirred the pot, an enormous grin splitting her face.

Will groaned internally. Cook didn't miss a damned thing.

He knew perfectly well that she was referring to Louisa's display of bosom the night before and his reaction to it. "Why don't you tell me the menu, Cook, and what order I should present it in. If you'll be so kind, I need you to instruct me as we go along as to the proper methods of presentation." Will had to suppress a laugh at this. He'd spent the majority of his life being served. If he didn't know how it was done by now, he never would.

"I'll guide you every step of the way, my lad, indeed I will, for you're a good boy, you are, and I know you'll do justice to my meal. To start with, you must be sure that you are silent in everything you do . . ."

Carrying in the first course of terrine, Will felt as if he were going to his own execution. He kept his head bent as he pushed open the door between kitchen and dining room.

Louisa sat at the head of the table, Lady Samantha at her right, both engaged in conversation. He carefully slid the plates in front of them and filled their wineglasses from the decanter he'd prepared earlier.

Louisa briefly glanced up at him as he poured her wine, her face expressionless, but she immediately lowered her eyes.

Samantha Davenport didn't look at him at all, and he breathed a sigh of relief as he moved over to the sideboard, lost in the shadows. Maybe it wasn't going to be so difficult after all. Still, he kept his head bowed, just in case. Keeping his ears closed was not so easy, and for the first time he pitied the footmen who had stood in his place. He'd never stopped to think before about what they heard. Half the reputations in England would be broken if footmen had been in the habit of talking.

". . . And my *dear*, you never would have believed Gertrude's face when Rothingford denied in *public* that they'd ever been affianced. She practically swooned, had to be carried off to a private parlor by her friends and fanned all the night. Of course, Gertrude Hunnicut always was a bit of an idiot, and to believe that a proposal privately made by someone like Rothingford had any legitimacy was the height of stupidity. To declare it in public before it had been announced amounted to social suicide." Lady Samantha put down her knife and fork and patted her gray hair, already perfectly in place. "Shocking, I call that. Absolutely shocking."

"Which, Lord Rothingford's denial or Gertrude Hunnicut's announcement?" Louisa asked. "Both of them sound incredibly foolish in their behavior."

"Indeed, my dear girl, indeed, although one expected Rothingford to behave in such a manner, and naturally he can get away with it. Gertrude should have had far more sense, whatever he'd promised her in private, and I can almost guarantee that a seduction was involved." She pressed a heavily ringed hand to her cheek. "I wouldn't be surprised if she doesn't vanish to the continent for six months to recover from a supposedly broken heart, but we both know what *that* sort of disappearance means. One more bastard for Rothingford, I suppose, and Gertrude will be lucky to secure a younger son of some lesser family with an income of a thousand a year, if that."

Will, forgetting for a moment that he was supposed to be a footman, shook his head. Nothing changed. Why should it? Society had been marching along the same fashion for hundreds of years. He'd only been removed from it for ten of them.

"I can only feel sorry for Gertrude," Louisa said. "No one deserves to be so ill-used."

Lady Samantha sighed gustily. "You are gracious, my dear. Your own husband did not use you well."

"Why would you say such a thing?" Louisa asked, her fork half raised. "Mr. Merriem was nothing but kind to me."

Will flinched. He hurt for her, for her need to protect her pride, although he strongly suspected she was about to find out that Lady Samantha already knew the full story.

He was right, or at least in part.

"My dear Louisa, you forget that you and I are friends and as such speak the truth to each other." Lady Samantha took a sip of wine, then dabbed delicately at the corner of her mouth with her napkin. "I know that Valentine was not kind to you. If you'll forgive my speaking plainly, I am aware of what he got up to when away from the Hall. Gambling, loose women, they were all part and parcel of his life in London when you were not there."

"Yes, it is true, but that is not uncommon behavior in young men," Louisa said, raising her chin. "In the end, he realized his responsibility and went off to fight for his country. He died a hero, Lady Samantha. Will you condemn him for that?"

"My dear, I will condemn him for nothing until I have facts, but your father had a large fortune. You left the Hall around the same time that Valentine left for war. I heard that your father suffered a reversal on the 'Change, and really, Louisa, I cannot help but think that Valentine had something to do with that loss, given his sudden and unexpected departure."

"I can assure you, Val did not run off with Papa's money, if that is what you are thinking."

"No, that is not what I am thinking. I am, however, think-ing that Valentine was somehow involved in your leaving the Hall and this change of lifestyle."

Will's head came up as something Louisa had said about her father echoed in his memory.

I think he has never been able to forgive himself for taking the advice of someone he ought not to have trusted . . . Val lost most of what we had in the same venture.

So. Was it possible that Val had been responsible for giv-ing the advice? Will thought that scenario more than likely and waited impatiently for Louisa's response. She was busy fiddling with her wineglass, turning it round and round on the tablecloth.

"Yes, very well," she finally said. "I suppose there's no harm in telling you, since you seem to have already reached that conclusion. Val did convince Papa to invest in shares that in the end were worth nothing more than the paper they were written on. The stock crashed, but the setback was not enormous."

Louisa's face looked as pink as the roses in the vase on the center of the table, and he knew that she hated the lie she'd just told. He understood perfectly well why she had, though, knowing she was trying hard to protect her father as well as Val. Louisa was hell-bent on taking responsibility for everyone and everything.

He should know. He suffered from the same inclination. "I see."

Lady Samantha imperiously raised her empty glass and Will jumped to attention. He moved to her side, staying well behind the woman, and refilled it. Louisa's was mostly untouched, so he quickly moved back into the shadows.

"I was right, then. Your Valentine ran off to war rather than face your father, is that it?" Lady Samantha continued.

"How very typical of him, but I thought as much. My dear Louisa, I did warn you against the marriage, but you would not listen, as many young girls do not when they fancy themselves in love."

Louisa looked down at her plate. "I was wrong," she said in a low voice. "I should have listened to you, but I've always been headstrong. Papa and I were speaking about it just two hours ago, and he said the same." She looked over at Lady Samantha with a slight smile. "Still, we have everything we need, as you can see. As I told you in my letters, Papa's health had been precarious for some time, and the Hall was really too much for him to manage, which is why he sold it."

"I was surprised he would let something go that has been in the family for generations, but I suppose with no wife, he found keeping it all up difficult. The farmhouse is charming, Louisa. You've made it such a warm home."

"Thank you."

"You brought your cook from the Hall, I believe. Very wise. She is excellent, and one does not let go of good cooks, for they are few and far between." She cast a glance in Will's direction. "The footman I do not remember, though. Is he new?"

Louisa nearly choked, and Will went weak at the knees, holding his breath.

"Er . . . yes," Louisa said quickly, her cheeks turning an even brighter pink. "Cutter came to us only a month ago."

"He has a familiar look about him. Did he come from a house I might know of?"

"I doubt it. Cutter is not experienced. He is still in training, as you might have noticed." Louisa looked as if she might slide off her chair in mortification.

"Come here where I can better see you, Cutter," Lady Samantha demanded.

Will whispered a quick prayer of protection under his breath, then stepped forward, trying to convince himself that Lady Samantha would never in a million years put two and two together.

"M'lady?" he said, bowing low.

"Where do you hail from, my man?" She looked him up and down, her gaze settling intently on his face.

"Norfolk, m'lady." He was placing himself far too close to home for comfort, but he could hardly say anything else—Louisa wouldn't understand a subterfuge for no good reason.

"Were you in service there?"

"Yes, m'lady," he said, searching desperately for some reasonable story. "I was in outside service, but then I went off to fight the war," he said, making his accent as country Norfolk as he could. "Now that I'm back, I'm trying to improve meself, and Missus Merriem's been good enough to take me on, what with all the unemployed soldiers looking for work."

Louisa stared at him as if he were off his head, but then she wasn't to know that he was doing everything he could to throw Lady Samantha off the scent.

"Mrs. Merriem has always had a kind heart," Lady Samantha said. "You are a fortunate man. Very good, Cutter, you may remove the plates and bring in the next course. Louisa, I simply must tell you about my visit to Lord and Lady Cirencester. As I told you, I'm on my way back to London from their country place—it's an absolute nightmare, my dear! Not a single extra blanket to be had, and the lack of candles was appalling. We were dining in near darkness.

The Cirencesters have obviously fallen on hard times, but then so many have . . ."

Will gathered up the plates and beat the hastiest retreat of his life, practically throwing the plates into the kitchen sink and sagging into the nearest chair.

"Whatever's the matter, Mr. Cutter?" Cook asked, saucing the lamb. "You look pale as a ghost. You didn't go spilling, did you?"

"Not in the way you think," Will said. "My nerves aren't up to this, Cook."

"Never you mind that Lady Samantha. She's just like you and me underneath that grand breeding. If I didn't know for myself that she was a duke's daughter, I'd have made her out to be an opera dancer in her early years—just look at those rouged cheeks. She's flamboyant as they come, but she can get away with it since no one would dare to say a word and she knows it."

Will stared at Cook, then burst into laughter. Cook had put her finger on Lady Samantha exactly. "You have a point, Cook, you have a point."

"I'll tell you something else, Mr. Cutter. She's got a heart as big as the world and no pretensions, not really. Why, she's even come into my kitchen and told me how much she enjoyed her meal. You can't fault a woman like that, no you can't, so don't let her unnerve you." Cook planted her hands on her hips. "Now you get right back in there and serve up the main course, lad. She won't bite on anything more than the lamb. You're safe enough."

He nodded and reluctantly rose. Oh, God, what had become of him? He'd gone into battle time and time again and never had anything more than a queasy stomach. But now he felt utterly sick.

All it would take was a few more long, probing looks from Samantha Davenport and she'd have him on his knees, the tongue that acted as her sword ready to deal the mortal blow. Louisa would never speak to him again.

To his amazement, the rest of the meal went smoothly. Lady Samantha never cast him another glance, talking on incessantly about one piece of gossip or another, all of which informed him well about what had been happening in society since his absence. As he stood at the ready at the sideboard he couldn't believe his good luck. She'd actually bought his ridiculous story, but then why shouldn't she?

Just as he originally anticipated, she'd seen what she expected to see, a humble footman.

Feeling confident that he was out of the woods, he cleared off the table, then carried the tea tray into the sitting room. He carefully placed it down in front of the sofa where Lady Samantha had arranged herself next to Louisa, who was regarding him nervously, as she had done all evening.

"Nicely done, Cutter," Lady Samantha said in an approving tone. "You will go far. Should Mrs. Merriem no longer require your services for whatever reason, apply to me in Upper Brook Street, London. I enjoy being surrounded by attractive footmen. One of the finer benefits of being a spinster is being able not only to choose but also to admire the help with impunity."

"Thank you, m'lady," Will managed to say, making a huge effort to keep a straight face. She really was outrageous. He couldn't help but wonder how many footmen Lady Samantha had managed to persuade into her bed.

"That is all, Cutter," Lady Samantha said with another wave of her hand. "Your mistress pours. You will learn these details soon enough. You cannot be expected to know everything in a month."

He bowed. "Your ladyship."

Will managed to contain himself until he'd reached the safety of the hallway. His shoulders shook with silent hilarity. Life had grown so bizarre that he couldn't make sense of it anymore, and didn't care to, lest he lose his mind entirely.

Considering his duties more than done, Will made his way back to the stables to rid himself of his footman's clothes and get some well-deserved rest.

10

A sharp rapping at his bedroom door woke Will from a deep sleep and he sat up, wondering who on earth could be wanting him at this hour. He could only think that something had happened to Charles Fleming.

"I'll be right there," he called, pulling on his trousers and a shirt and splashing his face with water to wake himself fully.

He walked to the door and pulled it open, his jaw dropping at the sight of Lady Samantha Davenport. "M-m'lady," he stammered, thinking that he had to be dreaming still. That's what this was, another nightmare. A very, very bad nightmare, one of his worst, and he'd had more than his share.

"Why, Lord William Fitzpatrick as I live and breathe," she said, folding her arms over her ample bosom. "Fancy finding you here. May I come in?"

She didn't give him a chance to reply, marching into the room and looking around her. "The last time I checked, this was not an officer's billet," she said, settling herself into the single chair near the bed, looking like a cat who had gotten into the cream pot.

Will was unable to summon any words to his tongue, Oh, *God*, couldn't anything go right in his life?

"Did you sustain a blow to the head at Waterloo?" she asked. "You were mentioned in dispatches, which also said that you'd received minor injuries, but nothing about incurring amnesia."

"My head is in perfectly good order, thank you," he replied dryly.

"I have to wonder about that if you're masquerading as a footman and thinking that I wouldn't notice." She tapped her foot impatiently on the floor. "Come, come, my man, out with it. What are you doing here at Broadhurst Farm playing at being a country yokel?"

Will sat on the bed, knowing there was no longer any point in pretending. Samantha had him by the short hairs and she was pulling without mercy.

"The game is up, William. You cannot possibly believe that you can flummox me now."

"No," he said shortly. "The problem is that I don't even know where to begin."

"At the beginning would be sensible. Something must have brought you here and something important, if I know anything about it. Does this have anything to do with Valentine Merriem? You served in the same regiment, and I cannot believe you arrived here by accident."

He nodded, as miserable as he'd ever been in his life. Samantha would go straight to Louisa and he'd be out by morning, all of his good intentions up in smoke, and Louisa would be left with no one to help her out of her scrape. The absolute truth was the only thing that would serve if he was to convince Lady Samantha to leave well enough alone.

"I came to bring Val's letters to his wife. She mistook me for a laborer responding to a notice she'd posted at the pub, and one thing led to another. I've been serving as her man-of-all-work."

Lady Samantha fixed him with her sharp gaze. "I gather Louisa knows nothing of your real identity?"

"Not a thing. I admit that the accent I put on tonight

took her by surprise, since she knows I speak as well as she does, but I affected that in an effort to mislead you. No, she knows nothing else, nor can she."

"Why is that, William? There must be reason behind this madness, for you've always been a practical boy, if a little too noble for your own good."

His head shot up. "Why would you say a thing like that?"

"Simply because I never believed for a moment the story that your brother told about that poor girl and your part in her death. Your father was a fool for having taken your brother's word, although I cannot understand why you didn't defend yourself."

Will released a heavy sigh. "How did you hear?" he asked with resignation, although Mary Potter and her tragic death was the last thing he wanted to discuss, the memory still raw after all these years. "My father and brother swore they would keep the story to themselves if I joined the army and left the country."

"Neither said a thing to me. I heard it from my maid who heard it from the butler when I was up at Alconleigh a month or two after you'd gone."

"I see," Will said. "I should have expected as much."

"Look here, William, if you think I've ever been blind to the situation between your brother and yourself, you must think me a fool indeed. I've always thought it a pity that you were the younger twin, for you were much better suited to inheriting the responsibilities of the marquessate than Rupert. You and he no more resemble each other in nature than you do in looks, and if I'd known how it was going to turn out, I'd have advised your dear mother to stand on her head for a few hours to shift the two of you around."

Will smiled reluctantly. "I doubt my mother would have listened, given how uncomfortable she must have been at the time. How is Rupert?" he asked even more reluctantly, although something deep inside of him really did want to know. Rupert was still his brother, despite the bad blood between them.

"Unmarried and more irresponsible than ever, if that is possible," she replied tartly. "Now that he is marquess, he behaves as if the world should fall at his feet and treat him like God Himself. He's neglecting the estates, from everything I can see, hot in pursuit of his own pleasures and spending money like water."

"I'm not surprised," Will said, although he was surprised by the deep pain he felt. He'd never expected Rupert to care about Alconleigh or the other properties in his trust, but he'd hoped his brother might eventually learn to take his responsibilities seriously.

"Have you considered that if Rupert carries on in this dissolute fashion, he might die? One cannot frequent the opium dens—oh, yes," she said at Will's look of disbelief. "That and more. Incessant whoring never was good for the health, and he might contract any manner of disease if he hasn't already."

"It's nothing to do with me," Will said. "I cannot change him at this late date."

"No. You cannot. But Rupert has no heir, and he's not likely to get one soon, not a legitimate one in any case, which leaves you next in line. You must think about that eventuality, which means you must do something about taking yourself back to where you belong. Forgive my bluntness, but I can only believe that you keep yourself here as a farm laborer or footman or whatever because you resist facing the trouble that your brother will give you when you do return to your proper place in society."

Will shook his head. "No, that's not it. I was on my way

home, albeit with reservations, when I became waylaid here at Broadhurst. Louisa's problems are far larger than any I might have, and she had no one else to protect her. I cannot leave until I have done what I can."

"Ah," Samantha said, looking supremely satisfied. "So finally we get at the truth. I have suspected for some time that Louisa was in trouble and that her pride prevented her from telling me about it. How bad is it? Perhaps I can help."

Will hesitated. He could do with some help, and it had just occurred to him that Samantha Davenport might be the answer to his prayers, but he couldn't risk Louisa's finding out that he'd revealed her situation. "Do we speak in confidence?" he asked. "Louisa would murder me if she knew I told you anything of her affairs, and she'd have every right to the act."

"Naturally. My tongue only wags when the parties are deserving, which is not the case here. Tell me all, my boy, and leave nothing out."

Will made a decision. He had no choice but to trust Samantha Davenport, not if he was to convince her to keep his secret. He took a deep breath and embarked on the entire story, or at least as much as he knew or had pieced together. When he'd finished, Samantha was silent for a few minutes, probably a record for her.

"A problem indeed," she finally said, nodding to herself. "Yes. Yes, I can see exactly why you have taken on this silly charade, for Louisa will accept help from no one she considers part of our circle. She fears that her father might be disgraced by his foolishness."

"That is it exactly," Will said, grateful that Samantha had picked up the salient points so quickly. "I don't know that Louisa will see it that way, but that's not the problem. She shouldn't be isolated like this, terrified every waking moment that she's going to lose the little that's left and cause her family to go to the poorhouse. I've thought about fiddling the books so that I could put money into the farm without her knowing, but she's far too smart for that, and in any case, she goes over those books with a sharp eye."

"The girl has never been anyone's fool, with the exception of her deciding to marry Valentine Merriem—but that's another story. I knew his family well and Valentine was the worst that particular breeding produced in at least three generations."

"What do you mean by that?" Will asked, wondering how he'd completely missed seeing Val's true character in all the years he'd known him. He still struggled against accepting what Louisa had told him, not that he doubted her word, but to hear the same assessment from Samantha Davenport was condemnation indeed.

"I mean that the boy had charm aplenty, but he was as selfish as they come. He did as he pleased and took what he wanted without regard to anyone else. He broke poor Louisa's heart, not to mention what he did to her dear father—now there is a *real* tragedy." Lady Samantha absently toyed with the three priceless strands of pearls that ringed her neck. "Such a handsome, dashing man he was, so strong and self-assured with a fine, upstanding character. From what Louisa tells me, not only has his health been damaged, but I imagine his pride has suffered a terrible blow as well."

"Why, Lady Samantha, if I didn't know better, I'd say that you have a soft spot in your heart for Charles Fleming," Will said in a teasing tone.

She flushed. "Nonsense, my boy. I merely said that I

admired him and cannot help but be saddened by his suffering. I have known him since my girlhood, and naturally I want to do whatever I can for him."

Will regarded her with fascination. Was it possible that Lady Samantha, who to his knowledge had never even considered marriage, held a *tendre* for Charles Fleming? That would explain why Samantha had taken Louisa on as her protégée . . . and it might also explain why Charles Fleming had refused to join them for dinner. Perhaps he hadn't been able to bear the thought of having Samantha see him as he was now. An outrageous idea occurred to Will, worthy of some serious consideration at a later date.

Lady Samantha cleared her throat loudly. "Well, never mind all that. The past is done and we must look toward solutions. Louisa cannot continue in this fashion, and dear Portia must have a proper upbringing. I don't suppose you'd consider marrying Louisa yourself, would you? You obviously must be fond of her to have gone to such lengths, and you do have a sizable fortune of your own."

Will wanted to scream. Lady Samantha had managed to miss the one most important point—Louisa would never accept him, even if he did offer marriage, which he'd have done in a heartbeat if he thought it would do him any good. "I'm afraid that is not a possibility," he said. "If Louisa knew that I'd deceived her about my identity, she would never forgive me."

"You might be surprised by how much a woman can forgive when her heart is involved."

"Her heart is most assuredly not involved," he said heavily. "Louisa is no more interested in me than she is in the man in the moon."

"Then make her interested. I will never tell, William, but

something leads me to believe that you have more invested here than an interest in Louisa's hay and livestock. Do not be a fool and let something wonderful slip between your fingers just because of your pride. This is a match I would be happy to encourage."

"Thank you," he said. "I appreciate your support, but I assure you it is in vain, for there is no match to be made. I will do my work here and then I will leave, and that will be the end of it."

"I doubt that very much, but fool yourself as much as you please. You have always been too stubborn for your own good."

He smiled. "And I begin to suspect that underneath your crusty exterior you are a devoted romantic."

"Nonsense. I know a good match when I see one. I don't suppose you've considered what will happen when you do leave here and reclaim your identity? Louisa is bound to discover your deception. What then?"

"I cannot see any reason why she should ever learn the truth," he said, although that possibility had occurred to him more than once. "She never leaves Broadhurst."

"You think her situation will stay this way forever? I can assure you that it will not, not by the time I'm finished, and if your goal is also to put Louisa back on her feet, then you had better consider the consequences. If I were you, I'd start thinking of how to sort out my own predicament."

"There is no predicament. As I said, I will eventually leave, Louisa will forget all about me, and if we should ever cross paths again, which is highly unlikely, I will deny any knowledge of ever having met her."

"You're a bigger fool than I thought," Samantha said with undisguised disgust. "Really, William, the last ten years should have taught you more. You cannot run away from your problems, as you did when you left Alconleigh, no matter how noble you thought you were being at the time."

"I didn't exactly leave Alconleigh willingly. My father offered me no choice."

"No, because you refused to set him straight, just as you are doing now with Louisa. Personally, I am hard-pressed to understand why you didn't just march up to Louisa's door, announce yourself as the gentleman you are, and offer your resources as her husband's fellow officer. Isn't that how one usually goes about it?"

Will opened his mouth to reply, then shut it again. He had no reasonable explanation, or at least not one he could give to Lady Samantha without telling her about the letters, about the fantasy he'd built around Broadhurst, about wanting to taste that life for himself, to be in Louisa's presence if just for a brief time.

Samantha was right. He'd behaved like a damned idiot, but it was too late now to change anything.

"You take my point, I see. Never mind, William, what's done is done, and I see no point in admonishing you any further. I leave it to you to find a way to set Louisa straight, for it simply won't do to carry on deceiving her like this. However, you may rest assured that your secret is safe with me."

"Thank you," he said.

"Don't thank me, you big blockhead. I love Louisa—I have from the moment I met her. She doesn't deserve any more ill-treatment. Valentine Merriem gave her enough for a lifetime."

Will merely nodded, knowing he deserved every bit of the censure she'd doled out.

"In the meantime," she continued, "I will get onto this business of David Cumberland. As you said, something is not right, and I suspect that I might be able to discover much in the next fortnight from my bankers."

"Tell them to look back five or six years," Will said, relieved that she'd let the other, more difficult subject drop. "I strongly suspect they will find some interesting stock dealings on Cumberland's part directly related to the sudden fall in price that brought Mr. Fleming down."

"Yes . . . and I will also think about poor Charles Fleming's situation. It is not right that such a fine man should have made himself an outcast just because of a reversal of fortune. He has so much still to offer."

"I'll be interested to hear what you come up with," he said. "You have always had a resourceful mind."

"Yes, I have," she said, rising with a grunt. "Now I am tired and want my bed."

"I am grateful for all your help, Lady Samantha."

Will stood and bowed, then saw her to the door. "I shall probably not see you in the morning as my duties take me out early and far afield. I pick up the Merriems mail each morning at the Hart and Hound in Maidencombe so, if you need to contact me, write to me there—and under the name of Will Cutter, if you please."

"Naturally, my dear boy," she said, resting her gloved hand against his cheek. "I will protect your cover by all means. Give me time to investigate. The very minute I know something, I shall write. In the meantime, do whatever you can to ensure Louisa's affections."

She winked at him in a conspiratorial fashion and slipped out the door like a spy into the night.

———

"My dear Louisa, how sad that I must leave you so soon, but London awaits with all its attendant responsibilities. We have only another month left to the Season and I must be there to oversee matters." Lady Samantha climbed into her carriage. "Thank you so much for your hospitality."

"I am only sorry it was so humble," Louisa said, thankful that Lady Samantha's social engagements forced her away so quickly. She didn't think that Will could have endured another evening of playing at footman. "Thank you so much for thinking of me and taking the time to stop."

"We must meet again very soon, my dear. Won't you come to London, if only for a brief while?"

"I cannot, I regret. Pip and my father need me here, and life on a farm is most demanding this time of year. I must supervise the operation."

"Naturally. Well, if you change your mind, you know my direction." She reached out the window and took Louisa's hand. "You must marry again, Louisa. It doesn't do to pine away out here in the country, not when there are men who would be happy to give you a good name and security."

Louisa shook her head. "I think not, Lady Samantha. I am done with men. I have everything I need in my father and Pip, honestly I have."

"Nonsense, child. You are still young and lovely, and you must grasp with both hands whatever fate puts in your path. One never knows what direction that fate might come from, but do not be blind to good fortune when it presents itself in whatever guise."

"I would never turn my back on good fortune," Louisa said. "I just don't think it is going to appear in the form of a husband."

Samantha smiled broadly. "Ah, but I have the utmost hopes for you, Louisa. Your life will have a fairy-tale ending so long as you embrace the possibilities, just mark my words."

Reaching up, she rapped sharply on the roof of the carriage. "Get on! What are you waiting for?" she bellowed to the coachman.

As the carriage sprang forward, Lady Samantha leaned her head out again, waving her handkerchief. "Do not forget, Louisa! Life is never as it seems!" she cried, and then something else, but her last words were carried away by the wind.

Louisa scrubbed the floor of the front hall with a vengeance, her mind thoroughly preoccupied with her father's health. He had taken a turn for the worse since Lady Samantha's visit three days before, and he'd refused to leave his room, the draperies drawn against the light, accepting only the most modest nourishment.

He said that he suffered from an attack of the migraine, and although he was prone to the painful headaches, she couldn't help wondering if the problem had not been brought on by Lady Samantha's unexpected appearance and his inability to face her.

Hadn't Will said he believed her father's real problem to be in his heart and not in his body?

She wished she could talk to Will about her concerns, but harvesting the hay kept him busy from sunrise till sunset. He only stopped to grab something to eat from the kitchen before going back to the fields, so there had been no time for conversation.

Sitting back on her heels and pushing a damp strand of hair out of her eyes, she thought hard. Something had to be done or her father would waste away, the rest of his life nothing but an unhappy progress of meaningless days until he finally died for lack of anything better to do.

Will had also said his own father had done the same, although his case had perhaps not been so extreme. She couldn't deny the evidence in front of her eyes and felt sure that Will was right—her father's nerves were the cause of his problems.

Her brow furrowed. Having defined the problem was all well and fine, but what was to be done about it? True, her father had cheered up that one night at dinner when Will had engaged him in philosophical discussion, but it hadn't been nearly enough to make any real difference. He was back in bed, unwilling to leave it, lost in a dark despondency that no one could touch, not even Pip.

If only Lady Samantha was right and her luck would change, that good fortune was only around the corner . . .

Louisa shook her head hard, as if she could toss the seductive thought right out of her head. She had enough *if onlys* to last her the rest of her life. Nothing was to be done but to continue on one day at a time, praying that she could somehow find a way to see them all through.

A knock came at the front door and Louisa, startled, jumped to her feet, drying her hands on her apron and trying to tidy her hair. She couldn't think who had come calling unless it was a bill collector. Too bad for him, she thought acidly. He'd have to go away empty-handed since there was nothing to be had.

She moved to the door, and took a moment to compose herself since it wouldn't do to let her panic show, then yanked the door open.

A gentleman in his middle years stood there, and Louisa knew without doubt that he was a gentleman. His impeccable dress, his manner, and the smart carriage in the drive told her everything she needed to know in that regard.

What he was doing on her doorstep was another matter . . . maybe horrible David Cumberland had sent him to take the farm away for nonpayment of rent. "May I help you, sir?" she said, desperately trying to hide her fear.

He took off his hat. "Is Mr. Peter at home?" he asked, an amicable smile creasing his face.

"Mr. Peter?" she asked in confusion.

"This is Broadhurst Farm?" he said, looking around him. "The sign outside did say as much."

"Yes, but I think you must have . . . Oh!"

Louisa stared at him incredulously. The only Mr. Peter she knew of was the person she'd invented as author of her novel. Which meant this man had to be Mr. Sandringham, publisher. Who else would be looking for a Mr. Peter at Broadhurst Farm?

She nearly keeled over in shock. "Oh, you mean Mr. *Peter*. Mr. M. J. Peter."

"Yes. I thought that was what I said," he replied as he handed her his card.

"I—er, won't you come in?" Louisa glanced down at the card, which confirmed her suspicion, and stood back, wondering what she was going to do now. In desperation, she took his hat and coat and led him into the study, her brain working frantically to come up with some possible excuse for the missing, not to mention nonexistent, Mr. Peter.

She couldn't let the opportunity slip away, not now. If Mr. Sandringham had come this distance, he must have a business proposition in mind.

"Mr. *Peter* is not at home at the moment. May I take your card, sir, and have him contact you?"

"Do you not expect him any time soon? I have traveled some distance to meet him. Indeed, I have news of import that I am certain he will wish to hear."

"Oh," she said, one hand going to her pounding heart. That could only mean that Mr. Sandringham wanted to publish her book, actually publish it! Money—it meant desperately needed money, a way out of her immediate problems.

Elation surged in her. She'd achieved an impossible goal as well as finding a solution to her dilemma, but it swiftly dimmed as she realized that if she grasped the moment, she would be exposed for an utter fraud.

How was she ever going to explain?

"May I offer you some refreshment?" she asked, trying to buy time. "Tea and biscuits, perhaps? Madeira?"

"No, thank you. Mr. Peter does live here, does he not?" Sandringham asked, looking thoroughly confused. "His address is clearly stated."

"Oh, yes. Yes, he does. Er, he is a tenant, that is to say, a boarder. He comes and goes, comes and goes. I never know what he will do next—I am Mrs. Merriem, his landlady." She laughed nervously, hating the lie and herself for telling it. "Would you be here on business, perhaps? He told me he had submitted a novel and was impatiently waiting for a response," she said, desperately digging for information. "I thought you might be a publisher."

"Oh, dear, how awkward, but I suppose if Mr. Peter has told you about it there is no harm in relating my business. You see, I wish to publish his novel, but time is a constraint. I have an immediate opening in my schedule, but I must proceed quickly or there will be no room for the next year or so." He smiled broadly. "I believe I can make a great success out of Mr. Peter, and I am anxious to move ahead—the time is right for this book and I would hate to see the opportunity lost. I cannot delay."

"Oh." Louisa bit her lip. "Maybe you could leave a letter for Mr. Peter, outlining the particulars. I would see that he received it immediately."

"No, that will not do. I must talk to Mr. Peter personally. We have details to work out as soon as possible, which is why I have made this journey. It's such a pity that he is not here, but perhaps in another year we can try again."

The blood drained from Louisa's face as she saw her great stroke of luck slip away. She'd have dragged her father from his bed to masquerade as Mr. Peter if she thought it would do any good, but her father was the last person on earth who should know about her publishing efforts. Not only would he forbid her to proceed, but the shock of knowing she'd done such a brazen thing would finish him off for certain.

"But—but Mr. Peter could be back as early as tomorrow," she said, wanting to curl up into a little ball and die. So much work and all for naught. Next year would be far too late. She needed the money now.

Mr. Sandringham shook his head. "I must return to London directly. I will write Mr. Peter a letter from there, expressing my regrets."

"No need. I am here now."

Louisa spun around, her mouth dropping open. Will stood in the doorway, looking as if he knew all about Mr. Peter, was Mr. Peter, and had always been Mr. Peter.

"Good afternoon," he said. "Forgive my appearance, but I have just returned from a walking tour of the south of Devon. Lovely country, wouldn't you agree?"

"Delightful," Sandringham replied, looking as if the moon

had just fallen out of the sky and directly into his lap. "You are M. J. Peter?"

"Indeed I am," Will said, strolling into the room. "I trust I find you well, Mrs. Merriem?"

"I—yes, very well, thank you, Mr. Peter," she replied, her head spinning. She couldn't begin to imagine what Will was up to, but she wasn't going to ask for explanations. M. J. Peter had just been delivered to her in the unlikely form of Will Cutter, and she wasn't about to throw away what seemed to be an act of God. She could question his motives later. "Your walking tour was a success, then?" she asked, trying to sound like an interested landlady.

"An enormous success, thank you. I made a number of notes for my next piece of fiction. Devon is such a fertile corner of the country for creativity." He looked at her, a laugh lurking in the back of his eyes. "Perhaps you find it so yourself?"

Louisa nearly choked. "I wouldn't know," she managed to say, wanting to kick him for funning with her at such a crucial moment. "This is Mr. Sandringham, a London publisher. He has come about your . . . your novel." She barely managed to get the words out, mortification burning in her throat. Will had caught her out once again, and she had no choice but to put herself at his mercy.

He turned to Sandringham. "Good heavens," he said, stepping forward and shaking the man's hand vigorously. "I am delighted, simply delighted to meet you, sir. How absolutely marvelous. I expected nothing more than a letter to inform me one way or the other of your decision."

"I could not help myself, Mr. Peter. Your novel was so compelling that I have come personally to make an offer. I hope you will find it satisfactory."

"Offer away, Mr. Sandringham. My terms are steep but negotiable."

Louisa's knees nearly collapsed. What was Will *doing*? He'd negotiate her right out of a contract. She had to force her lips together to keep a protest from escaping. Will was her only hope now, and she'd just have to pray that he didn't do anything stupid. He knew as well as she what was at stake.

Will looked over at her. "If you'll excuse us, Mrs. Merriem, I have business to discuss with Mr. Sandringham."

His eyes bored straight into her, demanding that she obey him, but he smiled at the same time as if silently asking her to trust him.

Trust him with her very future? He might as well ask her to cut off her right arm, but she knew she had no choice but to leave. "Of course," she said, feeling as if she were entrusting not only her future but her beloved book to a man who knew nothing about it at all. How in the name of heaven was Will going to pull off a monumental charade without her help?

"Thank you," he said, moving to her desk—*her* desk—and taking a seat. "Won't you sit down, Mr. Sandringham?" He indicated the chair opposite.

Louisa gave him one last, long suspicious look and then, with no other option left, turned and walked out, shutting the door behind her.

She might just as well have been shutting the door on all of her hopes and dreams.

Will settled more firmly into his chair, determined that he would somehow find a way to bluff his way through negotiations on a book he hadn't even known existed until a few minutes before, when he'd happened along to speak to Louisa and had overheard a good part of her conversation with Mr. Sandringham. He couldn't believe he was in the situation at all, but what was another charade at this point? He was becoming an expert at dissembling.

Trust Louisa to drop another shock into his lap, although he wasn't surprised that she'd managed to write a book that a publisher wanted to buy badly enough to come directly after it—he knew well enough how beautifully she put images and characters onto paper.

He thought he understood why she'd kept her book a secret until now, but what he didn't understand was why she'd chosen a male *nom de plume* and refused to confess to it. He imagined he'd find that out soon enough. In the meantime, he needed to put all of his energy into negotiating a good contract for her.

"Now that we are alone, sir," he said, folding his hands on the desktop, "why do we not proceed?"

He sent a silent prayer up to Michael, archangel of mercy and protection and Will's personal favorite of the heavenly hierarchy. This was not the first time he'd made a desperate plea to Michael and probably wouldn't be the last, although this was the first time Will had appealed to him outside the heat of battle. He'd not even asked Michael for mercy when Samantha Davenport showed up, but then that hadn't required divine intervention. This did.

"As I said," Mr. Sandringham said, "I wish to purchase your book, Mr. Peter. I found it a most compelling work and believe a wide audience will find it the same."

"How much are you prepared to pay?" Will said, going straight to the heart of the matter. He guessed that Sandringham's story about time constraints was no more than that—a story. If he wanted the novel badly enough, he would move heaven and earth to see that it was published. Will just wished he knew what the blasted thing was about, since he was masquerading as the author.

"How—er, how direct you are, Mr. Peter," Sandringham replied, his fingers fluttering together.

"I see no point in wasting time. You wish to buy my book, I wish for you to buy it. We are in agreement on that matter. The only thing that stands in the way of each of us achieving our desire is your inability to offer me what I require."

"Just what is it you require, Mr. Peters?" Sandringham asked, his eyes shuttering.

"Give me your offer and I will tell you whether it is what I require or not," Will said.

"Fifty pounds," Sandringham said. "I think it a highly generous offer for a new author."

"Ludicrous," Will shot back. "You will earn at least ten times that, if not more, and if your expressed confidence is any indication, as well as this unnecessary trip into the country, your expectations of an enormous profit are apparent. I am not a fool, Mr. Sandringham."

Sandringham looked down, hiding a smile that Will didn't miss. "You are as astute as your work, sir," he said. "Your assumption is correct. I should have realized I was dealing with no greenhorn, but one tries one's best."

"Try a little harder, Mr. Sandringham," he said, leaning back and crossing his arms. Lord, the things he did for Louisa. "Four hundred pounds and no less."

Sandringham gaped at him. "Impossible!" he gasped. "We have nothing to go on—you have no reputation, there are no guarantees. You cannot understand the nature of the risk we run in undertaking publication at all."

"I understand that you have a fine piece of work before

you and that you want very much to make a profit from it. You will realize no profit at all without my selling you this book, and I am not in the least bit desperate for the money," Will countered. "Three hundred and fifty. That is the least I will accept."

"Three hundred and not a penny more," Sandringham said, wiping his brow. "That alone is highway robbery."

Will laughed. "That is business, sir. I accept—if you make it guineas."

Sandringham paused, then nodded reluctantly. "Guineas it is. You strike a hard bargain."

"A fair one, I think," Will replied. "I'd like the payment by the end of the week as a guarantee that you will publish the work as quickly as you say. I would also like the bank draft made out to Mrs. Valentine Merriem."

Sandringham stared at him. "Isn't—isn't that a little unusual, having such a large amount made over to your er, your landlady?"

Will grinned. So Sandringham thought Louisa was his mistress, did he? Perfect—it only added to his image. "Unusual, perhaps, but practical. She looks after my affairs for me as I prefer to concentrate on my work when I am not traveling in search of new material. I assure you, Mrs. Merriem is as honest as the day is long and I trust her implicitly. If, however, you take exception to my request, I will simply find someone else to publish my work."

"No, no. I shall naturally do as you ask," Sandringham said, wiping his brow again.

"Thank you," Will said, leaning back in his chair in relief.

He couldn't believe his absurd ploy had worked. Louisa should bloody well kiss his feet for what he'd done for her this day, he thought, enormously pleased with himself.

A horrible prospect suddenly occurred to him and his back stiffened.

"There's just one more thing," Will said, deciding that he might as well make Mr. Peter even more of an eccentric. "I am a recluse by nature. I do not wish to be involved in publicity of any sort. No author appearances, is that understood? I must insist—my nerves would never stand the strain, and I cannot create when my nerves are on edge."

"Excellent, Mr. Peter, excellent," Mr. Sandringham said quickly, as if Will were a fish he'd snagged on his line and might still get away before being netted. "We have a bargain, then. If you'll just sign the contract? I took the liberty of having it drawn up in London." He produced a folded paper from inside his breast pocket. "If I might borrow your pen, I will write in the agreed amount."

"That is fine, but I cannot sign the contract until I have read it thoroughly," Will said. "I shall do that this evening and send it on tomorrow, if all is agreeable."

"You couldn't manage to read it now?" Sandringham asked, his eyes glazing over, his own nerves no doubt stretched to the breaking point. "It is not very long or complicated."

Will shook his head, as much as he would have liked to get the whole business over and done with. "I never read anything important unless I have due time to consider it."

The truth was that he wasn't going to sign the damned thing at all. Louisa would have to do that herself, just as she would have to read the contract. He had no right to act on her behalf in any further capacity.

"I see. Well, if you will just attend to it at your earliest convenience and send it directly back to me, I would be very grateful. Naturally I cannot write a bank draft until the signed contract is delivered."

"Naturally," Will said, wondering if a signature in a false name was legally valid. He doubted it. "Mrs. Merriem must sign as well, given that the draft will be made out to her," he added. "I do not wish any legal complications to arise down the road."

"Whatever you wish," Sandringham said, looking thoroughly exhausted. "If there's nothing else, let us move on to more creative matters—I like the title you have chosen."

"Oh?" Will said, praying for fortitude, since he had no idea what the title was. "I wasn't sure of it myself."

"No, no—*The Adventures of Jack Kilblaine, Pirate* has a certain ring to it. It will appeal to both men and women, I believe."

Will nearly choked. *The Adventures of Jack Kilblaine, Pirate*? What the devil had Louisa been up to? He'd expected something along the lines of a drawing room romance, not a story about a brigand on the high seas.

"I—I trust your judgment," he managed to say, desperately suppressing the desire to burst into fits of laughter. Ah, Louisa, only Louisa. So *that* was why she'd chosen a male pseudonym.

"It does have a certain ring to it, I suppose. Er, is there any editing that is necessary?"

"Hardly a thing. I suggest that you might want to add a little more detail to the final battle between the British excise officers and Jack and his crew to heighten the tension, but that is all I can think of. You did a splendid job, Mr. Peter, simply splendid. You will win a legion of enthusiastic readers."

Will went weak at the knees as the implication of Sandringham's words sank in. Oh, God. If Louisa won a legion of enthusiastic readers, he'd be stuck with the role of Mr. Peter to the end of time, and that just wasn't a viable possibility.

He was already stymied enough trying to figure out how to make Will Cutter vanish.

"Mr. Peter? You have gone pale. Was it something I said?"

"Only that you are too kind," Will murmured faintly. "I am overwhelmed by the ramifications."

"I can imagine," Sandringham said. "Not every day does an author hear such exciting news. So. You need time to absorb your good fortune, and I must start back to London. Just think, in a few months your novel will be on the shelves and with luck, on the tongue of every reader in England."

Will nodded, feeling sick. He had the most awful feeling that Sandringham was right. Louisa's book was going to be a huge success and the implications were far greater than anything Mr. Sandringham could appreciate.

He walked Sandringham to the front door, shook his hand, said all the correct things, the whole time thinking of the disaster he'd just managed to create for himself.

Really, he thought as he closed the door again, he had to get over this bad habit he had of helping Louisa.

11

*I*n an agony of anticipation, Louisa forced herself to stay in the shadow of the staircase where she'd been lurking until she heard the door close on Mr. Sandringham's back.

"What happened?" she said, practically jumping on Will. "What did he say? Did he buy my book?"

Will gave her a hard look. "Come with me," he said, pulling her into the study and slamming the door shut. He sat her down in the armchair by the fireplace and glared at her.

"What is it, Will?" she said, her heart sinking lower than she'd ever thought possible. "Did Mr. Sandringham change his mind?"

"Do you think you might once, just *once* in your life, give me some forewarning, even some small inkling, of what you are up to?" he roared. "How can you expect me to be constantly picking up your pieces when I don't even know what they are!"

"But I—I didn't ask you to pick up anything," she stammered, stunned by his behavior. "You came in and offered yourself up without any invitation on my part."

"Yes, I did, because you had made such a tangle of things that someone needed to step in, and I was the only person around to do it." He slammed a fist against his thigh. "God's teeth, Louisa, but you've landed us both in a potentially catastrophic situation."

"I have?" she asked uncertainly, not sure why he was so furious with her.

"You have. You—or rather I, whoever that might be—have. I just sold your book for three hundred guineas."

Louisa gasped in complete shock. "No," she said, trying to draw breath into her body. "No—no. You're . . . you're trying t-to bait me, to make me sorry that you were forced to pretend for me."

"I'm not baiting you in the least. I'm telling you the hard facts. You will be receiving a bank draft for that amount in a few days. Mr. Sandringham thinks your book is going to take the country by storm."

No words came to her. She shook her head and shook it again, unable to absorb his words. Three *hundred* guineas? She's expected fifty, if that. This was impossible—she'd mis-understood him, that was all there was to it. No publisher paid that sort of sum for a novel, or at least not one written by her. Did they? Because if they did, she could pay off all her debts and still have a good amount left over. Her family would be safe. They all finally would be safe. . . .

Too overwhelmed to do anything else, she burst into tears, covering her face with her hands and sobbing uncontrollably.

Will instantly dropped to his knees and drew her shaking body into his arms. "Don't cry, Louisa, please don't cry. I didn't mean to speak so harshly—I was just momentarily beside myself. The news is good, very good."

She couldn't find her voice, so she just nodded against his strong shoulder, pressing her forehead against it as Will's hands stroked her back, her hair, her back again, soothing her, patiently giving her the time to regain her composure.

"I—I can't believe it," she eventually said on a hiccup. "I just can't believe it. I never thought . . . the idea was so far-fetched, an attempt to make a bit of money, but I did enjoy myself, so the effort didn't seem entirely wasted. Now, now to learn that the book sold, and for so much—it's incredible." She looked up at him through blurred eyes. "Oh, *Will!* How did you ever force Sandringham to such a point? Really, the sum is ludicrous."

"Maybe. Maybe not," he said, releasing her and drying her eyes with his ever-present handkerchief. "He came to terms remarkably quickly, which leads me to think he did not arrive unprepared to negotiate. He was surprised to be pushed so hard, I think, but then he didn't know he wasn't dealing with the author."

"What do you mean?" she asked, gulping back another hiccup.

"I had nothing at stake but seeing the best possible outcome for you. This book wasn't my work, so I had nothing emotionally invested, nor did I have a pile of debts to pay." He smiled at her, one finger stroking her cheek. "Something tells me you would have accepted his original bid of fifty pounds on the spot. Am I right?"

"In an instant," she admitted. "Thank goodness you arrived when you did. Mr. Sandringham probably would have made no offer at all if you hadn't come in and assumed the role of Mr. Peter. How did you ever know?"

"A little light eavesdropping. Forgive me, but when I first heard your voices I thought someone might be giving you some trouble about bills, and I thought it prudent to assess the situation to see if you might need some timely intervention." He grinned. "You cannot imagine my surprise when I realized that Sandringham was a publisher trying very hard to buy a book from a man who existed only in his imagination. It wasn't too hard to put the pieces together."

"So you decided to take on the role yourself? *Why*, Will?

Why did you do that, when you could have spared yourself a great deal of time and trouble?"

He loosely clasped her hands in his. "Because I didn't want you to lose an opportunity that I knew had to mean so much to you, and because I knew you needed the money on top of that." He dropped his gaze. "And also because I wanted you to have something that gave you happiness and a sense of accomplishment," he said, his voice very low. "That was reason enough."

Louisa squeezed her eyes shut, a fresh sob catching in her throat. No man had ever shown her such kindness or consideration, not ever, and she didn't know what to do with the deep ache in her heart. Will had rescued her for no other reason than he cared about her happiness. How could that be? Why should he care at all? She'd asked herself that question at least a dozen times now and never come up with a good answer, as hard as she'd tried.

"You did all that for me?" she asked in a small voice.

"I would do that and more to put a smile on your face, Louisa. If I had my way, I'd see you smile most of the day. The rest of the time I'd—ah, well. I'd just see you happy." He reached out one finger and traced the outline of her mouth, curving the corners up one at a time. "There. That's much better," he said, his finger lingering on her lips.

She shuddered at his warm, gentle touch, at the infinitely gentle expression in his dark eyes. She wanted him to draw her back into his arms again, to run his hands over her back and hair, to do all sorts of wonderful, outrageous things to her. She couldn't help but wonder how he tasted, what the feel of his mouth would be like on hers . . .

Her eyes widened in horror at her own thoughts, and she sat bolt upright. The road to ruin had never looked so tempting, but she was determined not to take one more step down it. She had her reputation to think of, and—and Pip, she reminded herself frantically, willing her heartbeat to return to normal.

"What is it?" Will asked, sitting back on his heels and regarding her curiously. "You look as if the sky just fell. Or maybe the ramifications of this deception we've just played with Mr. Sandringham are beginning to sink in."

"You mentioned that before," she said, infinitely relieved that he'd given her something to think about other than her own wanton nature. "What ramifications do you mean?" She primly folded her hands in her lap.

"I mean that because you chose to write a book about pirates—" He paused, rubbing his hand over his face. "Because you chose to write a book to which you felt you could not put your own name and because you also chose not to come clean with Mr. Sandringham about your being the author of that book, I am now you. Or rather, you are now me, or something ridiculous like that. Why didn't you just *tell* him? I'm sure he would have understood."

"No," she said adamantly. "He would not have understood. Most important, my father would not have understood. The novel is . . . it's . . . ." She blushed furiously and covered her face with her hands.

"It's what?" he demanded. "I think I have a right to know at this point." An expression of suspicion entered his eyes. "Just what have you done, Mrs. Merriem?"

"It is *heated*," she blurted out from behind the shield of her palms.

Silence.

Unable to bear the suspense, she finally risked a peek at him from between her fingers.

Will had averted his face, but his shoulders shook with what she strongly suspected was laughter.

"What amuses you so?" she said indignantly, dropping her hands to glare at him. "I didn't say salacious, I said heated."

He looked back at her, grinning broadly. "Heated. Are you referring to the heat of battle or to the heat of the bedroom?"

Louisa bent forward and pushed him hard on the shoulder, knocking him off his heels so that he landed on his rear. "I meant, you cad, that it is amorous. I wrote nothing improper. Or at least not exactly . . ."

Will leaned back and rested his weight on his hands, his eyes dancing with deviltry. "I see. You merely implied the improper, is that it?"

"Jack Kilblaine is a pirate, Will. He has to behave like a pirate, doesn't he?"

"Just what has he pirated, if you don't mind my being so bold as to ask?" He gazed at her with utter fascination.

"Nothing—I mean, he pirates all the usual things, but he's a good man at heart, just someone who has had a hard time in life and does what he must to survive—but he doesn't do anything wrong to ordinary people, just to the Crown, which treated his family unfairly." She rushed on, trying to make Will understand. "You see, his father was wrongly arrested, then tried and put to death, and Jack's mother died in poverty. So as a boy he swore to seek retribution, and now that he is grown he takes to the seas and waylays government cargo."

"Hmm," Will said, scratching the corner of his mouth. "What does he do with all this cargo?"

"Eventually he becomes a rich man and makes a place in

society, using a different name, of course, and he takes revenge on all the people who conspired to bring his father down."

Will wrapped his arms around his knees. "I assume that somewhere along the way he falls in love with a dazzling woman?"

"Yes, but sadly he falls in love with a noblewoman named Elizabeth whose father, Lord Grissham, was one of the conspirators. Only Jack doesn't know that at the time," she said, warming to her tale. "When he finds out that Lord Grissham, the only one left now, was part of the conspiracy, Jack has a terrible crisis of conscience. Does Jack keep the vow he made to his father before his father's execution to expose all his enemies and proceed to destroy Lord Grissham, thereby destroying the family name of the woman he loves, or does he give up his quest and his honor for her sake?"

"What does he decide?" Will asked breathlessly.

"I'd tell you to read the book," she said with a mischievous smile, "but since you're supposed to have written it, you tell me, Mr. Peter."

"He throws honor to the wind and takes her straight to his bed like any right-thinking man."

Louisa poked his knee with her foot. "Is that what you'd do?"

"Certainly," Will said, his face perfectly straight. "None of this honor nonsense for me. So what does Jack do?"

"He runs off and joins the army, avoiding the problem entirely," she said, bursting into laughter. "I borrowed from my own life."

"Very droll," Will said, but he didn't look amused. "I thought he was supposed to be a hero, not a fool."

"Sorry," she said. "I couldn't help myself. Jack does the heroic thing, of course. He goes to Lord Grissham and tells him the truth about himself, and then he challenges Grissham to an honorable duel to the death—only he allows Grissham to bring the challenge."

"Why would he do such a ridiculous thing? I thought this was all about Jack's honor."

"It is," Louisa said impatiently. "Don't you see? If his true love knows that Jack made the challenge and Jack kills her beloved father, then she'd never speak to him again. This way, Lord Grissham challenges Jack for what he claims was an insult—Jack having the nerve to ask for his daughter's hand when he's only a parvenu. That way the daughter can't blame Jack."

"And?" Will asked. "What then? Does Grissham agree to the duel?"

"He does. Grissham also thinks he's the better swordsman, but he doesn't know that Jack was a pirate and one of the most accomplished swordsman of the day."

"So naturally Jack bests him, Grissham is killed, Jack's vow is complete, and he runs off and lives happily ever after with Miss True Love."

"Not at all," Louisa said with supreme satisfaction. "That would never do. Jack has Lord Grissham at his mercy, his sword digging into Grissham's breast ready to drive home, and then at the last moment Jack steps aside and lowers his sword, honor satisfied. But Lord Grissham, being the coward he is, takes advantage of Jack's vulnerability and thrusts his own sword into Jack's heart."

"Why?" Will said, looking mightily disappointed. "Why can't Jack just kill Grissham and marry the daughter?"

"Because Jack is an honorable man and couldn't in the end kill the father that his true love adored. He wouldn't have been able to live with himself. He never expected Grissham to be so dishonorable."

"I call that the height of stupidity," Will said, leaning his chin onto his hands. He considered. "Elizabeth now has to live with the tragedy of her lover's death, knowing her father killed him in a contemptible fashion."

"Yes, and that's the point. It's all about the heroic quest, Will. Jack makes the decision to let Lord Grissham live, but his supreme sacrifice is his life."

"So Jack dies in Elizabeth's arms, I presume?"

"Yes. He does." She couldn't help the sadness she felt at relating that part. She'd cried buckets over it when she'd written it. "He dies, but Elizabeth goes on. In the end, it is she who finally discovers the truth and condemns her father for his black deeds. She leaves his house forever and retires to a convent for the rest of her days to pray for Jack's immortal soul."

"Really," Will said, by this time having comfortably stretched out full length on the carpet as if he'd always been there, his cheek resting on his hand. "I don't see why Elizabeth shouldn't pick herself up by her corset laces and find some other man to love."

"Because she loved Jack, you idiot!" Louisa shifted off the chair and dropped onto her knees next to Will as if she could drum the obvious into his head. "She feels responsible for his dying at her father's hand. She'll never love anyone else—how could she?"

"Because if your Elizabeth was clever enough to choose someone as fine as Jack, she surely wouldn't be silly enough to think there wasn't another man out there just as fine—once she'd recovered from her grief, of course."

"That defeats the purpose," Louisa said, wishing he'd see the point. "Jack dies for her and in the interest of true love, she must also make the ultimate sacrifice."

"Which is to wither away in a convent? I think Elizabeth would be far better served by building a new life for herself and using all her gifts of beauty—and I assume of intelligence—to carry on. Yes, she's been disappointed by her father's undoubted perfidy, and yes, she is understandably wary of men, but she's strong and she's resourceful." He looked up at her, one eyebrow raised in question. "If she wasn't all of those things, Jack wouldn't have fallen in love with her in the first place. Would he want to see her condemn herself to seclusion or would he want to see her carry on with her life and make it as full and bright as possible?"

"You think I should change the end of the story?" Louisa asked, chewing at her bottom lip. Will had a point. Elizabeth was strong and resourceful, after all . . .

"I think you should consider it. You might be able to make a whole new book out of Elizabeth's ongoing adventures."

"Yes! Why not?" she said, excitement stirring at the thought. A simple change at the end of the manuscript would send Elizabeth off into an entirely different direction, could launch her into a story of her own.

"Thank you, Will," she said, meaning the words with all her heart. "You've given me such help and encouragement, and such amazing inspiration. I think I could start straightaway."

He chuckled. "I think you might give yourself a month or two. We have other things to deal with, which is actually why I came to see you. I've been considering this problem of selling your crops to the miller."

"Yes?" she said eagerly. She'd been burning with anger ever since Will had pointed out that she was being cheated. "Do you have a solution?"

"A fairly simple one, actually. I'd like you to go to the market at Dawlish. The distance is not great, which is an advantage, but it's far enough that you won't be known there. I'll go around and talk to some of the merchants, see who I think will be fair."

He sat up and pulled one leg against his chest. "Then I want you to go to that merchant and bargain—I'll tell you what to say beforehand, but I feel it's important that you do this on your own—you need to establish yourself as a businesswoman. You'll be doing this for yourself soon enough."

Louisa paled, not at the thought of bargaining with merchants, but because Will had just made her realize he would be leaving, and probably by late autumn when the last of the crops were in.

For some reason the idea made her feel as if she'd just been kicked in the stomach. Will had become—had become a *fixture*, she supposed. They had all grown to depend on him, to enjoy his company. What would life be like without him? She shivered, not wanting to entertain the thought, for it left her feeling cold and empty.

"Louisa? Tell me if you don't think you can do this, for I have no intention of forcing you to something you find distasteful or daunting. This is your decision, not mine."

"N-no," she stammered. "I can do it. I want to do it. I have to learn sometime how to manage."

"Then why do you look so unhappy at the suggestion? I promise you, the proceedings are not so difficult and you're a clever woman. Good heavens, if you can write and sell a novel to an enthusiastic publisher, you can surely do some shrewd negotiating with a country merchant."

"I suppose I find the idea of venturing out a bit alarming after all this time. I haven't been farther than Maidencombe in five years."

"That absolutely needs to be changed," Will said, appalled. "Let me suggest this: Why do we not make an expedition of it, maybe take Pip with us and go to the seaside for a day? We can stay overnight at an inn, let her play by the water, have a little adventure of her own? She no more deserves to be shut up here at Broadhurst than you do."

Louisa's heart quickened at the prospect. To have uninterrupted time with Will, give Pip some pleasure, to actually have some fun herself—what a wonderful idea. But the money—could she afford even the luxury of a night's stay at an inn?

Will spoke as if he'd read her mind. "You've just sold a book, Louisa. You should do something to celebrate. If you're concerned about any impropriety, we shall have Pip with us. I am nothing more than your man-of-all-work, taking you to the market. I can stay at different lodgings, if you like, although I'd rather be in the same place so that I can keep an eye on you both."

"No—it wasn't that. I was wondering where to find the money to pay for this adventure."

Will laughed. "My dear girl, you will simply go to the bank and tell the manager that you are expecting a draft for three hundred guineas. He can advance you the funds. For that matter, I can advance you the funds."

"You—you can?" she said, staring at him. "But you haven't any more than I have. I haven't even been able to pay you."

"Nonsense. I have a tidy sum that I've saved up over time and nothing else to spend it on. You can repay me when you receive your bank draft from Sandringham."

"But you couldn't even afford to buy clothes," she protested. "You had to borrow my father's!"

"That was Pip's notion, not mine. By the time Pip had

finished with her grandfather, I had no choice but to accept his offer. He looked so happy to be able to help out that I couldn't refuse."

Her father. Louisa's excitement vanished as if it had been a wonderful balloon deflated by the prick of reality. "I can't," she said, looking away. "I cannot leave my father when he is in a bad way."

"Absolute nonsense. Leaving your father for a day or two might be just what he needs. He's a grown man, Louisa, and for all you know leaving him in charge could give him the incentive to get on with life."

"No. He needs me." For the first time, her father felt like a burden, and she was ashamed of herself.

Will took her hand, squeezing her fingers. "Don't you see that he feels impotent, unimportant? The idea I had about the intellectual discussions at dinner was an attempt to bring him out of himself, but I realize now that it is no solution in the long run. He has to become reinvolved in life, not just go through the paces."

"But I *told* you—"

"I know what you told me," he said, cutting her off. "You think he might crumple under the weight of any responsibility. I think he might crumple if you don't allow him some. We'd be making a small beginning, but it is a beginning."

Louisa hesitated, torn by indecision. "His migraine . . ."

"I have to wonder if your father doesn't use headaches as an excuse to hide himself away when he is tormented by feelings of uselessness. Give him a reason to live, Louisa, and he will. Better yet, give him a reason for happiness."

She bristled. "How can you say that? His headaches are very real. He suffers terribly."

"He might, but then again, did he ever have these migraines before Val's advice drove him close to bankruptcy?"

"No," she admitted reluctantly. "His health was sound in every way, but I've told you that before."

Will ran his thumb over her palm. "Yes, you have, but I'm not sure you've listened carefully enough to my response. Men are proud, Louisa, especially men like your father. He needs a purpose. Why not give him one—unless you are unwilling to relinquish complete control of the reins?" He regarded her intently, his eyes delivering an unmistakable challenge.

Every instinct made her want to rail at him, to deny the charge, but something in her heard the ring of truth and she couldn't refute it. Will was right—she'd been so busy taking responsibility for Val's mistakes, so busy protecting her father, that she had never given him a chance to help.

"Maybe, just maybe," she said, determined to be honest, "I have been a little heavy-handed in that regard. I felt that if I let anyone else make decisions, I'd be faced with yet another disaster. The only person I've been able to trust for all these years is myself."

"Exactly," Will said, bringing her hand to his mouth and pressing his lips against it.

Louisa nodded, her eyes stinging with tears. "You have made your point," she murmured, refusing to cry yet again. Until Will Cutter had come along, she'd cried hardly a day, holding all of her tears inside, turning her pain to anger and action. Since then, she'd watered his jacket more times than she cared to remember.

"It wasn't a point I particularly wanted to make as it has caused you pain, but it is a point I believe can create a difference for you both. You are part of a family, Louisa—no war has ever been won by an army of one."

"No . . . I see that now." She turned her cheek against his hand, hating herself for having been so proud that she'd shut her father out of the struggle of daily life. For the very first time she saw that her determination to be strong had robbed her beloved father of his own strength and will to act. "What can I do, Will?" she whispered. "What can I do?"

"You can find a balance. You can appeal to your father for his help, admit that you're not able to carry all the weight by yourself. That alone might do you both a great deal of good, don't you think?"

Louisa looked up at him, saw nothing but honest intention in his eyes. "Yes," she said, her voice strangled by emotion. "Yes. I've been a hardheaded fool, Will, but I truly didn't know how else to move forward."

He slipped his hand around her head and pressed it against his chest. "How could you? How do any of us know how to proceed under circumstances that seem impossible? We can only pray for wisdom and then hope against hope that wisdom is given to us—and that we have the courage not only to hear it but to act on it."

She breathed in a deep, shaky breath. "I wonder if I've ever acted wisely in my entire life. I begin to doubt it."

"My sweet Rosebud, you have acted with enormous courage," he said, dropping a kiss on the top of her head. "Wisdom only comes with experience. You can't have it all, not all at once at any rate. Life deals out its lessons, but it deals out its rewards as well—the trick is in keeping your arms open for those rewards."

Louisa leaned her face closer into his shoulder, breathing in the deep, musky, masculine scent that clung to his jacket. If she responded to her baser instincts, that reward would be Will, for she couldn't imagine anything better just now than being wrapped in his arms and letting him kiss her into oblivion.

He slid his fingers down her neck, which nearly caused her to faint.

"Tomorrow," he said, his breath soft and warm against her cheek. "Why don't we go tomorrow? The hay is in. That's the other thing I wanted to tell you. Given that, we could leave without a worry."

"Without a worry," she sighed. "What a wonderful thought."

"Then hold on to it. I'll see to the details."

Releasing her abruptly, he stood. "I'd better get back. The horses need to be fed. Why don't you have a word with your father? I'm sure he'll be pleased that you are taking some time for yourself and Pip." He smiled down at her. "Oh, and congratulations once again. Have a look at that contract. We can go over it later if you like, but if all is acceptable, you should post it first thing in the morning."

Louisa nodded absently. The last thing on her mind right now was the contract. Her head was too full of everything Will had said, all the truths he'd driven home. But most of all, her heart was filled with terror at the way Will made her feel and how powerless she was to resist those feelings.

As the door softly closed behind him, Louisa put her head in her hands and cursed the weakness of her nature.

Then she gazed up at the ceiling and exhaled. Oh, well, she decided. If she was determined to walk down the road to ruin, she might as well enjoy herself in the process.

12

"Look, Mama, the sea—oh, it's so lovely. I haven't seen it in so long that I can hardly remember at all, and it's so silly since we live only a few miles from the coast."

Will looked over at Pip and smiled in satisfaction. She'd been in a state of barely contained excitement since last night, and now her dear little freckled face reflected such happiness that he wanted to scoop her up in his arms and spin her in circles. He restrained himself, doubting that Louisa would appreciate such a gesture. She guarded Pip as closely as a mother lion did her cub.

"It is lovely, isn't it," Louisa said to her daughter, her own face solemn as she gazed over the water. "I'd forgotten . . . the crashing of the waves, the intensity of the salty smell. I spent hours as a child combing the beach, looking for seashells, watching the gulls swoop for fish or march along the beach as if they owned it."

"There, there are some now," Pip said, skipping down the beach toward the gulls that had landed with loud squawks to peck at something.

"Don't go too close to the water," Louisa called to her daughter, who ignored her, stopping only to pull off her shoes and stockings before sticking her toes in the edge of the surf.

Will put out a hand to stay Louisa as she started after Pip. "Leave her," he said quietly. "She needs this time, a little freedom to explore. We're here to watch, and getting her feet wet won't harm Pip. Come, sit with me and enjoy this beautiful day."

He took her hand and led her to a little hillock. Louisa reluctantly followed, but her eyes never left her daughter.

Will laid down a blanket he'd brought for the purpose and started to spread out a picnic that Cook had packed. He'd never seen Louisa so jumpy. She looked as if she were going to her own hanging, pale and distracted, not interested in conversation.

Thank God Pip was there for his own distraction or he'd have torn his hair out. He'd planned this trip as a diversion for Louisa, not as yet another torment in her life, but she behaved as if it was that and more.

He racked his brains for the cause. He knew her father wasn't the reason—Charles Fleming had given his blessing to the excursion and miraculously risen from his bed the next morning, ready to assume his temporary duties. Louisa had at least told Will that much, albeit briefly and without embellishment. They'd posted the book contract on their way, and she hadn't seemed concerned, but then again she hadn't been particularly enthusiastic.

She silently stared out to sea with an impassive expression, but he *knew* she was deeply troubled. Odd, he thought, how clearly defined her emotions had become to him, as if he was now highly sensitive to every mood, every shift of thought and feeling. He'd never before experienced another person in such a distinct fashion; he wasn't even sure when he'd started perceiving her in this way, as if an invisible rope linked his heart to hers.

When he'd first appeared at her door, he'd known her only from her letters. Now he knew her as a different person entirely, knew her strengths as well as her weaknesses, knew her as the flesh-and-blood woman she was, complete with fears and heartaches, hopes and dreams and unfulfilled longings.

Those longings hadn't escaped his notice—anything but. He'd practically bolted out of the study yesterday when he'd finally realized that her attraction to him was equally as strong as his for her, the pulse in her neck beating hard and fast under the stroke of his thumb, the flush in her cheeks an unmistakable indication of desire.

He glanced over at her, wanting to kiss that same pulse, to take her in his arms, to let her know everything he felt and show her the same with his touch.

Oh, *God,* how he wanted to touch her.

He quickly looked away, forcing his breathing back under control. Touching Louisa was not an option he had, now or ever, and he'd do well to remember it.

"I've never seen Pip so happy," he commented, trying to distract himself from his desire for Louisa, a fairly useless endeavor. His loins were definitely not responding to his brain and he shifted, drawing a knee up so that Louisa wouldn't see the distinct bulge that had appeared in the front of his trousers.

"She does look happy," Louisa replied, her voice wistful. "I was just thinking how unfair her life has been. I should have been able to give her so much more."

"And now you will. Just think, Louisa, you have a promising career in front of you. You might never want for money again."

Louisa looked over at him with a rueful smile. "I wouldn't go that far. First the book has to sell. For all you know not a single person will buy it and that will be the end of that."

"Mr. Sandringham didn't strike me as a fool," he said. "The book will sell, and you will write another, and that will sell even better, and before you know it, you won't be able to write fast enough to keep up with the demand."

Louisa shook her head. "How do you think I am to run a

farm and do all this writing?" she asked. "The last book took me two years of stolen moments. It's a miracle I managed to get it done at all."

"Ah, but you'll be able to hire a proper manager now and devote yourself full time to your work."

Dropping her gaze, Louisa shrugged. "I would have to find the right person, someone I could trust. That is not so easy."

Will gave her a long, hard look. Maybe this was what had been troubling her. He had told her he was leaving after the harvest, and she now worried over how she was going to cope without him. He, on the other hand, wondered how he was going to cope without her—the very idea of life without Louisa in it seemed impossible, at best an empty and meaningless existence.

How odd life's vagaries were, he thought. He'd appeared at her front door with the simple idea of giving her some letters, and the next thing he knew, he'd taken on an entirely different mission. And in attempting to accomplish that mission, he'd lost his heart to this woman.

He couldn't deny that salient fact any longer. He was well and truly in love with Louisa, and as hard as he'd tried to push her out of his heart, she was there to stay.

How he was going to live with his feelings was another question entirely, and one for which he had no answer.

He glanced up as Pip came running breathlessly toward them, her hands full of seashells that she tumbled onto the blanket. "Look, Mama, Mr. Cutter," she said, picking up a shell with a delicate pink sheen. "Isn't it beautiful? I'm going to paste all of these onto a piece of paper and make a picture to hang on my wall so that I never forget this perfect, perfect day."

"What a wonderful idea," Louisa said, smiling at her daughter, her eyes filled with warmth and love.

Will's heart turned over. He wished she'd look at him like that instead of constantly regarding him with wariness, as if he were a snake about to strike.

"Here, Mr. Cutter," Pip said, handing him the pink shell. "You keep this one. It's the prettiest I've found so far, and this way you will have something to remember this day by, too, forever and forever."

He took it from her little fingers, a lump forming in his throat at all that would never be. If he could have chosen a ready-made family, this would be it. He ached to watch Pip grow into womanhood, to help shape her and guide her on that path, and ached just as much to have children of his own, children with Louisa. What a fine life that would be . . .

"Thank you, Pip," he said, his voice tight. "You are very thoughtful."

"Oh, no, Mr. Cutter. It is you who is thoughtful, taking us to the seaside like this." She skipped back to the beach to gather more shells.

"You've done a fine job of raising Pip," he said. "Tell me, how did you decide on the name of Portia? Did you take it from Shakespeare's *Merchant of Venice*?"

"Yes . . . she was such a beautiful infant," Louisa said, gazing at Pip dancing about among the rocks. "And I'd always admired the character of Portia, who was independent, brave, and smart. I thought if I named my daughter after her that she might somehow bear the same traits. I was being foolish, I suppose, but I couldn't help myself."

"Oh, but she does have those traits, Louisa, she does— all of those and more. You named her well. She will grow into a beauty, but then she takes after her mother."

Louisa colored, the flush starting at her chest and running all the way up into her cheeks. "I do not think you should say such things," she replied, looking startled.

"Why ever not?" he said, loving her all the more for her embarrassment. "I only speak the truth. You have also passed on your intelligence and resourcefulness to her."

Louisa tilted her head. "You are flattering me shamelessly, Mr. Cutter. What do you hope to gain, I wonder?"

"A smile would be nice. You've been unusually quiet all day. Does something trouble you, or do you merely find my continuous presence tedious?"

"No!" She colored again, a sure sign that she felt acutely uncomfortable, which Will found fascinating. "That is to say that your presence does not affect me one way or the other."

"Ah." Will raised an eyebrow. "How reassuring. It's so nice to know that I am of absolutely no significance to you."

"I—I didn't mean that," she stammered, looking as if she wanted to sink straight through the grass into the sand beneath. "I only meant that—that . . ." She trailed off uncertainly.

"I know what you meant. You've said it a dozen times in a dozen ways. I am your employee and as such have no place in your life other than the obvious."

She nodded. "Yes, that is exactly it."

Will thought she looked more miserable than he'd ever seen her. He also knew as sure as he breathed that she was lying. A small whisper of hope stirred in him that she felt anything but indifferent, but he was afraid to trust his instincts. Physical attraction was one thing, and that it pulled at them both was undeniable. But that she might actually care—that was something else entirely. He could hardly believe he might be that fortunate, but even if that was the case, what could he do about it? His hands were tied, and not only would it be cruel to lead her on, but he'd be mad to torture himself any further.

Distance. He needed to create a little distance.

"Well, that's fine then," he said cheerfully. "We both understand each other perfectly, in which case we can now proceed to enjoy ourselves, which was the purpose of this exercise." He stood and reached his hand down to her. "Why don't we follow Pip's example and go exploring? I've been meaning to ask—who did come up with that perfect diminutive for her?"

Louisa, let him pull her to her feet. "My father. Pip came early and when he first saw her he said that she looked no bigger than a pip in an orange. The name somehow stuck."

Will grinned, imagining Pip as a tiny babe. "It suits her. She probably came early out of sheer impatience."

"She did," Louisa said, laughing. "From the moment I first felt her move she didn't stop leaping about, as if she couldn't wait to meet the world. She hasn't stopped leaping since." Louisa pushed blowing wisps of hair out of her face, her eyes alight as if memories of a happier time had wiped away all her troubles. "She might not have been conceived under the most joyful of circumstances, but she has been the biggest gift in my life and I am grateful that God gave her to me. I can only feel sad that the other side of her family doesn't know how much they miss in ignoring her."

Louisa suddenly paled. "I didn't mean to say that. It just slipped out."

Shocked, Will turned her toward him, his hands firmly grasping her shoulders. "Are you telling me that Val's parents have nothing to do with Pip?" He knew both parents were living. Why hadn't he thought before to ask about their role in Pip's life? "Surely they could have helped you in your struggles, especially since you've given them a granddaughter?"

"Lord Merriem is not interested in me or his granddaughter. He firmly believes that I drove Val away with my waspish ways and therefore am ultimately responsible for his son's death. Val would never have gone into the army if it hadn't been for me." She bit her lip, her eyes clouding over. "As far as Lord and Lady Merriem are concerned, Pip and I no longer exist—they never approved of the marriage to begin with."

"But Pip is their flesh and blood. Surely they would want to have contact with her, see to her future, especially knowing your difficult circumstances?" Will couldn't believe what he was hearing.

"Val's family cares nothing about anything but title and pedigree. I have none to speak of, and therefore it follows that Pip is entirely insignificant, even though Val was her father. If he'd married a woman of their choosing, they would have behaved differently after Val was killed, but they chose to close ranks." She shrugged. "I am only sorry for them. As far as I'm concerned, Pip is better off outside their sphere of influence. As I told you, Will, I have no liking for the aristocracy, even the minor fringes—I want nothing to do with any of them ever again, not under any circumstances."

Will ran a hand over his eyes. Oh, *God,* he didn't have a chance in hell, not when she felt like that, not that it was any surprise. "What about Lady Samantha Davenport?" he asked, grasping at straws. "You seemed happy enough to entertain her."

"She's different," Louisa said. "She has a heart."

So do I, Will thought. *Oh, Louisa, so do I, and it's practically killing me.* "You think she's the only person in the *ton* who possesses one?" he asked, already knowing her answer.

"She's the only one who doesn't care what anyone thinks." Louisa threw her arms out to the side. "Don't you understand? No, how could you? You think people make their own way and their own luck."

"I never said that, not exactly. I said I believed people were guided by God and His angels if they only had the good sense to listen. Or something like that. I wasn't referring to the aristocracy specifically, but they're not exempt from God's plan, Louisa, just because a majority think they dine nightly at His table by virtue of birth."

"Oh, you're back to the angels now, are you? Honestly, Will, sometimes I wonder if you're not hopelessly romantic."

"Have you ever seen an angel?" Will asked very quietly.

"Of course not. Have you?" she replied tartly.

"Yes. Yes, I have. Believe me, Louisa, if you ever have the experience, you won't question it."

She looked at him as if he'd truly lost his mind. "Angels. You've seen them. Very well, Will. Describe one—wait. Let me guess." She scrunched up her face. "Great white wings, flowing hair, halo, white robe."

"No," he said with a slight smile, remembering every last detail of their appearances, although he wished they'd been under better circumstances. Then again, angels only appeared when one was in the direst need, according to his experience.

"Then what? Tell me." Louisa's face burned with curiosity mingled with heavy skepticism.

"The first time I saw an angel was when my mother died. I was by her bedside and when she took her last breath her eyes opened so wide that I looked behind me to see what had so amazed her. Someone stood there, surrounded by the most glorious light I'd ever seen. I couldn't make out who or what it was at first, only that it had human shape and form—no wings, if that's what you're thinking—but there was nothing human about it, only something glorious and peaceful and it held out both hands to my mother." He pressed his fist against his mouth, the moment so clear in his mind that it might have happened only a minute ago, the emotions just as raw. "She stood and took those hands, and then she disappeared into the light. When I looked back at the bed, her body was still there, but the life had gone out of it."

"Will, I'm sorry," Louisa said on a whisper.

He cleared his throat. So much for keeping his distance, he thought wryly. It just wasn't possible, not with Louisa. "Sorry? Why? I cannot think of a finer testament to life eternal. I am happy to have witnessed my mother's spirit taking its leave, as grief-stricken as I was."

"And you really think that was an angel?" Louisa asked, her brow furrowed. "You said there were other times. What were they?"

He paused, not wanting to go back to that memory, that place and time. The pain had never left, and he'd never spoken of it since. Even now, so many years later, the ache remained in the depths of his heart.

"You needn't tell me if you don't want," Louisa said, resting a hand on his arm.

Will covered her hand with his own. "I don't want to talk about the circumstances, and bless you for not pressing me. I will tell you this much. Someone I loved died under the most appalling circumstances. I was too late to do anything about it. I was frantic, beside myself, powerless to save this person." He caught his breath, pain stabbing at him as if it were yesterday and he was the young man he'd been then, helpless and horrified. "I could only watch as the end came."

"Will, how awful for you." Louisa's voice came soft and close, pulling him back to the present.

"It was. But then I saw two heavenly beings appear out of nowhere and lift this—this person up and away. I can't describe to you how I felt. As with my mother, the body was left behind, but somehow I knew that the soul had been safely taken away to a better place. The light surrounding those heavenly beings was exactly the same as it was with her, leaving the sense of peace, of everything being as it was ordained." He covered his eyes with his hands. "How can I describe something indescribable without sounding like a madman? I must sound that way indeed, but I can only tell you that's how it was in both cases."

"Was that the last time?" Louisa asked, not sounding as if she thought him mad at all.

He slid his hands down his face, wondering how to tell her the truth without giving anything else away. Valentine. The last time had been Val, when he'd held him in his arms and watched the angels descend. How the hell could he tell Louisa the truth about that? But he wouldn't lie to her either, not now, not when they'd come so far.

"No, it wasn't the last time," he finally said, deciding to abridge the incident. "The last time was when another friend was dying. He knew it was the end, but he didn't believe in God or His angels or much of anything else." Will shook his head. "Quite honestly, I begin to wonder how much he valued his own life. I can only pray that at the very end he understood the truth."

How ironic, he thought, that he was talking to Louisa about her own husband and he couldn't even tell her that much.

"I'm sorry that you've suffered the deaths of so many people close to you, but I think God must have given you a special blessing if you can see His messengers."

"You don't doubt me, then?"

"I have no reason to doubt you," she said. "Indeed, you give me hope. So often we do not trust in the existence of that which we cannot see."

"Faith is a complicated thing," Will replied. "I think, though, that it's just as important to have faith in people as it is to have faith in God. Not everyone is as ignoble as you sometimes think."

"I didn't say that I thought everyone ignoble," she retorted. "I reserve that opinion for the aristocracy—with the exception of Lady Samantha, as I said."

Seeing that he wasn't getting anywhere, Will dropped the subject. "Why don't we join Pip," he said. "I could do with some simple shell-gathering."

Will did his best during dinner that night to amuse Louisa and Pip with stories, making them both laugh. He wanted more than anything to give them a little happiness, make memories that they could wrap around themselves in darker times, although he wished he could be sure there would be no more of those.

He'd secured the inn's best private parlor, and he and Louisa shared a bottle of wine while Pip drank lemonade, a special treat that he insisted on. He watched with fascination as the claret brought a sparkle to Louisa's eyes and a smile to her lovely mouth. How he loved hearing Louisa laugh. Leaning back in his chair, he listened as she regaled them with a story about an orphaned lamb who'd been fostered by a cow.

"No, no," she was saying, "I promise you it's true. The lamb never did understand that she wasn't a cow and used to line up for milking every morning. I finally gave up trying to convince her that she belonged with the other sheep, and until the end of her days she lived in the dairy with her foster mother."

Pip nodded her head. "It's true, Mr. Cutter. Her name

was Matilda. I think that every time a bleat came out of her mouth instead of a moo she was terribly shocked and embarrassed."

Will burst into laughter. "I can well imagine," he said. "When I was a boy I rescued a fox cub who had also been orphaned. He was taken in by my dog, who had just had puppies, and ever after he trotted about at my heels. The farmers were most disapproving, convinced that he'd get into the henhouse, but Harry—that was his name—never showed any interest in anything but trying to get onto my bed at night."

"Good heavens," Louisa said. "Do you mean he slept in your bedroom?"

"Naturally. He had a little basket by the fire—pride of place, you know. My father was convinced that there was something terribly wrong with me; in his eyes I showed a distinct lack of manliness, since foxes were meant to be destroyed, not pampered." Will grinned. "I had an ongoing menagerie of wild animals and birds that drove him absolutely mad. I think the last straw was the owl. Now she was a character . . ."

They talked and laughed until Pip's eyes grew heavy and he scooped her up into his arms and carried her upstairs to the room she and Louisa were sharing.

"She'll sleep like a log tonight," Louisa said, as he lay her down on the bed. "Thank you, Will, for such a fine evening— for such a fine day. I'm glad you convinced me to get away from Broadhurst."

"So am I," he said quietly. "Sleep well, Louisa. I'll be right next door if you need anything."

"I cannot think of a thing," she said, suddenly blushing as if he'd suggested something improper. "Thank you anyway. I'll see you in the morning bright and early."

Will cast one last glance at Pip, who'd curled up in a contented ball. "Tomorrow," he said and quickly left, wishing with everything in him that it was he who was sharing the bed with Louisa.

He stripped and washed, then climbed into his own cold, very empty bed and stared up at the timbered ceiling.

For someone who'd just had a perfect day with the woman and child he loved, he felt remarkably despondent. He had absolutely no right to self-pity—he'd gotten himself into this mess after all, but the knowledge didn't help to ease the ache in his heart or in his loins, for that matter.

He couldn't go on like this, that much was clear, but what could he do? He'd written the script and played his part beautifully, which left him with absolutely nothing.

For that matter, it left Louisa and Pip with nothing either. He still burned with anger over Val's parents' deserting their grandchild. Pip needed a father, that much was clear, and Louisa could do with a husband. Here he was, ready and willing to take on both roles—indeed, he wanted nothing more, but he'd break Louisa's heart if he told her the truth about himself at this late date.

You might be surprised by how much a woman can forgive if her heart is involved . . . do not be a fool and let something wonderful slip between your fingers just because of your pride.

Samantha Davenport's words came drifting back to him unbidden and Will sat up abruptly.

If her heart is involved . . . as of today he was as sure as he could be that was the case. Hadn't Louisa's behavior given him every indication that she did have feelings for him? Her sweet confusion, her blushes, her willingness to confide in him as well as the struggle she put up to keep a wall between them, all gave him reason to hope.

Maybe he really *was* a fool.

Why the devil shouldn't he pursue her, give them both a chance at happiness? He had time to bring her around if he carefully laid the groundwork. Surely he could make her understand the reasons behind his charade?

The task would be a difficult one, given how she felt about aristocrats and army officers, not to mention men in general, but he loved her and that had to count for something. She might not love him, not yet, not truly, but even that was not an impossibility. He'd made a beginning.

He'd have to tread very softly for fear of scaring her away. Louisa was like a frightened mare, ready to bolt at the slightest sign of danger. He needed to make her feel comfortable and unthreatened.

Will lay back down, his hands behind his head as he considered his course of action. Val was finished in both their lives and the time had come to put the painful memories behind and move forward.

There was absolutely nothing standing in the way of his marrying Louisa save for Louisa herself.

He'd set himself an enormous challenge, but he'd never met a challenge he hadn't overcome. Will closed his eyes and finally drifted off to sleep.

The ground shook as if with thunder, the mud sucking around Maestro's feet, threatening to pull them both down as the streaming rain and smoke obscured his vision. Screams of men and horses nearly drowned out the sound of the cannon fire, but that was impossible. Nothing could shut out that dreadful, unceasing roar.

Will felt himself falling and falling, Maestro falling with him with an unearthly shriek until he thought the falling would never stop.

Blood. There was so much blood. He looked down at his hands, running red as if the flesh of his hands had opened and created a river, his life pouring out of them.

He lay on his back, Maestro above him, but instead of a horse's head, he saw a death mask, the eyes wide open and staring, the mouth pulled back in a skeletal grin, mocking him.

You see, you could not save me any more than you could save yourself, the voice said, and he realized it was Val's voice, taunting, it was Val's face that stared down at him, the flesh gone, the empty eyes accusing.

He was lost, so lost, would never find his way home. But Will didn't know if it was Val who was lost or himself. The two had blurred into one until they were one flesh and that flesh was rotting, buried under the mud that blocked his nose and mouth, left him powerless to move, mud that buried him alive . . .

Will woke with a cry, his body shaking, his flesh cold and covered in sweat.

He forced himself back to reality, struggled to catch his breath and convince himself that he was safe.

As soon as he had a semblance of a grip on himself he threw on his trousers and shirt and headed straight for the door.

Sometimes walking was the only cure, and he suspected he'd be walking for a good long time.

13

$\mathcal{L}$ouisa woke abruptly from a sound sleep, a noise of some kind penetrating her consciousness, although the sound was muted. She instantly reached for Pip, but Pip's breathing was deep and soft and her face untroubled.

She heard it again, another low moan, then a sharp cry, abruptly cut off. The cry had come from Will's room, and her hands flew to her throat as panic gripped her heart, sending icy spikes throughout her body.

Will—dear God . . . someone had broken into his room and attacked him. Leaping out of bed, she ran to the connecting door and pressed her ear against it, but she heard nothing, certainly not the sound of a scuffle. Lifting her hand to knock, she thought better of it and dropped her hand again. She leaned her forehead against the door and willed her pounding heart to steady.

Obviously he was safe, although she couldn't think what would make him cry out in the night. Unless he'd had a nightmare. . . . For some reason the idea struck her as strange—Will was so strong, so sure of himself. But why not? He wasn't exempt from the dark corners of the soul just because he looked after everyone else.

She frowned as she heard the scrape of feet on the wood floor and then his door opening and closing. Where could he possibly be going at this late hour?

Very quietly she opened her own door, only to see him disappear down the staircase just opposite. Quickly she ran to her window and looked out over the courtyard. Sure enough, Will emerged, wearing only a shirt and trousers.

Pausing, he raised his head to the sky, his face caught in a shaft of moonlight. He drew in long gulps of air as if starved for it.

Her heart caught at the stark, naked expression on his face. She could only describe it as haunted, as if he were suffering deeply from some terrible emotion that threatened to consume him.

He lowered his head and walked off in the direction of the beach, his gait not the easy pace she had grown accustomed to, but stiff and fast as if he tried to outpace whatever dark thoughts troubled him.

Every instinct Louisa possessed told her that something was very wrong, and without thinking twice, she threw her cloak on over her nightdress and impatiently tied a ribbon around her loose hair.

Whatever Will's trouble, he did not need to be alone with it. He had offered comfort to her so many times that he deserved the same.

Stopping only to stroke Pip's head and make sure that she still slept deeply, Louisa headed straight out the door and carefully locked it behind her.

She found a maid folding linens down the hallway and slipped a coin into her hand. "Will you listen for my daughter? She won't wake, but I must go out for a bit and I don't like to leave her without someone to watch over her."

"Yes, mum, surely, mum," the maid said with a curtsy.

"Thank you. The door is locked, but here is the key. Stay close. I do not know how long I will be, but there's another sixpence for you if you are here by the door when I return."

The maid, her eyes wide with her good fortune, dropped another curtsy. "Indeed I will be, mum. Don't you fear, your little girl's safe with me, you can count on that."

Louisa nodded, then shot down the stairs and out the

door, ignoring the stares of the people in the smoky tap-room behind.

She walked quickly, thinking hard as she went, grateful for the bright light of the moon that guided her way over the rough path to the beach.

Odd, she reflected, that she'd spent the entire day running away from Will, terrified by the strength of her feelings, and now she was running straight toward him without any hesitation. She was either mad or a victim of her own impetuosity, but she didn't care. Will was in need, and she was going to try to help him whether he liked it or not.

He wouldn't like it.

She knew that as surely as she knew that the sun rose and set every day. As enigmatic as Will was, he was a proud man, and that was just too bad. High time he was on the receiving end of a sympathetic ear. She owed him that much and more.

Tonight seemed a good time to repay him, as much as the idea terrified her.

Louisa quickened her pace and finally reached the rise of dune that led onto the beach. She spotted Will instantly.

He stood at the edge of the water, his strong, beautifully made body incredibly still as he looked out over the waves that rolled in toward shore in a gentle wash and sucked back out again. Their never-ending movement had always made her think of life and death, and had given her comfort from the time she was a small child. She wasn't surprised that Will had sought out the sea.

Moonlight caught in his thick hair, silver threads running over the dark, creating the image of a halo. This wasn't the first time that she'd pictured him as a dark angel—a small irony, since this very day he'd told her that he saw divine beings.

The real irony lay in her not doubting his word for one moment. She should have known from the beginning that Will was capable of seeing things that were invisible to most people. He'd been the only one to see into her heart, after all, with such clarity and compassion. Little wonder that she'd been running so fast and furiously in the opposite directions since he'd first arrived at Broadhurst.

The time had come to stop fighting him, to set aside her fear and give him whatever he needed—anything he needed—as best she could. The only question left was how to relieve the burden he carried that had woken him in the night with the cry of a wounded animal and forced him to the sea.

Standing quietly, she took in a few deep breaths, respecting his solitude before she broke it, then said a quick prayer for guidance.

That done, she finally got up the courage to approach him. "Will," she said softly, coming up behind him and laying a hand on his shoulder.

He spun around, his expression one of shock and dismay.

"It's a lovely evening, isn't it?" she said, for lack of anything better.

He ignored that polite opening. "What—what the bloody hell are you doing here?" he demanded, his voice hoarse.

"I felt the need for some exercise after such a large meal," she said, the lie sticking in her throat.

"You can't—you can't come out on your own like this. It isn't safe."

"I'm not alone," she calmly pointed out. "I'm with you."

"Which you shouldn't be." He dragged his hands

through his hair. "What about Pip? She *is* alone and that isn't safe either. You must know that." He looked ready to murder her.

"I left her in the care of a maid, although Pip is sleeping soundly. If experience rings true, nothing but cathedral bells going off in her ear will wake her."

Will glared at her. "I saw you both safe to bed and now you choose to take a little stroll on the beach at this time of night? Are you out of your mind?"

"I think I'm in my right mind for the first time in a long while," she retorted. "I knew I'd be safe, Will. I saw you leave the inn and I followed you."

"Why? Why in the name of God would you do such a thing? Did you think *I'd* be set upon by brigands?"

"No," she said, taking a deep breath and plunging in, "but when I heard you cry out from the next room I thought that maybe you had been. When I realized that you were not in mortal danger, I then thought that maybe you were in another sort of trouble, so I came after you."

"And what sort of trouble would that be?" he asked, his gaze falling to the ground as his hand went to the back of his neck.

"The sort that would drive you out of bed and send you fleeing to the beach," she said, waiting for the next blast of anger.

To her surprise it didn't come.

"I'm sorry you heard that," he said, meeting her gaze squarely, although he looked extremely uncomfortable. "Sometimes I don't sleep well. I came out here to try to clear my mind."

"From what, Will? I've learned from you that talking about one's problems can help. I'm happy to listen."

He smiled grimly. "Thank you for the thought, but this is

something that is best kept to oneself. Trust me, Louisa, there's nothing you can do."

"I don't believe that," she said stubbornly, refusing to let him off the hook. "I tried the same tactic with you when you first arrived and you wouldn't leave me alone until you'd elicited all my secrets. Why shouldn't I take a page from your own book?"

"Because it will do you no good at all. You'd be wasting your time."

"That's not fair play," she said. "Why should I tell you everything and you tell me nothing?"

He reached his hand out and cupped her chin, his eyes so dark that even with the light of the moon she couldn't read them. "I could tell you a great deal, but I don't think you really would wish to hear any of it."

"Do not assume, Will Cutter," she said, lifting her chin within the embrace of his hand, her entire body trembling. "I could very well surprise you."

He laughed at that. "I doubt that there's *anything* that you could do that would surprise me."

"Really?" she said, taking another step closer. She reached her hands up and took his face between them. "Not even this?"

Startled by her own audacity, but helpless to stop herself, she reached her face up to his and softly pressed her mouth against his, tasting the salty warmth of his lips.

Will pulled away, his eyes reflecting his astonishment. "Louisa?" he whispered, grasping her hands.

"I was just trying to help," she said on a gulp, thoroughly shaken not only by what she'd done, but by the effect his touch had on her. She'd never imagined just how heavenly his mouth would be, so soft and sweet and—and utterly male.

"Might I suggest that you help from about five feet away?" he said with a tight smile. "Or perhaps this is your way of forcing me to talk."

"N-no—I thought only to give you some comfort," she stammered.

"You call that comfort? Rosebud, you have some very strange ideas about what will comfort me."

"I'm sorry," she said, utterly mortified. She should have known better than to act on impulse. Now look at what she'd done—she'd embarrassed them both. "I didn't mean to offend you," she said in a small voice.

"*Offend* me? Anything but. You should know, though, that you've set light to a powder keg. Do that again and I'll not answer for the consequences."

She risked a glance up at him. "Do you mean you didn't mind?"

He groaned. "No, I didn't mind. That was the nicest thing you could have done. I'm only saying that you can't kiss a man like that and not expect him to respond."

"You want to respond?" she asked with a shiver that ran from head to toe.

"I'm not dead," he replied, his smile broadening as he ran his hands up her arms. "My mind might be a little unsettled at the moment, but the rest of me is in perfect working order." Will's smile faded as he gripped her shoulders and searched her face in the moonlight. "Louisa. You have hit on a way that's certain to make me forget my problems, but if I do what I'm inclined to do, you might never forgive me. Maybe it would be best if you let me walk you back to the inn."

The inn was the last place she wanted to be. Will's arms were so much more inviting. "No," she said. "That won't help anything at all."

Will looked down at her, his eyes suddenly blazing. "Is this really what you want? God knows I do, but be warned, Louisa: If I kiss you now, that won't be an end to it."

In answer she moved straight into his arms, lifting her face to his, every instinct she possessed telling her this was what they both needed, that this was an end and a beginning, and whatever lay on the other side she would deal with later. She'd never wanted anything more in her life than she wanted Will in that moment.

Will stroked a hand over her hair, his gaze intense and unwavering. "I hope you're sure," he said softly, cupping her head. "I meant what I said. This won't be the end."

"I don't want it to be. Please, Will?" She reached her arms around his neck and twined her fingers through his soft hair, loving him all the more for his restraint.

With a low groan, Will lowered his head, his mouth opening over hers as he possessed it fully, his tongue seeking her own in a sensuous dance that overcame her senses, leaving her helpless to do anything but cling to him as if she were drowning.

She distantly heard a moan and dimly realized it was hers. Fire consumed her body and obliterated everything but the feel of Will's hands and mouth on her, the hard contours of his body pressed against hers by the force of his arm tightening around her waist, the hand knotting in her hair.

She couldn't taste enough of him, couldn't even absorb the violence of the physical urge that swept over her and threatened to engulf her. Nothing else mattered, nothing else would ever matter again, and for once she didn't care about consequences. She'd gone up in flames, and for all she knew, only ashes would be left by morning, if she lasted that long.

She bit his lip with a gasp. "I can't—I can't breathe."

He didn't say a word, only scooped her up in his arms and carried her over to the dune, where he eased her down, spreading her cloak out around her to form a blanket.

Lowering himself over her, he gazed down at her, his arms trembling with restraint, his eyes aflame with his own desire as they locked with hers.

"Are you absolutely certain, Rosebud?" he whispered hoarsely. "God knows I want you, but there's no turning back, not from here. Can you deal with the consequences?"

"Please don't say anything else," she said, her arms wrapping around his back and pulling him down to her. "Let this be enough."

He didn't deny her, taking her mouth in an impassioned frenzy, drinking deep as he tasted her sensitive inner recesses, and she drank of him just as thirstily, desire running riot in her blood.

Will's hands stroked and smoothed over her face, tracing the line of her jaw, then slipped lower, cupping the sides of her breasts. She moaned as his palms slid to cover her swelling flesh, exquisitely sensitive, his thumbs caressing her nipples, which instantly formed hardened peaks as if they had only been waiting for his touch. "Lovely," he murmured. "Ah, Louisa—how I've wanted you."

Another gasp escaped her throat as he bent his head and lightly bit a stiffened nipple through the thin material of her shift. His breath came hot on her flesh, his lips soft and sensitive as he pulled her breast into his mouth, his tongue flicking lightly across the surface.

She writhed under him helplessly, feeling the sand give beneath her, cradling her body as Will cradled her. Clouds passed over the moon, obscuring the stars, and a chill wind blew in from the sea, but Louisa barely noticed, their bodies generating more heat than a scorching summer day.

She was lost in sensation as her hands restlessly moved over his back, the strong, defined musculature shifting under her fingers. Never—never had she felt anything as powerful and compelling as Will's touch on her body, or the feel of his flesh under her eager hands. She couldn't get enough of him, couldn't feel enough, couldn't drink in enough of his scent, so warm and musky.

Shifting impatiently, Will pulled up the cambric of her nightdress over her hips and breasts and lifted her to toss it to one side, leaving her naked to his gaze. She felt no shame as his eyes raked hungrily over her body, drinking in every detail.

"You are so very beautiful," he whispered, kissing her belly as he undid the buttons of his shirt and tossed that aside as well. "God must have been a fine frame of mind the day he created you."

Louisa couldn't catch her breath to speak. Will had renewed his assault, his palms smoothing over her hips and reaching behind to her buttocks, stroking and lifting, while his mouth roamed over her breasts again, suckling her nipples hard until the breath truly did leave her body and she fought for air.

He raised his head and looked down at her, his eyes full of tenderness yet at the same time filled with banked fire, his breath coming in hard gasps. "Louisa . . . ah, Louisa, we must both be mad."

"I've—I've never been more sane," she said, breathing just as hard, her fingers kneading his back, his flesh burning under her touch. "You don't have to protect me from myself."

Will shut his eyes for a moment, then rolled to one side, releasing the front of his trousers. Louisa shivered with anticipation, but the sight that greeted her was enough to make her eyes widen. As with everything else about Will, his erect member was in perfect proportion to the rest of his body, but she hadn't expected anything quite so—so *large*.

She didn't know whether she ought to be terrified or excited. Her only other experience had been with Val, and she'd found him perfectly adequate when he did get around to the act. Will's size was something else entirely. Her body involuntarily tensed.

"Rosebud?" He hesitated, then pressed his brow against hers. "You look as if the devil just came riding in on horseback. Should I button myself back up?"

If Louisa could have flushed any deeper than she already had, she would have turned a deep magenta. "No," she murmured. "It's just—it's just that it's been so many years, I don't know if I remember how to do this."

Will didn't bother to respond to that piece of idiocy. Instead he captured her mouth with his own and kissed her deeply and very thoroughly, making her forget that she'd ever been worried. He stroked and caressed the upper part of her body, then set light to the rest of her, his hand running up the inside of her thigh and tangling in the curls at the juncture, his fingers gently seeking the secret folds between.

"Oh, so soft, so silky, so utterly perfect," he whispered, stroking back and forth until she writhed beneath him in desperate need, heat pooling in the depths of her belly, a mindless need driving her to a place she'd never been before, a place where there was nothing more than their bodies twining together, so absolutely right.

"Now," she cried, her back arching and her thighs wantonly parting to receive him. "Take me now!"

Will smoothly lifted himself and slowly penetrated her with a low moan, partially entering her, allowing her tight flesh to stretch and open to him. He hesitated, kissing her deeply, then slowly eased deeper, his shaft filling her completely, his eyes locking with hers, urging her to respond.

Slowly he began to move, each thrust wringing a strangled gasp from her throat. Time ceased to exist as Will drove her beyond herself to a place where they were one flesh, one mind, their bodies moving in perfect unison, flesh slick with sweat, their breath one breath, their hearts pounding in unison. His mouth took hers in a frenzied dance, his tongue stabbing in and out of her mouth in imitation of his body pounding into hers, searing her, claiming her.

He quickened his pace, his hands lifting her hips up to his, plunging hard, over and over until she thought she might die with pleasure. Trembling violently, she kneaded his hard buttocks, her legs wrapping around his lean waist as she reached toward the unbearable tension that had gathered deep inside her.

Her head tossed back and forth on the sand, sharp cries of need breaking from her throat as the tension gathered like a wave swelling to an impossible crest.

A second later, though it seemed an eternity, that crest peaked and crashed, shattering every last sense she possessed. Convulsions seized her as she contracted around his shaft, rhythmically milking his steely flesh with her own.

She vaguely registered a desperate cry and somewhere in her addled mind realized it was her own.

"Louisa," Will choked. "Louisa! Oh, God . . ."

He pulled back and then plunged hard and deep, straight toward her heart. The searing heat of his seed pouring into her sent her straight back over the crest of another wave, Will's cries mingling with hers, both carried away by the breeze that blew in from the sea.

He exhaled hard against her cheek as he collapsed in her

arms, rolling slightly to his side to take his weight off her chest.

"My God," he gasped. "My God . . . that was extraordinary. I think I just died in the nicest possible way."

Louisa smiled against the corner of his mouth, feeling utterly sated and blissfully complete. "I think you're very much alive," she whispered. "Very, very much alive. Oh, Will, I've never felt anything like that."

He gathered her into his arms, his heart still pounding in a slow, heavy beat against her breasts. "I haven't either," he whispered, dropping a kiss on her temple.

They lay quietly in each other's arms, the only sound the constant roll of the waves echoing the steadying beats of their hearts.

"No regrets?" Will finally murmured against her cheek.

Turning her head, Louisa kissed his mouth softly. "How could you ask such a thing? Regretting what just passed between us would be like regretting the magic of a thunderstorm or the rainbow that follows."

Will laughed. "How eloquent you are." He lifted himself up onto his elbow, one hand lightly caressing her still swollen breast. "You *are* the rainbow, Louisa. Thank you for your generosity—you truly did make me forget my troubles."

"That wasn't generosity, that was an act of pure selfishness. Your troubles may have driven me out here tonight, but I cannot deny that you've had me in a state of longing for some time." She grimaced. "I suppose that sounds terribly promiscuous?"

"That sounds very human," he replied, gazing down at her. "I've been in a state of longing myself from the first moment I set eyes on you."

"You have?" she said, immensely gratified. "Truly?"

"Truly." He stroked the hair off her face. "If you wondered why I was tongue-tied when you opened the door that first afternoon, it was because I was so stunned by your beauty that I couldn't put two thoughts together."

Louisa colored, but answered his honesty with her own. "I—I have to admit to the same. I didn't expect anyone to respond to my notice who was quite so . . . so compelling."

"Compelling. Hmm. Is that what made you so prickly?"

"Yes. I didn't know you personally, of course, but I did know you were dangerous."

Will grinned. "Dangerous? Surely you didn't think I was going to behave in an untoward fashion? I was beneath your touch, after all, nothing more than a man-of-all-work."

She looked away. "I hope you do not think me such a snob as all that."

"Given what I've learned of your low opinion of the aristocracy," he said, tracing his finger over the line of her jaw, "I have to consider you positively proletarian in your attitude. No, Louisa. You are no snob—anything but. But I do think you should tell me where we go from here."

Her body stiffened. She hadn't thought further than tonight. "I don't know," she said truthfully. "I don't see why we cannot go on as before."

"Suppose I've gotten you with child?" Will asked, practical as ever.

"Oh—oh, no. That's not possible," Louisa replied hastily.

"Why ever not? As a matter of fact, this might be the appropriate moment for me to ask you to marry me, since I've just thoroughly ravished you."

Louisa stared at him, appalled. She sat bolt upright. "*Marry* you? But Will, I don't ever wish to marry again, surely you must know that."

"I can understand your reasons, but it won't do to give birth to a child out of wedlock, Louisa, however determined you are to retain your independence."

"I won't," she insisted. "I—that is, it's the wrong time of the month for conception."

"There's never a wrong time of the month for conception," Will replied, looking entirely unperturbed. "I won't have a child of mine born outside the sanctity of marriage."

Louisa narrowed her eyes. "Is this why you complied so easily? You thought to ensnare me in marriage?"

"No," Will said, lightly grasping one of her wrists. "I would never ensnare you in anything. However, when I mentioned consequences, a possible child was one of them. Let me remind you that I did not seduce you, my sweet—you played that role all by yourself. Not that I'm ungrateful."

"How can you be so callous?" she demanded, fury rising quickly.

"I see nothing callous about wanting to ensure your reputation and welfare, but I have no control over you. I am still your employee and you are still my employer no matter how intimate we've just been."

She drew in a shaky breath. "Then let us leave it at that."

He graced her with a lazy smile. "As you wish. You are a widow—there's no reason why you shouldn't take your pleasure where you will. Widows do it all the time."

"I suppose you know all about it, do you?" Louisa glared at him, reaching for her discarded shift and hastily pulling it on.

"I know nothing at all about widows, save for you. I do, however, know a little about the conventions of society. An unmarried woman must never let herself be touched. A married or widowed woman may choose to do as she pleases so long as she does not flaunt those choices in society's face. Is that not correct?"

"Yes it is," Louisa retorted, drawing herself up. "I am in a position to do as I please, when I please."

Will burst into laughter. "You do mount a high horse, Rosebud." He grasped her around the waist and lifted her, turning her into his arms. "I'd far rather you mount me, though, for I have no objection. I only thought I'd offer you respectability, being the small-minded man I am, a victim of my sad breeding." He reached out both hands and clasped her by the waist, pulling her down to him. "Shall we put your liberal thinking to the test? I can think of all sorts of ways to try it out, and since you're so intent on pleasing yourself, I am more than happy to oblige you in the endeavor."

Louisa couldn't resist him. After all, he'd just relinquished all claim on her. "If you insist," she said, laughing against his mouth.

"Ah, but I do," Will said, lightly biting her lower lip. "I do, Louisa, I do . . ."

14

Will sang along merrily with Louisa and Pip, who sat beside him on the box as he drove the carriage to Dawlish, his heart as bright as the sky.

Pip had her own notion of what she liked in music, not the least of which was "The Farmer in the Dell." They'd had a number of rounds of that. Will couldn't help thinking the song was particularly appropriate to their venture.

He glanced over at Louisa, whose cheeks held roses.

She looked happy, content, as if she didn't have a worry in the world, and for that he offered up a prayer of thanks.

Although no words of love had passed between them on the beach, their bodies had spoken volumes, and he was as certain as he could be that Louisa's heart was his—even though she would resist the notion for as long as she possibly could. She wouldn't be his Louisa if she didn't, he thought with a wry grin.

She'd taken him entirely by surprise last night. He'd never met a woman before who didn't flirt and simper and pretend astonishment at desire—either his or hers. That Louisa had come to him, made her needs known, set him reeling. She was honest and open and he could only love her more for her directness—and her trust, although he wasn't entirely deserving of it.

The passion with which she'd responded only heightened his love for her. His only task now was to bring her to the point of admitting her feelings and agreeing to marry him.

"Will, why are you looking at me in such a fashion? Anyone would think I'd grown two heads," Louisa said, turning toward him as if she felt his gaze on her, but her warm smile belied her tart words. "Shouldn't you be watching the road?"

"Probably, but I am too distracted," he replied. "How often do I have two lovely ladies sitting on the box with me?"

Pip laughed. "You think us lovely ladies, Mr. Cutter? I should have a fan to flap in my face. Mama says there is an entire language of the fan."

"No doubt you will one day use it to bring society to its knees," Will retorted, looking back at the road, although he trusted Maestro to take them in a straight line. "I should be thankful that I will be too old to suffer the consequences of your flirtations. My heart could not stand the strain."

Pip doubled over. "You are very silly. I shall settle for John Henry, and he would never stand for such foolish behavior. I'll be a farmer's wife and there's no place for fans in that sort of life." She pointed at the sky. "Look! More seagulls, Mama! Aren't they wonderful? I would so like to be able to fly."

"Fly in your heart, my darling. That's more important than wishing to sprout wings. Your heart will take you on journeys that wings never could."

Will tore his gaze from the road and regarded Louisa with interest. Maybe she was coming along faster than he'd imagined. "How right you are," he said mildly. "For the moment, though, I think we should concentrate on what you're going to say to the merchants. Let me give you a small tutorial in how you're going to go about this—it's important that you appear knowledgeable. To begin with, properly cured hay, cut at the correct stage so that it retains its leaves, has twenty percent moisture or less . . ."

The Dawlish market teemed with people, the crowd moving in a tight pack among the stalls. Louisa kept a tight grip on Pip's hand as the child's head turned and craned up to take in every sight and sound, her little body quivering with excitement.

Will turned to Louisa. "I'm going to go off and start my inquiries," he said, pressing threepence into Pip's hand. He leaned over and whispered in her ear. "Buy yourself some ribbons or whatever else you like, as long as your mama doesn't object."

"Thank you, Mr. Cutter," she whispered back, giving him a quick hug.

Will smiled at her, then straightened. "I'll meet you both back here by the well in an hour's time. Keep your ears open, Louisa. You can learn much from the conversation around you."

"I'll feel like a spy," she said, but her cheeks were flushed and her eyes bright with excitement. "An hour then. Come along, Pip. Let us see what adventures Dawlish holds."

Will watched them disappear into the crowd, then made his way over to the town hall, where the grain brokers did their business.

As promised, in an hour he returned to the well, where Pip was skipping around with a handful of bright ribbons and a twist of licorice.

"Look, Mr. Cutter—I bought all of this with your three pennies, and I still have a penny left over!"

"Then you are a very clever girl," Will said. "I can see the businesswoman in you already. Now it's your mama's turn. Louisa—there is a certain Mr. Peabody who pays by the quarter. His price is the highest of anyone if the crop is good, and he strikes me as an honest man." Will nodded toward one of the nearby benches. "Do you see him? He is the man with the round face, eating a bun. Now here's what you must say . . ."

Will rattled off his instructions to the last detail. "Make sure you tell him that you have had it on best authority that he is the man to deal with and that you have barley, wheat, and alfalfa to sell if the price is right," he emphasized. "He'll try to bargain, but tell him your price is fixed and that you'll go elsewhere if he cannot meet your demand. Tell him that if he is willing to work with you, he will have three sacks of free sheep's wool thrown in."

Louisa nodded and straightened her back. "Wish me luck," she said, nervously running the tip of her tongue over her bottom lip.

Will's knees nearly buckled at the gesture as he remembered just what she'd been doing with that tongue only a few hours before. "All the luck in the world," he somehow managed to reply, although his voice sounded hoarse. "You can do this."

Reaching out, Louisa squeezed his hand. "You make me believe I can do anything."

Will, touched to his core, didn't dare risk a reply, knowing he was in imminent danger of saying something that would give his true feelings away. Instead, he took her by the shoulders and turned her around, gently giving her a push in Mr. Peabody's direction. "Go, before you miss the opportunity. We'll be waiting right here."

Louisa released a breath and walked off, her slim hips swaying ever so slightly. That would do no harm, he thought with amusement. Mr. Peabody would most likely take one look at Louisa and offer her the world just for the pleasure of it. God knew Will would and planned on it.

"Come, Pip," he said, taking her hand and leading her over to the park that bordered the market, where he had a clear view of Louisa and Peabody. They settled on the grass and Will produced two Cornish pasties from his pocket, handing Pip one of them.

"Oh, thank you, Mr. Cutter," she said with delight, looking at the pasty as if it were manna from heaven. "I've never eaten so much, even though I was just getting hungry again." She took a big bite into the still steaming crust. "First we had an enormous dinner last night, and then a huge breakfast this morning—and now this! I think I might swell up into a huge balloon and burst."

"What an alarming vision," Will replied dryly. "But never fear, sweeting. You need some meat on your bones if you're going to grow into a fine lady and attract all those gentlemen I was mentioning earlier." He pulled out his handkerchief and wiped crumbs off her face.

"Mr. Cutter?" she asked through another mouthful. "Are you going to marry my mother?"

Will nearly dropped his pasty. "Why would you ask that?" he said, trying to hide his astonishment.

"Because you like her and she likes you—I can tell. I'd like you to marry her so that she wouldn't be so lonely. Most of all, though, I'd like you to be my papa. I haven't had one in the longest time, and I don't even remember the one I did have." She gazed up at the sky. "I know Papa's in heaven now, so I don't think he'd mind. He was killed in the war. Did you know?"

"I did," Will replied, not at all sure how to deal with the subject. Pip took care of that.

"He was killed at Waterloo. Mama says he was a great hero, but I don't know that she really believes that. *I* think she's angry with him for something. Her face always goes all tight when Papa's name comes up."

She polished off her pasty and Will wiped her fingers

and mouth, carefully thinking about what to say. He didn't in any way want to disillusion Pip, but she was too bright for lies. "I would think that your mother isn't angry with your father so much as the situation he left her in," he said cautiously. "It's very hard to be a widow left on one's own to raise a family."

"Oh, I know that," Pip said. "Mama has already said as much, but I think she isn't telling me everything. She wants to protect me."

Will, surprised by the depth of Pip's perception, didn't say anything for a moment. When he did, he measured his words carefully. "Pip, your mother's been trying her very best. I know that she loves you with all her heart and wants nothing more than your happiness. If she tries to protect you, that is because she's your mother, and that is the most important role in her life."

"I want her to be happy too, Mr. Cutter. Can't you just marry her and make us a proper family? That way we'd all be happy."

Although he wholeheartedly agreed with Pip, Will felt completely stymied. He couldn't tell her of his plans, nor could he in good conscience tell her a lie. "I care for your mother," he said. "I won't tell you otherwise. The problem is that your mother is an independent woman and has a mind of her own. She has no wish to marry again."

Pip pulled a face. "That's just foolish. She needs a husband as much as I need a father. I cannot tell her that, but maybe you can."

"I don't think so," Will said, reaching his arm around Pip's shoulder and pulling her close. "As much as I would love to be your father, that is your mother's decision to make. You cannot force people to your will, sweeting, as much as you might wish to. Marriage is a sacred covenant that needs to be based on trust and love. I hope that when the time comes for you to decide whom you will marry, you will remember that."

Pip shrugged. "As I said, I will marry John Henry. I see no reason to worry. He bullies me sometimes, but on the whole he listens to what I have to say when I make a point of it."

"I am sure that you make a point of it often." Will glanced over toward Louisa, who was engaged in conversation with Peabody. Much to Will's satisfaction, the man already looked smitten. "Tell me," he said, looking back at Pip, "does John Henry ever annoy you?"

"Oh, often," Pip replied with a giggle. "He is the most annoying creature when he chooses to be. He likes to march around as if he owns all the land in sight and talks about when he will be king of his domain. I think he's very silly, but I like playing with him too much to object—he's just a boy, after all, and will soon enough learn that his domain extends only to a few fields."

"And you, Pip?" Will asked, fascinated by her perspicacity, not to mention her fatalistic attitude. "How do you really see yourself in the years to come?"

"I shall guide John Henry," she said, as if that was already a given. "I shall teach him how to expand his holdings, just the way Mama and Grandpapa have taught me."

"And how is that?" Will asked, intrigued.

"One never sells at a loss, one uses one's savings to buy and improve the land. Principal property is never to be touched, only the income, and as little of that as possible. *That* is how I will instruct John Henry."

Will nodded, thinking Pip already on her way, although John Henry would not be in the picture by the time she reached adulthood. God help the man she did choose, for Pip clearly was going to rule her own roost. He sensed Louisa's hand in that.

"Very good," he said. "All of those principles are sound. There is something else I urge you to consider, however. Do not marry without deep and abiding love and respect, for without that all else suffers. Know your own mind and heart in that regard, Pip. You have much to offer and much to lose if you choose wrongly."

Pip crinkled her brow. "Do you mean that John Henry might not be the right person for me?"

"I will say only this, not having had the pleasure of meeting the boy. If John Henry cannot work out these basic principles for himself, then he is not worthy of you. You have the advantage of a fine education, Pip, so use it in all aspects of your life."

He sighed and looked down at his hands. "You are young for me to be telling you these things, but I believe you are also able to understand what I am saying."

Pip regarded him gravely. "I think you are telling me that you have had many misfortunes in your life, Mr. Cutter. I am sorry for that, for they must have caused you pain." She wrapped her fingers around his. "I still wish for you to be my papa, if you can possibly manage it."

Will closed his eyes against the stab of pain that penetrated his heart like an arrow hitting its mark. *If he could manage it.* He wished he could reassure this dear child that he would manage it, that her mother would understand his deception, that all would be well. Unfortunately he could make no promises, not to Pip, not when the outcome was still so uncertain.

Pip had penetrated his elation and made him realize

the cold, hard facts. Everything was in Louisa's hands now, and Louisa might never understand, not when the truth came out.

"Sweetheart, let well enough alone," he said, taking her hands, still slightly greasy, between his. "Whatever transpires, know that I love you dearly. That will never change. Let's go to the pump next to the well and rinse you off, shall we?"

Pip jumped up. "I love you, too, Mr. Cutter," she said, then dashed off to the well, rubbing sudden tears from her eyes as she went.

Will stood, intending to go after her and offer her some comfort when he heard a great shout that made him spin around.

"Major! Major! What are you doing here?"

His heart sank as he saw Sergeant Tibbins running toward him, Tibbins's face wreathed in a huge smile, his hand waving wildly, hailing him with enthusiasm. Will had never felt more like a coward, desperately wanting to flee, hide himself in behind the nearest stall before Tibbins exposed him entirely.

He was too late. Tibbins reached him before he had a chance to act on the impulse.

"Major Fitzpatrick! My lord!" Tibbins threw out his arms and grasped Will hard by the shoulders, his fingers digging into Will's flesh. "I can scarce believe my good luck—I've wondered about you so often! But what are you doing here? I thought you were safe with your family in Norfolk." His face fell. "I hope you were not rebuffed after all you have done for the Crown."

"I never ventured beyond Devon," Will said, wondering how the hell he was going to get Tibbins away before either Pip or Louisa spotted them. He'd have dragged Tibbins off to a tavern if he didn't have Pip to worry about.

"Never ventured beyond Devon?" Tibbins asked with a puzzled frown. "Why is that? You were very clear about going home to Alconleigh."

"I was," Will replied, "but I first went to visit Captain Merriem's widow near Maidencombe, hoping to give her some comfort. What I discovered there caused me to stay."

"What was that, Major?" Tibbins took off his cap and scratched his head.

"I haven't time to explain—listen, Tibbins, Mrs. Merriem and her daughter know me as Will Cutter. Just plain Will Cutter, do you understand?"

Tibbins slowly shook his head. "I can't say that I do, Major."

"Major? Were you in the army, Mr. Cutter?"

Will spun around to see Pip standing behind him, her eyes wide and shining with excitement. His heart dropped farther than he'd ever thought possible. Oh, he was *really* in a pickle now. Before he had a chance to reply, Tibbins jumped in.

"He was indeed, little miss, and a finer soldier you could not imagine, brave and true. All his men were devoted to him."

Will wanted to strangle Tibbins, even though he knew the man's heart was in the right place. "I was just an ordinary soldier, Pip, doing my job."

"Oh, but how wonderful! Did you fight at Waterloo, Mr. Cutter?"

"He did, he did, little miss. He and his magnificent horse Maestro led the charge and put paid to a whole pack of Frenchies."

"Enough, Tibbins. You embarrass me. Allow me to present Miss Portia Merriem. Pip, this is Sergeant Tibbins."

Pip executed a quick bob that marginally passed as a

curtsy. "I am honored to meet you, Sergeant Tibbins. My father was a soldier too. He died at Waterloo. Did you know him? His name was Captain Valentine Merriem."

"Many died at Waterloo," Will said, before Tibbins had a chance to put his foot in it even further. "Your leave must be drawing to a close, Sergeant. When do you return?" He glared at Tibbins, willing him to say nothing more incriminating than he already had.

"Er, next Monday . . ." Tibbins replied uncertainly, looking back and forth between Will and Pip. "I've enjoyed my time with the family—they live only three miles hence— but I am anxious to get back to the regiment and the life."

"Understandably. Well, it's been a pleasure running into you, Tibbins, but we must be on our way."

"As you say, my l—I mean, as you say, sir." Tibbins put his cap back on his head. "Good day to you both."

He quickly walked off, but he paused once, looking over his shoulder with a puzzled face, before he disappeared into the crowd.

Will watched him go, then breathed a sigh of relief. He'd hated having to treat Tibbins in such a dismissive fashion, but he'd really had no choice. Turning to take Pip's hand, he met only thin air.

Pip had vanished, and after a brief moment of panic as he wondered how he'd managed to lose her, he finally spotted her running toward Louisa, talking a mile a minute, her hands gesturing wildly.

If he'd been dismayed earlier, that was nothing to the horror he felt now as Louisa's eyes met his through the crowd, her face as cold and white as marble. Pip had clearly imparted all the pertinent facts, and Louisa was not pleased. Not that he'd expected anything else.

He thought frantically, trying to put together some reasonable explanation of why he'd deceived her about such an important matter. He needn't have bothered.

Louisa marched up to him and stopped a good six feet away. "Mr. Peabody has agreed to the terms," she said coldly. "We can return to Broadhurst, and not a moment too soon. We won't be stopping over as planned."

"As you wish," Will said, internally cringing against the disdain in her eyes. "May I have a moment to speak privately with you first?"

"That will not be necessary, Mr. Cutter. My business is complete and I want only to see to my father."

Will spent the entire journey back alone on the box, cursing himself for having lied to her in the first place. Louisa had every right to her anger, he told himself. He'd betrayed her, an unforgivable sin in her eyes and one she would not easily forgive.

When he finally pulled Maestro up outside the farmhouse, Louisa refused his hand, exiting the carriage with Pip firmly in tow. She didn't even bother to spare him a glance, leaving him to bring the cases inside.

Pip shot him an apologetic look over her shoulder as her mother pulled her into the house, slamming the door behind her.

Will blew out a long breath. Red hair and temper definitely went together, he thought, wondering how long the ice would take to thaw. Walking up to Maestro's head, he stroked his neck.

"I've really done it now, my friend. The lesson is never to misrepresent yourself. Perhaps you should tell your friend Theodora all about the war before she gives you a swift kick on the legs."

Maestro tossed his head with a snort. Will would have laughed, but he didn't have the heart. He felt as if the world had come to a halt and he with it. Life without Louisa's laughter, her boundless energy, her affection, was no life at all. But he wasn't about to let this setback stop him or drive him away with his tail between his legs. He'd persevere, give her time and the room to realize that he'd never meant her any harm, that he'd only been protecting both of them.

Setting the cases inside the front door, Will climbed back onto the box and guided Maestro toward the stables. He knew he had another sleepless night in store.

15

$\mathcal{L}$ouisa stood at the edge of the meadow, the waxing moon staring pale in the night sky, desperately trying to put her confused thoughts into order, with little success. Her hands clenched into fists by her sides, her emotions in turmoil. As much as she wanted to find a reasonable explanation for Will's deception, the bare fact was that he'd lied to her. There was no way around that cold, hard truth, the only truth she had left about him.

He'd lied to her from the beginning, made her believe that he was her friend, that there were no secrets between them. He'd even made love to her last night, had taken the gift of her body and her trust and turned it into a mockery.

Even Val's desertion hadn't hurt her like this, but then she had long since ceased loving him. Will had deserted her without ever having left her side.

He'd been a major in the *army*? All this time he'd led her to believe he had been moving around the countryside, working on farms, and she, gullible fool that she was, had believed him—had no reason to doubt him. If Pip hadn't come running to her and spilled his secret, she might never have known.

It wasn't as if Louisa hadn't given Will ample opportunity to tell her the truth about himself—he'd had every chance, but still he'd chosen to lie to her. Not once, not twice, but over and over again.

Why? Why would he do such a thing?

She must have been born with a fatal flaw that attracted her to rogues, their charm obscuring their darker nature. At least this time she'd learned the truth in a matter of hours rather than years. Her luck must be improving, she thought grimly, although she felt no better.

"If I could toss you out directly on your ear, Will Cutter, I would," she muttered between gritted teeth, "but I need you to see the harvest through. Then I shall take supreme satisfaction in running you straight out of town. In the meantime I shall simply ignore you as best I can and you can just suffer the consequences."

She would forget all about Will and focus on her new book, that's what she'd do. She'd give Elizabeth an entirely new life, one in which she had wonderful adventures and flicked men about like flies.

She thrust her chin forward in determination. "I shall become a renowned author and a wealthy woman, and I shall never need anyone like you again."

But her brave, angry words offered no solace. Louisa sank onto her knees, the soil soaking up the tears that dripped between her fingers, the wind carrying away the sound of her sobs.

A week later, Will led Maestro into his stall and gave him an extra helping of oats. They'd just come back from the Hart and Hound, where Will had hoped to find a letter from Samantha Davenport, but had returned home empty-handed. At least he'd had a nice dinner for his trouble, and he supposed it was really too soon to expect her to have turned up anything on David Cumberland.

He'd hoped to have more success with Louisa, but she still stubbornly refused to give him the time of day.

He shook his head with a smile. She really was the most

hardheaded woman he'd ever come across. The more he thought about it, the more he concluded that his transgression really wasn't so great. He just wished Louisa would see it that way, but he knew better than to push her.

Wearily he checked on Theodora and Achilles, then blew out all but one of the lanterns, which he took to light his way up the stairs to his room. All he wanted was a good night's sleep—well, that and Louisa's forgiveness, but that obviously wasn't going to be forthcoming for some time yet.

He opened the door and nearly dropped the lantern.

Betsy Robbins sat in his bed, the covers pulled up around her bare shoulders, her yellow hair tumbling loose.

"Mrs. Robbins," Will said, blinking in total shock. "What on earth are you doing here?"

"I thought you might want a little company," she said, smiling in invitation as she let the covers slip a little lower, exposing the tops of her ample breasts.

Will passed a hand over his face. "Mrs. Robbins . . ." he murmured, wondering how in hell to deal with the situation. "I—forgive me, but I do not recall inviting you to my room."

"No, but sometimes a man needs a little push in the right direction," she replied, but the saucy smile slowly left her face.

"You were mistaken. I need no push in any direction, nor am I in need of company," Will said, anger replacing his shock. "If you please, remove yourself from my bed and put your clothes back on. I will go back downstairs and wait for you to leave. I think it would be best if both of us forgot this ever happened."

"But—but, Mr. Cutter," she said, her eyes filled with confusion, "I don't understand. Surely you have your needs like any man . . ."

Will ground his teeth together. He had needs indeed, but only one woman could meet them and that woman was most assuredly not Betsy Robbins.

"My needs are no concern of yours," he said, glaring at her. "Now please, do as I ask." He turned abruptly and marched straight back down the stairs, wondering what awful thing he'd done that God felt the need to make his life a living hell.

He sank onto a pile of hay well out of sight of the stairs and put his head in his hands.

A few minutes later he heard the sound of Betsy Robbins's feet on the stairs and then the door opening and shutting.

Moving to the window, he looked out. Betsy was still buttoning the front of her dress and the expression on her face, caught in a shaft of moonlight, was one of thorough indignation. She turned to the right and headed off toward her cottage.

Will, suddenly in need of some fresh air, went outside and leaned against the stable wall, watching Betsy sashay across the field.

The absurdity of the situation struck him and he chuckled softly. He was having absolutely no luck with women, that was certain. Louisa wouldn't look at him and Betsy Robbins wanted to look a little too much.

He shook his head, then shook it again, deciding the only thing he could do was go to bed and pray for a few hours of oblivion.

Standing in the shadows of the trees that bordered the path to the stables, Louisa pressed her hand hard against her mouth, feeling sick, as if she'd been kicked in the stomach.

Will and Betsy Robbins? She couldn't believe it, but

she couldn't deny what she'd just seen, as much as she wanted to.

Betsy had emerged from the stable door, buttoning her dress, and Will had come out only moments later and watched her leave, a broad smile on his face. She could only draw one conclusion, and it wasn't one she wanted to consider.

HOW *could* he? How could he sleep with that woman only a week after he'd been with her? He was—he was a blackhearted cad!

She'd thrown her pride to the wind and come down to make peace with Will, having decided that maybe she'd overreacted to his deception. She'd actually been stupid enough to miss him, to regret that she hadn't given him a chance to explain himself.

Oh, she was a fool indeed. He'd probably been cavorting with Betsy Robbins all this time, taking his pleasures where he found them.

Blind rage boiled up and flowed over, leaving her shaking. She'd never felt so humiliated in all her life, not even when she'd found out about Val's other women. She had been so sure that Will was different, but she had seen the proof with her own eyes.

She couldn't believe she'd shed tears over him. She never would again, she swore that to herself there and then.

The lonely hoot of an owl sounded from somewhere in the wood and echoed in her wounded heart. Drawing in a painful breath of the soft, sweet air that carried the scent of cut hay, she pressed her hands hard against her face, then turned and walked back toward the house, feeling more alone than she ever had in her life.

———

Will stopped plowing and wiped the sweat off his brow, looking up at the blazing sun. He'd never known time to drag by so slowly, each day seeming to last a week. He took no pleasure in the work that had previously given him such reward.

Instead, a deep, nagging unhappiness ate away at him, along with an acute sense of guilt that he'd hurt Louisa this deeply when he'd intended the exact opposite. But as the saying went, the road to hell was paved with good intentions.

Three weeks, and she still hadn't given him a chance to explain. On the rare occasions when he did see her, she spoke to him about only the most mundane matters, rarely meeting his gaze. He might have been a complete stranger.

He knew that the entire household silently wondered what had caused the chill between them.

Louisa kept mostly to herself, taking her meals in her study. He imagined she had lost herself in writing her new book, not that she was about to discuss that with him. That hurt too. He missed their conversations, the ease they'd had with each other, the sharing of life's small details as well as its larger problems. She'd shut the door so firmly in his face that he doubted he'd ever get a foot back in it. His fault, only his.

Betsy Robbins was no help. She continued to sashay about, finding any excuse to run into Will and display her wares, as if she'd not heard a single word he said to her the night she'd appeared in his bed.

Contrary to her intentions, she only set his teeth on edge. He wanted no one but Louisa, and the vivid memories of their lovemaking only haunted him and made him ache for her all the more.

"Mr. Cutter? Mr. Cutter, are you daydreaming? I've been trying to get your attention for the last minute."

He blinked and looked down to see Pip standing at his side, a basket in one hand, her face screwed up in a quizzical frown. "Sorry, Pip," he said. "I believe I was."

"I've brought us something to eat. Will you share the basket with me or are you going to send me off yet again? You no longer seem to have any time for me." She regarded him with sad, solemn eyes that made him feel as if he'd betrayed her as well.

Will ran a hand through his wet hair. "Have I been that remiss?" he said, forcing a smile to his mouth. "Forgive me. I've been busy, trying to keep the farm moving along."

"I understand," she said, although he knew perfectly well that she didn't.

He supposed that Pip was accustomed to being abandoned by the people she loved and dealt with it as best she could. Her father had deserted her, her grandfather was too wrapped up in his own unhappiness and regret to give her what she needed, and her mother . . . her mother had shut herself away behind her study door for her own reasons, reasons that Will was entirely responsible for. If he hadn't been so concerned about the harvest, he'd have departed Broadhurst and left Louisa in peace. As it was, he owed Pip a great deal more than his own preoccupation.

"I'd enjoy sharing lunch with you," he said, taking the basket from her and leading her over to the shade of the trees that bordered the field. "What have you been up to today?" he asked, settling on the grass.

"Nothing much," Pip said with a shrug. "I did my lessons, although I didn't have much to do since Mama believes that summers should be for playing outside. Then I took Apple out for a ride. Grandpapa is in one of his moods, so he didn't care to play chess with me, and Mama is working as usual so I didn't want to interrupt her. I'm supposed to meet John Henry in a little while down by the dairy, so at least that's nice."

Pip exhaled loudly and handed Will a piece of cheese and bread along with a tankard of ale that she'd carefully poured from a flask. "I don't know what it is about adults, Mr. Cutter. They're always too busy to enjoy themselves. When I grow up, I shall be sure that I find time in every day to have fun."

"I think that a fine aspiration," Will said. "Keep to it and you will live to a ripe old age."

"John Henry says that life is meant to be enjoyed and that enjoyment can be taken from the smallest things. One doesn't need grand carriages and houses, for a good climbing tree is just as important and makes as fine a house as any. Do you agree, Mr. Cutter?"

Will smiled fondly at her. "Your John Henry has wisdom beyond his years. I do agree. One makes one's own happiness, Pip, and although material things can give one the ease that simplifies life, nothing is more important than finding that happiness. As far as I'm concerned, we can live in a palace and be entirely miserable if we're not with the people we love."

Pip nodded thoughtfully. "If you believe that truly, Mr. Cutter, then I think you should do something about my mama."

Will nearly dropped his bread. "What do you mean?" he asked carefully.

"She cares about you, Mr. Cutter. I know she's been behaving in a very peculiar fashion, but I think it's because she's afraid of something. She was fine before we went to

Dawlish, and then I told her that you were a soldier in the army." Pip gazed up at him, her face very serious. "Do you think she's afraid because she thinks you might go back to the army and be killed like my papa, leaving her all alone again?" Her words came out in a rush and she ducked her head to disguise the tears that had started in her eyes.

Will instantly put down his meal and wrapped Pip tight in his arms, infinitely touched. "I don't think so—she knows that the war is over. I think, Pip, that your mama is very angry because I didn't tell her I was a soldier. I should have, but when I first arrived she said that she wouldn't have anyone working for her who had been in the army, so I held my peace." He dropped a kiss on the top of Pip's head. "I shouldn't have misled her, sweeting. That was my mistake, and she has every right to be angry with me."

Pip raised her head and met his gaze squarely. "Thank you for telling me. I didn't know that she dislikes soldiers. I suppose I shouldn't have said anything if it got you into trouble, but I thought she would be pleased, since Papa was a soldier." Pip chewed on her lip, then blurted out her next question. "Why doesn't she like soldiers, Mr. Cutter? Was it because Papa died?"

Will wished to hell that he could duck the question, but he'd had enough of lies. He thought of how to frame his answer without giving Pip more information than she needed. "I believe your mother doesn't like soldiers because your father didn't tell her that he planned to become one. As I told you before, he left her alone to cope, Pip, and that was a hardship for her. Perhaps she thinks that all soldiers have a habit of vanishing."

"Will you vanish, Mr. Cutter?" Pip asked, clutching at his hands. "I don't know if I could bear that."

Will's throat tightened into a hard knot. "I cannot stay

indefinitely, sweeting. Your mama would not wish me to. Don't you worry, though," he said, releasing her. "You'll forget me soon enough and someone else will come along who shall entertain you."

"I don't want someone else to come along," Pip said, her voice catching on a sob. "I want you to stay, Mr. Cutter. Please, please stay? I don't need to be entertained, really I don't. I—I'm not very much trouble, really I'm not."

A stab of pain shot through Will's heart. How he loved this little girl, far more than he could tell her and for reasons that stretched far beyond the time they'd spent together. He felt as if he knew every detail of her early childhood, all etched by Louisa in her letters and fixed firmly in his mind.

He loved Louisa for the same reason. She wasn't just the woman he'd fallen in love with in person, whom he'd held in his arms, whose body he'd joined with his own. She was also the woman who had imparted so much of herself on paper without ever realizing it, the descriptions amazingly explicit as she painted a picture of her inner self, her thoughts, the way she saw the world, her life, her beloved daughter.

Pip was so thoroughly a part of the fabric Louisa had woven with words. Now that he knew Pip for himself, he only loved her more. She had become everything to him, entangled in his love for Louisa until the two could not be separated.

If he lost Louisa, he lost Pip as well. For the first time he realized how devastated he would be. He'd come to terms as best he could with Louisa's severing him from her life, but Pip—he hadn't gone so far as to think of the heartbreak that would cause him.

Will ran his hand over the top of Pip's hair with a soft sigh. "I shall do my best to find a way around this difficulty, little one, but give me some time. I can't work a miracle overnight, and a miracle is what it will take."

Pip sniffed hard and wiped her nose on her sleeve. "Whatever you can do, Mr. Cutter. My mama is difficult sometimes, but she is not impossible."

"No," Will said with a sad smile. "Not impossible. Your mother is a good, fine woman and she does her very best to give you everything she can. Her life has been difficult these last few years, and she has had to work very hard to provide for all of you."

"I know that," Pip replied. "But you see, I know how she is when she's with you—or how she was, anyway, before she became so angry with your soldiering. You make her happy, Mr. Cutter, happier than I've ever seen her before."

Out of the mouths of babes, Will thought wryly. Pip really didn't miss a thing. "I think," he said slowly, "that I have taken some of the burden from her shoulders. If that has lightened her heart I am glad, but do not read too much into it, Pip. I only work here."

"You do so much more than that, Mr. Cutter. You have since the day you arrived. Grandpapa is so much better, even though he still has his bad days, but just in the last month he's been happier, busy with the books that Mama's given over to him and making plans for next year."

"Yes," Will said. "I've seen that for myself." Indeed, he felt nothing but gratitude that Louisa had at least listened to him in that regard. Charles Fleming was becoming an entirely different man.

"Even Cook is positively pleasant at times. I know she looks forward to dinner so that she can listen to your silly stories. Mr. Trueboot and his daughter do, too—they talk about you all the time in the dairy."

"Do they?" Will said. "How very unsettling. One cannot help but wonder what people say when their subject is out of earshot."

"Oh—nothing but nice things," Pip said. "They think you are very wonderful, but they also think you have a mysterious past and possibly a great tragedy that happened to you and drove you here. They've come up with all sorts of wonderful stories, but I think they're all nonsense."

Will laughed. "Good for you. I am constantly amazed by the scope of people's imaginations when it comes to other people's business."

Pip ferreted around in the basket and produced two apples, handing Will one of them. She crunched into the sweet flesh and chewed thoughtfully. "Violet says that *she* thinks you're the bastard son of a lord who refuses to acknowledge you."

Will nearly choked on the bite of his own apple he'd just taken. "She thinks *what*?"

"As I said. Mr. Trueboot says that's just silly. He thinks you're the son of an impoverished vicar, for that's the only way you'd have come by your education—your 'edification,' he calls it," she added with a giggle.

"And what do you think, Miss Pip?" Will asked, raising one eyebrow, fascinated by all the speculation about which he'd been utterly unaware. A bastard son indeed. If they only knew.

"Oh, I think you're probably just one of the last of a lot of boys in a family not unlike our own. There wasn't enough to go around, so you went into the army and then the war ended and you came back to England and took up the first thing you could think of." She looked over at him with a mischievous twinkle in her eyes. "After all, you didn't know the first thing about milking cows when you came to Broadhurst."

Will burst into laughter. "You're absolutely right, Pip. I didn't know a blasted thing. I suppose I was very brazen to think I could learn, but I've managed well enough, don't you agree?"

"Yes, indeed. Now Tessie practically runs to you when she sees you coming in the morning. I think she likes the touch of your hands. Cows are particular that way."

"They are, aren't they? I have to admit, I never thought I'd find milking cows soothing, but there you are. As long as you do it right they leave you alone to think your own thoughts, or so I've discovered."

Pip brushed off the front of her pinafore and stood. "I hope you think some more about staying here at Broadhurst, Mr. Cutter. We'd all miss you, the animals included."

"You're very kind to say so," Will said.

"It's only the truth. I'd better be off. John Henry will probably be waiting. We're going to play pirates in the hayloft."

"Pirates, is it?" Will said, thinking that Pip had more of her mother in her than Louisa realized. "Have a good time."

Pip nodded. "I always do with John Henry. He has a prodigious imagination." She picked up the basket and sped off with a backward wave of her hand.

Will watched her go, a sudden feeling of unease pricking at him. He had an urge to call her back, but no good reason for it.

Releasing a heavy breath, Will went back to his plowing, but he couldn't help feeling unsettled.

16

$\mathcal{P}$ushing her foolscap to one side, Louisa stood and stretched her back. She had made no real progress with Elizabeth today, but she wasn't surprised. She hadn't been able to think of much of anything but Will, as much as she'd tried over the last three weeks to push him out of her mind.

The dairy needed her attention, for the end of the week approached and the cheeses needed to be ready for the small Maidencombe market on Saturday.

Walking slowly, Louisa tried to take pleasure in the brilliant blue sky and the warm day, but she felt numb inside, just as she had ever since she'd discovered Betsy Robbins leaving the stables and realized what sort of man Will really was.

The sound of Pip's laughter and shouts coming from the hayloft cheered her slightly. At least Pip was enjoying the summer, she thought, trying to count her blessings. Pip was healthy and happy, they had money in the bank thanks to Mr. Sandringham, she'd finished her corrections on Jack Kilblaine's book, and . . . and to her infinite relief she'd found out last week that she wasn't carrying Will's child. Those were all things to be pleased about.

So why did she feel as if her world had come to an end?

Louisa shivered, forcing her dark mood away. If she wasn't careful, she'd sink into despair the way her father had done and be of no use to anyone. At least her father seemed to be improving. There. Another blessing. Will had been right about her father, anyway. He thrived on doing the books, even though Louisa had not told him the truth about the three hundred pounds, letting him assume they'd been there all along.

"Mama!" Pip called, waving at her from the open door of the hayloft. "Look! John Henry and I have the best new game. You jump from here onto the pile of hay below. Watch!"

Before Louisa could call out in alarm, Pip opened her arms wide and leapt into the air, landing high on the hay and sliding down with a squeal of delight.

But her squeal turned into a sharp cry as she reached the ground and her face suddenly turned pale. "Mama—Mama, come quickly! I've hurt myself! Oh, Mama—I think it's bad!"

With horror, Louisa saw Pip double over, clutching her foot, her hands covered with blood, the red dripping between her fingers.

She tore to her daughter's side, her heart pounding in panic as she pulled Pip's hands away. A slash ran through the top of Pip's foot, and blood pumped in a stream from the wound. A scythe that had lain hidden in the bottom of the hay was covered in the same blood.

"Stay still," Louisa said, grabbing Pip's foot and trying to pull the edges of the open cut together, but with no success. The blood just kept pumping and pumping, soaking the hay, Louisa's dress, Pip's chest and legs.

"Oh, dear God," Louisa sobbed as Pip grabbed onto her arm, her eyes wide with fear, her face ashen. "We have to stop this. I don't know how, God help me, I don't know how."

John Henry appeared at her side, his face white as chalk. "It looks terrible bad, Mrs. Merriem," he said in a small, shaking voice. "What should we do?"

"Get Mr. Cutter," Louisa demanded. Will. Will could fix it. He could fix anything. "He should be in the south field."

"In the south field," John Henry repeated, staring at the blood spurting from Pip's foot as if transfixed.

"Yes," Louisa said on a sob. "Go now, John Henry! Run as fast as you can. It's not far, but everything depends on your speed."

John Henry tore off, running as if Pip's life depended on it, and Louisa thought it very well might.

"Mama, Mama, *do* something," Pip said, her voice weak. "I'm frightened."

"Mr. Cutter will come, darling, any moment he will," Louisa said, putting all her weight on the wound, thinking that maybe she could stop the bleeding that way. She managed to slow the stream, but not enough, and with a sense of disbelief Louisa watched the blood leave Pip's little body as her eyes rolled back in her head and she lost consciousness.

Louisa cried out in fear and covered Pip's body with her own, calling her name over and over, her hands still clamped to Pip's foot.

"I'm here, Louisa," Will's voice said from over her shoulder after what seemed like a lifetime but could not have been more than a few minutes.

"Oh, Will, thank God, thank God," she sobbed, sitting up. "Please do something? Save her, Will, save her. She's cut the top of her foot and I can't make the bleeding stop."

Will stripped his shirt off and gently moved Louisa away, quickly wrapping the linen tight around Pip's calf and twisting it hard.

"Not there, Will—I told you, it's her foot!" But as she spoke the words, she saw the blood trickle to a near stop. She stared in astonishment. "How—how did you do that?" she said in a choked voice.

"John Henry, go to the stables and into the supply room,"

Will said, his face grim. "There's a box there on the shelf with bandages and so on for the horses. Bring it to me in the house. The kitchen would be best."

John Henry, his eyes huge, dashed off.

Will looked up at Louisa. "We'll get Pip through this, don't you worry."

She could only nod her head, tears streaming down her cheeks. She'd never felt so helpless or so relieved. Will was there. He would get Pip through, she knew he would.

He scooped Pip up in his arms and carried her carefully all the way back to the house, laying her still body down on the kitchen table as Cook stared aghast, her mouth opening and closing but no words coming out.

"Please put some water on to heat, Cook," Will asked calmly, taking a clean kitchen towel and wrapping it around Pip's foot.

"Whatever you say, Mr. Cutter." His voice somehow steadied her, for she moved instantly to the stove and put the kettle on. "Should we call for the doctor?"

"There's no time. I cannot keep the bandage so tight for much longer."

Louisa swallowed hard. "What are you going to do, Will?"

He glanced up at her. "I'm going to stitch the wound. Do you have any objections?"

"Do—do you know how?" she asked, sinking into a chair, clutching one of Pip's hands in hers.

He straightened and regarded her steadily. "Despite what you might think, there are some advantages to having been in the army, Louisa. I spent time in field hospitals and learned from the doctors there. This is a relatively simple procedure as long as it's done quickly. Pip nicked an artery, which is what caused so much bleeding."

He bent back over Pip, his hand stroking her pale brow. "If you'd rather wait for a doctor to be summoned from God knows where, though, that is your decision."

"No—no, I trust you, Will."

"Do you?" he said, not bothering to look at her.

Louisa colored, not missing the inference. "Please— whatever you can do."

"You must know I will do what I can. The rest is up to God."

Louisa bent her head into her hand, trying very hard not to cry. She couldn't lose Pip. She just couldn't. Pip was her entire life.

John Henry came racing in with the box and put it on the table. "Can you save her, Mr. Cutter?" he said, panting hard.

"I hope so," Will said, opening the box and taking out a smaller box that contained a needle and waxed thread. "Thank you for your help, but I think it's best if you wait outside now. You as well, Louisa."

"No. No, I will stay. Pip needs to know I'm here."

"Very well. Cook, may I have that water now and some soap?"

Cook, as white as the rest of them, brought a basin over and put it by his elbow. "Anything else, Mr. Cutter?"

"That will be all, thank you. Leave us now." Will washed his hands and then the needle, then dried both off. Threading the needle, he removed the towel and sat down, carefully beginning to stitch Pip's wound closed.

Louisa finally had to look away. She couldn't bear the sight of Pip's flesh being pierced, although the way Will went about it, he might have been doing very fine petit point. Every now and then he dabbed blood away with the towel before going back to his stitching.

Finally he looked up. "That's it," he said.

Louisa couldn't believe it. Only ten minutes had passed. "Are you sure?"

Will unwrapped his shirt from Pip's thigh and watched her sutured foot carefully. "I'm sure," he said a minute later, covering the closed wound with an ointment from the box and then binding her foot with a long strip of linen. "Now we wait. I'll carry Pip up to bed, but it will be some time before we know anything. As I said, she lost a good deal of blood, but she's young and strong and her pulse is good, considering."

"Thank you," Louisa said on a gulp. "Thank you so much."

"You owe me no thanks. I love your daughter, Louisa, and would do anything for her, although this I would have done for anyone." He picked Pip up, holding her with infinite gentleness as he took her out into the hall and up the stairs.

Louisa hurried ahead to open Pip's door and pulled the covers of the bed back, watching anxiously as Will lay her down.

"Could you help me take her dress off?" she asked. "I—I think I should put her in her nightclothes so that she'll be more comfortable when she awakes." *If she wakes,* Louisa thought with a shudder.

"Of course," Will said. "I'll just go downstairs first and get some more hot water so that we can wash her off. Keep her covered until I get back. She needs to stay as warm as possible."

He was back in an instant with towels and a clean basin, and together they cleaned Pip up and put on her nightclothes, exchanging no words beyond the necessary.

As soon as they'd settled Pip back under the covers, Will lit a fire in the hearth and pulled up a chair next to her bed.

"Go and change your own clothes now," he said. "Pip doesn't need to wake up and find you covered in blood. I'll stay here with her."

Louisa looked down at herself, surprised to see that the front of her lavender dress was now brick red. "Yes," she said, standing unsteadily. "Yes. That is what I should do. Of course I should."

Her knees wobbled as her head spun in dizzy circles, and Will moved around the bed and caught her just before she collapsed.

"That's it," he said. "I'm taking you to your room and you're going to lie down. You're in as much shock as Pip and of no use to anyone in this state."

So saying, he scooped her up as if she were as light as Pip and carried her down the hall, kicking open the door to her bedroom with his knee. He lay her down and rolled her over onto her side, undoing the tapes of her gown and pulling it over her head.

"What are you doing?" she asked in alarm, her head still going around in circles.

"I'm undressing you. There's no point in pretending modesty now, Louisa, for I've seen you naked before this. I don't have lust on my mind, if that's what you're thinking."

She couldn't find the strength to object. She felt as weak as an infant, her entire body shaking with delayed shock. "Pip—I have to be with Pip," she murmured.

"I will stay with Pip, and I promise to alert you the moment she awakens. For now you need to lie down. I don't expect you to sleep, but I'd far rather not have two patients on my hands."

He pulled a mound of blankets over her shivering body and drew the draperies shut. "Be quiet now and know that Pip is in safe hands. When you feel steady enough, wash and ask Cook to make you some sweet hot tea. I'd send for it myself, but I don't want to leave Pip alone for another moment."

Louisa couldn't fight him. Pip was the only person who was important, and she knew deep in her heart that Will would take the best of care with her. He'd just saved her life, hadn't he?

The door shut behind him, and to her surprise, despite her worry, her eyes closed and she slept soundly for the first time in weeks.

Will prayed as hard as he'd ever prayed in his life. God and His angels would protect Pip—she was blameless in this world, only a small child whose life was still ahead of her.

He bent his head and pressed his hands together. "The Lord will send His angel to be with you, Pip, and to keep you safe," he whispered. "He said: 'See I am sending an angel before you, to guard you on the way. Be attentive to him and heed his voice.' " Will swallowed hard, his throat so tight, he could hardly get the words out.

"God our Father," he continued hoarsely, "in Your loving providence You send Your holy angels to watch over us. Hear our prayers, defend us always by their protection . . ." He paused for a moment, pressing his folded hands against his mouth. "Please, Father, send Your angels to watch over Pip. Send them to give her life, not to take it from her. We need her here with us."

He leaned forward and cupped one of Pip's small, cold hands in both of his, willing her to fight her way back, to open her eyes and smile at him. He of all people knew how fragile life was, how suddenly it could be taken, and he truly didn't think he could bear watching the angels descend to take Pip's spirit away—not this time, not an innocent child who only an hour before had been laughing merrily.

She lay so still, her face pale as marble, her lips slightly blue, the shallow rise and fall of her chest the only sign of life.

He raised her hand to his lips and kissed the fragile skin, wishing he could give her his own life force. He'd hoped never again to see blood like that pouring from anyone. Battles were one thing—men created their own nightmares. But the scene that greeted him at the dairy had horrified him to his core. Things like that weren't supposed to happen to small children, let alone a child he loved.

He didn't know where he'd found the strength and clarity of thought to do what was needed. He could only be thankful for what he'd learned on the battlefield, and if that was his reward for all the years of bloodshed he'd endured, then every moment had been worth it—if Pip survived.

"Please don't leave us, sweeting," he murmured, gently stroking a hand over Pip's hair. "Your mother needs you. I need you, and so do your grandfather and—and just think how lost John Henry would be without your guidance. Be a soldier and fight for us all, will you? Come home, Pip, please come home."

He brushed his hand across his eyes, his vision clouded, then lowered his head and started praying all over again.

Will didn't know how much time had passed when he felt a strange prickle at the back of his neck, as if someone had entered the room. He sat up abruptly, expecting to see Louisa at the door, but it was shut. He looked over his shoulder toward the window, but saw only twilight through the glass. The room was empty save for Pip and himself.

Something felt odd, though. He rubbed his tired eyes and looked down at Pip. She hadn't moved. He looked around once again, thinking that shock had scrambled his brains, for a strange light began to fill the room, a shimmering gold like sun breaking through clouds after a thunderstorm, only this was like nothing he'd ever seen before.

Light saturated every corner, clear and bright, and Will felt a sense of infinite peace fill his soul. A whisper sounded in his ear, so soft that it might have been only the breeze blowing, but the words were perfectly distinct.

Fear not, for the Father giveth and restoreth. Hold tight to faith, for it is faith that heals both soul and body. Be of good heart, William, for you have been a faithful servant and all your prayers will be answered . . .

The whisper faded away as the light dimmed and became simple twilight once again.

Will shook his head as if he could clear it. He didn't know what had just happened, only knew that it was as real as anything he'd ever experienced.

Rubbing his hands over his face, he looked back at Pip. His breath nearly left his body, for Pip watched him steadily, her mouth curved up in the smile he'd thought he might never see again.

"Pip? Pip?" he cried, catching up her hands. "You are—you are awake!"

"Did you see them, Mr. Cutter?" she asked, her voice weak but steady. "Did you see the angels?"

He slowly shook his head. "The angels? No . . . just a light. A beautiful light."

She nodded solemnly. "Yes. A beautiful light. The angels carried me through it straight back home. They said I belonged here with you and Mama. I had a very nice time, though, while I was gone."

Will gazed at her, forcing back tears. "Did you, sweeting?"

The door flew open and Louisa ran into the room, her face white. "Will? I heard you cry out Pip's name . . ." She stopped and her hands flew to her mouth as she took in her daughter's smiling face. "Pip. Oh, darling, you're back with us. Thank God. Thank God!" Running to the bed, she caught Pip up in her arms and held her tight.

"Mama, I talked to the angels," Pip said, disentangling herself and looking at her mother with shining eyes. "They were very wonderful. They took me to a place with flowers and waterfalls and lots and lots of horses, and they said that I could decide whether to stay with them or come home, and I said if you please I would like to come home because you and Mr. Cutter and Grandpapa and John Henry would be too sad if I didn't."

She only stopped to catch her breath. "Mr. Cutter kept saying so, over and over. So I thought I'd better come back quickly before you missed me too much. Did you?"

Louisa looked up over Pip's head and met Will's eyes, her own filled with bewilderment.

Will smiled at her, then chucked Pip's chin. "We did, Pip. We missed you very much and worried about you."

"Oh. That's right, I hurt my foot. Is it better now? It feels awfully sore," she said, looking down at the sheet. "It didn't hurt at all when I was with the angels," she said accusingly. "Maybe I should have stayed a little longer."

Will burst into laughter. "No, I think you came back right on time. Staying too long with the angels is a bit like staying out after dark—you might be having a fine time, but everyone who loves you starts to worry."

"Oh. I suppose that makes sense."

"Here, drink some water," Will said, handing her a glass, "then let's have a look at that foot of yours. You did manage to do a thorough job of cutting it, but if you will jump off lofts into loose haystacks, you take your chances."

He pulled the covers back and gently picked up her bandaged foot. "Can you move your toes for me?"

To his relief, she easily obliged him. He'd been worried that she might have severed some nerves, but that wasn't the case. "What about moving your ankle about in a circle? Very slowly, sweeting, since you have a nice line of stitches that you don't want to pull apart."

"I have stitches?" Pip said, her eyes wide. "John Henry will be very impressed. He did nothing but brag when his pony cut her leg and had to be stitched, saying the whole time how brave she was." Her brow furrowed. "Was I brave, Mr. Cutter? I cannot seem to remember anything about being stitched."

"You were very brave indeed," Will replied. "Do oblige me, though, and move your ankle?" He waited, holding his breath, praying the tendons were still intact.

Pip winced with the effort, but she managed to turn her foot from side to side.

Will exhaled. Pip had been a lucky girl indeed. She'd have a scar, but that was a small price to pay. "Excellent. The good news is that you'll be just fine. The bad news is that you absolutely have to keep your weight off your foot for a good week, which means you have to stay in bed. No cheating as you do at cards."

He didn't add that she'd be too weak from blood loss to get out of bed for at least that amount of time, or that infection was still a concern—although something told him that Pip's recovery had already been seen to.

Pip didn't protest. She handed Will the glass of water

that she'd finished. "I'm tired," she said, sinking back onto the pillows. "I think I'd like to sleep now." She closed her eyes and tucked her face up against one hand.

Louisa kissed her cheek. "That's a good idea, darling. I'll sit here with you for a while."

"Sleep well, Pip," Will said, kissing the top of her head. "I'll come and see you in the morning."

He glanced over at Louisa, but her attention was fully occupied with Pip as she adjusted the covers over her daughter's sleeping form.

If she needed him, she knew where to find him, he decided, quietly letting himself out. As for him, he was suddenly seized by a ravenous hunger. He'd go down to the kitchen and charm Cook into producing something from the larder before going back to the stables and mulling over the miracle that had been given to them all.

17

$\mathscr{S}$taring at the upper stable window, Louisa released a deep breath. She owed Will a very large debt of gratitude, and she didn't want to wait until morning to repay him.

No matter what else he'd done, he'd saved Pip's life that afternoon. However, she didn't know if she could bear walking up those stairs and discovering him in bed with Betsy Robbins.

The window was dark, but that could mean anything. An idea struck and she picked up a pebble and threw it at the glass, then waited a few moments. Nothing.

She threw another, this time with more success, for the window opened and Will leaned his head out, his hair tousled.

"It is I, Louisa," she called up.

"Louisa," he said, running his hand over his face. "What is it?" Alarm shot to his eyes. "Pip—has something happened?"

"No. I'm sorry—I didn't mean to worry you. Pip is sleeping soundly. My father is sitting with her."

"Oh . . . well, that's good. In that case, what are you doing down there? It must be close to midnight."

"I came to speak to you, but I'd rather not do it with my head craned back."

"If you'll give me few minutes, I'll come down." He pulled his head back in and shut the window again.

Louisa glowered. He probably did have Betsy Robbins up there and didn't want her to know or he would have asked her up.

She owed Will her thanks, but that was all he was going

to get, she decided bitterly. He might have saved Pip's life, but he was still the same cad he'd been that morning.

True to his word, Will came out only three minutes later, buttoning his shirt with one hand, his other brushing hurriedly through his hair. "Come," he said. "Let's sit on the bench."

She followed him over and gingerly placed herself as far from him as she could, her hip pressed up against the bench arm.

"What's all this about?" he asked, regarding her quizzically.

"Will . . . I—thank you for what you did. That's all, really. Without you I don't think Pip would be sleeping peacefully in her bed."

"You came all the way down here at this hour just to say that?" He leaned back, resting one arm on the top of the wooden strut, and watched her, his eyes steady.

She wished the moonlight wasn't quite so bright, since she was sure he could see the flush on her cheeks. She might think poorly of his character, but his nearness affected her every bit as much as it ever had.

"I—I also came to say that I cannot be so angry about your having been in the army, since as you pointed out earlier, your experience saved Pip."

He dropped his gaze, his fingers moving back and forth on the wood. "True. But I do owe you an apology for not having told you. I've tried to find an opportunity all this month to make it, but you haven't given me a chance."

"I was angry," she said, trying to ignore the way his fingers stroked the back of the bench. She wouldn't have minded being that piece of wood just now . . . Horrified with herself, she quickly chased the thought away and clung to her indignation. "You lied to me, Will. You deliberately misled me."

"I saw no point in telling you something that would only

distress you. You made your abhorrence of army officers perfectly clear, and I suspected that if I did tell you, your reaction would be far from favorable. You cannot deny that I was correct."

Louisa glared at him. He made perfect sense, the last thing she wanted to admit. "Why didn't you just say so at the very beginning?"

"Would you have given me the job?" he asked logically.

"No. No, I wouldn't have," she allowed. "Or at least I don't think I would have." She bit her lip, determined to be honest. "No, I'm sure I wouldn't."

"Which would have gotten neither of us anywhere." Will smiled faintly. "So you see, although I regret keeping the truth from you, I do not regret what came of it—or at least I didn't until Sergeant Tibbins showed up and exposed me. Are you still very angry?"

"Not about that. I was going to tell you three weeks ago, but I changed my mind."

"Why?" he asked softly, his eyes puzzled. "I have to admit I was growing impatient with you, for the issue didn't seem so important as all that. Especially after what passed between us on the beach."

Louisa, enraged by his cheek, jumped to her feet. "How could you say such a thing?" she cried. "You sound as if you attach some importance to that night, when I know perfectly well that it meant nothing at all to you!"

Will stared at her, looking as if she'd just slapped him. "You cannot believe that. You were there with me, Louisa. We both know what it meant—we acknowledged what it meant."

"Oh? And I suppose that it meant so much that you took up with another woman only a week later, if not before. You probably said the same thing to her."

He looked at her as if she were a sheet short. "What in God's name are you talking about?" he said. "What other woman? I haven't even thought about another woman since I first set eyes on you."

"Don't you think to lie to me now, Will Cutter. I know the truth. I saw her with my own eyes the very night that I came down here to speak to you!"

Will paled. "Oh, dear God. You surely don't mean you saw Betsy Robbins leaving . . ."

"I did indeed," she said, trying not to let him see the pain she still felt in her bruised heart. "I saw everything, Betsy leaving, your coming outside half dressed, I even saw the satisfied smile on your face as you watched her go."

Will stood and took two paces over to her, grabbing her hard by the shoulders. "You little fool," he said. "Why the *hell* didn't you just say something then instead of causing us both so much anguish the last three weeks?"

"What did you expect me to say?" she snapped, pushing his hands away. "That I didn't mind, that I understood? I don't understand, Will, and I don't care to. You and Val are cut from the same cloth—you wouldn't know loyalty if it fell on your head."

"I didn't lie with Betsy Robbins," he roared. "I found the blasted woman waiting for me in my bed and I threw her out. My God, what is the matter with you? I thought you knew me far better than that—I would never do such a thing, not ever!"

Louisa gazed at him uncertainly. His anger seemed true enough, although Val had displayed the same indignation when she'd first confronted him about his fancy dancers.

"For all I know, Betsy Robbins is in your bed now," she said, folding her arms across her chest and standing her ground. "You probably are just trying to mislead me yet again so that you can have it both ways, Betsy one night, myself another."

Will's hand flashed out and he grasped her by the wrist, pulling her straight toward the stable door. Without a word he dragged her upstairs and kicked his bedroom door wide open.

"There," he shouted, pointing with his free hand at the empty bed, the sheets tousled. "There, Louisa," he said, drawing in a steadying breath and releasing her wrist. "Does it look to you as if I've been doing anything but sleeping? Alone, I might add?" He shoved his hands on his hips. "Damnation, woman, I've missed you every single night of the last month, longed for you so much that my body hurt, wished that you were in that bed with me so that I could show you how much I love you."

Louisa gaped at him. "Wh-what?" she choked. "What did you say?"

With a groan, Will turned his back. "I said that I love you," he murmured almost inaudibly. "Shoot me if you will, but that's the truth. I've loved you for a long time now."

She tried to catch her breath but couldn't manage. Her heart hurt too much, but this time with happiness. "You—you never said," she finally gasped.

He turned to her, his eyes blazing. "How could I? You weren't ready to hear. I didn't mean to say it even now. The words just came out." He sighed. "You're nobody's fool, Rosebud, but you've been badly hurt and the last thing I wanted to do was frighten you away."

"I . . . I love you too, Will," she said, tears starting to her eyes. "I don't know when it happened exactly, only that it did. I could never have given myself to you on the beach, not like that, if my heart hadn't already belonged to you."

Will gathered her into his arms, pressing his cheek

against her hair, his hands stroking her back. "I know," he murmured. "I knew that then. If I hadn't, I never would have continued." He cupped her chin and lifted her face to his. "Will you let me love you now, let me show you how much I mean every word I've said?"

In answer she turned her face up to his, and Will's mouth instantly descended, claiming her own in a deep, overwhelming kiss, his tongue moving against hers, his warm lips tasting her until her knees went weak and her entire body shook with longing.

He picked her up in his arms and carried her over to the bed, laying her down on the rumpled sheets. His fingers swiftly unbuttoned her dress and stripped it from her as his mouth traced a line of heat down her neck. Her chemise quickly followed the dress.

Louisa's fingers fumbled at the buttons to his shirt in her haste, finally stripping it off. Her hands hungrily explored the hard contours of his chest, so familiar, not a single detail forgotten. His nipples tightened under her fingers and he groaned, lowering his head to her breasts and suckling hard as she writhed in unbearable pleasure under the insistent pull of his mouth and tongue.

Somehow he managed to divest himself of his trousers without ever lifting his head and, cupping her buttocks, he pulled her close against him, his erect penis pressing insistently against her belly. Heat pooled where he touched and fire flamed between her thighs, an unbearable need building until she writhed beneath him with little cries of pleasure.

"I want you, Rosebud, God how I want you," he whispered, his breath hot against her cheek, his fingers slipping low and finding her cleft, sliding between, finding the most sensitive part of her and circling it until she moaned and her legs fell apart, urging him to go deeper.

He thrust two fingers into her willing flesh and rocked them in and out until Louisa thought she would explode with desire. "I—I can't bear it," she cried. "Oh, Will, I am going to die."

He instantly shifted over her and positioned his tip against her entrance, his dark eyes holding hers. "I love you," he whispered as he slid into her, filling her, completing her. "I love you, Rosebud, now and forever."

Pulling his hips back he plunged hard and deep and then withdrew only to drive into her again and then again, as if he could brand himself on her very heart. With each powerful stroke, with every deep kiss, Will's body told her the truth of his words.

She gave the same truth back to him, her own body molding to his, matching his rhythm, her frantic cries urging him to take all of her, everything she had to give and more.

Will caught her mouth, biting lightly at her lips, his tongue tangling with hers, his hands cupping her buttocks as he drew her impossibly close.

An unendurable knot of pleasure built deep inside her and broke apart, sending her falling over the edge of a precipice that threatened to have no end.

Louisa cried out as her body spasmed over and over, the intensity of sensation too much to tolerate. A long, keening wail escaped her throat as Will thrust deep and hard, staying still as she rode out the storm of ecstasy.

With one last thrust he groaned, the rhythmic waves of his own release just as powerful, his body racked with shudders.

Lowering his forehead onto her breast, he exhaled a few huge deep breaths. "I . . . love . . . you," he managed to say before collapsing onto his side and pulling her over against him, his heart pounding in strong, slow beats.

"If you ever . . . *ever* mention Betsy Robbins's name again in this context, I shall . . ." He pulled in another gasp of air. "I shall shake you till your teeth rattle."

"Never again," Louisa said, half laughing, half crying. "I am truly sorry that I ever doubted you."

After a few minutes Will weakly lifted himself up onto his elbow and stroked the damp hair out of her face. "Don't ever doubt me. There's *so* much I need to tell you, but I can't, not now. You have undone me, Rosebud, you truly have." He dropped a light kiss on her mouth. "Please, no matter what happens, know that you and Pip mean the world to me."

He dropped another kiss onto the top of her breast. "You'd best go now before your father begins to wonder where you are. I'll stop in and see Pip first thing in the morning, but then I have to go into Maidencombe for supplies. Is there anything you need?"

She shook her head in the cup of his shoulder. "Nothing. Just you, Will."

"We'll speak again tomorrow evening when the work of the day is behind us." He kissed her gently, then picked up her chemise and slipped it over her head. After helping her into her dress, he pulled on his trousers and walked her down the stairs.

"Good night, Rosebud," he said, covering her mouth with his and holding her close for a moment. "By the way," he murmured against her ear, "Pip was right about the angels."

Louisa pulled back and looked up him, her eyes wide

with fear. "The—the angels? You *saw* them? Were they coming to take her?"

"No," he said with a gentle smile, stroking her hair. "They were bringing her back. I've never seen anything like it in my life. I only saw their light, Louisa, but it was so beautiful. I wish I could describe what it looked like, but I can't, not properly." He sighed. "I knew I was in the presence of holiness, though. For the first time I realized that prayers truly are answered and miracles really can happen."

She wiped hot tears from her eyes with the back of her hand. "Thank you," she said, her voice choked. "Thank you for telling me. I think you are the miracle, Will Cutter. God must have sent you, His angel on earth, to watch over us."

"I wouldn't think anything so dangerous," Will said with a broad smile. "Let's just be grateful that he brought us together and that I happened to be here when Pip was in need."

Louisa's lips tightened. "I'd like to find the fool who left the scythe under the hay and shake him until his teeth rattled in his irresponsible head."

"I imagine it was one of the laborers," Will said, "but I think a word of warning to all of them will suffice. Pip shouldn't have been jumping off the loft, after all, although something tells me that Bassanio was responsible for that piece of ill-advised adventure."

"Bassanio?" Louisa crinkled her brow, then laughed as his meaning became clear. "Oh, you mean John Henry. That's right—Bassanio was Portia's true love in *The Merchant of Venice*."

"He was. By the by, I had a word with young John Henry earlier, and I don't think he'll be encouraging Pip toward any more escapades in the near future. The near-disastrous ending of this one shook him to his marrow, so there's no need for you to take him any further to task—he appeared sufficiently sobered."

"As he should be." Louisa wrapped her arms around Will, breathing in his warm scent with contentment. "Pip is fortunate to have you as her champion."

He chuckled. "I am fortunate to have Pip as mine. She seems to think I can walk on water, and I dread the day when she realizes that I'm an ordinary flawed mortal."

"There's nothing ordinary about you," Louisa said, reluctantly pulling away from him. "I must go back to Pip now."

"Give her a kiss for me. I'd walk you back, but I'd rather not take the risk of someone seeing us together at this hour. I'll see you in the morning."

Louisa started up the path to the house, stopping once to look back.

Will still stood there, bathed in moonlight, his face thoughtful. He raised one hand, then turned and went into the stables, the door closing behind him.

Tethering Maestro to a mounting post, Will walked into the Hart and Hound, intending to ask if he'd received any letters. Before he had a chance to ask, a familiar voice spoke from over his shoulder.

"William. How fortuitous. I was about to write a note to you, although your unexpected appearance is much more convenient."

Will turned in astonishment to see Lady Samantha Davenport standing in front of him. "Lady Samantha— what in heaven's name . . . I had no letter saying you would be arriving."

"No, I decided it was best to come straight down rather than waste the time exchanging letters. Come with me. I have bespoken a private parlor and we have important things to discuss."

She practically dragged him into the parlor and shut the door firmly. "Sit, William. I have news of great import. David Cumberland has wrapped a noose around his own neck and we are about to hang him from it, figuratively speaking, of course."

"Of course," Will replied, trying to absorb the implications of Samantha Davenport's unexpected appearance. "What news do you bring that requires such urgency?"

"Do not ask stupid questions, my boy, just listen." She lowered her bulk into a chair. "I simply must buy another carriage. My bones are positively shattered with all the jostling I've had to endure, although we did come at a cracking pace."

"Perhaps a drop of Madeira might help?" Will asked politely.

"Don't be absurd. This is no time for indulgence. Now see here. My banker has been brilliant, although he took his time about it. Nevertheless he has uncovered a nasty trail of treachery on David Cumberland's part. Here are the details . . ."

She breathlessly told her story, embellishing it with a good amount of hand-waving and bosom-patting. "So you see, we have him!" she finished triumphantly. "All that is left is to corner him in his lair, confront him with his misdeeds, and force him to restore everything he took from those dear people."

"Let me see if I have this correctly," Will said, his head spinning. "Cumberland deliberately inflated the price of the stock, then sold it short once he'd convinced Valentine Merriem and Charles Fleming to buy. The stock then tumbled and became nearly worthless."

"That's it, that's it," Samantha said impatiently. "He didn't exactly commit a crime, but he did ruin the family out of vengeance. You and I have enough influence to bring him to his knees and ruin him in the eyes of the *ton*. He has no choice but to comply."

"I have no influence," Will said quietly. "You seem to forget, Lady Samantha, that I am all but disgraced."

"Don't be ridiculous. You are anything but. In any case, you will be the next marquess in a matter of days, if not less."

Will paled. "I—I beg your pardon?"

Samantha clapped her hands to her mouth. "Oh—my dear boy. I did not mean for the news to come out that way. Forgive me. Sometimes I speak without thinking."

"Perhaps you had better explain," Will said, his body suddenly cold. "You refer to my brother, of course. Is he ill, injured?"

"William, I am afraid that the news is very bad. This is the true reason I came down to Devon so quickly, as the other could have waited." She leaned forward and took his hands between hers. "Your brother is dying. He has an advanced case of consumption. I myself did not know until I happened to stop by on my way to visit relatives nearby. The Stanleighs—do you know them? Lord Stanleigh is my cousin by—"

"For the love of God, woman," Will shouted, "never mind the damned Stanleighs! What of my brother?"

"He lies near to death," she said in a hush. "Do keep your voice down, William, unless you wish the entire world to hear of your brother's sad plight. As I was saying, he lies near to death and wishes to see you. Once I said I had word of you he became agitated in the extreme and begged me to send for you." She patted at her hair. "Naturally I told him nothing about your circumstances, only that you had returned to England and had sequestered yourself in the south. I said I would do my best to convince you to go to him."

Will pressed his palms hard against his eyes. His brother, dying? Not possible—it just wasn't possible.

Rupert was the marquess, the twin who had been born first, the one designated to take on the responsibility of the lands, the estates. Rupert was the ordained son. Will had merely been the afterthought, the brother who had made his appearance in the world already in second place.

"You do realize what this means, William?" Lady Samantha said. "You will be the next marquess, and the eighth at that. You cannot avoid the responsibility, as much as you might enjoy being Louisa Merriem's farm laborer."

Will raised his head, his eyes hot and dry from unshed tears. "The point did not escape me," he managed to say in a civil tone. "Despite the problems between my brother and myself, I do love him. I must go to him at once. David Cumberland will simply have to wait for his hanging."

"No, my boy. David Cumberland will not wait. I know for a fact that he is in residence at the moment, so you and I will go now to see him. Have you not thought of the consequences of leaving Broadhurst Farm without restoring Louisa and her father to their rightful place and fortune?"

Will hesitated. "I see your point," he finally said. "If we force David Cumberland to give everything back, that means Louisa and her family will be able to manage with no trouble."

She shoved herself to her feet. "Exactly. Furthermore, I *need* you to help me confront Cumberland. You, with your position as the next marquess, will have an enormous amount of influence over him. Combined with mine, we can bring him to the point."

Will could not argue with her. If he didn't do as she suggested, Louisa would never be able to bring in the harvest, not with him gone. But how would she manage in any case? There would be so much to be done, so many details to be looked after.

"I shall stay with the family, William," Samantha said, as if reading his mind. "I shall stay for as long as they need me. A new tenant farmer will have to be found to take over Lower Broadhurst and then there is the return to the Hall to consider. I think we should give Cumberland no more than a fortnight to vacate."

Will nodded absently. Samantha had a point and he valued her help, for he had no choice but to go to his brother. But what would he tell Louisa?

How could he possibly explain the reason for his abrupt departure without having to confess everything else—she was in no way ready to hear the full truth now, and he wasn't in any shape to tell her, not with this tragic situation on his hands.

He nodded. "Very well, I'll do as you ask as long as you give me your word that you will stay with Louisa until she's back on her feet. Her daughter's been hurt and Louisa will need all the help she can get."

"You have my word," Samantha said, making a cross over her heart. "I promise I will stay and see to everything. Now into my carriage, William, and let us make haste to Broadhurst Hall."

He looked down at himself. "I am not dressed in precisely the correct manner to be presenting myself as Lord William Fitzpatrick."

"Never you mind that—you will do well enough. All you need to do is assume an imperial manner. The rest will take care of itself."

She marched out of the parlor and called for her carriage.

Will followed, deep in contemplation of life's very strange twists and turns.

18

"Is Mr. Cumberland at home?" Lady Samantha demanded of the footman at the door, giving him a searing look that brooked no argument. "Tell him that Lady Samantha Davenport and Lord William Fitzpatrick have stopped to pay him a morning call." She produced a card and shoved it at the footman.

"Certainly, your ladyship. Immediately, your ladyship." He showed them into the hall and vanished.

A moment later he returned, practically scraping the ground with obsequiousness. "Mr. Cumberland is pleased to receive you. If you will just follow me into the drawing room?"

Samantha plowed ahead like a battleship under full sail, and Will strode after her, feeling like a rowboat being pulled in her majestic wake. Really, he wondered if she needed him at all.

"Lady Samantha, this is an unexpected pleasure," David Cumberland said as they entered, his round face wreathed in a welcoming smile as he moved forward to kiss her gloved hand. "What brings you to this part of the world?"

"That will become clear in a moment. May I present Lord William Fitzgerald, brother of the Marquess of Alconleigh?"

"I am delighted to make your acquaintance, Lord William." Looking him up and down but without commenting on his unusual manner of dress, David Cumberland executed a neat bow. "Won't you both sit down? May I ring for refreshments?"

"Thank you, no," Will said, deliberately moving over to the fireplace and casually leaning one elbow on the mantelpiece. "We have come on a business matter, Mr. Cumberland."

"A business matter? Ah. Perhaps you are seeking investment advice, since that is my specialty." He smoothed one hand over his coat. "You were recently in the King's Dragoons, were you not, Lord William? I follow the dispatches and read that you had distinguished yourself most particularly at Waterloo, if memory serves correctly."

"I am more interested in discovering how well your memory serves a certain business transaction that occurred five years ago. I refer to a large investment you had in corn futures. You advised Mr. Charles Fleming through his daughter's husband, Valentine Merriem, to put virtually everything the family had in this particular stock."

As Will spoke, the color drained from Cumberland's face. "The risk was high, but the potential profits great," Cumberland said. "A pity that the strategy failed."

"You sold all your stock only days after Charles Fleming and Valentine Merriem had bought stock at a premium price. Since you owned a majority of shares, cleverly held in a company name other than your own, panic ensued and the price of the stock dropped steeply, becoming as good as worthless. Am I not correct?"

"I do not know how you have come by this information," Cumberland said coolly, "but I cannot see why you have any interest in the incident. Things like this happen all the time. I did nothing illegal."

"That is a matter of interpretation, Mr. Cumberland. The fact is that your actions caused Charles Fleming to lose nearly everything. What I find particularly interesting is that you were then willing to jump in and immediately buy

Broadhurst Hall and most of its holdings for well unde
market price so that Fleming would not be left completel
destitute."

"I thought it only the right thing to do," Cumberlan
said, lowering himself into a chair.

"I suppose you also thought that taking your revenge o
the family in such a shoddy manner was also the right thin
to do."

"My—my revenge?" He reddened. "Lord William, yo
overstep yourself. I do not know what sort of foolish sce
nario you and Lady Samantha have concocted between your
selves, but I assure you that I am nothing more than .
businessman who sold shares in a stock when it appeare
as if it might become unreliable. I then did what I could t
make reparation to Mr. Fleming, who had not had the fore
sight to do the same."

"I've never heard such claptrap," Samantha said, wavin
her hand in dismissal. "You never forgave dear Louisa Mer
riem for rejecting your suit in favor of Valentine Merriem
and don't you try to tell me anything else, for Louisa con
fided in me. She told me just how enraged you were an
how you swore to make both her and Valentine sorry."

Will's gaze sharpened. He hadn't realized that David Cum
berland had been stupid enough to actually threaten Louisa
and he was infuriated. "So," he said, making an enormou
effort to keep his anger in check, "your having made you
intentions clear does simplify matters."

"I did no such thing," Cumberland protested, his fac
turning even more crimson. "I behaved like a perfec
gentleman."

"I was not aware that perfect gentlemen set out to ruin
the families of women who spurned their attentions," Wil

said, his voice icy. "I shall make a point of asking my acquaintances about it."

"What—what do you mean?" Cumberland asked, his fingers gripping the arms of the chair in which he sat, his knuckles turning white.

"I mean, Mr. Cumberland, that although you might not have strictly broken the laws of trading, you broke the most basic laws of decent behavior. I doubt very much that you will be able to hold your head up in society should Lady Samantha and I decide to inform the polite world of your dishonorable actions and the reason behind them."

"No one will believe a word of this absurd story," Cumberland said, beads of sweat shining on his brow. He licked his lips, then pretended a large yawn. "This conversation becomes tedious. I suggest you choose someone else to bore with your fantasies."

Lady Samantha thoughtfully tapped one finger against her cheek. "I have often thought how fortunate I am to be so well connected. I do enjoy having the ear of the entire *ton*. Oh, and Mr. Cumberland, did you know that Lord William's brother is gravely ill?" She shook her head sadly. "He is not expected to live much longer, although one can only pray for a miraculous recovery. Since that seems unlikely, Lord William will have to step into his brother's shoes. You know how the *ton* reveres its marquesses."

David Cumberland looked back and forth between them. "Do you think to threaten me?" he said, his voice indignant but his eyes reflecting his panic. Will had seen that look a hundred times before on the field of battle.

"How astute of you, Mr. Cumberland," Will said smoothly. "That is our intention exactly. On the other hand, should you decide to correct the wrong you have done and hand over the deed to Broadhurst here and now, as well as restore every last penny that Charles Fleming and Valentine Merriem lost, Lady Samantha and I can safely promise you that society will never be the wiser."

"This is—this is blackmail!" Cumberland cried. "I should call for the bailiff and have you brought up on charges!"

"Dear me," Lady Samantha said. "You are even more of a paperskull than I'd previously thought. You do not seem to realize the seriousness of your predicament, Mr. Cumberland. I've always known that you had social aspirations far beyond your station and were greedy to boot, but I never believed you to be entirely stupid."

She pushed herself to her feet. "Very well, have it your own way. You shall soon find that every door you have worked so hard to open will be shut to you and your name will be wagging on every blue-blooded tongue, but not in the way you had hoped." She beckoned to Will. "Let us take our leave, Lord William. This man will simply not save himself from social ruin."

Will straightened. "I regret to say that I agree with you. Such a pity, for one always wishes in hindsight that one's vision had been more astute."

"No—no, wait," Cumberland said, jumping to his feet. "Although I admit no culpability in Mr. Fleming's misfortunes, I naturally do not wish him or his family to suffer any further. I was not aware that the situation was so dire, and if I can help by returning Broadhurst Hall and its land to them, naturally I will."

"How generous of you," Will murmured, disgust for the man bitter in his mouth. "Then there is the small matter of restoring the family fortune. My understanding is that your pockets are deep enough that you will not suffer unduly."

"I—I can perhaps see my way to giving them a thousand pounds," Cumberland said, looking as if Will was pulling his fingernails out one by one.

"I think not. The entire sum, Mr. Cumberland, which I believe was in the region of one hundred twenty-five thousand. Would that be correct, Lady Samantha?"

"One hundred and seventy-five thousand if you include Valentine Merriem's use of his wife's dowry. I have the papers right here in my reticule."

"But—but you cannot be serious!" Cumberland said in a choked voice. "That is a fortune!"

"And that is my point," Will replied. "It is a fortune that you caused to disappear. My suggestion is that you make it reappear again and within a fortnight, by which time you will have vacated Broadhurst Hall. My information tells me that you have another two hundred thousand pounds again in investments, so you won't be left penniless by any means." He shrugged. "Your choice, Mr. Cumberland—you can choose social ruin, or for the first time in your miserable life you can choose to act in an honorable manner and save your sorry face and name."

Cumberland's shoulders slumped in defeat. "Very well," he mumbled. "I will do as you ask."

"I'd like the deed now, if you please, signed over to Charles Fleming, as well as a promissory note that guarantees the one hundred and seventy-five thousand—consider yourself fortunate that I do not ask for five years of interest on top of that."

Cumberland moved slowly to his desk and, taking a key from his pocket, opened the bottom drawer and pulled out a document. He wrote on it with a shaking hand, blotted the ink, then shoved it across the desk. "There. You have what you want. Now go."

"Not before you produce the promissory note," Will said. "I'll tell you precisely how to word it."

Cumberland pulled out a piece of paper from the front drawer, the muscle in one cheek twitching. "Proceed, Lord William, and damn you to hell."

"I've already been there and back. I have no intention of returning," Will said, starting to dictate. When Cumberland had finished, Will pulled the document over to his side of the desk. "Lady Samantha, would you be so kind as to act as witness?"

"With pleasure," she said, taking the pen from his hand and signing with a large flourish.

"Our business is concluded, Mr. Cumberland," she said, handing the pen back. "I am delighted that in the end you managed to see reason. There is one last item of business, however: I must insist that you never mention to anyone how this transaction came to pass. We would all be best served by letting the world believe that you behaved in this fine manner because you possessed a conscience."

Cumberland glared at her. "As I said, I want only to see to the welfare of those who suffered from a bad financial loss. Is that all?"

"That is all." Will picked up the documents and deposited them in the safety of the pocket of his inner coat. "Good day, Mr. Cumberland. We shall see ourselves out. Do not forget—you have a fortnight to vacate the premises, and you will leave everything—*everything*—as you found it."

Cumberland walked to the window and stared out, his shoulders stiff. "I want nothing from this place. I suddenly find that it fills me with distaste."

"How convenient for us all, but should I learn anything to the contrary, you will regret crossing me. I am more than capable of making your life acutely difficult."

"Go. Everything will be as you wish." David Cumberland abruptly turned, his face a picture of rage. "You might both think yourselves paragons of virtue, but I will find something to bring you to your knees, depend on it."

Lady Samantha burst into peals of laughter. "Oh, my dear misguided man, you will not only find nothing, but you will also make a greater fool of yourself than you already have. Your only hope is to retire quietly somewhere and live off the fortune—the now much smaller fortune—that you have made for yourself." She tucked her hand into Will's arm.

"Despite your best efforts, you never have made much of an impression on the *ton*," she continued, "and you must know that we tend to detest those who reach above their grasp, no matter their financial gains. True gentlemen, however, are excluded from that censure."

Cumberland bared his teeth. "You have taken your pound of flesh," he said in a low, vicious voice. "Leave or I'll have my servants eject you from the premises—they are still mine for the next fortnight."

"Take care the premises remain intact," Will said. "I advise you to behave with caution, no matter the violence of your feelings. I meant what I said, Cumberland. Any act on your part against the welfare of this family and I will put the full power of my influence toward bringing you to justice as well as exposing you for the dishonorable cad that you are."

He didn't wait for a reply, leading Lady Samantha from the room. As they crossed the hall the sound of glass crashing on the floor came from inside the drawing room.

"A vase, no doubt," Samantha said without pausing. "I would say that expresses the violence of Mr. Cumberland's feelings nicely."

Will grinned. "I have to agree. I only hope that Mr. Cumberland follows my directive and leaves it at that."

"I believe he realizes he has no choice. A job well done William. You managed an imperious attitude with no trouble at all."

Helping Lady Samantha into the carriage, Will joined her and settled back against the red velvet squabs. "How do you wish to proceed from here?" he asked as the carriage started back to the Hart and Hound. "You surely see that I cannot go to Louisa or Charles Fleming with these papers without giving myself away."

"Certainly not. I will take them and say merely that on my last visit I was alarmed to find them in such a sorry state and did some looking into the matter with this result. The part you played remains between us."

She reached out her hand for the documents and Will pulled them from his coat and gave them to her. "Lady Samantha . . . I think I should tell you that I plan to marry Louisa if she'll have me."

"As I expected. When?"

"I thought that over on the way here. I must go immediately to Rupert, and if he is truly on his deathbed, then I shall have a great deal on my hands. I can obviously do nothing about marrying Louisa for the three months of necessary mourning, but after that time, I'd like you to bring Louisa to me."

"Bring Louisa to you? By all means, but what do you wish me to tell her? She might find such a suggestion odd if she has no idea why she is invited to pay a visit to the Marquess of Alconleigh. Do you not intend to reveal yourself before that time?"

He sighed heavily. "No. How can I? I don't have any idea what she'll do when she does learns the truth—for all know she might very well turn her back on me for all time, but that is a risk I must take."

"If she loves you, she will understand."

"That is easy for you to say," he replied dryly. "You know the situation and the reasons for my deception. Louisa does not, and it's going to take a great deal of explaining. She does not appreciate dishonesty in any form—I had the devil of a time bringing her around when she inadvertently discovered I'd been a major in the army, although she still isn't aware that I was in the King's Dragoons and knew Valentine well."

"Dear me. Yes, I can see that you have an enormous problem on your hands. Never mind, William." She patted his arm. "You'll find a way. In the meantime, write to me at Broadhurst and keep me informed. I see no difficulty in Louisa's knowing that I am receiving letters from the Marquess of Alconleigh, for that is most likely what you'll be, given your brother's condition at the moment."

"Tell me, Lady Samantha," Will said, drawing in a deep breath and releasing it. "What did Rupert say when he asked you to send me to him? Did he mention anything of the past?"

"Only that he had serious regrets about what passed between the two of you before you left for the army and wished very much for your forgiveness before he died."

Will rubbed the bridge of his nose, his heart squeezing painfully in his chest. "He wishes for my forgiveness," he said in a flat voice. So his brother had finally developed a conscience. "He told you nothing more?"

"Nothing." She fixed him with a piercing gaze. "William, what really did happen? I heard that the Potter girl had drowned herself when she found herself pregnant with your child and you refused to marry her. I also heard that you saw her go into the river and did not lift a finger to save her. As I told you, I never believed a word of it, but if your brother wants your forgiveness, that can only mean he lied about your part in her death."

Will squeezed his eyes shut for a brief moment. "I suppose you have a right to know, given all you have done to help me," he said reluctantly. Talking about Mary's death would force him to relive the agony, but he supposed that was something he'd have to do anyway with Rupert.

"You needn't tell me if you don't wish to," Lady Samantha said in a gentle voice that surprised Will. He'd never heard this tone from her before, accustomed as he was to her bark.

"I will tell you," he replied. "Perhaps talking about what happened will help me to put my thoughts in order." He ran his hands over his hair. "As you probably heard, Mary was the daughter of Alconleigh's blacksmith. We'd been friends since childhood, even though our stations were far apart."

With a breaking heart he thought of Pip and John Henry's friendship, as he had so many times. He and Mary had shared the same closeness, the same sort of adventures. "Mary grew into a beautiful young woman," he continued, "but I never was drawn to her in that respect. We loved each other as old friends do, but Rupert mistook the relationship, and his jealousy ate at him. He thought I possessed something he didn't have, and he was determined to take it away from me."

"I have always wondered," Samantha said, "if your brother's being born with a deformed foot didn't cause much of the trouble between you. He was always jealous of you, William, and determined to make your life difficult."

"Yes, I know," Will said with a heavy sadness. "Rupert

resented all the things I could do that he could not. He never ceased reminding me that he was the heir, and I could never convince him that I didn't care. In some ways that only seemed to exacerbate his enmity toward me."

"Yes, I see. He would have been so much happier if he'd felt that you did mind. At least that way he could have something to hold over your head."

Will nodded. "I've often thought that if our mother had lived, everything might have been different. As you know, she died when we were still so young, and my father didn't cope well with her death. Unfortunately for Rupert, I more closely resembled her than he did so my father favored me. I'm sure that only caused more bitterness on Rupert's part and he set out on a campaign to discredit me, using my aversion to hunting and shooting to try to convince my father I was a coward, not worthy of the family name."

"I remember," Samantha said. "You always had an entourage of animals about you. Your father was such a fine shot and he told me that he could not understand why you had no interest, especially when you had the ability while Rupert physically wasn't able to pursue blood sports—or sport of any kind."

"Exactly," Will replied, "which leads directly back to Mary Potter. I knew something terrible had happened to her, because one day the light went out of her eyes and she became quiet, withdrawn. She refused to speak of it, and I cannot help but believe that Rupert raped her, taking what he thought was mine."

"William—oh, my dear boy. How very dreadful . . ." Samantha's hand slipped to her cheek. "Are you saying you think Rupert fathered the child she carried?"

"I think he must have." Will shook his head. "Mary talked always about how much she wanted to fall in love and have a houseful of children. She wasn't the sort of girl who would have given herself to any man, not when she valued marriage so highly."

"Yes . . . and then one day your lovely friend Mary suddenly withdrew into herself and refused to tell you what had happened. You make sense, William, you do make sense. And the rest? The drowning?"

A cold shudder ran through Will's body as the memory of that dreadful day came back to him far too clearly. "Mary must have realized she was with child. The coroner had no doubt. I suppose she felt she would be disgraced, that her life was over, her dreams destroyed."

He pressed his hands against his thighs, his fingers tightening. "I—I remember riding down toward the river, something drawing me . . . a sense of uneasiness is the best way to describe the feeling. Then I saw Mary. She'd already walked into the water but was still in the calm part, before the current begins."

"Did you see Rupert anywhere near?" Samantha asked, covering one of his hands with her own, steadying him.

"Yes. Rupert stood on the bank above," he replied, his voice tight. "He said nothing, only watched. I called out to Mary, for she was wading out of the shallows toward the deeper water where the current picks up and becomes swift and dangerous." He swallowed hard. "She knew better. We both knew the river well. I shouted to her, but she paid no heed, even though I knew she heard me."

"What did you do then?" Samantha asked quietly.

"I . . . I jumped off my horse and ran as fast as I could, diving into the river," he said, the horror and sense of disbelief he'd felt replaying itself with sickening clarity. He'd never forgiven himself for not taking the chance and going into the deadly current, being much stronger than Mary.

He'd always wondered if that had not been a fatal mistake costing Mary her life.

"But you didn't manage to catch her," Samantha said.

"No. No, she was gone," he replied, his voice choked. "The current had already swept her away as if she were nothing more significant than a tree limb. I climbed out of the river and mounted my horse, riding furiously down the bank, hoping to pull her out to safety once she'd passed into calmer waters."

He paused, one hand covering his eyes. "I finally found her downstream about a mile away, tangled up in weeds next to the bridge. She was dead."

"William. How dreadful." Samantha grasped his hand tightly in hers. "But you did your best. You did everything you could."

He dropped his hand and stared out of the window. "I don't know. Had I been a minute or two earlier, perhaps I could have saved her, but I wasn't and I didn't. And then Rupert claimed that I hadn't even tried to save her, that he'd seen the entire thing and I'd deliberately let her drown."

"Could he not have mistaken what happened?"

"No. There was no mistake. Rupert told our father that he'd overheard Mary and me having a heated argument, that I refused to marry her, and that she threatened to kill herself if I didn't claim the child as my own. All lies, of course, but my father wasn't to know."

"So your father's solution was to send you off to war?"

"He thought me guilty of cowardice, as Rupert had planned. My father decided my joining the army would at last make a man of me. It's a long-standing family tradition for second sons, you know." Will laughed bitterly.

"Oh, William, I am so terribly sorry. But why did you not come to your own defense?"

"I did proclaim my innocence initially, but my father believed Rupert. I couldn't bring myself to persist in accusing Rupert of the dastardly deeds, partly because Rupert was my father's heir, and also because Father's health was precarious and he could not have withstood the shock of learning Rupert's true nature."

"You were wrong to assume the blame for your brother's actions," Samantha said bluntly.

"Yes," Will said just as bluntly. "I believe I was, but I was young and idealistic and believed I was doing the right thing. I will say this. If there is any sort of divine plan, then my actions brought me to Louisa and for that I cannot be sorry."

"No. You have made your point, William, and I shall make sure that your sacrifice has not been in vain. We arrive now, and you must take your horse and return to Broadhurst. Know that I will look after Louisa and her family until such time as you send word for her."

"I thank you, Lady Samantha. I know that I leave them in the best of hands."

He waited for the footman to open the carriage door, then turned to her and picked up her hand, dropping a kiss on it. "Until Alconleigh," he said.

"Until Alconleigh," she replied as he climbed out. "I will wait here for another hour before arriving at Broadhurst Farm so that Louisa can make no possible connection between us and her sudden good fortune, but do not leave until she has a chance to tell you of it herself. That will make your departure much easier and your conscience can be clear."

Will smiled grimly. "As you say, Lady Samantha, although my conscience won't be clear until I am finally able to tell Louisa the truth."

He turned and started to walk toward the stables, where he'd left Maestro.

"Don't forget to write," Samantha called.

Will raised his arm over his head in acknowledgment, barely hearing her. He really didn't know how he was going to get through the next few hours.

19

"*You*—you did what?" Louisa stared in disbelief at Lady Samantha, unable to believe her ears. She looked over at her father, who appeared equally dumbfounded.

"As I said. I convinced Mr. Cumberland that his own best interests would be served by returning all of your holdings as well as the full sum of the investment he caused you to lose."

"But—but *how*?" Louisa had an absurd impulse to pinch herself to make sure she wasn't dreaming.

"I simply pointed out that I would destroy his name and reputation if he didn't agree." Samantha shrugged. "He wasn't pleased, but he did see reason. So you see, all that remains to be done is to organize your removal back to the Hall."

"Just a moment, Samantha," Charles Fleming said, clearing his throat. "How did you even know that our circumstances were so badly compromised? Louisa assured me that she made every effort to keep them from you when last you were here."

"I have eyes in my head, Charles, and am not easily fooled. Louisa did her best to pull the wool over my eyes, but I saw past it with no trouble." She chuckled. "Your supposed footman, for example, was a dead giveaway—anyone could see he'd never served at table before."

Louisa blushed with embarrassment. "Oh, I should have known better than to try to pass Mr. Cutter off as a footman, but the truth is that he is our man-of-all-work. I just didn't want you to worry about us, Lady Samantha."

"I understand, my dear child. Never you mind, for all's well that ends well, and I consider this a very fine ending indeed. You can now resume your life as it was meant to be. Naturally I shall stay on for a time to see that all goes smoothly."

"That is very kind, but entirely unnecessary," Louisa said quickly. "We do not wish to impose on you any further."

"Nonsense. I insist, and in any case, if Mr. Cumberland knows I am here, he will not dare to cross me. I shall enjoy a nice respite in the country."

Louisa sighed, seeing that Lady Samantha was going to be immovable, and although the strain of keeping her occupied would take its toll, Louisa did have to admit that Lady Samantha was a master organizer. "If you'll excuse me, I must go tell Wi—er, Pip, that is. I must tell Pip the incredible news. She is laid up in bed with a hurt foot, and this will cheer her immensely."

"Go, child, go," Samantha said, waving her hand in dismissal. "I wish to speak to your father privately."

Louisa looked uncertainly at her father, but he didn't appear at all dismayed by the prospect of being left alone in Lady Samantha's company. He smiled at her, then turned his attention to Samantha, who had already launched back into conversation.

Hurrying from the room, she dashed up the stairs, hoping Will had returned from Maidencombe by now and would be with Pip, for she wanted to tell them together.

Her wish was rewarded, for she heard Will's voice coming from inside Pip's room.

"Do not worry, little one," he was saying. "You and your mama will manage perfectly well without me, I promise you that."

Louisa halted abruptly, the blood draining from her face.

"But Mr. Cutter, will you ever come back?" Pip asked in a small voice.

"I don't know, sweeting, I don't know what is going to happen now, only that I must go."

All the elation that had filled Louisa only a moment before vanished, replaced by panic. Will was *leaving*? That couldn't be. He wouldn't do that—he loved her. Only last night he'd told her so. She must have misunderstood. Surely she'd misunderstood.

She forced herself into the room, steadying herself with one hand on the side of the door, her knees weak with shock. "Will?" she said, trying to sound calm in front of Pip. "What is this? You are leaving?"

He turned his head in surprise, then slowly stood, his expression bleak. "I was going to find you and tell you myself. I've just had news, Louisa, bad news."

"Wh-what sort of bad news?" she asked, her heart in her throat. Will couldn't leave, he couldn't. They'd only just found each other. Her life would be so empty without him.

"It's family trouble," he said, walking over to her and taking both her hands in his. "I received a letter today."

Her head was spinning.

"It's about my brother. He's ill, very ill. He might well be dying."

"Oh, Will . . . I'm so sorry," she said, sudden tears stinging at her eyes, although she didn't know whether they were for him or for herself. "Of course you must go to him. I—I know how much you have suffered over the rift between you."

"Thank you," he said, squeezing her hands hard. "You will understand then why I must make haste. Norfolk is a good distance and I cannot afford to delay."

"No . . ." she said, the single word of acceptance tearing

her heart to shreds. "Don't worry about us—we shall be fine. I have . . . I have just had the most amazing news. We are to return to Broadhurst Hall. David Cumberland is giving it back to us along with our fortune."

"Really! That's the most wonderful news you could have told me," Will said. "But how did it happen?"

"Lady Samantha Davenport came just an hour ago to tell us—she found out that David Cumberland had manipulated the stock, and faced him with his crime. In order to keep from being ostracized by society he agreed to return everything to us."

"I like your Lady Samantha. She obviously has your best interests at heart. I'm relieved, for I can go with an easier heart—I worried about how you would get on."

"We will manage beautifully, really we will." She looked down at the ground as her tears spilled over, and hastily wiped at her cheeks, not wanting him to see her distress when he had enough of his own to bear.

"Let me just say a final farewell to Pip, and then we'll speak alone." He walked back to the bed where Pip lay, her face wet with her own tears.

"Good-bye, little sweetheart. Look after yourself and don't go jumping off any more haylofts."

"I won't, Mr. Cutter, I promise," Pip said on a sob. "I'll be very good. Please don't forget about us."

"Never. Never, Pip. I love you—always remember that."

"I will," she said, throwing her arms around his neck. "I love you too. Thank you for saving my life."

"Thank you for saving mine," he murmured, kissing her temple and stroking one hand over her hair. "You did, you know. You reminded me of what life was all about at a time when I'd nearly forgotten. I need you to be brave, Pip, and strong for your mama."

Pip nodded, then abruptly released him, lying back and turning her face into the pillow, her slight shoulders shaking with her sobs.

"Come, Louisa," he said, holding out his hand.

She put her hand into his, and she folded his fingers around it. He silently walked with her down the stairs, not saying a word until he stopped her on the outside steps.

Maestro waited, tied to the mounting post, filled saddlebags straddling his sides. She couldn't help but think of the day Will had first arrived, of how Maestro had stood just there as she had seen Will for the first time, her breath catching in her throat.

But she hadn't known him then, hadn't known how completely he would change her life and take possession of her heart. Now he was leaving, and she didn't know if she'd ever see him again.

She looked away, her throat tight with pain.

"Louisa," he said softly, taking her face between his warm hands. "Look at me."

She risked a glance up at him, his face blurred through her tears. Drawing in a deep breath that caught in her chest, she released it. "You must go."

"Yes, I must, but know that I love you. That will never change, no matter what else does." Stroking his thumbs back and forth over her cheeks, he looked long and hard into her eyes. "I honestly don't know what is going to happen, but if you have ever believed in anything, believe me when I tell you that you mean everything to me. I might not be able to be in touch for some time, but have faith, sweetheart. Have faith."

She nodded into the cup of his hands, tears streaming unbidden down her cheeks. "I love you, Will. I pray that Maestro carries you home safely and swiftly."

He smiled and drew her into his arms. "I never told you that my father gave Maestro to me when I went into the army," he murmured against her ear. "Maestro has carried me safely through many battles. He incurred that scar on his side saving my life. He won't fail me now."

She raised her head, trying to look brave, even as her heart broke. "Godspeed, Will Cutter," she whispered.

In answer he lowered his head and kissed her gently, his lips lingering on hers for a long moment. "God keep you safe and well until we meet again," he said, releasing her.

He walked swiftly down the steps and untied Maestro, mounting him in one easy movement. Kicking him into a canter, he started down the drive, his hand raised in farewell.

Louisa watched until he turned the corner and vanished, leaving only a cloud of dust behind. Only then did she sink to the steps, her face buried in her hands, weeping for the love she'd just lost.

Four days later Will arrived at Alconleigh, his clothes stained from travel, exhausted almost beyond endurance, as was Maestro. They'd stopped only for food and water, and the few short hours of necessary sleep they'd taken in fields along the way.

As he rode through the imposing Alconleigh gates and up the long drive that led to the even more imposing house, Will slowed Maestro, then pulled him to a halt, drinking in the sight.

Alconleigh. He hadn't laid eyes it for so very long. Odd, he considered, that the last ten years or so might never have been, for everything felt so deeply familiar, as if he might have left only yesterday and the intervening years had never happened.

Memories came flooding back unbidden—the time he'd found his little orphaned fox cub just over in the woods to the left, or the time that Mary had come running to him from the stables, a laugh on her lips, to tell him that the barn cat had just delivered seven kittens.

Such simple moments, and yet so many complicated, painful memories as well. His mother's death . . . his father coming to him in tears to tell him that she and the baby daughter she'd delivered were dead. He looked over at the chapel where they both were interred, where Rupert might soon by lying alongside them.

Will cleared his head, remembering his purpose, and urged Maestro forward toward the front of the house.

"Is—is that you, Lord William?" Gransby, the butler who had been with the family for as long as Will could remember, came rushing out of the house, his eyes practically popping out of his head. "Oh, my lord, this is a day, a fine day indeed!"

Will clasped the elderly man's shoulders hard. "Gransby. I am happy indeed to see you."

"And I you, my lord. I am only sorry that the circumstances under which you return are so painful. You do know that your brother is ill?"

"I know—Lady Samantha reached me with the news. Tell me," Will asked, praying hard that he hadn't been too late. "How does my brother fare?"

"Not well, my lord," Gransby replied with a mournful expression. "He has not long to live, I fear, but he will be so happy to see you. He has done nothing but ask for you this last fortnight."

"I am here now. Please, will you take me to him—and

sk someone to look after my horse? I have pushed Maestro
ard and he needs attention."

"Indeed, my lord." Gransby snapped his fingers and a
ootman instantly appeared. "See to Lord William's horse
nd make sure that the groom understands the animal needs
ery particular care," he commanded. "A warm blanket
vould not go amiss, nor a nice hot gruel."

"Thank you," Will said, relieved that at least Maestro was
n good hands. "Now to my brother. Tell me, Gransby, how
ritical is his health? Does he have decent doctors attend-
ng him?"

"He has," Gransby said, leading Will inside. "They hold
ut no hope, I am sorry to say, but have been attempting to
nake him as comfortable as possible."

Will stopped abruptly, absorbing the shock of being
ack inside the house in which he'd spent the first twenty
ears of his life. So much the same . . . nothing had changed,
ot really. If anything or anyone had changed, it was he.

He breathed in the heady scent of beeswax polish and a
ertain mustiness that had always permeated the place, but
n a pleasant way, the way only a house that had existed for
wo hundred years could smell. Glancing around, he took
n all the old family portraits, the suits of armor in the hall,
he tapestry chairs by the fireplace.

The only new addition was a portrait of Rupert that now
ung over the mantelpiece. Will moved closer and studied
t, trying to discern what he could from the expression cap-
ured on his twin's face.

The figure that stared back at him from the canvas looked
nuch older than Will remembered, indicating that the por-
rait had been painted relatively recently. A sardonic smile
urled Rupert's lips, but that didn't surprise him, since Ru-
ert had always possessed a certain arrogance. What shook

him were the eyes: they looked haunted, even distant, as if Rupert had been trying to avoid the painter's acute gaze.

So, he thought with great sadness. Rupert had never stopped running from himself. But that came as no surprise either. Samantha Davenport had indicated as much with her description of Rupert's debauchery. Now he was paying the price with his life.

Will turned and placed his hand on Gransby's shoulder. "Take me to my brother," he said.

"My lord," Gransby said with a slight bow. "He is in his bedroom. If you will follow me?"

Steeling himself, Will walked through Rupert's door. He'd seen more men close to death than he cared to remember, but nothing had prepared him for what he saw now.

Rupert lay in his bed, his face white as the sheets that covered him, his breathing heavily labored, his hands clutching the bedclothes as he struggled for air. His eyes were closed, the lids as thin as tissue paper, his dark lashes a terrible contrast to the pallor of his skin. Beneath the covers his body appeared wasted, the once vital form no more than a skeleton, the flesh wasted away.

Will exhaled sharply, determined not to let Rupert see his shock. He moved to the side of the bed and sat down, taking one of Rupert's cold hands in his own. "Rupert," he murmured. "It is Will. I'm here now. I'm home, Rupert."

Rupert's eyes fluttered open, and he gazed at Will as if he were seeing a ghost. "Will," he whispered, passing his tongue over his dry lips. "Is it really you, or am I dreaming again?"

"Not dreaming, Brother. Lady Samantha tracked me down and told me of your condition. I came immediately."

"Thank God," Rupert said, weakly gripping Will's hand. "I was so afraid . . . I thought I might never see you again, that I would die before I could tell you."

"Tell me what?" Will replied softly. "If you refer to what happened all those years ago, that is behind us now and I bear you no grudge."

"You always were the good twin, weren't you?" Rupert said with a tight cough, a touch of the old irony in his dark eyes. "I hated you for that. All that honor, that nobility—everyone loved you and despised me."

"No one despised you. No one despises you now, least of all myself. You are my brother and I will always love you."

"There's no point wasting your love on me. I'm done for, Will. My lungs are eaten away with this damned consumption."

"Hush," Will said, forcing back tears. "Save your strength."

"For what? Another day of pain and misery? I waited only until I could see you and beg your forgiveness so that I could die with a clean conscience, although that probably won't do me any good now. I'm bound for hell, Brother, which is precisely where I belong."

"I don't believe in hell," Will replied, his heart breaking for Rupert, for himself. Whatever their differences, whatever Rupert had done, he didn't deserve this.

"No, you wouldn't," Rupert murmured, then grimaced. "Would you hand me that glass of water on the bedside table? It contains my medicine."

Will reached for it, then supported his brother's head as he drank in deep gulps.

"Thank you," Rupert said as Will took the glass from his lips and lay his head back on the pillows. "So, how have the years treated you? You look well."

"Fighting a war was not what I might have chosen for

myself, but I survived it. Since then I've been working on a farm, helping the widow of a fellow officer."

"You'll have far more than a farm on your hands when I'm gone. I've made a mess of things, Brother, and you'll have the devil of a time sorting everything out."

"I'll manage." Will couldn't bring himself to speak platitudes, tell Rupert that he'd be around to sort things out for himself. His brother clearly had very little time left to him, and Rupert knew it. "Rest now. Let the medicine take effect."

"I have no time for rest. Don't you want to hear my confession, Brother dear? I would have thought you'd be anxious for it after all this time." He coughed again.

"As I said, that is behind us. There's no need for a confession."

"Yes—yes, there is, damn you!" Rupert said with surprising strength. "I cannot rest in any peace until I tell you . . . tell you what I did. I took that girl, Brother, took her against her will because I was jealous, and when she told me she was pregnant with my child that last day, I laughed in her face and said no one would believe her. She walked into the river in despair and I didn't lift a finger to stop her."

"I worked all that out for myself," Will replied quietly.

"Perhaps you did, but then I accused you of being the guilty party and a coward on top of it." Rupert's eyes burned into Will's. "Don't you understand, Brother, I did it all because I loathed you, because you were everything I wasn't and I wanted you to suffer. I convinced our father that the only hope for you was the army, and then I prayed for years that you'd be killed so that you would be out of my life once and for all. Do you forgive me for that as well?" He fixed Will with a challenging glare.

"I forgive you for all of it," Will said, meaning the words in every fiber of his being. "How could I not? You are my twin. We were conceived together, born together, raised together. You are bound to me not just by blood and loyalty, but by something deeper."

Rupert laughed faintly. "Damn you to hell. I'd feel much better if you'd stop being so blasted noble and take my head off for having made your life a living misery for as long as I can remember."

"Rupert." Will sighed heavily. "I won't tell you that I haven't carried my fair share of bitterness, but somehow over time that disappeared. I saw more men than I can count die alone and in agony, and life became incredibly precious to me. Why waste time being angry and resentful when there are so many better things to do?"

"Such as?" Rupert asked, his brow drawing down. "I do not understand you. I suppose I never really have."

"No, you haven't, but I cannot feel that is important. You are my only brother, Rupert, and I love you. I wish you had managed to find happiness in your life, but perhaps you will find it in heaven."

Rupert shook his head. "Heaven. The concept is entirely foreign to me. I imagine the only heaven that will be had is by the worms when they feast on my flesh."

Will couldn't help smiling. "You might be very surprised, but I see no point in trying to impose my point of view on you at this late date."

"No. You'd be wasting your breath." Rupert gripped Will's hand. "I—I am sorry, if that counts for anything."

"It counts for everything, and I imagine God will think so too. Your eyes grow heavy, so sleep. I'll sit here with you, never fear."

Rupert nodded, his eyes closing. "Believe me or not, I am truly glad you are home."

"So am I," Will said. "So am I."

The hours ticked by as Will sat in the chair by the bed. Unlike the time he'd spent keeping guard over Pip, he felt no sense of urgency or panic, only a deep sadness that Rupert's life was winding down to nothing.

If he wished anything, he wished that Rupert's life had been fuller, that he might have found peace and happiness, a woman to love, that he'd had children to dote on and give him completion and contentment. That was not to be. Not for Rupert, not now.

Will couldn't help thinking of Louisa and Pip. They had become his entire world, had given him a taste of what fulfillment could be. He could only pray that love would carry them through, that Louisa would not turn her back on him when she learned the truth.

Somewhere around two o'clock in the morning Rupert woke with a terrible fit of coughing, bright red blood dribbling from the corner of his mouth. Will cleaned it up and gave him some more of his medicine, then held him in his arms and rocked him as if he were a small child while he struggled for breath.

Eventually Rupert slept again. Will dozed on and off, knowing the end was very close now.

As dawn broke, Will woke suddenly, aware that he and his brother were no longer alone in the room. He sat upright, his hand reaching for Rupert's as two beings of light descended.

"It's time, Brother," he whispered.

Rupert's eyes opened and he stared up at the ceiling. "God's teeth, what are they?" he cried.

"Angels," Will said very gently. "They've come to take you home. Go with them, Rupert. Know I love you and will see you again."

Rupert's eyes opened wide. "I—I've never seen anything so beautiful . . ."

The breath left his body in a long sigh, and Will watched as his brother's soul rose into the angels' arms and vanished with them into the light.

"Go in peace," he said in a choked voice, his throat burning. "God keep you safe."

Leaning forward, he closed his brother's staring eyes, which still held wonder, then pressed his head into his hands and wept for all that might have been.

20

"The afternoon post is here, Mrs. Merriem," announced the butler, carrying a silver salver filled with letters into the drawing room.

"Thank you, Collier," Louisa said, although she had no interest in going through the pile. She'd given up all hope of hearing from Will. He'd said he might not be able to write for some time, but three *months*? No, she doubted she'd ever hear from Will again, and the thought only served to make her heavy heart ache all the more.

"You don't mind, my dear?" Without waiting for an answer, Lady Samantha jumped up as usual when the post came in and shuffled through the letters. "Ah," she said with satisfaction. "How lovely. Three for me."

Louisa looked over at her. "I suppose you have yet another letter from the Marquess of Alconleigh?" She was beginning to wonder if the marquess didn't have a *tendresse* for Lady Samantha. He wrote to her at least twice a week, and Samantha always wrote straight back.

"Naturally I have," Lady Samantha said, breaking the seal on the letter and scanning its contents, all the time making little hums of interest.

"I cannot see why the marquess feels he has to write to you quite so often," Charles Fleming said with barely concealed annoyance.

"I cannot see why he shouldn't write to me as often as he pleases," Samantha retorted tartly. "I have known him these last twenty-some years, after all, and we are good friends."

"You never mentioned him particularly when we were

London," Louisa said, digging for information. She had
wonderful feeling that her father had become extremely
ond of Samantha Davenport and she of him. However, Samantha had been surprisingly silent on the subject of the
marquess.

"Why should I? He was not in London during your Sea-
on and did not figure in your social calendar, my dear.
How very nice. He says he would like me to come for a visit
up at Alconleigh. Heavens! He also wants you to come
with me, Louisa." Lady Samantha peered at Louisa over her
lorgnette.

Louisa stared at Samantha. "What?" she said in astonishment. "Why in the name of heaven would he want me to
come along?"

"He has been following my news of you with great interest and thinks you might enjoy a change of scenery now
that the harvest is in. I think him most kind to offer the invitation." She sighed happily. "Alconleigh is most beautiful,
and now that I think of it, he is absolutely right. A change of
scenery would be good for you after all the hard work you
have done."

"But—but I couldn't . . ." Louisa stammered, taken aback.

"Why ever not, child? If you are concerned about your
reentrance into society after all this time, you are being
foolish. The marquess does not entertain lavishly. He has
been in mourning these last months and most likely wishes
for some quiet company."

"No. No, I simply cannot accept an invitation from a
complete stranger." Louisa didn't know why she felt so panicked, unless it was because she feared missing a letter from
Will in her absence. She dismissed that thought abruptly.
Will was no longer a consideration in her life.

"But he's not a complete stranger, Louisa. He is my friend,

and will soon enough be your friend if you would give him half a chance. Really, my girl, anyone would think you were skittish."

"I'm not skittish," Louisa protested. "I—I'm trying to be responsible. I can't just leave Pip and Papa and go off to . . to wherever."

"Norfolk. Alconleigh is not so far from Norwich, a lovely town with an impressive cathedral that you really must see."

Louisa's head shot up. Norfolk? Will lived in Norfolk, or at least his family did.

"If you're worried about me, Mama, you needn't be." Pip spoke up from the corner of the room where she'd been bent over her sketch pad. "Grandpapa and I will be perfectly fine on our own, and Lady Samantha is right. You should have a holiday."

"I don't need a holiday," Louisa protested. In truth, she didn't know what good a holiday would do her. She'd be just as miserable as she was now.

"You do, my dear daughter," her father said, putting down his book and walking over to her, resting his hand on her shoulder. "As reluctant as you are to admit it, you are tired. And as reluctant as I am to see you and Lady Samantha depart, and I shall miss you both, I think you should go."

"Shall you miss me, Charles?" Lady Samantha patted her bosom. "Goodness, I believe I have gone breathless."

He scowled at her. "I do not know what business you have with the marquess, and I do not care to know unless you have made your mind up to marry the man."

"*Marry* him?" Samantha burst into peals of laughter. "My dear Charles, the thought of marriage never crossed my mind. I thought I made my position clear. The marquess is a close friend."

"Good," Charles said gruffly. "In that case, you must come back to Broadhurst when you are done with your visit."

To Louisa's astonishment, Samantha blushed to the roots of her hair. "Why, Charles," she said with a remarkably girlish smile, "how very generous of you, when I've already taken such advantage of your hospitality."

"Never mind my hospitality, Samantha. I do not look forward to the coming winter months, and I would be happy for your company."

"Then how can I possibly refuse? Besides, there's still so much that needs to be done with the Hall, now that the farm is running smoothly." She turned to Louisa. "What about it, my girl? Will you come with me? The journey is so tedious on one's own and you would be a comfort to me. Besides, you've been looking peaked recently."

"I—I don't know," Louisa said in an agony of confusion. "I have to think about it."

Pip jumped up. "I'll help you think, Mama. Let's take a walk, and you can think aloud. I'll fetch your cloak."

Feeling that she had no choice, Louisa nodded. "Very well, Pip. A walk would be nice."

They set off down the lane toward the south fields, the farm where they'd lived until so recently only a small patch in the distance.

"Look, Mama, doesn't the farmhouse make a cozy picture with the smoke curling up from the chimneys? I'm so happy that John Henry lives there now with his family. His father is very pleased that you turned it over to him." She took hold of her mother's hand. "He's a very clever farmer, isn't he?"

"Very clever," Louisa said, but all she could think of was the time she'd spent there with Will. If she could wish those days back, she would, even if they meant a return to poverty.

"Mama, I know you've been unhappy since Mr. Cutter left and that you haven't wanted to talk about it, but I do believe he still loves us and thinks of us all the time, even if he hasn't written."

Louisa looked down at her daughter. "Sometimes I think you see far too much, my sweet."

"Not really. I know you were happy together. I even hoped you might marry." She shot Louisa a quick smile. "I know you are always telling me that I am precocious, but I am not blind. He'll write, Mama, I know he will when he can, and we can't guess at what has happened."

"No. No, we can't," Louisa said with a heavy sigh. "I confess, Pip, I do miss him. I miss him terribly at times." She blinked back the sting of tears.

"So do I. He's the nicest man I've ever known, and the kindest."

"Yes, he is," Louisa said, her voice choked. "But I think it would be wisest for us both not to expect anything. He has his own life to lead and I doubt we have any part to play in that any longer."

"I think you should have more faith, Mama. I also think you should go to Norfolk with Lady Samantha. If Mr. Cutter should come back while you're away, I will write to you and you can come back straightaway."

Louisa's heart tugged hard in her chest. "I love you, my Pip."

"I love you too, Mama," she replied with a squeeze of her hand. "Look—there's John Henry. Do you mind if I go?"

"Go, sweetheart. I'll be fine."

Pip looked at her hard and then, apparently satisfied with what she saw, she released Louisa's hand and dashed off.

Louisa watched her as she ran down the lane and across the grass toward John Henry, braids flying. She looked as free as a bird and Louisa was glad for it. She couldn't remember the last time she'd felt that free—or perhaps she could. When Will had last held her in his arms, holding her safe and tight against the night, against all fear, all worry.

Choking back a sob, she forced her feet forward and continued on her path, trying to put her scrambled thoughts in order with little success. She couldn't carry on like this, she really couldn't, but she just didn't see how going to Norfolk would change anything. Will might be there, but Norfolk was a large county and she had little hope of finding him there, even if she knew where to begin. He'd told her almost nothing, save that he lived in a small town. There were more small towns in Norfolk than she could count.

Even if she was able to track him down, she had no way of knowing if he'd be happy to see her.

Lost in thought, Louisa nearly plowed over an elderly man who had stopped in the middle of the lane, apparently admiring the view over the valley.

She stopped just short of knocking him down. "Oh," she said, startled. "I beg your pardon. I didn't see you."

"It is of no import," he said, steadying himself with his cane. "I cannot complain if a very attractive young woman wishes to mow me down. Indeed, I should count myself lucky." He chortled. "At this time of my life, I am fortunate to attract any attention at all. Perhaps I should stand in the middle of the road more often."

Louisa smiled at him, instantly at ease. "I wouldn't recommend such a practice. A thoughtless woman is one thing, but a carriage going at a fast clip is another."

"True, true," he said. "But I suppose one might take one's chances, don't you agree? One never knows what life might bring one. Just now it's brought you to me for a moment and I consider myself fortunate for this brief but delightful encounter."

"Oh. How nice of you to say so . . ."

Flustered by the elderly man's courteous but rather gallant statement, Louisa colored. He was a fine-looking gentleman, his clothes slightly shabby and outdated, but it was his face that drew her interest. His eyes were light blue and clear as a fine summer's day, and they held a wonderful twinkle as if he knew all the secrets on earth and possibly in heaven too.

"Do I know you?" she asked, for he had a vaguely familiar look about him, although she couldn't place it.

"Very possibly, my dear, but it's always hard to say, isn't it? Allow me to present myself." He doffed his hat, exposing a full head of white hair, and bowed from his waist. "Raphael, Mr. Raphael."

"I am Louisa Merriem," she said, making a small curtsy. Oh, she *did* like him. She felt as if he might have been the grandfather she'd never known, white whiskers and all. "Are you visiting Devon?"

"In a manner of speaking. I have interests in these parts but come only when I am needed."

"What sorts of interests would those be?" she asked, her curiosity piqued.

"I am in the business of futures. Investments, you know."

"Yes, I do know," Louisa said, hoping that he knew what he was doing, for she knew full well what could happen when one invested impetuously.

"Hmm, I wonder. Tell me, my dear, what brings you down this particular road looking so sad, with tears in your eyes no less. Have you lost a dog, perhaps?"

Louisa shook her head. "Only a dream."

"Only a dream? Oh, dear. That does sound serious. What sort of dream was it?"

"The unattainable sort. I—I thought I held it between my hands, but it vanished." She couldn't imagine what made her speak so freely to a stranger, but in a way she was relieved to be able to put her feelings into words.

"Ah. A vanished dream. That is difficult. Of course, dreams are only dreams. It's what you make of reality that is important." He leaned both hands on his cane and gazed up at the sky. "I have always believed that one must take one's destiny into one's own hands. *Carpe diem* and all that. Life is not just a series of coincidences, but must be taken as a whole, for surely that is what God intends, that we guide our own destiny with a little help from Him."

Louisa squeezed her eyes shut for a brief moment as she heard an echo of Will's voice from what seemed like a lifetime ago.

What sense is there in living a life that is nothing but a series of blind coincidences while we wait for our heavenly reward, when God might very well have given us the gift of making and rectifying mistakes so that we can learn from our humanity?

She shivered. "Yes. Yes, of course," she said. "The problem is that I don't know how to do that."

"Oh, that part is not so difficult. All you have to do is ask for God's help. The rest follows as night follows day. A little courage goes a long way, my dear child." He tilted his head and regarded her. "For you, I believe, the hardest part is relinquishing your pride. You don't like to ask for things, am I correct?"

Louisa couldn't help laughing. "You are so very correct," she said, "although how you fathomed so much in so short a space of time is beyond me."

"As I said, I am in the business of investments. One has

to have keen instincts if one is to succeed." He chuckled "Never mind, Louisa, for all you need to realize your dream is to look to the future and invest yourself in it. Looking back will do you no good at all. I must leave you now, and you must move forward. Good-bye, my dear."

"Good-bye, Mr. Raphael," she said, sorry that their conversation had been so brief. "Good luck in your investments."

"Thank you, although I have great faith in them, as I have in yours. Do not look back, Louisa. Do not look back."

He set off past her, tipping his hat once again as he went. Louisa resumed walking, wondering at their strange encounter but oddly enough, feeling much lighter of heart for it. She abruptly stopped and turned, wanting to thank him.

As she looked down the long stretch of lane, she saw nothing but empty road and trees gently swaying in the light breeze.

Mr. Raphael had vanished as if he'd never existed.

Louisa drew in a long breath of amazement, then threw her head back and crowded with laughter. If she wasn't very much mistaken, she'd finally been visited by an angel of her own, although he hadn't been anything like the angels that Pip or Will had described.

She promptly turned around and headed straight back toward Broadhurst Hall, her mind made up. She would go to Alconleigh with Lady Samantha and see what the future held. Who was she to argue with an angel?

Picking Samantha Davenport's letter out of his correspondence, Will opened it with shaking fingers. He'd been waiting in an agony of anticipation to see whether Louisa would accept the invitation he'd offered forth, even though she had no way of knowing that it came from him. He quickly scanned the hastily written lines and breathed a huge sigh of relief, pressing the paper against his forehead with both hands.

Louisa was coming. She was actually coming. Somehow Samantha had convinced her and they'd be here this very day, according to Samantha's calculations.

Will couldn't believe it. He hadn't expected Louisa to capitulate so quickly or easily, but Samantha had worked her magic and that was what he'd prayed for.

His life had been chaotic since Rupert's death as he'd tried to put to rights the complete disaster his twin had made of everything from the various estates to business affairs, but Samantha's constant letters telling him every detail of the happenings at Broadhurst had been his calm in the midst of the disorder, giving him enormous satisfaction, a feeling that he was missing nothing.

Odd, he thought, that it was Samantha who now gave him those details about life at Broadhurst that he'd once read in Louisa's letters with such avid interest, a calm amid the chaos of war. But in reading Samantha's letters, he knew the reality now, the people.

He knew all about Pip's uneventful recovery, the move up to the Hall, Charles Fleming's return to vitality, and the successful harvest. He also knew how unhappy Louisa had been, and for that he felt a huge responsibility. He could now only hope that she would hear him out and understand, find a way to forgive him, for he had been equally miserable without her, aching for her day and night. He'd worked out how he intended to approach her, but he still wasn't entirely prepared.

With a start, he realized that he was daydreaming. To-day . . . Louisa was coming today.

Leaping to his feet in alarm, he tried to work out what had to be done first. Rooms had to be readied. Louisa might be arriving at any moment. Flowers, he thought, dashing out the door. Lots of flowers, and fruit. Fruit would be good. . . .

21

"$\mathcal{M}$y dear Louisa, I cannot tell you how happy I am that you decided to come with me," Samantha said, turning to Louisa as the carriage barreled down the road toward Alconleigh. "I promise that you will simply adore the place."

"I trust you," Louisa said with a tired smile. "Are we very close now?"

"We'll be turning into the gates any moment. You must remember, the marquess is only just coming out of mourning."

"Yes, you've told me that several times." She rubbed a hand over her aching brow. "You said he is mourning for his brother?"

"Indeed. Such a sad story, really. Did I tell you they were twins?"

"No," Louisa replied, glancing over at Samantha with renewed interest. "Twins? How very much more difficult that must make his loss."

"Yes, although they were not identical—anything but. Their natures could not have been more disparate. Indeed, an animosity existed between them, entirely created by the elder brother, who envied his younger, more attractive and accomplished twin." She fluttered her fan. "Perhaps I should tell you the sad story so that you are better prepared. My dear, it is so tragic, my heart could break. This is what happened . . ."

By the time Samantha had finished relating the sorry tale, Louisa wanted to cry. No matter who this marquess was, he surely had never deserved such terrible treatment at the hands of his own family. That by a trick of fate he happened to have inherited his brother's title seemed to be a bit of redemption, but really—to be accused of cowardice when the opposite was the truth, and then to be forced to join the army when he abhorred killing, that was truly horrible.

She decided to like the poor marquess whatever sort of man he was, for no one should have suffered such unfairness.

"Look, Louisa. We approach."

Pulled from her thoughts, Louisa gazed out of the window and beheld the most magnificent house she'd ever seen. Huge, stretching over at least an acre of land, Alconleigh possessed the parkland surrounding it rather than the other way around. She gasped, trying to take it all in. The great gray stone expanse stretched forever, three full stories of long windows reflecting the lowering sun. The front boasted a massive portico and endless steps leading up to the front door.

"Shall we?" Samantha said as the footman, clad in red and gold livery, lowered the steps of the carriage. "Really, Louisa, there's no need to look as if you were walking into the lion's den. I am certain that you and the marquess will get along perfectly. You will find that you have a great deal in common."

Louisa wasn't so sure, but she obediently followed Samantha out of the carriage and walked up the steps, her heart in her throat, her nerves in shreds. She'd never in her life been to such a grand place, and she hoped she wouldn't disgrace herself in any fashion.

"Wait here," Samantha commanded as they walked into the vast entrance hall. "I would like to speak privately to the marquess before I introduce you."

Louisa just nodded, then sat down in one of the chairs

near the huge fireplace, tightly twining her fingers together as Samantha disappeared behind one of the doors that led off the hall.

Only a few moments later she returned, smiling. "He would like to see you now, Louisa. Just go through that door there." She pointed in the direction she'd just come from.

"He wants to see me? Alone?" Louisa's mouth went dry, and her heart started to pound in panic. "But why? Surely he would like you to introduce me to him?"

"No, he feels no need for such formality. You must stop being so skittish, my girl. He's a perfectly nice man." Samantha adjusted her hat and pulled an errant feather into place. "He feels as if he already knows you well. Go, Louisa, go," she said, practically pulling Louisa to her feet. "I am sure he does not like to be kept waiting."

Louisa stumbled across the massive hall, wishing in that moment that she'd never left the safety of Broadhurst; she hadn't been out in society for so long that she barely remembered all of the niceties.

A footman opened the door for her with a bow, and she stepped into the room, her body trembling. After the darkness of the hall, her eyes took a moment to adjust to the brightness of the sun streaming through the windows.

A tall, well-built man stood with his back to one of them, then moved forward.

"Louisa," he said quietly. "I cannot tell you how happy I am that you have come."

Her eyes opened wide with shock. Will. It was Will, standing only a few paces away from her. Her mouth opened in disbelief. She looked around the room for the marquess, but they were alone.

"Will?" she whispered, thinking she must be dreaming.

Her heart started to pound erratically. "What—what are you doing here?" she asked, trying to make sense out of the senseless.

He smiled. "I live here. This is my home."

"But—but it *can't* be," she protested. "This is the home of the Marquess of Alconleigh. Do you . . . do you work for him now?" she asked, sure that had to be the answer. "Why didn't you write to let me know? I wouldn't have minded that you'd gone to take on a better position." Her head spun with confusion. "But you told me that you went to look after your brother . . ."

"I did," he said, walking up to her and picking up both her hands in his. "Louisa, my love, do you not see the truth even now?"

"Wh-what truth?" she stammered, undone by his touch after so long, after thinking she'd never feel it again. Oh, he felt so good . . .

"My dear, sweet love, I *am* the Marquess of Alconleigh. My brother died shortly after I arrived, and I have inherited the title."

Louisa stared at him, then abruptly detached her hands from his and took a quick step backward. "No," she whispered. "No, this isn't possible."

If she'd been shocked a moment before, that was nothing compared to the shock she felt now. Will was just Will, plain Will Cutter, man-of-all-work. Surely he was. He was playing a trick on her, that had to be it.

"I'm so sorry, Louisa. I wish I could have told you the truth of the matter long ago, but I just couldn't find a way, not without creating all sorts of complications that you weren't ready for."

She looked him up and down, took in his fine clothing, his bearing, and as she did, she saw something ineffably different about him, about his demeanor, the authority with which he spoke.

Turning her back abruptly, she covered her face with her hands, knowing that he spoke the truth and feeling utterly betrayed. "I can't believe you deceived me," she said, her voice hoarse, her heart breaking all over again.

He rested his hands on her shoulders and gently turned her to face him, lifting her chin in his hand so that her eyes were forced to meet his. "I never meant to deceive you, please believe that. The day I arrived at Broadhurst Farm, I had an entirely different purpose in mind. When you mistook me for a man responding to your notice at the pub, I seized the opportunity and took the job."

"Why, Will, *why*?" she cried. "You could have told me the truth then and saved us both this pain."

"No. I couldn't have," he said gently, taking her hand and leading her to a chair, sitting her down. He pulled another up opposite and leaned forward, regarding her intently, his forearms resting on his knees.

"I had full intention of telling you the truth, but you'd already made the assumption that I'd come to work for you. Since I gathered you were in trouble, I thought I might be able to help you out."

"Why did you care at all? And why *did* you come? You said that you had a different purpose in mind." Her thoughts were so muddled that she couldn't sort out one from the other. She wanted to believe Will, wanted desperately for everything to be as it was, but that could never happen now. He was the Marquess of Alconleigh, and she had no place in his life. "I don't understand anything . . ."

He rose without a word and went to the mantelpiece, picking up a pile of letters tied with a ribbon. "This is your answer," he said, placing the bound letters in her hand.

She stared wordlessly down at them, recognizing her own writing, her body going cold. "These are the letters I wrote to Val," she finally said. "How . . . how do you come to have them?"

Will sat down again. "Louisa. Hear me out before you say anything."

She nodded, although she already had answered her own question. Will had to have been in the King's Dragoons, had to have known Val if he had Val's letters. She wanted to die, remembering all the things she had confided in Will, her innermost secrets about her marriage, her antipathy toward her husband—and Will had known Val all along and not said a word. She looked away, her throat hot and dry.

"I met Val five years ago when he joined my regiment," Will said quietly. "We became friends, good friends. He was a fine soldier, Louisa, if that helps at all, brave and true." Will released a heavy breath. "I didn't know the truth about him."

"But—but the letters," she said. "How do you come to have the letters? Did you *read* them?" she demanded, horrified by the thought.

"Yes. Val shared them with me, and I read each one as if it were a lifeline to sanity. In the process I felt as if I had come to know you, to know your family. I think I fell a little in love with you at the time." He smiled softly. "You were my angel, Louisa, my link to the world I'd left behind, and you wrote so beautifully, painted such evocative pictures, that I came to feel as if Broadhurst were home and everyone who lived there my family. Pip became like a surrogate daughter to me, and I looked eagerly forward to each detail of her progress, each new adventure."

Louisa looked back at him, but no words came. She didn't know whether to be flattered by his interest or infuriated that a complete stranger had violated her privacy. "So you came to Broadhurst to insinuate yourself into our lives under false pretenses?" she finally said, burning with outrage.

"No, I came to Broadhurst only to return your letters to you," Will said, leaning forward. "Everything changed the moment I saw you. It's true that I wanted—that I wanted so much to have a small taste of Broadhurst for myself, to make it a reality instead of a dream after the nightmare of the war. Can you understand that?"

"I don't know," she replied tightly. "I can understand a little of what you said, but I wish that you'd just been honest."

"And if I had been? Think, Louisa. Would you have given me the time of day?"

She paused, thinking. "No," she said. She had to be truthful, as reluctant as she felt, given all the lies he'd told her. "No, I wouldn't have. I imagine I would have shown you the door."

"My point exactly. I didn't expect to fall in love with you, sweetheart, I really didn't, but it happened, and then I was really and truly in trouble, for I knew I couldn't just walk away."

"You managed it anyway," she said shortly, her gaze falling to her clenched hands.

"Yes, but I left Samantha to look after you and I stayed in constant touch through her."

"Of course," she said, her anger building and coursing through her body so that she shook with it. "You and Lady Samantha have been in collusion all this time. She must have known from the time you appeared as footman who you really were. You—you probably schemed all of this together, bringing me here."

"Yes, that is true. But I have prayed all these last three

months that you would understand when I told you the truth."

"What is it that you expect me to *understand*, Will? That you misrepresented yourself the entire time you were at Broadhurst, that you led me to believe you were a simple man with a few family problems?" She glared at him. "Do you expect me to understand that you were a good friend of Val's, that you read all of my letters, that you knew every detail of my life over the last five years and never let on for a moment?"

"Yes," he said quietly. "I do expect all of that and more. You are not only an intelligent woman, Louisa, but a thoughtful one. Put yourself in my position and think about what you might have done under the same circumstances."

"You are asking the impossible!" She rubbed her hands over eyes that infuriatingly brimmed with tears. "You deliberately deceived me, you—you made love to me as someone else entirely. How am I supposed to forgive that, let alone understand it?"

"I made love to you as the man that I am," he replied. "My name didn't seem important at the time. As I said, I planned on telling you the truth when the time felt right, Louisa, but I didn't expect circumstances to change so drastically." He stood and walked over to the window, his back to her. "I had no idea my brother was mortally ill until Samantha told me that last day. I had to leave immediately. I barely had time to pack my bag, let alone give you explanations." He turned around. "I would have written—God knows I started ten letters before tearing them up again, realizing that you would have recognized my writing from the letters I wrote to Samantha. The last thing I wanted was for you to learn the truth from anyone but myself, so I chose to wait until my period of mourning had finished before I asked you to come."

Louisa shook her head. "Why did you bother? What good can it do now, Will? You are still Will, at least?" she asked in a biting tone.

"Still Will," he said with an amused smile. "Always Will to you, I hope. Louisa, do jump off your high horse and try to remember that I love you every bit as much as I always have."

Louisa couldn't believe his nerve. "You behave as if nothing has changed save for a little adjustment to your station in life and expect me to bound into your arms in joy?" she said, thoroughly outraged. "You seem to forget that you *lied* to me, Will. For instance, you knew Valentine well and never bothered to tell me. I think that calls for a bit more explanation, don't you?"

"Yes," he said, crossing his arms over his chest. "You are absolutely right. I considered Val my dearest friend. Brace yourself, for there is something else of importance I have to tell you."

"Brace myself? I cannot think of anything else you could possibly say that would shock me any more than what you have already told me," she replied bitterly, her entire world in shreds. She might have expected such deception from anyone else, but not from Will. Never from Will.

"I believe there is," he said, looking her square in the eyes. "Louisa, Val died in my arms. That was another thing I came to Broadhurst to tell you."

"He—he died in your arms?" Louisa swallowed hard. This the very last thing she'd expected to hear. She leaned forward, staring at him. "You were at Waterloo with him?"

"I was." He looked away for a long moment. "I can't

describe to you how horrible that day was, but I can tell you that Val fought with enormous courage."

"Tell me what happened," she said in a small voice, her anger forgotten. "I had a letter from the colonel of the regiment, but he didn't give me any details. I've always wondered what the end was like for him."

"Are you sure you want to know?" Will said, dropping his arms to his sides. "It's not a pleasant story."

"I'm very sure. Val might have been a coward in other ways, but I did hope that he died bravely."

Will hesitated, then nodded. "He did," he replied, his eyes turning distant and filled with memory. "When the bullet took him in the chest he called out for me. Eventually I found him." He paused for a long moment. "Val and I both knew he was done for, so all I could do was to hold him close in my arms."

"He must have been in terrible pain," Louisa said, suddenly feeling awful for Val. Whatever he'd been, he didn't deserve to die in anguish. At least Will had been there with him, and she could only be grateful for that. She could see how horrible it had been for Will too. Perhaps this was the source of his nightmares.

"Yes, he was in pain, but too far gone to feel it, really. He only said he was cold."

"Did he—did he say anything else?" she asked hesitantly, wondering what had been on his mind at the end, whether he'd felt any remorse, had even thought of the family he'd left behind.

Will frowned. "He said he didn't believe in God, but then he cried out for Maria. I assume he meant the Holy Mother and prayed he'd had a vision that sustained him."

Louisa stared at Will in disbelief. "He cried out for *Maria*?

And you thought he meant the Holy Mother?" She sank back into the chair. She would have laughed if she hadn't been so upset. "Will, don't be absurd. You know that Val liked his ladies. He was most likely calling out for his latest paramour."

Will rubbed his hands over his face, then dropped them. "How stupid of me," he said. "I suppose I never went back to that time with the realization that your husband was a— well, that he was what he was. Forgive me, Louisa. I thought only to comfort you. I forgot what I've learned about him since."

"You weren't to know," she allowed grudgingly. "I'm sure he drew you in just as much as he did me. I suppose he did have a few good points."

"Yes, he did, and that is most generous of you to admit." Will grinned at her, and the sight caused her heart to quicken. How many times had she seen the same grin, the same laugh in his eyes that invited her to laugh with him? She could easily spend a lifetime looking at that smile.

But his smile quickly faded. "I was undone at the time," he said, "but I have since learned to put those feelings to one side. If I can tell you anything comforting at all, it is that the angels did come for him."

"They did?" she said, slightly surprised, given Val's conduct during the course of their marriage. "You saw them?"

"I did. I told you about it, although I didn't give you the actual circumstances at the time. Do you remember when I said that the last time I saw the angels was when a friend had died?"

"Yes . . . yes, of course I do."

"That was when Val died. Seeing them descend was the greatest comfort I had in the midst of what felt like hell."

"So you think that Val is at peace?" she asked, for some unfathomable reason really wanting to know.

"I cannot imagine that he is not. Perhaps I should also say that they came for my brother, too, and he was no saint, so maybe we should feel reassured that our sins, whatever they are, do not necessarily keep us from the kingdom of heaven. But what do I know?" Will walked over to the window.

Louisa couldn't help smiling. "I have to think that you know a great deal, given what you see." She hesitated, then very quietly said, "I saw an angel, too, Will. He was nothing like any of yours." She sighed in memory. "I met an old man on the road, a Mr. Raphael, and he gave me advice, then vanished—literally vanished."

Will regarded her with keen interest. "Do you mean he was real to you at the time? Did he have any light around him, anything that might indicate he was sent to you from above?"

"No," Louisa said, forgetting that she was supposed to be furious with Will. She felt as if no time had passed at all, for they'd slid easily into conversation of the sort they'd always had. "He was there one minute, and he was absolutely lovely. We talked a bit, and then when I turned around to wave a final good-bye, he'd disappeared. There was nowhere else for him to go, Will, so what else could he have been but an angel?"

Will looked down. "I don't know. I've never had the good fortune to be visited by an angel personally. I only seem to see their presence when people are in trouble. Did he give you good advice?"

Louisa's spine tingled as the angel's words came back to her. *All you need to realize your dream is to look to the future . .*

"Yes, he did," she said on a whisper, knowing in her heart that Mr. Raphael had been right. Will was her future, her destiny, although she didn't know if he felt the same way now that he was a marquess. "He gave me very good advice."

Will cocked his head, regarding her curiously. "Do you mind telling me what it was?"

"He just said that I shouldn't look back, and that we guide our own destiny with God's help. You said that once, or something like it."

Will walked back to her, reaching down to take her hand, smoothing his thumb over its back, his touch sending electric shocks shooting down her spine. "I still believe that with all my heart. Louisa, can you find it in your heart to forgive me? I should never have misled you as I did, but I cannot help being grateful for the circumstances that brought me to you, even if I had to be Will Cutter for a time."

She gazed into his eyes for a long moment. "I loved Will Cutter," she answered softly. "I imagine I can love Will Alconleigh. You haven't changed *that* much."

A grin flashed across his face. "I don't think I've changed at all, save for having acquired a large house and a title. I love you too, Louisa, I love you with all my heart." He picked up her other hand and held them both tightly between his. "I don't suppose you could see your way to marrying me?"

"M-marrying you?" she stammered, completely unprepared. "You want me to *marry* you?"

"That is what people usually do when they love each other, isn't it?" He sounded amused, but his eyes held anxiety. "That's what I've wanted all along, but I wasn't free to ask you until now."

She stared at him, so overwhelmed with happiness that she couldn't speak. To live out the rest of her life with Will . . . the thought was too wonderful to grasp all at once.

"Would that be a *yes* or a *no*?" he asked, frowning. "Please say something, sweetheart, and put me out of my misery. My heart can't take the strain."

"Oh, Will, of *course* I'll marry you," she said, bursting into laughter. She jumped to her feet. "How could I not? I'd have married you as Will Cutter, man-of-all-work, and I'll marry you as Will, Marquess of Alconleigh, just so long as I can lie in your arms every night and wake up to your face every morning, and—and have children with you and—and talk to you until I'm blue in the face."

"All of that and more," Will said in jubilation, picking her up in his arms as if she weighed no more than a feather. He swept her around in a circle, then deposited her back on the ground and drew her tightly into his arms.

"I swear to you, Louisa Merriem, that I will never give you a moment's doubt about me, that I will love you until the day I die and make you the happiest woman on earth until that day comes."

He lowered his head and kissed her hard, his mouth claiming hers in a fashion that left her breathless and trembling.

"When?" she asked as she finally caught her breath.

"Tomorrow," he said, laughing. "A special license has been burning a hole in my pocket these last two weeks. The next time I bed you it will be as your husband, and I really don't think I can last any longer than a day."

"But what about my father and Pip?" she said, her head spinning. "They surely will want to be here for the occasion?"

"They will understand," Will said decisively. "Samantha will be here and can be counted on to give them every last detail after the fact."

Louisa smiled. "Indeed. Lady Samantha has become something of a fixture at Broadhurst. I cannot help but wonder if there's not another wedding in the making. My father has become a different person entirely since she ensconced herself."

Will dropped a kiss on her forehead. "I am happy to hear it, but the only wedding I can bring myself to think about is ours. Come, my love, and let us give Samantha the good news. She has waited a long time to hear it."

He took her firmly by the hand and led her toward the door, his other arm tight around her waist. He paused before reaching for the door handle. "One last thing, Louisa," he said, looking down at her, his face grave. "I need to extract a promise from you."

"What is it?" she asked, willing to promise him anything.

"You must write to Mr. Sandringham and confess all," he said with a sudden grin. "I cannot be your Mr. Peter for a moment longer, since I now have a position to consider, and it does not include being the author of pirate adventures on the high seas. You will have to be Mr. Peter, Marchioness of Alconleigh, all on your own."

"Oh, very well," she said with a sigh. "If truth be told, I've already written to Mr. Sandringham and confessed, since I didn't know if I'd ever see you again. He didn't mind in the least. Indeed, he wrote back and told me that he'd suspected as much all along."

Will hooted with laughter. "That's my Louisa. Always resourceful. Have you started on Elizabeth's adventures?"

"Oh, yes," she said with enthusiasm. "You were exactly right about the convent. She didn't belong there at all.

Instead I started with her taking instruction in the art of pistol shooting."

"Excellent. I've been thinking," he said as he opened the door. "What if Elizabeth decides to become a pirate herself in order to spirit the beleaguered aristocrats away from France . . ."

Epilogue

Watching fondly as Lady Samantha Davenport, now Lady Samantha Fleming, soundly kissed her new husband to seal their marriage vows, Louisa smiled with satisfaction. She couldn't remember the last time she'd seen her father look so happy, or Lady Samantha for that matter.

Pip roared with laughter at the sight. "Grandpapa is done for now," she said. "Lady Samantha is going to rule Broadhurst."

Will looked down at her with a grin. "Lady Samantha is not only going to rule Broadhurst, she's going to make your grandpapa into a new man. I've never seen him look so well."

"I couldn't have asked for a better ending," Louisa said, leaning into the arm Will had wrapped around her. "Who would have thought that Samantha would give up her endless house visits and parties to retire to Devon for love of my father?"

"She found happiness, much as we have," Will replied simply. "Do you want to sit down, sweetheart? You've been on your feet for too long."

"I'm not ailing, Will, only carrying a child," she retorted, loving him all the more for his concern. "I am perfectly well, really. Ask me again in four months' time when you'll barely be able to get me out of a chair."

"I cannot wait," he said, stroking a hand over her expanding belly. "What do you think, Pip? Boy or girl?"

"A boy," Pip answered decisively. "I want a brother and Mama is always so obliging when I ask her nicely."

Will fondly smoothed a hand over her head. "We shall

see. The baby is in the hands of the angels, still in the making."

"We are all in the hands of the angels," Louisa said with a soft smile, remembering Raphael, who had never really left her. She felt his unseen presence often, especially since she'd conceived her unborn child. "Now and forever."

Will tightened his hand around her waist. "Now and forever," he murmured against her hair. "Now and forever, but in the meantime, let's go off and eat some of the cake Cook made. The thing looks like a carriage wheel, it's so huge . . ."